Of Mind and Madness

A Detectives Daniels and Remalla Mystery Thriller

J. T. Bishop

Eudoran Press LLC

Eudoran Press LLC

6009 W. Parker Rd. Su. 149, #205

Dallas, TX 75093

www.jtbishopauthor.com

Publisher's Note: This is a work of fiction. Names, characters, places, and incidents are a product of the author's imagination. Locales and public names are sometimes used for atmospheric purposes. Any resemblance to actual people, living or dead, or to businesses, companies, events, institutions, or locales is completely coincidental.

Author Photos by Nick Bishop and Mayza Clark Photography

Book Editing by P. Creeden and G. Enstam, C. Marquis and C. McGuire.

Cover Design by J.T. Bishop

Of Mind and Madness/ J.T. Bishop -- 1st ed.

ISBN 978-1-955370-16-5

To my lovely team friendship ladies, dinner buddies and confidants – you make me laugh and I adore your company. Here's to many more years of hysterical fun.

Chapter One

AN OWL HOOTED IN the woods. Manny stopped short and grabbed a tree trunk. His head spun with the movement, and he almost puked. Taking a breath to settle his stomach, he leaned over. "Are we almost there?" he asked.

Amy stopped beside him. "I think so." She took a pull from the flask she was holding. "It's a little farther in. At least that's what my brother told me." She handed him the flask.

Manny straightened, took the flask and leaned back against the tree. "If I drink anymore, I'm gonna pass out in these damn woods. Hopefully, they'll find my body, only I'll have shit my shorts and barfed my guts out." He put his hand on his stomach, feeling the pressure of his full bladder. He eyed his surroundings, wondering where he could relieve himself and questioned whether he could hold out long enough to get back and use a bathroom.

Unsteady, she leaned against him. "Don't be so dramatic. Your drunken stupor doesn't equate to being attacked by an animal."

"You mean a hell hound. There's a difference." The need to puke faded and he took another drink. The alcohol burned his throat, and he grimaced. "God. What is this stuff?"

"It's from Jimmy," she said. "The bar owner. He makes it in his backyard."

"If anything's going to kill me tonight, it's going to be this." He shook the flask.

"Just wait till the hangover. Then you'll wish you were dead." She grabbed his arm. "C'mon. Let's go."

Manny eyed the creepy woods around them. The farther in they traveled, the thicker the foliage and trees became.

"You sure you know where we are?" She yanked on him, but he resisted.

"Hell," he said. "When I came out here, I was hoping to get laid. Not get killed."

She giggled. "We can have some fun later, silly." She pulled on him again. "But I want to keep going." When he didn't move, she pressed against him and whispered. "I promise. I'll make it worth your while."

The alcohol on her breath almost made him grimace again, but she slid her hand down and squeezed his ass, and his other body parts responded. Manny had figured hanging out with a hot girl and hunting for a witch and her pet hellhound at night where others had disappeared might be kind of exciting, especially if Amy promised more than just booze and a late-night hike. Smiling, he tried to kiss her, but she pulled away.

"Not yet, handsome. We've come this far, but we're not finished." She stepped back and yanked on his hand. "Rumor is the witch lives out here."

Manny moaned. "This better be worth it." The owl hooted again, and a breeze blew through the trees, rustling the leaves. He pushed off the tree and almost stumbled into a thick patch of vines but righted himself and followed her.

"Baby, you better believe it is." She took the flask from him, closed it and put it in the back pocket of her tight jeans. "My brother said he saw something, but I think he's full of shit. The whole damn town's full of shit. The rumors are nothing but overblown hysteria. It's probably just some run-down old house and a stray dog."

"Then why not do this during the day?" asked Manny. The wind made the branches creak, and the sound made his heart thump.

"Because it doesn't count when the sun's up. The challenge is to do it at night." She walked down the dark path using the flashlight on her phone.

"Challenge?" He stayed beside her, hoping her battery would hold out long enough to illuminate their walk home.

"Yeah. It's a rite of passage. You come out here and face the witch and her hellhound. You have to make it down the path and back. It's a little over four miles."

Something snapped nearby, and he startled, telling himself it was probably a raccoon or a deer. "How many have succeeded?"

Amy's light created crazy shadows that made him recall a recent horror movie he'd seen. "Nobody," she said.

"Nobody?"

"Well, the dead people may have made it all the way, but we'll never know. They never made it back."

He stopped. "Hold up. *Dead people?*"

She turned and swayed. "Don't freak out. They never came back so we have to assume they're dead, but nobody really knows for sure."

"Are you serious?"

She giggled again. "It's no big deal. It's just stories that people have made up over the years. Nobody even knows the truth anymore. To be honest, the rumors are that one guy died but I think he just disappeared. We did have somebody get lost once and another hiker who broke an ankle, but they made it out. The others that didn't return probably just got lost and died of exposure. It happens."

Manny frowned at her. "How many didn't make it back?"

"C'mon. We've got to be close." She resumed walking.

Manny heard another rustle and debated whether to continue, but Amy had the light, so he hurried up beside her. "Maybe we should go." Another creak to his right made him turn and look, but all he saw was darkness. "I don't like this."

"I think it's cool as shit. I can't wait to tell Brandon I completed the challenge and didn't see a damn thing other than bear scat and some spooky trees."

"Bears? Are there bears out here?"

She smiled. "You're such a city boy. Of course, there are."

His alcoholic haze was wearing off fast. "How much farther?" He stuck close to her, his mind now alert and darting his gaze around, looking for any movement. His bladder protested, and he groaned. "I got to take a piss."

"So take one."

Manny eyed his ominous surroundings. "You sure?"

She giggled again. "You're not scared, are you?"

Manny spotted a nearby tree in the shadows and did his best to walk confidently up to it. "Give me a sec." He unzipped his fly.

"I'll be right here."

Forcing himself to relax, Manny sighed as he peed in the woods. Feeling better, he zipped his pants and turned, but didn't see Amy. "Amy?" he asked, his heart rate speeding up. "Amy?" He heard her say something in the distance and he started down the trail when he heard a scraping and scampering beside him. His voice locked up when he saw an animal dart out of the trees, run over his foot and disappear into the shadows.

Manny bit back a scream and ran backward into a tree trunk. Something hit his shoulder and scampered down his arm. Screeching, he saw a big hairy spider run down his wrist and hand. He lost it and shaking his arm to detach the spider, he spotted the same animal run out of the trees at him. Panicked, he turned and ran, sure that the animal was chasing him. A small part of his brain told him to slow down. That it was just a raccoon, but he was certain the animal was right behind him, and he kept going until his breath caught and he had to stop. He hunkered down behind a dead log and looked behind him but didn't see anything.

Breathing fast and cursing at himself for being so stupid, he realized he had no idea where he was. "Amy," he yelled loudly. "Amy? You out there?" He reached for his cell, wondering if he could call her, but saw there was no service and his battery was almost dead. He put it away. "Amy?" he yelled again. He didn't hear a response. "Shit." He squatted and sat in the dirt. What was he going to do now?

A few seconds passed and figuring he was stuck there until the sun came up, he heard Amy call his name in the distance.

"Manny?"

He straightened and hearing her call out again, he stood. "Amy? I'm here."

"Manny?" She was getting closer. "Where are you?"

He heard footsteps crunching through the leaves. "I'm over here." He waited, praying she'd find him, and breathed a deep sigh of relief when her light flickered through the brush and she stepped out of the shadows. "Thank God," he said.

"What the hell is the matter with you?" she asked. "Why'd you take off?"

"I...I saw something." He didn't want to tell her he'd panicked at the sight of a spider.

She smirked. "What was it? A rabbit?"

"No. It was way bigger."

"Sure it was." She turned back. "C'mon, Superman. We need to get back to the trail."

His heart returning to a more normal rhythm, he followed. "I hope you know where it is, because I'm totally lost."

"I know these woods. I think I know where we are." She turned back and Manny stuck behind her as they walked. Several minutes later, they were still looking for the trail.

"Do you know where we are?" asked Manny.

"I thought it was this way," said Amy. She stopped and looked around. "Shit, Manny. Why'd you have to run off?"

"I told you. I saw an animal." He wiped sweat off his forehead. Everything around them looked the same. "Are we lost?" His attempt at sounding confident failed.

Amy turned. "Let's try this way." She shined the light and walked in another direction.

Manny felt certain she had no idea where she was. He followed her again but after another several minutes, he stopped. "Admit it. We're lost."

She flipped off the light and darkness enveloped them. "If you had stayed put, we wouldn't be in this mess."

"Now what do we do?" Manny's heart thumped against his chest.

Amy pulled out the flask. "We sit tight until morning. When the sun comes up, I can tell what direction to go. Until then, though, we might as well have a drink."

Manny dropped his jaw. "We're staying out here all night?" An owl hooted and he jumped.

"Do you have a better idea, because I don't." She drank from the flask and handed it to him.

His fingers shaking, he took it and swallowed a healthy sip, wishing he'd been smart enough to stay home. "This sucks," he said, capping the flask. The alcohol burned but he barely noticed.

"Tell me about it. I wanted to complete the damn challenge." She took the flask from Manny, returned it to her pocket and turned her light back on. "There's a clearing by that tree. We can wait there." She took a few steps, but then stopped and Manny almost bumped into her. She went still and her eyes narrowed. "What's that?" she whispered.

Manny froze. "What's what?"

She pointed. "There." She ran up to a small fallen log and squatted beside it. "Do you see it?"

He squatted next to her, and she flipped off the light.

"I can't see shit," he said.

"Beyond the trees. Over there." She pointed.

He blinked, waiting for his eyes to adjust, and then spotted it. A dim light in the distance. "What is that?"

Amy darted out from the log. "Let's get closer."

"Son-of-a..." He followed, terrified of being left behind. "Are you crazy?"

Her footfalls crunched against the leafy ground, and she scooted up beside a large tree. "Look."

He put a hand on the trunk, trying to control his breathing, although his adrenaline was rushing through him. In the darkness, he could see what looked like the haunted house of his nightmares. Silhouetted in the murky light of the moon, he could see a two-story structure, with two windows on either side of a front door on the first floor, and two windows on the second floor beneath a dilapidated wooden roof. Soft red light emanated from the windows below. More details were impossible to make out in the darkness. The owl hooted again, and Manny almost bolted. "Okay. We saw it. Let's go back."

"Hell, no. Let's go check it out." Amy stepped out from the tree.

Wishing he'd never agreed to this, Manny reluctantly followed. They moved slowly toward the house, and Manny prayed he could find his way back if he had to make a fast exit. Getting closer, he noted the silence of the woods. The crickets had stopped chirping and even the breeze had gone still. "Wait," he said and went to grab her arm when he heard a soft, but distinct, low growl. His blood ran cold, and Amy stopped and turned.

"What was that?" he whispered.

Her eyes wide, she shook her head. "I don't know."

Hearing the fear in her voice, his own fear surged.

"It's probably nothing," she said. She grabbed for her phone when the growl rumbled again, this time closer.

"Oh, shit," said Manny, his voice shaking. "Is it a bear?"

Amy managed to flip her phone light back on, but it shook as her fingers trembled. "I don't see anything."

Another growl, this one deeper, sounded again, but this time from behind them. Amy swiveled and Manny pressed against a nearby tree, too scared to even look. "Shit. It's close. We have to get out of here."

"If we run, it will chase us."

Manny closed his eyes. "Oh, hell. I should have listened to my gut and stayed in town." He looked up toward the sky. "I swear. I'll never be swayed by a hot woman again. I'll go to church every Sunday. I'll even become a priest, or a minister, or a rabbi. Just get me back to civilization."

"Would you shut up?" She swung the flashlight through the trees. "It's...it's just trying to scare us."

"It's working." He forced himself to push away from the tree. "Let's go."

"But we're so close."

"I don't want to be the next couple to die out here."

"We are not going to—"

The growl, deep and menacing, returned, and Manny swore it was now between them and the house. He went rigid and Amy swiveled again, just as her light flickered and went out.

Manny's brain went fuzzy with terror. He didn't know whether to scream, run, or cry.

"Shit." Amy banged on her phone. "Shit. Shit. Shit."

Manny squinted, hearing the soft crunch of footfalls grow closer. "A... Amy." His chest tightened, and his heart pounded. "Wha...What is that?"

Amy stopped messing with her phone and eyed the woods. Two red glowing eyes stared back from just beyond a thicket of trees. Manny dropped his jaw, hearing his silent scream in his head, but unable to verbalize it.

The growl came again, and the eyes encroached.

Amy stepped back into him, and almost tripped. "It's...it's..."

He muttered away as the eyes neared. "It's what?" His throat had dried up and he was surprised he could speak. The eyes advanced and another growl, this time louder, almost made him puke, but not from Jimmy's booze.

She walked backwards. "I think...I think it's the hellhound." She spoke so low, Manny could barely hear her.

The eyes flashed, the growl bellowed, and Manny took off in a dead run.

Chapter Two

CAPTAIN FRANK LOZANO SAT at his desk and eyed his laptop. Detective Mellenbuehl sat across from him. "What do you think, Mel?" asked Lozano. "You think he's guilty?"

Mel sipped from a cup of coffee and chewed on a donut. "I think he's dirtier than O.J. We just need to prove it. His girlfriend's his only alibi. I say Garcia and I push her a little harder. See if a little pressure gets her to open up. I don't think she quite realizes what lying to us could do to her if we catch her."

"She might also clam up and protect him. We've seen it before."

"Yeah. I know. But it's worth a shot."

"You talk to his mother?" asked Lozano. "She might have something interesting to say, too."

"Going today. Just waiting for Garcia."

Lozano nodded. "Go on, then. Let me know how it goes." He checked his watch. "I've got a meeting. Keep me posted."

Mel nodded and stood. He tossed his empty coffee cup and napkin in the trashcan beside the door. "You got it." He took the last bite of his donut and left.

Lozano closed his laptop and sat back in his seat. His blinds open, he looked out the glass portion of his office wall into the squad room. Various detectives sat at their desks, and he observed the usual comings and goings of his men and women working. Spotting the empty desks of Daniels and Remalla, he wondered about each of them, and considered calling when the outer squad door swung open, and Detective Gordon Daniels walked in. He looked around, and then saw Lozano through the glass. Lozano waved him over.

Daniels, his blonde hair gelled back and perfectly in place, strode toward him. He wore his usual casual, but ironed, slacks and a long-sleeved collared blue shirt. His attire stood in stark contrast to his partner Detective Aaron Remalla's, whose clothes were usually wrinkled, his jeans worn, and his shirts stained. While Daniels had the book smarts and the look of a wrestler, Remalla resembled more of a track and field athlete and had the street smarts. Together, they were a formidable team, had forged an indelible friendship, and were two of his best detectives.

Daniels opened the door to Lozano's office. "Hey, Cap."

"Come on in. Have a seat."

Daniels shut the door behind him and sat. "How are you?"

"Good. The crazies are a little more settled at the moment, so there's a brief lull."

"Glad to hear it."

"How're Marjorie and J.P.? You been enjoying a little time with the family while you're on leave?"

Daniels propped an ankle on his knee. "We actually took a couple days and got out of town. We needed it."

Lozano nodded, recalling Daniels' and Remalla's last case and how it had ended. Daniels was currently on leave pending an internal investigation after firing his weapon in the use of deadly force. "I know you did. You guys have been through a lot. I'm glad you could get away."

"Any news on my current status?"

"I spoke to the Chief a couple of days ago. You should hear something soon about getting back to work. Everything's looking good, so hopefully, you'll know something next week."

"That would be great. As much as I've enjoyed getting some time off, I think I'm ready to get back. Relaxing isn't my strong suit."

"Funny, isn't it? You have a hellish case, wonder how you do this job, but then get some time away, and you miss it."

Daniels chuckled. "We're all a little crazy, aren't we? Otherwise, how else could we do what we do every day?"

"You got that right." Lozano sat up and tossed a folder on his desk into a pile. "How's Rem doing? You talk to him?"

"I was about to ask you the same thing."

"You came at a good time. I'm actually about to meet with Kate Schultz, the prosecutor on the Allison Albright case. Said she learned something and wanted to talk to me. She should be here any minute."

"Kate's coming?" Daniels frowned. "Is it something serious?"

"I don't know. Said she didn't want to discuss it on the phone."

"Did she talk to Rem about whatever it is?"

"I didn't interrogate her, Daniels. I figure if she needed to talk to Rem, she has his number."

Daniels rubbed his jaw. "Has he been okay while I've been out? He hasn't said much, but I know he didn't want to bother me while I was gone. You know how he is."

Lozano tipped his head. "Why are you asking me?"

"Because you've seen him more than I have." He sat up and looked out the glass. "Is he here? Don't tell me you paired him up with Silvers. Rem will be bitching like an angry cat, and I'll never hear the end of it."

"What the hell are you talking about?" asked Lozano, confused. "Remalla took some time off. I haven't seen him in four days."

Daniels swiveled in his seat, his face serious. "What?"

"You heard me. He took some time off."

"When?"

Lozano scowled. "Are you suddenly deaf? I told you. Four days ago. Didn't he tell you?"

Daniels shook his head. "Cap, he didn't say a word. He told me that he's been here, either doing desk duty or helping out with various cases. Are you saying he hasn't been here at all?"

"I think that's what taking time off means. No. I haven't seen or heard from him."

Daniels pulled out his phone. "Shit. Why in the hell wouldn't he tell me?" He dialed a number and put the phone to his ear.

"He's your partner. You tell me."

Listening, Daniels set his jaw. "He's not answering." He waited and then left a message. "Rem? I'm in Lozano's office. Where are you? Call me." He hung up. "What did he say when he asked for time off?"

Lozano shrugged, thinking back to his last phone call with Remalla. "He said he'd gotten word that his aunt was sick. He wanted to go see her.

I told him to take the time he needed. Considering what he's been through, he needed to get away as much as you."

"His aunt? Which one?"

"Hell if I know, Daniels. I'm not his mother. I expected him back at the end of the week."

Daniels texted. "Well, he's not in hiding anymore. I'm on his trail now and he better damn well tell me where he is." He sent the text. "I don't get it. Why—"

A knock sounded and Lozano saw Kate Schultz through the glass. He raised his hand and waved. "Come in."

She entered, carrying a briefcase and wearing a two piece, fitted dark green suit. "Captain," she said. She eyed Daniels. "Gordon."

"Hi, Kate," said Daniels, standing, but holding his phone.

Lozano raised a brow at their familiarity. Daniels tipped his head at Kate. "Kate's aunt and uncle lived down the street from my parents when we were kids. We used to ride our bikes around town during the summer when she was visiting."

"Small world," said Lozano.

"It is," said Daniels. He looked back at Kate. "How are you? How's the case?"

She looked between the two of them. "I've been better. I'm glad you're here. I can kill two birds with one stone." She set her briefcase on the chair beside Daniels. "I don't suppose you know where your partner is?"

Daniels lifted his phone. "I'm trying to find out right now. Why?"

"Something to do with the Albright case?" asked Lozano.

"You could say that," she said. "But just how much, I can't say. Not yet anyway. I've been trying to reach Remalla, but he's not returning my calls."

Lozano could see the shift in Daniels' posture. Something was up, and Daniels could sense it just as fast as Lozano could. "How can we help?" asked Lozano.

She opened her briefcase. "I became aware of something this morning. Allison's attorney contacted me."

"You mean Greasy Measy?" asked Daniels. "That guy's a toad. What'd he want?"

"He kindly informed me that your partner," she pulled out a file folder and opened it, "visited Allison Albright in jail four days ago."

Lozano tensed, and Daniels' jaw dropped. "He did what?" asked Daniels. "There's no way. He wouldn't go near her in a million years."

Kate pulled out a sheet of paper. "I didn't believe Measy either, so I contacted the warden. He sent me this." She handed the paper to Lozano.

Lozano studied it, his heart racing.

"What is it?" asked Daniels.

"Copy of the visitor log where Allison is being held," said Lozano. "Remalla signed in at nine sixteen a.m. and signed out at nine twenty-four, four days ago." He handed the sheet to Daniels.

"That's not possible," said Daniels. He read the paper.

"Oh, it's possible," said Kate. "I've requested the video to see what was said. He better pray he didn't do something stupid. Measy was almost salivating on the phone, so it doesn't bode well. Any of you talk to Remalla because I sure would like to."

"Has Remalla texted back?" asked Lozano.

"No. He hasn't." Daniels handed the paper back to Kate. He paused for a second, and then headed for the door.

"Where are you going?" asked Lozano.

Opening the door, Daniels barely stopped to answer. "I'm going to find my partner." He walked out, passed his and Rem's desks without a second glance, and left the squad room.

Chapter Three

REM HEARD THE BUZZING of his phone and groaned. He pulled the pillow tighter over his head and ignored it. Trying to go back to sleep despite his pounding headache, he heard his familiar text notification tweet at him and cursed. He cracked an eye open and moved the pillow enough to see the sunlight and winced. His head throbbed, his mouth felt like he'd chewed a bar of sand, and his crusty eyes didn't want to open.

After debating whether to ignore his phone, he decided he ought to check it since he'd received a call and a text in close proximity. Guessing it was his mother since he hadn't called her on Sunday, he reached out and grabbed it off the chair beside the bed. The room he occupied was too small for a nightstand, so he'd used one of the two chairs there to act as one. He had no idea what time it was, or when he'd fallen into bed. There was a vague recollection of getting drunk at the local bar, but after that, he...

His memory engaged and sucking in a breath, his previous evening rushed back at him, and he regretfully remembered the details, not just of the previous night, but the last three days.

Moaning, he reflected on his last few nights. Not long after his arrival, he'd found the town watering hole where the locals drank but not the tourists. It was off the main road and right down the street from the miniscule fishing shack Rem had rented, which had cost next to nothing since the fish weren't biting yet, or maybe because the room had space for only a pull-out bed, a toilet and shower, a tiny kitchenette and a small table with two chairs. Rem didn't care about the size though. He just needed a place to sleep.

The local bar was called Jimmy's and he'd gotten stupid drunk there every night since leaving San Diego. The first night, he'd stumbled back to his aunt's after closing and had barfed in her rose bushes and passed out on the front steps. The second night, after she'd kicked him out and he'd rented the shack, he couldn't find his way home, and the sheriff had found him and taken him to the jail to sleep it off. Rem squeezed his temples at the memory. He'd woken in a small cell on a narrow cot, not recalling how he'd gotten there. The sheriff had been kind enough not to charge him with public intoxication, and had let Rem go, but Rem recalled the deputy not being so thrilled. He'd sneered at Rem, called him a stupid drunk, and argued with Sheriff...what was his name? Rem clenched his eyes. Whistler. Sheriff Joe Whistler, and the deputy was...he sighed, forgetting the deputy's name, but he recalled sneering back at him on his way out and shooting him the finger. Shaw. Randal Shaw, thought Rem, remembering the deputy's nametag.

Night three had been more successful in terms of getting back to the shack, but more regrettable in terms of what had occurred in the bar. His stomach churned at the memory.

He'd met Sharon his first night at Jimmy's. She was a recent transplant to the town and had been working as a teller at the local bank on Main Street, and she hung out at the bar in the evenings. She and Rem had hit it off and had spent the last three nights getting plastered, singing to tunes on the jukebox and dancing, or more like weaving, on the dance floor. It had stayed friendly until the night before, when Rem had gone to the bathroom, and she'd followed him in and locked the door behind her.

Barely coherent, he'd tried to fend her off when she'd drunkenly backed him up against the wall and started to kiss him. Images of Allison Albright straddling him had flashed in his head, and he'd almost gotten sick, but then a switch had turned in his brain and he'd ignored the warning signs telling him to leave. With her body pressed against his, his anger had unexpectedly flared and then he'd stopped caring. He'd let her kiss and touch him, and before he knew what was happening, his body took over and he'd pushed her up against the bathroom sink. She'd pulled on his clothes, and he'd pulled on hers, and then she'd grabbed his crotch and spoken the same words Allison had–she wanted him to tell her that he wanted her.

Everything had gone ice cold in that moment. The urge to be sick returned, and Rem had shoved Sharon away. Confused, she'd tried to pull him back, but he'd yelled and told her to leave. Cold sweat had popped out on his skin, and he'd unlocked the door and forcefully shoved her out. She'd cursed at him, but he'd ignored her and barely had time to close and lock the door before racing to the toilet and heaving up the copious amount of liquor he'd imbibed since that afternoon.

It had taken him several minutes to pull himself together enough to return to the bar and resume his drinking. Sharon had been cold toward him, but when Rem continued to buy her drinks, she'd warmed quickly, and they'd resumed their partying as if nothing had happened.

Rem's stomach flipped at the memory, and he berated himself. This wasn't him. He'd been about to have random drunken sex in a bar bathroom with a stranger. And worse, he'd had a flashback at the mention of a few stupid words.

But just as quickly he argued with himself. Why not have sex with a stranger? What did it matter? Nothing he'd ever done had worked out, so why not do whatever the hell he wanted, and screw the consequences? Life was short and damn hard. Why not have some fun?

But was this fun? He asked himself.

No. Not really.

But then he recalled Allison and the news she'd given him. He was going to be the father to her unborn child, and she wanted him to raise that child with or without her presence but definitely with her involvement. If it was true, Rem knew he would never be rid of Allison whether she went to prison or not. His stomach lurched again. How had he fallen into such a deep hole in such a short period of time? Three years ago, he'd been the happiest he'd ever been, and now it was all gone.

His thoughts continued to war against each other. He told himself he should pull it together and go home. People had been through worse. But just as fast, he countered, telling himself he was a loser and could have avoided this whole thing. All of this was his own damn fault.

Remaining in bed, he felt depressed, lonely and infinitely sad, and wanted a drink. Right now, hiding appealed to him. His plan had been to disappear for a few days, get a grip on his life, and head back without anyone knowing where he'd gone. He didn't tell Daniels because his partner would worry and want to keep tabs on him. Mikey had called him a few times, too, but he hadn't called her back. She'd want to know what was wrong, and he wasn't strong enough to have that conversation.

After seeing Allison, he'd just driven away. He'd hit the highway and after a few hours, found himself in the small town where his Aunt Genevieve lived. After finding her house, he'd knocked on her door and, happy to see him, she'd let him stay with her until he'd barfed and passed out on her lawn, which hadn't gone over well. She'd asked him to leave if he couldn't pull it together and he hadn't spoken to her since.

His head pounding, he forced himself to look at his phone. At some point, he would be required to reconnect with the outside world, but he wasn't feeling the need yet. He wanted more time.

The screen lit up and squinting against the light, he moaned when he saw who had called and texted him. Daniels.

Shit, he thought to himself, and listened to the voicemail and read the texts. His partner was aware of his absence and knew Rem had been lying about his whereabouts. Daniels would be looking for him now.

Lowering the phone, Rem debated whether to call his partner, and imagined the conversation. Daniels would want to know why, and Rem wasn't ready to talk. Not that it mattered. Everyone would hear the news soon enough anyway.

Sighing, he returned the phone to the chair, rolled over, pulled the covers over his head, and went back to sleep.

• • • • • • • • •

Daniels entered Rem's home and shut the door. The house was quiet and undisturbed. Looking around, he noted that everything looked as expected, until he went into the kitchen. It was clean except for a mug sitting on the counter. It was filled with cold coffee and the coffee machine was turned off, but the pot was almost full. Rem never wasted coffee, so Daniels knew he'd left in a hurry.

He walked through the house, thinking about where his partner might have gone. He'd called and texted again since leaving Lozano's office, but Rem still hadn't answered. Putting the timeline together, Daniels surmised that Rem had left home fast enough to abandon his full cup of coffee and visit Allison, but why? He stopped at the thought. Rem had no intention of ever seeing Allison, except for...

Daniels cursed himself for not realizing it sooner. The only reason Rem would have ever agreed to see her was if she'd threatened him, or someone close to him. She'd already tried once by using Rudy Halpern, the man who'd kidnapped Josh Lambert and had almost killed Rem and Daniels. She'd almost succeeded, until he and Rem had taken care of Rudy, but obviously Allison still held some cards and she'd used them to her advantage.

Daniels thought back and recalled Rem being drugged at the police station. He'd been dosed with a hallucinogenic in an attempt to make him look unstable and unreliable in hopes of damaging his testimony at Allison's upcoming trial. Daniels thought they'd eluded that threat, but had they? Had Allison found a way to use that against Rem? It was the logical conclusion. The question was what had happened once she'd gotten Rem there? And why had he disappeared?

Some part of him wanted to visit Allison to find out. Daniels believed she would gleefully tell him, but he realized that would be a bad idea. He'd find out soon enough when Kate got a hold of the video.

Trying to think like his partner, he walked through Rem's home, hoping to get an idea of where he might go. He entered Rem's bedroom, seeing his rumpled bed. Looking around, he turned back toward the wall and saw the bureau with a set of drawers beneath. A stack of folded clothes sat atop it next to a lamp and beside the lamp was a framed photo of Rem and Jennie. He picked it up and smiled, recalling when he'd taken the picture. The four of them had been on a double date–Rem and Jennie and him and Marjorie, not long after he and Marjorie had started dating. They'd gone to an artist festival at a park and had stopped to get seafood on the way home. The picture had been taken at the park, with the park's large pond behind Rem and Jennie, who stood on the bridge that traversed it. Rem had his arm around Jennie, and he'd been teasing her, and she'd turned and poked him in the ribs. Daniels had taken the shot and inadvertently captured The Look. The one that had conveyed how much they'd loved each other and which they'd only shared with each other. It was Rem's favorite picture of the two of them and he'd framed it soon after. After her death, he'd boxed it up with the rest of Jennie's things, but at some point, the picture had reemerged.

Daniels studied the photo, remembering Jennie's laugh, and closed his eyes, wishing she were there. If anyone could help him locate Rem, it would be her.

I need a hand to find our boy, Jen, he thought to himself, and opened his eyes. His gaze fell on the top drawer, and he had the sudden urge to open it. Still holding the photo, he slid the drawer out and saw Rem's address book sitting on top of a pile of t-shirts. His heart thumping, he took it out.

He set the picture down and opened the book, seeing the names, numbers and addresses of Rem's numerous family members. By the fragility and worn look of the pages, he'd had it a while. Daniels flipped through it, wondering which aunt Rem had gone to visit, assuming Rem had told Lozano the truth about that much.

Some of the names were familiar to him, and he recalled meeting a few, but most were just letters on a page. There was no telling where Rem could have gone. He stopped on the section where Rem's mother was listed. Her address was in Florida and for a moment, he considered calling Mrs. Remalla but then wondered what he would say to her. The possible conversation flashed in his head. *Hello, this is your son's partner, Gordon. I have no idea where Aaron is, do you?*

He could only imagine her response and the worry that would ensue if she didn't know where her son had gone. Daniels recalled speaking to Mrs. Remalla once when Rem had handed him the phone to go handle a botched delivery at his front door. Daniels had talked with her for the next thirty minutes while she chatted about her garden, a potential hurricane, and her various nieces and nephews. He'd had to tell her that Rem needed his help in order to get her off the phone. The last thing Daniels needed right now was to upset his friend's mother and then hang up on her. Calling her would have to be a last resort.

He flipped through the rest of the pages, but no names stood out. Frustrated, he closed the book and eyed the picture of Rem and Jennie again.

"Any ideas?' he asked out loud.

Tense, he rubbed his neck, and Jennie's face appeared clearly in his mind's eye. She smiled and then he had a strange thought. *Close your eyes and open the book.*

Daniels wasn't sure what to think of the odd feeling and vision, but instead of questioning it, he closed his eyes and opened the book to a random page.

Now point, said the voice in his head.

Daniels pointed and opened his eyes. His finger was on a name.

Aunt Genevieve in Merrimac. A number and address were listed.

Merrimac rang a bell with Daniels. It was a quaint little town about three hours north. His family had gone fishing there once when he was a kid. Over the years, it had developed into a charming bed and breakfast stop with outdoor cafes, pricey retail shops, and an array of artists who displayed their wares along the main street. Marjorie had gone on a girls' trip to Merrimac a few years back and had loved it. Daniels had been meaning to take her there for a long weekend, but they hadn't yet made it.

He eyed the name and number and then stared at Jennie in the photo. *Call it,* he heard clearly in his mind.

The urge was so strong that he pulled out his cell and dialed the number, wondering what in the hell he was going to say when Aunt Genevieve answered, but figured he'd just have to wing it.

The phone rang three times, and he debated what to do if she didn't answer when someone picked up. "Hello?" he heard a woman say.

"Uhm, yes," he said. "Is this Genevieve?"

"Yes. It is. Who's calling?"

Daniels dove in. "My name's Detective Gordon Daniels. You don't know me, but I work with your nephew, Aaron Remalla. I'm his partner. I've been trying to locate him and I was hoping you could help."

She snorted. "What took you so long, Gordon?" Daniels gripped the phone and heard her sigh. "It's about time you called."

Chapter Four

DANIELS TOOK THE HIGHWAY exit toward Merrimac. The sun had set, and it was dark, but the road signs and directions were clear. Eyeing the clock on his dash, he noted he'd made good time.

After speaking to Aunt Genevieve and confirming Rem was in Merrimac, he'd rushed home to talk to Marjorie and ensure J.P. had childcare so he could take a few days to find Rem. He'd debated leaving the next morning, but something told him not to wait. Genevieve hadn't said much on the phone. Only that Rem had showed on her doorstep unannounced four days earlier. She'd been happy to see him, and had welcomed him, but it hadn't taken her long to realize that something was troubling her nephew. She didn't go into specifics but had told Daniels that Rem was no longer staying with her although he was still in town. Genevieve said she would explain more later and that if he was coming, he ought to hit the road.

After updating Marjorie, he'd packed a quick bag, made a sandwich, dropped J.P. off at Marjorie's mom's and left. Genevieve had given him directions to her home and between that and his navigation system, he knew he was about thirty minutes away.

The farther he drove, the quieter the road and the denser the trees became. Merrimac bordered the Merrimac River, which was still a popular fishing stop at certain times of the year. After her girls' trip, Marjorie had told him that the woods around the town were beautiful and provided for lovely hikes during the day, but that they'd been warned away from the forest at night. Something about it being haunted and that it should be avoided after dark. She'd assumed that the locals loved to spook the tourists with tales of strange creatures in the woods. Daniels hadn't paid much attention, but as he neared the town and the tall trees and thick foliage grew heavy, he could see why it would unnerve people. He recalled his stay at his grandfather's house in Dumont where he and Rem had had their own spooky encounters and had almost died after revealing Dumont's secrets. Shivering at the memories, he said a small prayer that Merrimac wouldn't hold any surprises. He didn't expect any, though. This town was way bigger, safer, and more popular than the tiny town of Dumont.

Nearing his turn, he slowed and noted the increasing number of pretty homes and manicured lawns. Many of them had lighted signs advertising them as bed and breakfasts. He made the turn and drove down another street which led him into the heart of the town. Shops and restaurants lined the road, and he could see why this was a popular place to visit. Couples walked along the sidewalk, hand in hand, and others sat in outside diners, eating, drinking and laughing. Driving past a square with a large fountain spraying jets of water, he saw a big sign above him advertising the upcoming Dandelion Festival. He halfway hoped he would find Rem and maybe they could spend a couple of days here while Rem got his head together about whatever was bugging him, and then they could head home.

After passing through the center of town, he drove another mile, and upon seeing Genevieve's street, he turned. Large trees with long branches lined the road and more houses with big front porches, green lawns and gabled roofs made him envious. The town's attractive charm, beautiful surroundings and peaceful setting made it the perfect getaway and idyllic place to live. He wondered if Marjorie would ever want to settle in a place like Merrimac.

His navigation system indicated he'd arrived, and he pulled up and parked in front of a white two-story house with a cozy porch holding big cushy furniture. Green shutters flanked the windows, a weathervane on the lawn pointed east, and a short, black, rod-iron fence enclosed the property. A sign hung from a post. It read *A Little Piece of Heaven Bed and Breakfast.* White clouds poked out from the sides and a small angel sat on one of them. Daniels hadn't known that Genevieve ran a B&B. and he hoped he wouldn't be disturbing anyone with his visit.

He grabbed his bag and got out of his car. Hearing the rustling of the large trees, he noted a few other B&B signs along the street. Genevieve wasn't the only one who opened her home to guests. Walking to the front door, he wondered if Rem was there. It would put Daniels' mind at ease to at least know his partner was physically okay. He rang the bell and waited.

After a few seconds, he heard footsteps, the knob turned, and the door opened. A middle-aged woman in a purple house dress, white sandals, short brown spiky hair, big earrings and red lipstick stood at the entry.

"Gordon?" she asked with a smile. Her eyes twinkled in the porch light.

He immediately recognized the Remalla grin. "Aunt Genevieve?"

"You made good time. Come on in." She opened the door wide.

He stepped into a lovely home with wood-paneled walls, wooden floors with thick rugs, ornate velvet furniture, an intricately carved banister that ran up carpet-covered stairs, delicate antiques and pretty landscape art on the walls. "Thank you." He looked around. "You have a beautiful house."

"Thank you, dear. I have to give props to my third husband, though. He had the artistic eye and the money. I got this place after the divorce, and he got the rest, plus his twenty-two-year-old fruitarian lover. I think I got the better deal." She laughed and waved. "Let's go in the kitchen. You can leave your stuff here if you want."

Daniels left his bag beside the staircase and followed Genevieve into the kitchen. It was spacious with a large island, and it smelled like cinnamon and apples.

"Have a seat," she said. "Can I get you some tea?"

Daniels sat at the small breakfast table. "I thought Remallas were coffee drinkers."

"I'm not a Remalla. I'm Natalie's sister. She's Aaron's mom. I'm a Reverton. I went back to my maiden name after the last divorce and don't plan to abandon it again." She rifled through some tea packets. "I have peppermint, chamomile, hibiscus..."

"Peppermint is fine," said Daniels. "Thank you."

"I'd offer you coffee but it's much too late. Unless you're like Aaron. That boy can drink coffee at all hours and sleep like a log." She pulled out two bags and set them aside.

"You know him well."

"I'd like to think so. I hadn't seen him in a while, which is why it was so nice when he showed up the other night."

"Is he here?" The house was quiet, and Daniels wondered if she had any guests.

"No. He isn't. He's out at the shacks."

Daniels raised a brow. "The shacks?"

She nodded. "Yes. There's a row of fishing shacks down near the river. They rent for cheap during the off-season, and I told him that would be a better place for him to stay. At least for now." She pulled out two teacups and set them on the counter.

Daniels wondered why Rem leaving had been the better option. "You said over the phone that he was troubled. Did he not want to stay here?"

She picked up a large silver kettle and began to fill it with water from the faucet. "No. I asked him to go. That's why he's at the shacks."

Daniels raised a brow. "You kicked him out?"

After the kettle was filled, she turned off the water and put it on a burner. "The water will be ready in a minute." She came over and sat beside Daniels. She held his gaze. "Aaron holds you in high regard. You two have been partners a long time."

"We have. We're best friends. We've been through a lot together."

She nodded. "Aaron is struggling with something." She paused. "I just want to be sure it has nothing to do with you, and you're not here to make it worse."

Daniels appreciated her honesty. "You may not be a Remalla, but you certainly have the Remalla penchant to protect the people you love."

"That's not a Remalla thing, dear. That's a family thing." She narrowed her eyes, and he felt oddly exposed. He squirmed in his seat. "You have the same penchant, don't you?" she asked. "You want to protect him."

"I'm trying but I seem to be failing."

She continued to study him. "Sorry for the inquisition, but I had to be sure. I don't get a feel for people until I get them talking." She patted his hand. "I'm getting the sense you may be the only one to pull my nephew out of the hole he's dug for himself."

Daniels straightened. "What happened? Why couldn't he stay here?"

Sighing, she stared off. "When he arrived, he tried to act as if everything was fine. We caught up, and I made him lunch. But I knew something was wrong and I confirmed it when he didn't eat the apple fritters I offered him. He loves those things."

Daniels chuckled. "I bet he does."

"I tried to get him talking, but all he would say was that it was a work thing and he just needed to get away for a while and clear his head. I offered to let him stay in one of the upstairs rooms and he accepted." She slid out of her seat and returned to the kitchen.

"I didn't know this was a bed and breakfast," said Daniels. "Do you rent out the rooms?"

"I do on the weekends. I also have a separate area out back with a small gazebo. I leave everyone a breakfast basket at their door each morning. It's a lovely place to stay. Are you married?"

"I am."

"You should bring your wife sometime."

"I'd like that."

"Aaron stayed once with Jennifer a few years back." She grabbed a plate from the cabinet and set it on the counter. "Such a shame. She was a lovely girl."

The familiar grief bubbled up, and Daniels swallowed. He figured he must have met Genevieve at the funeral, but those days were a blur and he couldn't recall her. "She was."

Sighing, she opened up a tin and set some cookies on the plate. "Aaron's never been quite the same since she died."

"He's come a long way, though. He's battled through highs and lows, but I can see why you'd say that."

She brought the plate over and set it in front of Daniels. "Some homemade short bread cookies. Another one of Aaron's favorites. Help yourself."

"Thanks. They look delicious." He reached for a cookie. "You were saying Aaron took one of the upstairs rooms?" He bit into the cookie and understood why it was one of Rem's favorites.

"He did. But he had nothing with him. No luggage or overnight bag. I asked him about it, but he didn't explain. He said he'd get some stuff in town, then left for a bit and came back with a shopping bag. He stayed upstairs and later that evening, he came down and asked where he could go to sit by himself and get a drink."

Daniels nibbled on his cookie. "Did you tell him?"

"I did, but it came with a warning."

"Warning?"

The kettle began to whistle, and she took it off the burner. She filled the two teacups with hot water and set the kettle down. "I know the Remallas and how they cope with their problems. Aaron's father was no exception." She brought the teacups and the teabags over and set them on the table. "I was never a fan of Raymond, but Natalie loved him so I dealt with it."

Daniels took a cup and opened his teabag. "What does this have to do with Aaron going to get a drink?"

She opened her own teabag and set it in the water. "Raymond Remalla was a functional alcoholic, although I use the word functional loosely. Natalie denied it, and I suspect Aaron knew but never acknowledged it. He idolized his dad, at least until he was a teenager."

Daniels knew that Rem's father hadn't been around much when Rem was growing up, but his partner had never said much about it. "What are you trying to tell me?"

"I saw how Raymond handled his problems. He'd stumble home late at night drunk, barely coherent, and Natalie would have to clean him up, praying Aaron wouldn't wake up and see the mess. My first husband had similar issues. I was young and stupid back then and thought I could change him. Eventually, I figured things out and took matters into my own hands." She paused and dipped her tea bag. "I kicked my ex out and told myself I'd never put up with that shit again, and I haven't." She picked up a cookie. "I saw a similar look in Aaron's eyes before he went out that night. Despair. Anger. Maybe even hatred. I told him he was a grown man, and he was going to do what he was going to do. But if he came home a mess, it would be his last night here. He told me he understood."

Daniels leaned back in his seat, recalling several drunken nights with Rem over the years and a few Rem had all on his own. They weren't usual, but when they happened, they were memorable. "He came back drunk, didn't he?"

"He vomited in my shrubs and passed out on the stairs. I left him there, and he woke up with an aching back and a crushing headache. I asked him if he planned to do it again and, to his credit, he didn't lie. He said he probably would. That's when I suggested the shacks, and he left. I haven't seen him since, but I've heard things. Small towns talk. I know the locals and I'm good friends with the sheriff."

Daniels held his breath. "The sheriff?"

"Aaron's been frequenting Jimmy's. It's a small bar across from the shacks. Probably the perfect place to go to get stupid drunk and then stumble home. Except he didn't make it one night. Joe picked him up and brought him to the jail and let him sleep it off in a cell." She nibbled on her cookie.

Daniels set his cookie down, trying to fathom what could have Rem in such a miserable state that he'd get drunk several nights in a row. What had Allison told him? "Joe? He's the sheriff?"

"He is. He and I...we've been seeing each other. He could have easily arrested Aaron, but I asked him not to, and he was kind enough to go along, but I can't keep asking for favors. And that deputy of his...Randal Shaw...he's a...well, pardon my French, but he's an asshole. If it had been up to him, Aaron would still be in jail."

Daniels dunked his tea bag and then just let it sit in the water. He tried to think about what to do next. "You think Aaron's at Jimmy's now?"

"I'd bet my shortbread cookies on it. And I don't take that wager lightly." She put her hand on his wrist. "I'm worried, Gordon. I expected him back after a couple of nights or at least a phone call. But he hasn't reached out." She paused. "Did he do this after Jennifer died?"

Daniels recalled those days with sadness. Rem had barely left his bed after Jennie's death, other than for the funeral arrangements and the funeral itself. Back then, he could hardly get Rem to eat, much less drink. The drinking had come later. "He had his moments, but he didn't disappear for days without telling anyone where he went."

She set her teabag on the saucer and held her cup. "You think you can reach him? Because I certainly can't." She hesitated. "But I sense I'm not the one he needs to talk to."

Daniels studied his drink. After a pause, he picked it up, took a sip, and set it down. "Thank you for the tea, but I won't be able to finish it." He held his cookie and stood. "Where can I find the shacks, and this Jimmy's?"

Chapter Five

REM SHOT BACK THE rest of his tequila and banged the glass on the bar counter. "Another round, Jimmy."

Sharon shot back hers, too, and put her glass down. "Don't forget me."

Rem laughed. "And one for the lady."

"Thanks, babe." She hung an arm over his shoulders and whispered in his ear. "Care to dance with me again?"

She slurred a little, but Rem figured his words weren't much better. He swiveled around, and she wrapped her arms around his neck. "I'm not exactly sure I can stand." He smiled at her. Loose tendrils of hair hung down her neck from a messy ponytail and he swiped a tendril back. A sheen of sweat shone on her face from their last dance to a fast-paced tune from some pop star, but her red lipstick was perfectly in place. He figured he had few of her lipstick marks on his cheek and jaw. "How about we rest a second?" he asked.

Sharon swayed against him. "I can find us a slow tune, and then we can cuddle." She giggled and squeezed his shoulders.

"That's tempting," he said. "Maybe after the next drink."

Jimmy set two shot glasses on the bar counter. "Two tequilas," he said.

"Get me a beer, too, Jimmy," said Rem. He reached for a tequila and handed it to Sharon, and then took the other for himself. He held it up, and Sharon clinked her glass to his. "What are we toasting?" He tripped over the word 'toasting' and had to repeat it.

She kissed his cheek. "You're so damn cute when you're drunk." She clinked his glass to hers again. "Let's toast to love."

Rem's stomach fell, and he frowned. "I'd rather not."

Sharon ran a hand down his arm. "Oh, c'mon, sugar. Everybody needs love."

"Not me. Let's toast something else."

Marvin leaned back and stared at them. He'd been sitting two bar stools down from Rem since Rem had arrived earlier. "My godson's wife just had a baby," he said. "You want to toast to that?" He blinked his heavy lids, and Rem suspected he'd fall over if he stood. He'd bought Marvin almost as many drinks as Sharon.

Sharon smiled. "Perfect." She said, holding up her glass. "To babies. And fatherhood."

Rem's stomach churned again, and he raised a hand. "Nope. No babies and no fatherhood." He glanced at Marvin. "Sorry, Marvin."

Marvin knitted his brow. "Why the hell not?"

Rem tried to think, but his brain wouldn't cooperate. "Because it's apple pie day. Let's drink to apple pie." It was the only thing he could come up with. He lifted his glass.

"Apple pie?" asked Marvin.

"Work with me, Marvin," said Rem. "You want another free drink?"

Marvin lifted his glass. "To apple pie."

"Apple pie it is, baby," said Sharon, and she downed her drink.

Rem shot his tequila back and wondered if he should eat. He couldn't recall if he'd had dinner or not. He didn't even know what time it was, but it was dark out. He was sure he'd been at Jimmy's for least a couple of hours, but it was probably longer. His stomach rumbled. "You got any more nuts, Jimmy?'" he asked.

"Coming right up," said Jimmy.

"You want to play some pool?" asked Sharon. A new song played on the jukebox, and she moaned in his ear. "I like this song. You sure you don't want to dance?"

Rem almost slid off the barstool but managed to right himself. "I think I need something to eat." He looked down the bar. "Jimmy, you have any food?"

Sharon slid a hand around his waist. "We can go eat later if you want. I'll sneak you into the kitchen at a restaurant where I know a guy. We'll raid the fridge."

"You said that last night," said Rem. "We never made it."

"That's because you got me so hot and bothered." She ran a hand up his thigh.

Rem took a sip of his beer but didn't stop her roving hand.

"You want to go back to the bathroom?" she asked. "Maybe try again?"

Rem set his jaw, remembering their previous escapade. "Let's just take it slow." He sipped more beer and then set the glass down.

Her hand moved higher. "You were so intense. I love it rough."

Her words made his body heat, and he told himself to relax, but his mouth didn't listen. "You liked that?"

"I did." She moaned into his ear, and she bit his lobe. "I want you."

He grabbed her wrist when her fingers almost reached his crotch. His mind and body warred with each other, and the additional shot of tequila made everything blur for a second and he blinked. For a moment, he had the desperate impulse to leave, and he almost pushed her away. The thought of getting out of the bar, finding some dinner, taking a hot shower, getting a good night's sleep and driving home in the morning almost won, but then that ugly pang of anger and regret returned, and he recalled what he'd be returning to. Deciding to man up and finish what he'd started, he grabbed her hips and yanked her close. "I never disappoint a lady." He growled at her, and she yelped and laughed.

"Time to show me what you got, sugar." Grabbing his hand, she pulled him off the barstool. He held onto the counter for support while his inner demons raged. *Don't do this. Go back and get another drink. Leave now and get some sleep.* He ignored all the warnings and suggestions, though, and stumbling, started to follow her. Passing a wall where a large pane of glass with a beer slogan etched into it hung, he stopped cold. In the reflection, the front door opened, and Daniels walked in.

· · • • · • • · ·

After Daniels left Aunt Genevieve's, he headed toward the shacks and had found himself on a quiet road lined with more big trees along a nearby stream and river, a row of shacks, and various local shops and offices. He'd driven down it to get an idea of what was nearby and passed the sheriff's office, the post office, a barber shop, convenience store and Jimmy's Bar. He'd almost stopped at Jimmy's, but before he did, he

wanted to check out the shacks. He'd turned around and found a sign to
the office and parked. The shacks were scattered back into the trees near
the water, and he'd gotten out and walked down a path that led to the
individual cabins. Genevieve had been correct. They were tiny, and it
didn't take long to spot Rem's car parked in front of one of them toward
the end.

He'd jogged over and knocked, but no one had answered. The door had
been unlocked and he'd opened it to find a messy interior with a small
unmade pull-out sofa bed, a tiny kitchenette, a table with two wooden
chairs, a trashcan filled with paper plates and cups and some fast-food
bags, a bathroom, and an almost empty bottle of tequila sitting next to a
cold and half-filled pot of coffee on the counter.

After surveying the room where Rem had been sleeping, Daniels
quickly deduced he'd have to find a shack of his own. He returned to the
office where he'd found the owner and rented the shack next door. After
retrieving his car and parking in front of his rented cabin, he dumped his
bag and started walking toward Jimmy's. As he neared, he could hear loud
music playing and laughter, and he strode up the stairs and entered.

Jimmy's had a long bar with several round barstools. Mirrored neon
signs hung above and along the wall, and there were several tables–many
of which were occupied with patrons sitting and drinking. Two men
played pool in a back room where a big TV was mounted on the wall, and
a lively country song played from a jukebox. Two couples danced and
swayed to the music. Looking around, he stopped when he caught sight of
Rem. His partner was standing and wobbling toward what Daniels
guessed were the restrooms. A woman with light brown hair up in a
ponytail wearing tight jeans and a tighter spaghetti-strapped top guided
him by the hand. Studying him, Daniels held his breath. His partner's
disheveled hair hung loose around his face, his dull skin had a sheen of
sweat, and his puffy eyes drooped. He was unshaven, his clothes were
wrinkled, and his jeans bagged on him. Daniels blinked, unsure he was
seeing his partner.

He caught Rem's reflection in a mirror on the far wall and Daniels
didn't miss the subtle shock on his partner's face. The haunted look told
Daniels how far down the well Rem had fallen. It communicated a sadness
that Daniels had not seen since Jennie's death. But just as fast as Daniels

had caught it, it vanished. Rem stilled for a moment, but then he'd smiled and turned.

"Look who's here," he said, his smile wide. He put a hand on the bar to support himself. "Everybody, this is my partner. Gordon Daniels. Say 'hi' everybody."

Daniels watched some people turn toward him, including the bartender, an older man sitting at the bar, and a few customers at the tables. There was a muffled 'hi,', but then they looked away. The only exception was the woman with Rem, who stared at him with an unreadable expression, and a man sitting alone at one of the tables, who looked between him and Rem with a sneer.

He walked farther in and up to Rem. "Hey, partner. You forget how to answer a text or voicemail?"

Rem snorted and waved a hand. Daniels could see he was well past more than a few drinks. "Whatever," said Rem. "You found me, obviously."

"I did, with a little help." Daniels thought of Jennie and her instructions.

Rem's face fell. "Please tell me you didn't call my mother."

"No. I spared her the trouble." He looked Rem over. "But I may reconsider. She wouldn't be too pleased with the state you're in, or that you disappeared without telling anyone where you were going."

Rem swayed, and Daniels almost raised a hand to support him, but the woman beside him was faster. She wrapped an arm around Rem. "C'mon, baby. Let's go." She tugged on him.

"Hold up," said Rem. "This is my partner."

Her gaze traveled over Daniels. "What partner?"

Rem held his stomach and laughed. "We work together. Didn't I tell you?"

She leaned close and whispered in his ear. Rem blushed. "Not that kind of partner," he said.

"We're detectives," said Daniels.

She scowled. "Detectives? Like cops?" She shot a look at the man sitting alone. The man shot a stern look back and returned to his beer.

"Yup. Like cops. We catch bad guys, or we try to," said Rem. He pointed. "This is Sharon. She and I, uh, well, we're friends."

By the way Sharon clung to Rem, Daniels had to wonder if they were more than friends. "Nice to meet you," he said.

She nodded at him. "Sure."

A woman walked by wearing jeans, a clingy short-sleeved t-shirt, chunky earrings, and an apron. She held a tray and her nametag read 'Amy.' She stopped beside them. "Can I get you something to drink?"

"No, thanks," said Daniels.

"Yes. Get us all something," said Rem. "We want another tequila." He nodded at Sharon, then tilted his head toward the bar. "Marvin? You want a tequila? We're celebrating."

The older man at the bar lifted his head. "Fatherhood? Love? New babies?"

Rem frowned. "None of the above. We're toasting partners."

"Partners?" asked Marvin with a shrug. "Okay."

"Jimmy. Get Marvin a tequila, too," said Rem.

"No tequila for me," said Daniels, wondering how he was going to get Rem out of the bar. His partner was showing no interest in leaving, and it didn't help that Sharon was surgically attached to him.

"Oh, c'mon," said Rem. "You need a drink. You need to relax, like me."

"You relax anymore and you're going to fall over," said Daniels.

Rem grinned. "I'm holding up so far." He eyed the waitress. "He'll take a beer."

Amy nodded and walked away.

"Let's sit," said Rem, waving toward the barstools.

Sharon slid her hand down Rem's arm and pulled on him. "I thought we were going to the bathroom," she whispered.

"Later," said Rem. He walked toward the bar and slid into a stool next to Marvin.

Daniels wondered why Sharon was so eager to visit the restroom with Rem when the likely reason occurred to him. His stomach dropped, and he wanted Sharon away from his partner. He took the stool next to Rem. "You mind if we talk?" He looked back at Sharon who'd remained at Rem's side. She slid her arm over Rem's shoulders. "Alone?"

Sharon glared while Rem reached for a half-filled beer on the bar, took a sip and ate a peanut. "Talk? Whassis talk about?" He belched.

Daniels faced him. "Why you disappeared and didn't tell me? Why you've been sitting at Jimmy's the last four nights getting stupid drunk? Why you went to see Allison Albright?"

Rem went still at the last question and gripped his beer glass.

"Who's Allison, baby?" asked Sharon, grinning. "She your girlfriend?"

Rem tensed. "No." He went quiet and then that relaxed look returned. "She's not. Where's that tequila?"

Amy appeared on the other side of the bar and handed out three tequilas and a beer.

"Thanks, Amy," said Marvin.

"Rem." said Daniels. "Let's get out of here."

Rem raised his tequila. "To partners."

"To partners," said Marvin, slurring the word.

Daniels sighed.

Aiming a dirty look at Daniels, Sharon took her drink and shot it back. Rem and Marvin did the same.

Daniels sipped his beer, debating what to do and studying the man at the table who continued to watch the bar and sneer at Rem and Sharon. He was young with a chiseled jaw and a muscular build. His short reddish-brown hair was cut close to his scalp, and he had a big tattoo that ran down his neck. He sipped on his own beer, and when Daniels caught him looking, he looked away.

Rem went back to drinking his beer. "You talk to Aunt Gin?"

"Who?" asked Daniels. "You mean Genevieve?"

Rem nodded.

"Yeah. She told me you'd be here."

"She okay?"

"She is, but she's worried about you." He paused. "So am I."

Rem offered him a sideways glance. "Nothing to worry about. Just needed to get away for a few days."

"Right after talking to Allison? And without telling anyone?"

"Not anybody's business." Rem drank more beer.

"The hell it isn't," said Daniels. "If I'd pulled a stunt like this, you'd be all over my ass."

Rem furrowed his brow. "If I want to get away for a few days, I sure as hell can. I don't need to tell anyone or get anybody's permission."

"That's right. You don't have to do anything. But you've never done it before, so why start now?" asked Daniels. "What the hell happened, Rem?"

Rem looked away. "I don't want to talk about it."

Daniels set his jaw and told himself not to get frustrated. "I'm here to help you."

"I don't want your help," said Rem, his voice quiet. "I don't want anyone's help." He raised his glass and drained it. "Another beer, Amy...or Jimmy. Whoever." He set the glass down with a bang. "I'm beyond help, anyway, so you might as well go home."

Daniels put his hand on Rem's forearm. "Whatever it is, we can figure it out. Let's get out of here and get some food. Then you can get cleaned up and hopefully sleep, and tomorrow we'll tackle whatever ghost is haunting you."

Rem eyed Daniels' hand on his arm. "No thanks."

"What is it?" asked Daniels. "What is eating at you?"

"It's nothing."

Daniels shut his eyes. "If you talk about it, it will help." He opened his eyes. "You know it will."

Rem shook his head. "I...I...don't want to talk about anything."

Daniels prayed he was making progress. "Rem, God knows we've been through some shit and survived. We can do it again."

Rem hung his head. "I know, but that was different."

"Different how?"

The bartender, who Daniels assumed was Jimmy, slid a fresh beer to Rem. Rem grabbed it and took a healthy gulp.

A new song began to play, and Sharon squealed. "I love this song. C'mon, sugar. Let's dance." She tugged on Rem's arm.

Rem set his drink down. "Because, this time, partner," he paused, his eyes half-slits, "I just don't care anymore." His somber look made Daniels' heart hurt.

Sharon yanked on him again and Rem turned toward her.

"Rem—," said Daniels.

Rem stood and wobbled again, but Sharon held onto him. Rem looked back. "Go home, Daniels," he said. "There's nothing you can do for me."

He stared for a second, and then smiling, turned on the charm and grabbed Sharon by the waist. "Let's strike a pose, honey."

Sharon giggled, squealed again, and pulled Rem toward the dance floor.

Chapter Six

AN HOUR LATER, DANIELS sat at one of the empty tables, nursing his second beer. After refusing to leave, Rem had danced with Sharon through several songs. Daniels had taken the beer Rem had ordered for him and moved to a table not far from the man with the perpetual sneer. Knowing he wouldn't leave without Rem, he took his time to survey the bar and the people in it. The bar slowly began to fill as time passed. He'd finished his first beer while Rem and Sharon had slow danced, and tattoo guy continued to glare.

Amy had come by again, and he'd ordered the second beer. Eventually, Rem and Sharon stumbled back to the bar stools where they'd continued to talk and laugh. Daniels waited to see if his partner would join him, but Rem ordered another shot for him and Sharon. Marvin declined another drink, said he was leaving, and stood, but on his way out, he spotted Daniels, walked over and stopped at Daniels' table. He put his hand on the back of a chair and leaned on it. "He's usually here until closing, unless he gets kicked out."

Daniels eyed Rem and Sharon as they spoke to a couple who'd recently joined the fray at the bar. "You in a hurry, Marvin?"

Marvin raised a brow. "Hurry? To go home and sleep? Nah, not really."

Daniels pushed a chair out with his foot. "Have a seat. I'll buy you a water."

Marvin swayed and chuckled. "Big spender." He sat in the chair beside Daniels.

"You drink any more liquor and you'll never make it out the door, and you sure as shit better not be driving."

Marvin scoffed. "I live two streets over. I walk it."

Daniels nodded, figuring Marvin would be a good source of the information he needed, if he was sober enough to answer. "Good. You come here a lot?"

Marvin shrugged. "I come here enough. Jimmy's a good guy and a friend. I've lived in this town close to thirty years. My wife and I owned some of the shops until she passed a couple years ago. Then I retired, but I come here some nights just to get out and be social."

"You drink this much every night?"

Marvin belched. "I've drunk more this week than I have in a month since your friend arrived. He's been buying my drinks."

"Nothing's stopping you from saying no."

"Hey, if he's offering, I'm accepting."

"I can see that." Daniels chose not to argue with Marvin about taking advantage of Rem. "You know these people?"

He looked around. "I know 'em all."

A big guy with wide shoulders, a thick neck and tree-trunk legs walked into the bar. Jimmy yelled at him. "Hey, Big John. How are ya?"

Big John grunted and waved a hand. "I'm alive and breathing." He walked to the bar and spoke to Jimmy.

"Who's that guy?' asked Daniels.

Marvin raised a brow. "That's Big John. He comes here on busier nights and acts as a bouncer in case anyone gets riled up. This weekend is the Dandelion Festival. It will be more crowded than usual, so he'll be working."

Daniels watched Big John survey the bar, and then walk to the door and stand beside it. "Who's tattoo guy?" Daniels nodded toward the man still sitting alone a few tables down who continued to drink and glare at Rem and Sharon.

"That's Scott Herndon. He's a local. He works for his dad at the auto shop and does maintenance and handyman stuff for a lot of the B&B owners around here."

"Why has he been eyeing my partner?"

"Herndon?" Marvin glanced at Scott. "He and Sharon used to date, and she broke up with him last month. But those two are always on and off.

Right now, they're off and she's hanging all over your friend. I suspect she's doing it to piss Scott off."

Daniels sipped his beer. "Tell me about Sharon. She a local?"

"Not really. She moved here almost a year ago. She's a teller at the bank and she comes to Jimmy's because her friend is Amy, the waitress."

Daniels eyed the woman who'd served him earlier. She was taking an order from a couple sitting at a table beside him. "Is Amy a local?"

"Oh, yeah. I've known her since she was a kid. She works at the car dealership during the day and works here at night. She's saving up to go to school. Amy can be a bit of a troublemaker, but she's got a good head on her shoulders, that is, when she uses it."

"And Jimmy?" asked Daniels.

"Been here almost as long as me. He left town for a while after he got married, but then came back after he divorced, and opened the bar. He's well liked and well known around here."

Daniels recalled what Genevieve had said about the sheriff. "I heard my partner got picked up by the sheriff the other night."

Marvin smiled. "That's Sheriff Joe Whistler, but we just call him Sheriff Joe. Good man, but a sad story. I think a lot of us have spent a night or two in one of his cells."

"What's his sad story?"

Amy came over, and Daniels asked for two waters. She nodded and left. Rem and Sharon continued to drink at the bar.

"He's a local, too. His dad was the mayor for a while until he died of a heart attack. His brother is Rocky Whistler who runs the barbershop. Joe was deputy at the time of his dad's death, but then he ran for sheriff and won. He was married at the time to a woman named Sybil. Sybil wasn't from around here and she clearly hadn't planned on staying. She made Joe's life hell. He wanted kids but she didn't. She bullied townspeople, belittled Joe, and didn't hide that she hated Rocky. Nobody liked her but Joe didn't believe in divorce. She ran one of the retail shops in town and had a hard time keeping any staff. Nobody could work with her for long before she ran them off."

Amy returned with the waters and set them down.

Daniels thanked her and drank some water, recalling that Genevieve had said she was seeing the sheriff. "What happened to Sybil? She still around?"

Marvin drank some water, too, and rubbed his eyes. "No, she isn't." He put his elbows on the table. "She had a huge blow up with one of the town's most respected residents."

"Who's that?"

Marvin shot out a thumb toward the bar. "Your friend's aunt, Genevieve Reverton."

Daniels sat up. "Aunt Genevieve?"

"You know her?"

"Met her this afternoon. Nice lady."

"One of the best. Gin would give you the blouse off her back. When my Lila died, she kept me fed and checked in on me every day for a week. And she let family members who came in for the funeral stay at her house for free. She, along with the rest of the town, put up with Sybil because Joe was a friend, but then one day, Gin walked into Sybil's store. Nobody knows why, but she confronted Sybil. Sybil didn't like Gin, either, and she gave as good as she got. The two women ended up in the street, with Gin telling Sybil to do everyone a favor and leave town, and Sybil threatening Gin with a lawsuit if she didn't back down. Gin shoved Sybil into the big fountain on Main Street, and the sheriff had to break it up, but not before everyone in the area got a cell phone pic of Sybil in the water. She was furious and insisted Joe arrest Gin. He refused and just told Genevieve to go home. Gin told Sybil she'd been warned and then left. Sheriff Joe took Sybil home but the next day he had black eye and a broken nose. Sybil got in the last word and Joe paid the price."

Daniels tried to visualize the nice lady he'd met earlier who'd offered him a cookie threatening someone and shoving her into a fountain. "What happened after the fight?"

Marvin held his water glass. "A week later, Sybil was gone."

"She left?"

Marvin narrowed his eyes. "She went out at night, into the woods, and never returned."

Daniels didn't understand. "She walked into the woods? Did she die?"

"Nobody knows, Detective. But she did the one thing anyone who lives around here never does."

"What's that?"

"Enter the woods at night."

"Why not?"

"Because they're dangerous."

"Are there bears? Or wolves?"

Marvin paused. "That's what some like to think, but too many have encountered something else and it's not a normal animal, or normal anything."

Daniels hooked an arm over the back of his chair. "What the hell are you trying to tell me, Marvin?"

"The woods around Merrimac are haunted, Detective, and if you believe the stories, by a witch and her hellhound."

Daniels couldn't hold back a chuckle. "You have had a lot to drink tonight."

"I wish I could blame it on the alcohol, but I can't. Sybil wasn't the first to go into those woods and not come out, and she wasn't the last."

"When did Sybil disappear?"

"Almost four years ago, I think," said Marvin.

Daniels debated how far to entertain Marvin's delusions, but his curiosity got the best of him. "Okay. I'll bite. Who else disappeared?"

"A couple. Five years before Sybil. Before them, it was just the typical spooky stories. People would say they heard or saw things, like terrifying howls or ghosts. The couple had heard that stuff and were thrill seekers. They walked into the forest after dark, determined to expose the secrets of those woods, and never came back. The rumors took off after that. Some say they were attacked by animals, maybe those bears you mentioned, and were dragged off. Some say they just walked to the next town, caught a cab, drove away and are living on some Caribbean Island. Nobody knows, except the locals."

Daniels narrowed his eyes. "What do the locals believe?"

Marvin's expression darkened. "It's shifted over the years, like the stories. But most think they encountered the witch, and she sent her hound after them, but they didn't get out in time. A search party went looking, but all they found was the woman's hairband and the man's shoe. Nothing else."

Rem's laughter rang out from the bar, and Daniels saw him speaking to a patron sitting beside him. Leaning over, Rem almost fell off his stool, but Sharon held on to him even though she almost fell herself. Daniels realized that if he didn't get Rem out of there soon and back to the shack, he was going to have to sling his partner over his shoulders. "I'm sorry, Marvin. But I'm not buying it."

Marvin smiled with weariness. "Visitors always say that, but they avoid the woods at night, too."

"I bet they do. You say something enough times, it might as well be true."

"Merrimac sits on the edge of six thousand acres of dense forest, Detective. You go out there without knowing what you're doing, it's dangerous enough, but you add an element that doesn't want you there, it's damn scary."

"You obviously believe the stories."

Marvin squirmed in his seat. "I believe 'em because I've witnessed it myself. I went out there. I got drunk one night with a friend who was visiting. He heard the rumors and like you, he didn't buy it. After leaving Jimmy's, he dared me to walk into the woods. I'd told him about the challenge, and he wanted to do it."

"Challenge?"

Marvin nodded. "It's a thing. The high school kids came up with it. The locals know about it, and some have tried it."

"I'm afraid to ask."

Marvin sipped more water. "I should have gotten that last drink."

"Your liver is thankful you didn't. What's the challenge?"

"You head out on the trail outside of town after dark. You basically stay on it for four miles and then come back."

"That's it?"

Marvin nodded. "Pretty much."

"How many have made it?"

"None, including myself."

Daniels narrowed his eyes. "What happened when you did it?"

Marvin shuddered. "Scared me so bad, I almost pissed my pants. We got about a mile, mile and a half. You're not supposed to leave the trail because if you do, you may never find it again. We heard the standard shit. The creepy wind, the hooting owls, and the crickets, but then..." he paused, "...we heard something else."

Daniels could only imagine. "What?"

"A growl." Marvin's face paled. "Low and deep. And not a bear or a wolf. I tried to tell myself that's what it was, but it wasn't. We stopped and listened, and it came again, only closer. That thing was nearby. We started to back away, and...and that's when I saw it."

Daniels almost groaned. "Saw what?"

"The eyes. Two red glowing eyes. Watching us from the trees, and then we heard another growl, and we took off. We couldn't get out of there fast enough."

Daniels shook his head. "That's called the power of the mind, Marvin. Fear will make you see and hear things that aren't there."

"They were there. I'd swear it on my sweet Lila's soul." He tilted his head. "Ask Amy. She just went out there herself. Tried the challenge with some young fella. They didn't last long before they saw it, too."

Daniels sighed. "Let me take a wild guess. You and your friend were drunk, and so was Amy and her fella."

"Nobody would dare to go out there unless they were."

"You're proving my point, Marvin."

Marvin shrugged. "Suit yourself, but you've been warned. Don't go in the woods at night."

"You said someone else disappeared after Sybil," said Daniels. "They try the challenge too?"

"Almost two years ago. A man walked out there. Name was Doug." Marvin waved his fingers. "Doug...something. Said he was going to confront the witch and her hound and dispel all the stupid stories. He never returned." He sipped some water. "Some people believe he was murdered, but they never found a body. The rumors just morph over the years."

"Poor Doug." Daniels wondered if Doug had been hired to disappear into the woods to keep the town's ghosts alive and well. It probably brought in a few extra tourist dollars every year. "What about during the day? Can you hike then?"

"Just stay on the trail, and you'll be fine, and be home before you lose the light. People who go off trail during the day report getting disoriented and almost lost. And if you leave the trail after dark, then good luck and say your prayers."

Daniels thought of Sheriff Joe. "If there were all these stories, then why did Sybil go out there?"

Marvin eyed his water. "That's just it. Nobody knows. Joe said he got up in the night and she was gone. He went out looking and found her backpack at the edge of the woods just beyond the head of the trail. The next morning, Jimmy told Joe that he had seen her. He'd closed the bar and was driving past the trail on his way to some lady's house and he'd spotted Sybil's car. He stopped and saw Sybil standing near the trees. He called out to her, but she'd cussed at him to mind his own damn business, so he did. Nobody saw her again."

Daniels figured Sybil had found a way to escape while torturing her husband at the same time. Sybil had perhaps joined the couple on the Caribbean Island. "That's quite a story."

Amy stopped by the table. "You guys want anything else?"

Daniels looked up at her. "Not a drink, but Marvin here tells me you tried the challenge recently."

Her eyes widened, and her skin paled like Marvin's.

"You see the eyes and hear the growl?" asked Daniels.

Gripping the tray, she swallowed. Marvin waited and didn't say a word.

"I did," she said. "I saw and heard both...and I saw a house."

Marvin straightened. "A house? What house?"

"It looked old," said Amy.

Daniels was curious, too. "Abandoned?"

She shrugged, her body tense. "I don't know. Me and Manny, we wanted to be the first to make it all the way down the trail and back. We were stupid and we'd had too much to drink. We left the trail, but I didn't think it was that big of a deal."

"Shit," said Marvin. "The damn witch has a house."

Daniels almost rolled his eyes.

"We kept going deeper into the trees, and that's when I saw it," said Amy. "It looked scary as hell. It was two stories with some kind of a red glow coming through the windows. I don't know if it was abandoned or not. I wanted to get closer, but Manny freaked and that's when we heard the growl."

"And saw the eyes?" asked Marvin.

She nodded. "Both sets."

Marvin frowned. "Both?"

"I'll never forget it. I saw that creepy house, the growling started, and two sets of red eyes were watching us." She paused, and Daniels wondered if he should order Amy her own drink. "Whatever's out there," she said, her eyes round, "There's two of them."

Chapter Seven

DANIELS LOOKED BETWEEN MARVIN and Amy and didn't know what to believe. He figured it didn't matter, though, because as soon as he got his partner out of there and sobered up, they'd be getting out of town and heading home. He had no interest in taking the challenge and knew Rem wouldn't even walk into peaceful woods at night, never mind haunted ones.

Hearing loud voices at the bar, he saw Rem toast the couple beside him and down another shot. Sharon leaned across the bar, saying something to Jimmy and Rem stood, holding onto the counter, and by the look on his face, Daniels guessed he was headed to the bathroom.

Sharon saw him, eyed her ex, and ran up beside Rem. She slid her arm around him and whispered into his ear. Rem said something back and shook his head, but Sharon kept up her harassment. They headed toward the back and realizing that Rem could barely stand and seeing Sharon hanging all over him, Daniels had had enough. He took a guess as to what Sharon was up to and was fed up with these people taking advantage of his inebriated partner. An idea flashed in his mind, and he eyed Big John and Scott Herndon. Rem stopped to lean against the wall outside the restroom and Sharon pushed up against him. She slid her hands down his chest, although Rem grabbed her wrists to stop their descent.

Amy had walked away, and Daniels leaned over to Marvin, who'd gone back to sipping his water. "Listen, Marvin," said Daniels. "Whatever happens in the next few minutes, stay back and hug the walls. Don't get too close."

Marvin furrowed his brow.

Acting fast, Daniels stood and walked over to Scott Herndon, who was glowering at Sharon and Rem. "You Scott Herndon?" asked Daniels. He stood directly in Herndon's line of sight and blocked his view but knew Rem would be able to see everything.

Herndon set his beer down and looked up, his eyes menacing. "Who the hell's asking?"

Daniels pointed. "You've been sitting here all night, drinking and staring daggers at your lady, who appears to prefer my friend. What's your problem?"

Herndon tensed in his seat. "That's none of your fucking business. Sit your ass down, shithead."

The noisy bar quieted, and Daniels could hear murmuring. "The only shithead around here is you. You gonna sit there and cry into your beer or go find someone else who'll actually want an ugly asshole like you? I can see why she prefers my friend, because you look as dull as a mule and you probably smell like one, too."

Herndon stood. He was shorter than Daniels, but he made up for it in girth. "You think because you're some damn detective, I won't kick your fuckin' ass?"

Daniels sneered back. "Let's find out." He picked up Herndon's half-filled beer, lifted it, and poured it over Herndon's head.

The effect was instantaneous. Herndon knocked the glass out of his hand and rushed at Daniels. He wrapped his arms around him and shoved him backwards. Feeling like he'd been hit by an angry bull, Daniels stumbled backwards into the table behind him, which skidded, cracked and broke with the added weight. Hitting the ground with a thud, Daniels groaned when the air left his lungs in a whoosh. The people sitting at the table had darted away just before Daniels, with Herndon on top of him, had landed, but their drinks weren't as lucky. Glass shattered, and Daniels felt liquid soak his shirt.

Daniels raised an arm to protect himself, but Herndon was fast, and he slugged Daniels in the jaw. Daniels' head rocked back and hit the floor. Grunting, he forced himself to move and went to grab a piece of table leg to use as a weapon when a flash of dark hair flew out of nowhere and slammed into Herndon. The weight fell away from Daniels, and he sat up to see Rem wrestling Herndon.

A man Daniels had seen at the bar jumped in and grabbed Rem from behind. Rem flailed, and Daniels stood, grabbed the man's shoulder and pulled him off Rem. The man swiveled, and Daniels reared an arm back and hit the man in the face. Blood gushed from his nose, and the man stumbled back and fell into another table that had been vacated by whoever had been sitting there.

Unrestrained, Rem slugged Herndon in the face, but it barely slowed Herndon down. He shoved Rem back. If Rem hadn't been drunk, he would have had Herndon on his back with his arms pulled up behind him within seconds, but Rem lost his balance and fell sideways. Herndon was up in a flash, and reached for Rem, but before he could hit him, Daniels tackled and knocked Herndon back into a booth. He heard another crack, the table they'd fallen into collapsed, and grunting, he and Herndon fell to the floor again.

There was a distant scream, and Daniels managed to slug Herndon in the jaw before something grabbed him from behind and yanked him back. He struggled to free himself but failed. Turning, he saw Big John holding him in an iron grip. John dragged him away, and leaning over, John grabbed Rem by the arm and lifted him like he was a piece of broken furniture.

Rem protested, but Iron John didn't even blink. He pulled Daniels and Rem to the front door, kicked it open, yanked them to the porch and shoved them off it like they were high school kids. Daniels hit the dirt with smack, and he heard Rem curse and hit the ground beside him.

Iron John barely offered them a second glance. "You two come back in here," he said with a point and a sneer, "and I'll get mean." He turned and went back inside.

His jaw throbbing, Daniels sat up in the dirt. He brushed off his wet shirt and eyed Rem, who was on his back, staring up at the stars. Rem held his head and moaned.

"How you doin', partner?" asked Daniels, breathing hard.

Rem rolled to his side and got a hand beneath him. "Just peachy." He shoved himself up with a grimace. "Shit. That hurt."

"They don't call him Big John for nothing." Daniels rubbed a sore shoulder.

Rem held his stomach. "Did you do that on purpose?"

Daniels slapped an innocent look on his face. "Who, me?"

Rem scowled at him. "What the hell were you thinking?"

"I had to get you out of there, and I didn't feel like waiting around." He got to his knees and groaned. "I figured it would be effective."

"And painful." Rem attempted to get up. "You could have just—" He grimaced and even in the dark, Daniels could see his face pale.

"Uh...uhm..." Daniels looked around for a suitable spot. "...the bushes."

Rem barely had time to crawl over to a nearby shrub before he puked up the alcohol in his stomach. Daniels waited until he was finished before he stood, stretched his sore neck and squatted next to Rem. "You done?"

Rem moaned. "I feel terrible." He wretched again, coughed, and spit into the shrub.

"I bet. Just wait until tomorrow. Think you can stand?"

Rem clutched his belly and leaned his shoulder into a post supporting the porch. "Just leave me here to die. They can get my body in the morning."

Daniels looked down the quiet street. The music started up again inside the bar, and Daniels saw no sign of Herndon or Sharon. "Tempting, but how about we get you some place more comfortable?"

"I'm comfortable here," said Rem, his eyes closed, and his head on a strange slant against the wood.

"Yeah. You look it. C'mon, partner." He leaned low, took Rem's arm and put it around his shoulder. He hooked his own arm around Rem's back and side and lifted with a grunt. "God. You're heavier than you look." He got Rem on his feet.

Rem mumbled. "You're no lightweight either."

"Yeah, but you're not carrying me."

Rem made a snort. "Good point." He tried to take a step but stumbled. "Whoops."

Daniels held him up. "This is usually a simple procedure. You put one foot in front of the other."

"That's what they all say." Rem chuckled. "But they're all liars."

After a few steps, Rem got into a rhythm, and Daniels slowly walked him back toward the shacks, praying Rem wouldn't barf on him. Rem bobbed his head but managed to stay upright.

"Is okay," he said with a slur. "I can walk."

"Sure you can," said Daniels, holding Rem when he stumbled again. "You're doing great."

Rem's eyes widened. "I am?"

"Best walker in town." Daniels was grateful it was a cool evening because his partner was getting heavy, and Daniels was starting to sweat. "Almost there."

Rem made a soft laugh. "I am a good walker, aren't I?" He tripped on a root protruding from the ground, and Daniels almost dropped him. "Sorry," said Rem, righting himself. "Something ran in front of me." He giggled.

"Yeah. Better be careful out here," said Daniels. He got his arm back under Rem and continued walking.

Rem lifted his free hand. "It was like this big." He waved his arm.

"You're lucky to be alive." Daniels saw Rem's shack and headed toward it.

"That's what I said," said Rem. The word 'said' came out 'shed.' "It's dang...danger...out here."

"You mean dangerous?" Daniels thought of the haunted woods nearby. "You have no idea." He got to Rem's door and opened it, happy it was unlocked. He helped Rem inside, took him to the open sofa bed and sat him on it. "There you go. Take a load off." He straightened, wiped the sweat from his brow and closed the door. "You okay? You're not going to puke again, are you?"

Rem wobbled. "Great. Feel great." He started to tip over when Daniels grabbed him. "Hey, he said, "let's take this off before you crash." He wrangled Rem's jacket off before Rem fell to his side on the bed. "There you go." He grabbed Rem's feet and pulled them up on the bed. He took off Rem's sneakers and tossed them on the floor. "How's that? Better?"

Rem didn't answer, and Daniels realized Rem had passed out. Shaking his head as his partner started to snore, Daniels adjusted the pillow and blankets, covered Rem, and grateful to be out of that bar and ready to get some sleep, he slipped out of the shack and headed toward his own.

Chapter Eight

THE NEXT MORNING, DANIELS woke early, stretched and rolled out of his small, lumpy bed. Figuring Rem would still be asleep, he showered and put on some fresh clothes. His plan was to wake Rem, get him cleaned up and some food into him, hopefully get him to talk, and then pack up and hit the road. The sooner they could leave, the better. Daniels sensed it would help to get Rem home, where he could resume his routine and start to feel better.

His stomach rumbling, he left his shack and headed to Rem's. He wondered if there was a diner nearby where they could get some breakfast. Anxious to get his partner up, he didn't bother to knock and opened Rem's door.

He slipped inside but stopped when he didn't see Rem. His sneakers were gone, but his jacket was still where Daniels had tossed it the night before. "Rem?" he called. The bathroom door was open, but it was empty. "Rem?"

His partner wasn't there.

Scratching his head, Daniels turned and went outside. Rem's car was still parked in the same place and Daniels had seen his keys on the table inside. Had he gone for a walk?

Looking around, Daniels spotted a small dirt trail leading down toward the water. Nobody was around, and he jogged down it. "Rem?" he called. "You out here?"

He made it to the water's edge but didn't see anyone. *Shit*, he thought. *Where the hell did he go?* He walked along the bank, but then turned back. Rem was not the sort to head into any woods, and certainly not at night. A nudge of worry began to creep up his spine. He returned to the trail and headed back to the shack when he heard a soft moan.

He stopped and swiveled toward the sound. "Rem?" He stepped off the trail and heard the sound of shuffling leaves. Moving faster, he jogged around a big tree and almost tripped over Rem's legs. His partner was lying against a wide tree trunk, wearing the same clothes as the previous night. One sneaker was on, and the other foot was covered only by a dirty, purple-striped sock. Rem had dirt on his pants, leaves in his hair and a bruise on his forehead.

Daniels squatted next to him. "What the hell are you doing out here?" He looked over his partner, but apart from his bruised head, he didn't see any injuries.

Rem moaned again, rubbed his neck and blinked his eyes. "Where am I?"

The wind whistled through the trees and a bird sang in the distance. "You're in the great outdoors."

Rem squeezed his temples. "My head hurts."

"I bet it does. How'd you get out here?" He leaned closer. "You must have fallen and bumped your head."

Rem squinted and closed his eyes. "God, it's bright."

"It's called the sun. It tends to shine."

"It's killing me." He clutched his belly. "Everything hurts."

"Did you come out here to take a leak?" asked Daniels. It was the only explanation that made sense. "You know you have a bathroom?"

Rem opened his bloodshot eyes. "I...uh...I guess." He paused. "I don't remember."

"Where's your other shoe?" Daniels stood and looked around the area. "Did you lose it?"

"What shoe?"

"The one you wear on your right foot. It helps to wear one on each foot when you walk."

Rem wiggled the toes of his foot with the dirty purple sock. "I don't know."

"Here it is." Daniels pulled it from a pile of leaves. "You're lucky you didn't end up in the water."

"What water?"

Daniels handed Rem his shoe. "That big puddle over there." He pointed to the nearby rock-strewn stream that fed into the river. "Do you know where you are or do I have to tell you that, too?"

Rem grimaced. "I know exactly where I am." He took his shoe and held it. "In hell." He rested his head back on the tree trunk. "Just leave me here to die and turn to dust, and let my body blow away in the wind." He closed his eyes again. "Or let the wolves eat me."

Daniels studied his partner and squatted beside him again. "I hate to tell you this, but you're not in hell. You're in Merrimac." He took the shoe, grabbed Rem's foot and put it back on. "Imagine that. The slipper fits. Looks like you're the princess."

"And you're the prince?" Rem opened his eyes and glowered. "Lucky me."

"C'mon. Let's get you back to your favorite shack. There's a hot shower with your name on it."

Rem expelled a heavy sigh. "Just let me lie here."

"Sorry, I can't."

"What if I gave you a million dollars?"

"You don't have a million dollars, but even if you did, I'd still say no."

Rem scowled. "I really hate it when you're so damn dependable."

Daniels held out a hand. "No. You don't. It's what you love about me." He grasped Rem's palm. "Let's get you up."

Reluctantly, Rem stood with a deep groan, and Daniels slowly walked him back to the shack. Once inside, Rem sat on the rumpled bed.

"You got any clean clothes?" asked Daniels.

"Top drawer."

Daniels opened the drawer of the small bureau and found a pair of sweatpants and a t-shirt. "This is it?"

"I didn't exactly pack. I just grabbed a few things from the thrift store after I got here." Rem started to lean toward the pillow.

Daniels grabbed him by the arm. "No, you don't, Sleeping Beauty. In case you missed it, you're filthy and you don't smell so great either. Hop in the shower and toss out what you're wearing." He pulled Rem up and handed him the sweatpants and t-shirt. "I'll find a cleaner and throw your stuff in the wash while you're showering. I'll pick up some food, too. By the looks of you, you haven't had a decent meal in a while."

Rem stood and swayed. "You hate me, don't you?"

"Yes," said Daniels. "I tend to feed and clothe people I hate. You caught me."

Rem hung his head. "You don't have to do this."

Daniels spotted the tremble in Rem's fingers. "Yes, I do." He considered saying more but decided to wait. "You'll feel better after you shower and eat, and then we'll talk."

"There's nothing to talk about."

"Then we'll stare at each other in uncomfortable silence."

Rem finally met his gaze, and they shared a quiet look. "Fine," said Rem softly.

"Good," said Daniels, feeling as if he'd won one small battle.

Rem headed toward the bathroom. "There's a washer and dryer in the office. The owner lets the tenants use them."

"Even better. Thanks." He picked up Rem's dirty clothes hanging over the chairs. "And you better be here when I get back."

Rem hesitated, but then nodded and headed into the bathroom.

· · · ● · ● · · ·

Daniels left the shack, walked to the office and found the washer and dryer. About to toss in Rem's stuff, he spotted what looked like blood on the sleeve of the shirt Rem had been wearing. It was only a few drops, and Daniels assumed Rem must have scratched himself during his early morning jaunt. He threw in the clothes and started the machine. Recalling the small convenience store down the road, he eyed the time, and while the washer ran, he walked to the store and grabbed enough groceries to tide them over until they could get out of town. Holding the bags, he returned to the office. Seeing the washing machine had a few minutes left on its cycle, he was about to bring the bags back to Rem's when his cell rang.

He pulled it out of his pocket and saw it was Lozano. He answered. "Morning, Cap."

"Morning. You find him?"

"I did. He's visiting his aunt in Merrimac, but he's definitely got something on his mind."

"How's he doing?"

Daniels chose to keep Rem's drinking to himself. "He's been better. I'm going to try and figure out what's bugging him this morning."

Lozano sighed over the phone. "I just got off the phone with Schultz. She got a hold of the video of Rem's visit with Allison. We know why Remalla disappeared. You sitting down?"

Daniels gripped the phone. "No."

"Maybe you better."

Daniels opened his mouth to argue but spotted a bench outside the office. Wondering what Lozano would say, he walked over and sat. "Okay. I'm sitting. What is it?"

Lozano didn't hesitate. "Allison's pregnant, and she told Remalla the baby is his."

Daniels didn't move. He felt like he'd been hit with a bucket of icy water.

"She told him she believed the baby was a girl, that she planned to raise her with Rem's involvement if she was acquitted, but if she wasn't, that she wanted Rem to raise the child. Allison expects him to visit with their daughter if she ends up in prison."

Tongue-tied, Daniels opened and closed his jaw, but nothing emerged.

"Daniels? You there?"

Daniels' shock turned to anger. "She's lying, Cap."

"That was Kate's thought, too. But she checked with the jail's doctor. It's confirmed. Allison is three months pregnant."

"That doesn't mean it's Rem's baby. It has to be Victor's."

"Rem said the same. Allison told him D'Mato had had a vasectomy. I checked with the coroner who pulled the medical records. Allison was correct. D'Mato's not the father."

Daniels' mind raced to come up with another explanation. "Then it's somebody else's."

"Maybe, but maybe not. But there's no way to know until the baby is born."

Daniels set the grocery bags on the ground and dropped his head. "Shit," he said. "That means at least six months of Rem having to wait and wonder."

"And if there are no delays, Allison gets to walk into that courtroom before a jury nine months pregnant..."

"...telling the whole damn world that Rem is the father of her child. Son-of-a..." Daniels gripped his temples. "No wonder he's a mess."

"I can imagine what he's going through, but we still need him front and center. His testimony is required to put her away."

Daniels sat up and fell against the back of the bench. He thought of Allison's attorney, Kenneth Measy. "That's why Measy is so damn smug. Rem will be testifying against the supposed mother of his child. He's gonna use that to gain the jury's sympathy."

"It's not going to be easy. You know your partner. If he believes it's his baby, he'll fall over backward to protect his child. I just don't want that to extend to Allison."

Daniels blew out a breath. Now that he understood, it didn't surprise him that Rem had been drinking himself into a stupor since learning the news. "I'll talk to him."

"It'll be up to you to get him through this. It's going to be a long six months in addition to a difficult trial." He paused. "And if it's confirmed that the child is his..."

Daniels closed his eyes. "Yeah...I know." He tried to think about what he would say to Rem. "Don't worry, Cap. Rem will be ready. We'll figure it out." Thinking of Rem alone in his shack, he opened his eyes. "I need to go."

"Keep me posted and let me know when you're on your way. Schultz needs to talk to Rem."

"I will. I'll call you when we're headed out." He said his goodbyes and hung up with Lozano. Still in disbelief, he stood and returned to the office, where he moved Rem's clothes from the washer to the dryer, grabbed the groceries and headed back to the shack.

Chapter Nine

AFTER EMERGING FROM THE shower, Rem dried off, brushed his teeth and dressed in the clean sweatpants and t-shirt. His head still pounded, but he felt a little more human, and he eyed the unmade sofa bed. The urge to crawl into it and go back to sleep almost won, but he was sick of sleeping. He'd either been in the bed or the bar since he'd arrived. Determined to stay awake, he smoothed the sheets, closed the bed and sat on the sofa. Resting his head back, he shut his eyes, and waited. Fatigue took over though, and he dozed until he heard the door open and close. He opened his eyes.

Daniels entered, holding a couple of plastic bags. He stopped beside Rem and pulled out a bottled water. "Here. I got you some aspirin."

Rem took the water. "Thanks."

"Your clothes are in the dryer. They should be done soon." Daniels set the bags down. "How do you feel?"

"Only mildly horrible. The shower helped."

"That's progress." He cracked a bottle and shook out a couple of aspirin. "Here. Take these, and I'll make you a sandwich."

Rem took the pills and swallowed them down with the water. Feeling weary, he rested his head back again and closed his eyes. He heard the bags shuffling, Daniels moving and the clanking of whatever he was doing.

After a few minutes, Daniels spoke. "Come and get it."

Rem lifted his head and saw a paper towel with a sandwich on it.

"Peanut butter and jelly," said Daniels, sitting with his own sandwich. "Your favorite."

Rem pushed up. "It hasn't been my favorite since I was twelve."

"Well, there aren't any Taco del Fuegos in town, so it'll have to do."

Rem stood with his water and sat at the nicked wooden table. "Maybe I should open a taco stand. Make a killing in Merrimac." Eyeing the sandwich, his stomach flipped, and he played with the edge of the paper towel.

Daniels took a bite of his own sandwich and chewed. "Not hungry?"

Rem rubbed his belly. "I guess not."

"At least eat a couple of bites or that aspirin is going to upset your stomach."

"Yeah." Rem nodded. He picked up the sandwich and took a bite. It had no flavor, and he almost spit it out but forced himself to chew and swallow it.

"That good, huh?"

"Sorry. I haven't had much of an appetite." Thinking of Allison and his predicament, he put the sandwich down and drank some water.

Daniels finished his bite. "You want to talk about it?"

Rem set his water down and stared at the table. "Nothing to talk about."

"You keep saying that, but we both know that's not true."

Rem looked up and they made eye contact. Several seconds passed. "You know, don't you?" asked Rem.

Daniels wiped his lips with a paper towel. "Talked to Lozano while I was out. The prosecutor got a hold of the video from your visit to the jail."

Rem sank in his seat. "I figured."

"You still want to tell me there's nothing to talk about?"

Rem traced a water droplet down the side of his bottle. "What do you want me to say? Congratulations? You're about to be an uncle?"

"You don't know that it's your child."

"And I don't know that it isn't."

Daniels went quiet, and Rem pulled the crust off his sandwich.

"Why'd you go see her?" asked Daniels. "Did she threaten you?"

"She had a video of me walking through the halls of the station, high as a kite after Ginger dosed my coffee. I got an email with a copy, telling me it would be released to the press if I didn't see her that day."

Daniels cursed and sat back. "Why didn't you tell me?"

"Because you would have told me not to go, and I couldn't risk your career or Lozano's along with mine."

"You realize Allison or Ginger could still release it."

Rem pulled more crust from his sandwich. "I suppose, but Allison got what she wanted, so I'm sure they'll save it till they want something else from me. At this point, though, I don't know that I care anymore." The first bite had settled in his stomach, and he ate the crust and took another swig of water.

"Listen," said Daniels, leaning in. "I know you're reeling, and you've spent the last few days with a liquor bottle in your hand, but at some point, you need to go home and deal with this."

"Why?"

"Why? Because you have a life. You have family and friends who love you, and a job you care about." He interlaced his fingers. "And a woman you still need to testify against and put behind bars."

Rem considered Daniels' argument. "My family and friends will love me no matter where I am, and that job I care about has caused me enough pain to require sedating myself with alcohol, and that woman..." His breath caught. "The woman who..." He cleared his throat. "...who... sexually assaulted, abducted, and almost killed me..." He set his jaw. "... could be the mother of my child." He blinked watery eyes and tried to compose himself. "And regardless of whether she goes to prison or not, I'll never be rid of her." His voice had trailed to a whisper.

Daniels studied him, his face a mixture of worry and sadness. "Don't get me wrong, Rem. I can't imagine what you're going through."

"No." Rem dropped his head into his palm. "You really can't." He thought back to that day when he'd spoken to Allison and closed his eyes. "When I first heard, and I got back to my car, I—" He hesitated. "I...well..." he sighed, "...let's just say drinking to excess was an improvement."

A second of silence passed. "Rem," said Daniels tautly. "Where's your gun?"

Rem's chest tightened, but he answered. "It's in the trunk of my car." Weary, he looked up. "I had a moment...and I..." he struggled to speak, "...I put it there to be safe."

Daniels pursed his lips, and his gaze held a measure of concern. "That was smart."

Rem took a breath. "I figured my family and friends would prefer me drunk instead of dead. My preference, on the other hand, well, that's still up for debate."

Daniels' face tightened but then he sat straight. "You are not going to let this lady win."

"She's showed her cards, partner. I'd say she already has."

Daniels shook his head. "She may have stolen your flag, but she's not at the finish line. You put her away, and you'll win this war."

"And I'll be raising our child."

"You don't know that it's yours."

Rem tensed. "Call it a hunch."

"And what if it is? Is that so bad?"

Rem stared, not sure what to think. "I don't know."

"Just because Allison says something, doesn't mean you have to do it. If this child is yours and Allison goes to prison, you don't have to go anywhere near her."

Rem rolled his fingers into fists. "Don't you think I've thought of that? Don't you think I've considered every damn scenario in this whole fucking mess?" He stood. "If that baby is mine, then I have to put my child first. Not me." He started to pace.

"Rem—"

"Allison will be her mother. I can't deny my...my daughter the right to know her mother, no matter how evil her mother is." His breathing picked up. "And what happens if Allison serves her time and eventually gets out? Her first stop will be to see her kid. Unless I go into hiding, I can't prevent that, and I certainly couldn't prevent any of Allison's followers from harassing us, which Allison would instigate if I denied her any time with her child." He rubbed his forehead in frustration. "And what if she gets acquitted? Am I supposed to ignore the fact that I'm a father? Am I supposed to pretend that my child doesn't exist? I can't do that, either." He stopped and put his hands on his hips. "She's got me, Daniels, and she knows I've got no choice but to do exactly what she wants." He sat again and studied the tabletop. "And I have no idea how to handle it." His mind raged at him, and he didn't know how to shut it up.

"Yes, you do."

Exhausted, Rem rubbed his face and ran his hands into his hair. His body ached and he felt like he had a tightly wound cord wrapped around his shoulders. "I do, huh?" He chuckled softly. "Then maybe you can enlighten me."

"You do what you always do. You face it. You don't run from it."

"Running sounds pretty appealing right now."

"What are you going to do? Hang here in Merrimac with your aunt? Get drunk and sell Taco del Fuegos? It won't change the fact that you'll still have a daughter who has a crazy mom and who is going to need you, no matter what happens with her mother."

Rem held his breath and looked away.

"I know this sucks, but it's the cards you've been dealt. Allison is counting on this knocking you back ten feet so she can take a giant hundred-foot leap forward. Don't give her that satisfaction." He set his hands on the table. "Maybe you are going to be a dad, and if so, that's great. That little girl will be the luckiest kid in the world if it's true. Maybe you need to start seeing this in a positive light. Maybe you will have to take her to see her mother in prison, and you'll hate it, but don't forget what's important here. It will be your child, Rem. You'll be the one to mold her and raise her and teach her what's right. Not Allison. Not if you put her away for a long time."

Some of the tension eased, and Rem fiddled with the edge of the paper towel. "And what if I don't? What if Measy wins?"

"Then you fight like hell for custody. Don't let Allison decide what's best for you and your kid. If she wants to involve you, then let her dig her own grave."

Rem groaned. "God. Now you've got me in a custody battle."

"I'm not saying that will happen. All I'm saying is that Allison is counting on you to do exactly what she expects. She wants you scared and afraid. Don't give her that. You have to fight back, Rem." He paused and softened the tone of his voice. "Show her that messing with a Remalla is not as fun as she thinks."

Rem took a shaky breath. "I don't know if I'm strong enough."

"I don't believe that for a second. I've seen you when you're pissed, and that's just when the innocent are abused. God help the person who messes with your child."

"It will be her kid, too."

"And she's a cult leader who manipulated her followers, assaulted and tried to sacrifice you, and killed Victor. Judges tend to frown on that."

For the first time in days, Rem began to see a little light at the end of the tunnel. "There's something else." He set his elbows on the table and clasped his hands together. "If I do end up a single dad, I don't think I can stay a cop." He held Daniels' gaze. "It will be too dangerous, and the hours, plus the cost of childcare..."

"You have thought about this, haven't you?"

Rem closed his eyes. "I thought the booze would shut down my thoughts, but it only made it worse."

"It's only a temporary fix, if that."

Rem opened his eyes.

"If that's what you need to do, then do it. Don't worry about me. Even if we aren't partners, it doesn't mean I'm going anywhere. I'll have to give you lessons on diaper changing, burping and proper feeding anyway. I'll probably spend more time with you doing that than I do now."

A powerful wave of relief almost overwhelmed him, and he bit back tears. "I'd hoped you'd say that."

"What else would I say?"

Rem sniffed. "I haven't been thinking too clearly lately."

Daniels ripped off a piece of his paper towel and handed it to Rem. "I know, but I promise, it'll be okay. You'll see."

Rem dabbed his eyes with the towel. "Jennie always told me everything happens for a reason." He sighed deeply again. "I hated it when she said that."

"She was right though."

Pulling it together, Rem crumpled the towel into a ball. "I...uh...I'm gonna need your help for the next six months. I may be a little rough before and during this trial. Ah, hell. And afterward, too. Who am I kidding?"

"You've needed my help since the day we met. Nothing's changed."

A chuckle bubbled up. "I'd argue, but I don't have it in me."

"Then eat your sandwich. And try not to think the worst."

Rem eyed his food. "Okay." His stomach felt better, and he took a bite.

They ate for a few minutes, and Daniels finished his sandwich. "Once you're ready, we'll grab your clothes, and you can change. Then we'll pack up and hit the road. Lozano misses you."

His hunger kicking in, Rem took another bite. "Sure he does." Taking a full deep breath, he felt more of the tension leave him. "Before we go, though, I need to see Aunt Gin. I should apologize. I haven't exactly been an exemplary nephew since I arrived."

"Not a problem. We can head over on our way out. I'm sure she'll be pleased to see you're okay. She's been worried about you."

"Yeah. I know. And it's probably all over town that her nephew's been getting drunk every night at the local bar."

"Aunt Gin doesn't strike me as a lady who cares what others think." Daniels stood, grabbed his crumb-dusted paper towel and tossed it in the trash. He finished his water and tossed the bottle, too. "You well enough to safely carry your weapon?"

Rem eyed his partner. "Don't worry. I think I'm past the worst of it."

"Just promise me that if you ever go down that road again, you'll call me. I don't care where I am, what I'm doing, or what you think I might or might not do." He furrowed his brow and waited.

Holding the remains of his sandwich, Rem paused. "I promise. You'll be the first call I make."

"Good."

"And thanks for pulling me out of yet another shithole. I seem to be falling in a lot of them and can't find my way out."

"All you've ever needed is a helping hand to pull yourself from the muck, but once you take it, you manage just fine on your own. You'll see once you start changing diapers."

Rem hesitated and his stomach knotted again. "Hey."

Daniels turned as he started to put away the peanut butter and jelly. "What?"

"Before we start talking about late-night feedings and baby puke, can we just get through the next six months? There's a lot that can happen between now and Allison's trial, and I'd really like to not get kicked in the teeth again." He lowered his sandwich. "Let's just assume, for now, that my life will go on as is, and that that child, should Allison give birth, will live a happy life, whether it's with me or someone else."

Daniels nodded. "You got it. No more mention of dirty diapers or baby puke until we know."

"Thanks." Although tired and still a little worried, Rem felt better than he had in days, and wishing he had a Taco del Fuego, he finished his sandwich.

Chapter Ten

DANIELS KNOCKED ON GENEVIEVE'S door as Rem stood beside him. After Rem's shower, aspirin, food, talk and clean clothes, he looked human again. His weary eyes, narrow face and lean frame still revealed his delicate mental state, but Daniels hoped that after a few days of rest and getting back to work, he would be back up to speed.

Genevieve opened the door and smiled back at them. "Well, look who's here." She stepped back. "Come in."

"Hey, Aunt Gin," said Rem, walking in with Daniels.

Gin wore a long blousy dress cinched at the waist with a belt, big hoop earrings and bright red lipstick. "Glad you're back, Aaron." She closed the door behind them and gestured. "Come on into the kitchen."

Daniels followed her and Rem to the same table where he'd sat before. This time the kitchen smelled like cinnamon and chocolate. "We wanted to stop by before we left," said Daniels.

"Have a seat," said Genevieve.

They all sat at the table and Rem fidgeted. "I...uh...didn't want to leave without apologizing. I know I haven't been...well...at my best since I've been here."

Gin reached over and patted him on the hand. "You look better. Do you feel better?"

Rem hesitated. "I'm getting there."

"I'm glad." Gin eyed Daniels. "I heard about the bar fight."

Daniels touched his sore jaw. "Big John does his job well."

"He's big but give him some good food and he's putty in your hands," said Gin. "Much like my nephew."

Rem smiled softly.

Gin straightened. "Your apology is accepted. Now let's move on." She stood. "You can't leave yet. Not without some nourishment." She headed into the kitchen and opened the refrigerator.

"You don't have to do that, Aunt Gin," said Rem. "Daniels and I had a sandwich."

"Nonsense," said Gin, and she pulled out a covered dish. "I made a fantastic lasagna last night. How about some leftovers?" She set the dish down on the counter.

Rem's eyes widened. "Lasagna?"

"And afterwards, if you're very good," she grabbed a cloth-covered plate from the counter, brought it to the table and set it in front of Rem, "you can have one of these." She pulled off the cloth to reveal a stack of perfectly cut brownies.

Daniels met Gin's gaze, and she winked at him. Rem looked like he was about to drool on the table. "I think you had Rem at hello," said Daniels.

"I know what makes a Reverton happy," said Gin. She slid the plate to the middle of the table. "Aaron gets his love of sweets from our side of the family. His father hated chocolate."

"It's one of the reasons we didn't get along," said Rem. "But nobody separates a Reverton from a baked good without serious injury." He eyed the brownies and Daniels. "You mind staying a little longer?"

If it meant Rem would eat, Daniels would stay as long as needed. "Wouldn't mind at all. It looks delicious."

Rem reached for a brownie, but Gin smacked at his hand. "Lasagna first," she said with a smile.

Rem frowned and pulled his hand back. "You always were a stickler for rules."

"If I wasn't then you wouldn't be sitting there today." She returned to the kitchen.

Daniels heard footsteps on the stairs, and Gin stopped and peered out into the hall. "Give me a few minutes. I have a full house tonight and I told this lovely couple I'd give them the lay of the land and a few suggestions of what to do in Merrimac. I'll be right back."

"Take your time," said Rem.

"Help yourself to some coffee, but don't touch those brownies, young man," said Gin, closing the kitchen door.

Rem sighed.

Daniels chuckled. "What did she mean about her rules and you not sitting there?"

Rem sat up. "If it hadn't been for her, I doubt I'd even know you. I'd probably be best friends with some cell mate."

"Aunt Gin impresses me more and more. Why is that?" Daniels sat back in his chair.

Rem eyed the closed kitchen door. "It's a long story but I'll try and keep it brief." He looked back. "I told you when I was eighteen, I was a hellion. I'd graduated high school but didn't know what to do after that."

"I recall," said Daniels.

"Well, I was arguing with my mom, and, by that time, I barely spoke to my dad. And when we did speak, we just yelled. He and I got in a huge fight, and we both said things that took us years to get over." He stared off. "I left town. Kind of like I did a few days ago. I didn't know where to go, but I had to get away." Rem picked at a crease in the wooden table. "I had a full tank of gas and twenty bucks in my pocket, and I just drove. I ended up on Aunt Gin's doorstep."

"You're a creature of habit."

Rem shrugged. "I suppose. Gin let me stay with her. She was in Merrimac by then, but in a different house." Rem stood and went into the kitchen. "You want some coffee?"

"Sure. Thanks."

Rem rummaged through the kitchen and found two mugs. "She told me I could live with her on two conditions. One, I find a job and two, I behave myself."

"Did you meet those conditions?"

Rem found some coffee pods and grabbed two. He popped one into a coffee machine on the counter, hit a button, and it began to whir. "Yes and no." He opened a drawer, pulled out a spoon and set it on the counter. "She helped me find work. She recommended me to her bed and breakfast friends, and they gave me odd jobs around their houses. It paid decent and it wasn't too hard, but my stupidity reared its ugly head."

"I have some experience with that," said Daniels.

Rem smirked at him. "I got in an owner's face when he didn't like the way I painted something. I told him to go fly a kite, only my language was a little harsher."

"I bet."

"He fired me, and it wasn't long before word spread and everybody else fired me, too. Merrimac is a close-knit community. You piss one person off, you piss them all off." The coffee machine stopped whirring, and Rem slid the cup out and brought it to Daniels.

"Thanks," said Daniels. "Did Aunt Gin kick you out?"

Rem returned to the machine and added another pod. "No. She didn't." He hit the button again. "She gave me a warning and advice. Both of which still stick with me." Rem leaned a hand on the counter while he waited for his coffee to finish.

Daniels sipped his coffee. "I can't wait to hear this."

"She sat me down and told me I could be mad for as long as I wanted. That was my right. But if I wanted respect from others, that I would have to respect myself first. There were no shortcuts. Then she said that when she needed to clear her head, she'd found that the best way was to give instead of get."

"Smart lady."

The coffee machine slowed and stopped, and Rem pulled out his mug. "I didn't know what she meant." He opened a container, picked up the spoon and added sugar to his coffee. "But she quickly informed me." He stirred, opened the fridge and grabbed some creamer. "She suggested I work for free." He added cream to his coffee and stirred again.

Daniels sat up. "Free?"

Rem nodded, returned the creamer, put the spoon in the sink and came back to the table with his mug. "I thought she was crazy." He sat and sipped his coffee. "But I did what she said because I needed a place to stay. I went back to that owner I pissed off. He almost slammed the door in my face, but I managed to apologize and tell him I'd do whatever he wanted around the house for free. On one condition. That got his attention."

"What was the condition?"

"I'd do the work for nothing, but if he was pleased with it, he could offer whatever he wanted in payment. Money, food, or just a thank you. It would be up to him, and I wouldn't question it."

"Did he go for it?"

"Sure did." Rem leaned back. "He tested the waters, though. I fixed his fence, repaired the paint job, and replaced his air filters without even so much as that thank you. I was beginning to think Aunt Gin had that screw loose like my dad always said. But then I replaced the oil in his car. By then, word was getting around that I was working for free, so I started getting calls. It's amazing how fast free travels. Suddenly, I was in demand." He sipped more of his coffee. "I don't know if it was because of that, or he felt guilty, but after I finished the oil change, that owner handed me a check that covered all of the jobs put together times two. And then he finally thanked me." He smiled. "After that, I made a killing. I'd go to jobs, do the work, tell them it's free, and they'd insist on paying me, usually double what I would have asked."

Daniels set his coffee down. "Did that help you clear your head?"

Rem eyed his drink. "It did. I started feeling good about myself. People looked at me different and even said hello if they saw me in town. I stopped being the neighborhood hoodlum and became Genevieve's sweet nephew. That's when I understood the whole respect thing."

"Was that the game changer?"

"You'd think, but it wasn't the big one. That came later when I was doing a job at one of the small shops on Main Street. I stepped outside and heard a scream. I saw Mrs. Turner on the sidewalk trying to wrestle her purse from some guy trying to steal it. I'd just been at her house helping her hang some pictures and I knew she was fragile. Something flipped in my head and before I could think, I took off after him. He'd yanked the purse from her and took off. I chased him down."

"Your high school track medals paid off."

"They did. I tackled the guy and took the purse back. I sat on him until the sheriff arrived and then returned the purse to Mrs. Turner. I became the town hero." He smiled. "That's all it took for me to figure it out. Six months later, I enrolled at a community college. Got my Associate's and joined the Academy after that. And you know the rest."

Daniels smiled back. "How come you never told me all that before?"

"I don't know. Guess it never came up."

Daniels nodded and heard laughter come from the other room. "What's Aunt Gin's story? What makes her so damn smart that she led you to the straight and narrow? I know she's divorced. She have any kids?"

"She's been divorced three times and has two kids. "Her son, Sawyer, lives in Arizona and does real estate last I heard, and I have no idea where Simone is. My mother thought she'd married and moved to Europe."

"They're not close?" asked Daniels.

Rem picked up a crumb from the brownie plate and ate it. "It can be a touchy subject. Gin keeps it close to the vest when it comes to her past. I vaguely recall playing with Sawyer and Simone when I was little. They were older than me, and they always stole my toys. That's all I remember. But then Gin moved away, and I didn't see any of them again for years. I heard Gin had eventually divorced and came out here, remarried and divorced again, and by the time we reconnected, Sawyer and Simone had grown up and were gone." Rem sipped more coffee.

"That's too bad. I can't imagine—"

The kitchen door opened, and Gin reappeared. "Sorry about that. You two making yourselves at home? I see you got some coffee."

"We're good Aunt Gin," said Rem. "You get your guests settled?"

"They're on their way to a lovely lunch and a day on the town." She went into the kitchen and grabbed some plates. "I'd offer you two a place to stay if you wanted to enjoy the weekend. But I'm booked with the Dandelion Festival." She eyed the guest house in the backyard. "I'm expecting my next guest soon. They're taking the room out back."

"It's nice and quiet," said Rem. He paused. "Jennie and I loved it."

Gin smiled softly. "I remember. That was a wonderful visit."

"I like the added gazebo," said Rem.

"Me, too," said Gin. "It adds a touch of romance, I think."

Daniels followed Gin's gaze and saw a pretty one-story brick structure with a vine-covered trellis and gazebo out back. A butterfly fluttered among some flowers and a bird drank from a bubbling water fountain.

"You need any help, Aunt Gin?" asked Rem.

"I'm good, dear. You sit and talk with your partner." She uncovered the lasagna.

Rem gestured toward the backyard. "You should bring Marjorie next time you two want to get out of town."

Daniels recalled his weekend trip with Marjorie and J.P. "It would be nice, but it may have to wait. Marjorie's not too happy with me right now."

"Why? You two have a fight?" asked Rem.

Gin pulled a knife from a drawer and cut some lasagna.

"The trip went fine, and we had a good time," said Daniels. "But on the way home, she asked when I wanted to start trying for our second."

Rem widened his eyes. "Second? As in second baby?"

Daniels gripped his mug, recalling their argument. "I may have made the mistake of telling her I didn't want another one, and it went downhill from there."

"This is why I'm not married, nor intend to be ever again," said Gin from the kitchen.

"Did you guys plan on having two?" asked Rem.

"Kinda, sorta. But it wasn't definite," said Daniels. "At least that's how I saw it. Marjorie saw it differently."

"Why don't you want a second?" asked Rem.

Daniels was acutely aware of how this conversation might affect Rem and he tried to steer around the pitfalls. "It's just not the right time."

Rem narrowed his eyes. "And?"

Gin chimed in from the kitchen. "And they're a hell of a lot of work. They're expensive and once they're born, your life belongs to them for the next eighteen years. And it's hard enough if you stay at home with them, but if you're a working parent, it's double the stress, worry and time away. Never mind the guilt."

Rem held Daniels' stare. "Is that it?" asked Rem.

Daniels nodded. "She's pretty close."

"And then they grow up and you're lucky if you ever see them again." Gin cut two pieces of lasagna and put each on a plate. "But that's life. You play the cards you're dealt and move on." She sighed and glanced back at them. "Sorry. I'm just speaking to myself. Kids are a blessing and a miracle."

Daniels caught her eye roll and set his coffee down. "They are, which is why I'm conflicted."

"You guys don't have to decide now. You've got plenty of time to figure it out," said Rem. He traced the lip of his mug. "Who knows what might happen?"

"You're right." Daniels imagined what Rem was thinking. "Who knows?"

The microwave began to whir. "It'll be ready in a few minutes," said Gin. The doorbell rang, and Gin wiped her hands on a towel. "That must be my next guest." She tossed the towel next to the sink. "Hang tight."

"We can get the lasagna," said Rem. "No rush."

Gin left the kitchen and headed to the front door. She opened it, but Daniels watched her face fall. "Deputy Shaw?" she asked.

A man spoke. "Hello, Genevieve. I'm looking for your nephew. Is he here?" Daniels straightened, and Rem swiveled in his seat.

Gin hesitated at the door. "Well, yes. He's here. We're about to have lunch. What's this about?"

Daniels stood along with Rem, and they walked into the front parlor. "What is it, Aunt Gin?" asked Rem.

With a frown, Gin widened the door. "It's Deputy Shaw. He's asking for you, Aaron."

Rem approached the door and stilled. Daniels recalled Genevieve and Marvin telling him that Shaw was not well-liked and knew Rem had met him during his overnight jail stay. "Shaw?" asked Rem, his jaw tight.

Shaw took a step inside, and his face twisted in an ugly smile. "Detective Aaron Remalla."

"In the flesh," said Rem.

"Put your hands up and face the wall. You're under arrest," said Shaw.

Rem froze. "What is this? A joke?"

"Arrest for what?" asked Daniels.

"Are you serious?" asked Gin.

"Take the stance, Detective," said Shaw. "Now." He held out handcuffs.

Rem's jaw dropped. "Not until you tell me what for."

Shaw's eyes glittered in the sunlight and Daniels got the sense he was enjoying this. "For the murder of Sharon Belafonte."

Chapter Eleven

DANIELS' MIND RACED. "SHARON Belafonte? The woman in the bar?"

"Sharon is dead?" asked Rem.

Gin put her hand over her mouth. "Oh, no."

"Found her body in the woods this morning," said Shaw, eyeing Rem, "about a mile from where you were staying, Detective."

Rem gawked at him. "I didn't kill her."

"I heard you had a fight last night with her ex at Jimmy's," said Shaw. "Word is, it was over Sharon."

Daniels patted his chest. "I started that fight. I poured beer over Herndon's head. Everybody there saw it."

"We'll see about that." Shaw swung the handcuffs. "Let's go, Detective."

"Aaron would not do this," said Gin. "He wouldn't kill anyone."

"You can't arrest him over bar gossip and vicinity to the crime," argued Daniels.

Shaw smiled with narrowed eyes. "No, I can't, but I can arrest him for finding the murder weapon under the couch in the shack you were occupying."

"What?" asked Gin.

"That's not possible," said Rem. "I never saw Sharon after the fight."

"I've been with him the whole time," said Daniels. "I can vouch for his whereabouts. And that weapon was not in the shack this morning. If it's there now, it was planted."

"You've been with him the whole time?" asked Shaw. "Didn't you rent the shack next door?"

Daniels opened his mouth to answer, but realized Shaw was right. He hadn't been with Rem overnight. And worse, he'd found Rem outside the shack lying in the woods that morning. "He was too drunk to do anything after we left the bar. He passed out on the bed before I left."

"So you weren't with him the whole time, were you?" asked Shaw. "And as far as you know he passed out, but maybe that's what he wanted you to think."

Rem stared in shock. "I didn't kill Sharon."

"Have you talked to Joe about this?" asked Gin. "Does he know what you're doing? This is ridiculous. My nephew is a detective for heaven's sake."

"All the more reason why he would know exactly what to do," said Shaw.

"Which is leave a murder weapon under the couch where he's sleeping?" asked Daniels. "For you to discover?"

"I can't speak for his intelligence," said Shaw. "Maybe he's a lousy detective." He pointed at Rem. "Up against the wall."

Rem didn't move. "I can't believe this."

"You've got this all wrong," said Daniels.

"I'm calling Joe," said Gin.

Shaw's face fell. "Sheriff Whistler is out of town visiting his mother as you well know, Genevieve. I'll get him up to speed when he returns."

"And I'll get him up to speed right now," said Gin. She turned and headed toward the kitchen.

Shaw sneered at Gin, but then spoke to Rem. "Detective?" He gestured toward the wall. "I suggest you do as I ask, unless you'd like to add resisting arrest to the charges."

Rem held Daniels' gaze. "I...I don't even know what to say." He walked to the wall and put his hands up.

Daniels watched, his anger rising, as Shaw patted his partner down. "I'll tell you what to say. Nothing. I'll call Lozano. We'll get you an attorney."

Shaw pulled Rem's arms down behind him and clicked on the handcuffs.

"Where are you taking him?" asked Daniels.

"To jail," said Shaw.

"It's just down from Jimmy's," said Rem. "I've already been there once."

"It'll be so nice to have you back, Detective," said Shaw. "You struck me as a problem from the start. Guess I wasn't wrong." He pulled Rem out the door and guided him down the porch stairs.

Daniels followed. "I want to see him once he's booked."

"You can see him after I question him." Shaw looked back. "And if I'm in a good mood."

Daniels fought the urge to grab Shaw by the neck and bounce his face into the patrol car he was leading Rem toward. "You've got the wrong guy," said Daniels. "You better be sure you know what you're doing, because this is going to backfire on you."

Shaw opened the rear door of his car. "I know exactly what I'm doing, and two big city detectives aren't going to scare me off." He pushed on Rem's shoulder and head and Rem slid into the backseat of the car.

"Remind me why I should see the glass half full," said Rem, his face solemn. "Because right now, it's looking pretty damn empty." He sighed. "And I was worried about Allison."

Daniels leaned over. "Remember. Don't say a word. I'll be there as soon as I can."

Shaw shut the door, got in the driver's seat and started the ignition.

His heart thudding, Daniels watched as Shaw drove off.

· • ◆ • ◆ • ◆ • ·

Rem eyed the back of Shaw's head through the metal grate that separated the front seat from the back. "You know I didn't do this."

Shaw eyed him through the rearview mirror. "We'll see about that."

"You honestly think I'd be stupid enough to leave the murder weapon under the couch in my room, when there's a giant forest out there, not to mention a river and all sorts of babbling brooks and streams?" Rem shifted, trying to get comfortable. "I'd have to be the world's dumbest detective."

"Maybe you are." Shaw turned down the main road. "Stupid people are my business, detective. I see them all the time."

"You should talk to Herndon," said Rem. "He's your best suspect. He could have easily killed Sharon and dumped that weapon at my shack."

"When I want your advice, I'll ask for it."

"You're setting yourself up for a big fall," said Rem. "The killer is out there, running around, probably laughing his ass off that you fell hook, line and sinker for this charade."

"Laugh all you want, because it's your charade, Detective. You can sit there and pretend to be innocent, but you and I both know you've been nothing but a nuisance since you arrived. You and Sharon have been flaunting yourselves in front of Herndon since you got here, and I suspect she told you she wanted him instead and you murdered her." He glanced back. "You probably thought you'd be long gone before we found her body. And you probably planned to dispose of the weapon before you left town."

"I checked out this morning, you idiot."

"It would be easy to go back at night. The doors are rarely locked."

Rem scrunched his face, not sure he was hearing right. "Are you serious? That's your theory?"

"I've never been more serious about anything in my life." Shaw stopped at a red light. "You killed her, and I'm going to do everything in my power to prove it."

Rem stared back in disbelief. The light changed to green, and Shaw drove on.

• • • ● • ● • • • •

Daniels strode back into the house and into the kitchen, pulling out his phone. Gin held her own phone to her ear and lowered it. "Joe didn't answer but I left him a message."

Frustrated, Daniels punched the button for Lozano.

"His mother had surgery and he went up to see her. He's supposed to be back tomorrow." Gin eyed the front. "Shaw took Aaron?"

"Yes," said Daniels. "To the jail." Lozano answered and Daniels filled him in on what had just happened. After expressing his disbelief, Lozano said he'd make a few calls and would get in touch soon. Daniels hung up. He eyed Gin who paced in the kitchen, her face a mask of worry. "Tell me what you know about Shaw," he said.

Gin stopped beside the chair Rem had just been sitting in. His unfinished coffee sat near the plate of untouched brownies, and Daniels had to take a second to center himself.

Gin gripped the back of the chair. "I told you that Deputy Shaw is an asshole."

"Why?"

Gin rubbed her forehead. "He's Sybil's brother. Sybil used to be married to Joe. When she disappeared, Joe brought Shaw in as a deputy when Shaw lost his job elsewhere. I think he used to be a police officer in another town. I know Joe hired him out of guilt, but I don't understand why he continues to put up with him. I've told him time and again that Shaw can't be trusted. He doesn't care about right or wrong, he just likes to abuse his power." She studied her phone as if willing it to ring. "He's just like his sister."

"How does he abuse his power in a town like Merrimac?"

Gin lowered her phone. "He'll look the other way when you need help, or he'll make things difficult when you piss him off. Joe's told me that he can handle him, and he usually does. If someone complains about Shaw, Joe will look into it. Shaw and Joe have had it out on more than one occasion." She sat in the chair. "But this...this is something...I can't even grasp."

Frustrated, Daniels ran a hand through his hair. "If Shaw's correct and Sharon is dead, and the murder weapon was found under Rem's bed, Shaw sure as hell can make things difficult." He paced, trying to think. "What do you think Joe will do when he hears about this?"

"He'll want to talk to Shaw and get the details. He'll want to know exactly what happened to Sharon, and about the investigation."

Daniels attempted to put a timeline together. "If they found Sharon's body this morning, then there hasn't been a hell of a lot of time for investigating. How did they find the weapon so fast?" He blew out his cheeks. "A town like this isn't going to have a Forensic or Crime Scene unit. They'd have to call that in for help." He checked the time. "There's no way they've finished in such a short period of time. They should still be out there. How'd they zero in on Rem?"

"Probably the bar fight."

Daniels thought back. "Sharon was alive and well when we left. Rem went back to the shack with me and passed out." He stopped pacing. "The question is what happened after we left? Where did Sharon go and who was she with?"

"Don't you think Shaw should be asking those questions?"

"He sure as hell should."

"He doesn't like Aaron," said Gin. "That probably doesn't help."

"Why not?"

Gin set her phone on the table. "Joe stayed over the night before he left town. He was keeping me up to speed about Aaron because he knew I was concerned. He told me about letting Aaron sleep it off in the jail after he'd passed out in the street. Said Shaw made some comments about it. He called Aaron pathetic and a disgrace to the profession. Aaron overheard it and made a few comments of his own. Aaron didn't cower to Shaw, and Shaw didn't like it. Shaw wanted to charge him with public drunkenness and disorderly conduct, but Joe told him to get over it." She put an elbow on the table and held her head. "Shaw holds grudges, so he's probably gloating to Aaron right now."

Daniels set his jaw, wondering what to do next. "What do you know about Sharon?"

Gin raised her head. "Not very much I'm afraid. All I can say is she is... or was, messed up. Liked to party and get attention. Ever since she arrived in Merrimac, she's stirred up trouble. Kind of thrives on it, I think, like some do. She hooked up with Scott pretty quickly and they've pretty much been together since, unless they fight and break it off, but that's temporary. Once things cool off, they're back together again."

Daniels sat across from her. "What about Scott?"

She sighed. "He's not much better. He's lived here longer though, so I know more of his history. He's always been the sort to have big dreams that he never acts on. He was going to shake the town's dust from his shoes when he got older, but he never took the leap. His father owns the auto body shop, and Scott works there. He's good with his hands and he helps around town with odd jobs, too." She pointed down the hall. "He replaced my banister when I needed a new one. He did a good job. Too bad he can be such a shit."

"Is he shitty enough to kill?"

Gin stilled. "I don't know, but I suppose if you're pushed past your breaking point, it's possible for anyone." She slid Rem's coffee cup over and held it in her hand. "Why would he kill Sharon though?"

"Could anyone else have it out for Sharon?"

Her grip tightened on the cup. "I don't know, but you could ask Amy."

Daniels recalled the woman who'd served him drinks last night. "The waitress at Jimmy's?"

Gin nodded. "She works at the local car dealership, too. She and Sharon are roommates, although I suspect Sharon spent most of her time with Scott when they weren't fighting. If anyone would know something, it would be Amy."

Daniels stood. "Then that's where I'll start." He pushed his chair back in.

Gin's eyes widened. "Start what?"

"Somebody's framing Rem for murder, and if Shaw's not going to bother to find out who, then I am." Determined, he headed for the door.

"Gordon, wait." Gin followed him to the entry.

He put his hand on the knob and stopped. "What?"

She hesitated. "Just be careful, okay?" She clasped her hands together. "Merrimac is a safe place, but it has a way of protecting its secrets."

Daniels paused. "What do you mean? They'll protect whoever killed Sharon?"

"That depends on who killed her."

Daniels pointed. "Rem is not taking the rap for murder so Merrimac can maintain appearances."

"No," she said. "I know that. Aaron is innocent. But if someone went this far to frame him, who knows how much further they might go?"

Daniels opened the door. "Don't worry, Gin. I can handle myself. And whoever did this, better be prepared to deal with me."

"Just promise me something," she said. "Let me know where you are and...and stay in town at night."

Daniels stopped short, remembering Marvin's warning about Merrimac's haunted woods. "Witches and hell hounds are the least of my problems. If I have to take a hundred challenges to find a killer, then I'll do it, because I'm not leaving this town without my partner."

Chapter Twelve

DANIELS RAPPED ON AMY'S apartment door and waited. After leaving Genevieve's, he'd headed to the only car dealership in town. The owner had told him that Amy had called in sick after hearing about Sharon. Daniels got her address and had headed over.

When no one answered, he knocked again. "Amy?" he called, determined to talk to her. "I need to ask you about Sharon." Impatient, he rapped harder. "It's important."

He heard a lock turn, and the door opened but the chain was still on. He saw Amy's puffy eyes through crack of the door. "Amy? I'm Detective Gordon Daniels." He didn't have a badge because he was still on administrative leave and hoped she wouldn't ask to see it. "I need to ask you a few questions."

She stared at him. "I know who you are. You were at the bar last night."

"Can I come in?"

She bit her lip. "You're his friend, aren't you?"

Daniels gripped the door frame. Obviously, word was spreading fast. "Whose friend?"

"The man who killed Sharon. He was at the bar, too, buying all the drinks."

Daniels told himself to stay cool. Making enemies in Merrimac wasn't going to help Rem. "My friend didn't kill Sharon. That's why I'm here."

"To defend him?"

"To find the real killer."

She paused. "They arrested him."

"I know but he didn't kill Sharon."

"I saw him with Sharon last night. They were all over each other."

"Did you also see the fight? Me and Rem were kicked out, remember? That was last time either one of us saw Sharon."

Tears welled up in her eyes. "You're lying."

Daniels bit back a groan. He had to get through to her. "Listen, Amy. I'm sorry about Sharon. Nobody deserves what happened to her. All I want to do is find out the truth, but I can't do that without more information. That's why I need to talk to you."

"How do you know he didn't do it?"

"Because I was with him, and he'd passed out when I left him. You saw how drunk he was. He didn't kill Sharon, but I sure want to find out who did, and I suspect you do, too."

She wiped at a tear. "And what if you're wrong?"

Daniels paused. "If I'm wrong and I prove my friend's a murderer, I'll be the first to testify against him. I promise you that."

She sniffed. "You'd send your friend to jail?"

"If he's guilty, I will. But I know he's not guilty, so Sharon's killer is on the loose, and I'd like to find him...or her. Wouldn't you?"

Another tear slipped down her cheek. "How do I know you aren't the killer?"

Daniels hesitated. It was a good question. "I'm not, but if it will make you more comfortable, you can call whoever you want and tell them I'm here. Take a picture if it makes you feel better. I don't care. I just want to ask a few questions, that's all. We can even leave the door open. Or you can call my captain. He'll vouch for me."

She eyed him warily, and after a few seconds, she closed the door. He heard the lock slide and the door opened. Amy stood in baggy sweats and a big t-shirt. She held a tissue and swiped at her face. "You can come in."

"Thank you."

"I'm leaving the door open."

"That's fine."

She held a phone and started to type. "And I'm texting my boss, telling him you're here."

"He should already know. I stopped by there first."

She finished typing and sent the text. "You murder me, and you and your friend can roommate together in prison."

"All the more reason not to murder you. I spend enough time with him as it is."

She grabbed a blanket from the couch and pulled it over her shoulders. "What do you want?"

"First of all, I'm sorry about Sharon. I'm sure this is hard for you."

Fresh tears surfaced. "I can't believe it." She sat on the couch and dabbed her face with her tissue. "Why would your friend hurt her?"

"He didn't. He went back to his shack and crashed. Can you tell me what happened after the fight? Did Sharon stick around?"

She wiped her nose. "She did for a little while. She talked to Scott but then she left."

"By herself?"

She nodded. "Yes."

"What time?"

Amy held her head. "Probably around midnight."

"Anybody leave around the same time? Where was Scott?"

"He...uh...he left, too, but after Sharon."

"What time did he leave?"

Amy sniffed again. "I don't know. Maybe twelve thirty? I'm not sure. He made a phone call first, though."

"Do you know who he was talking to?"

"No. I don't. But he seemed upset."

"Scott was upset when he was on the phone?" asked Daniels.

"Yeah. He got upset with Sharon, too, before she left."

Daniels sat in a chair across from her. "Did they argue?"

Amy gripped the blanket and pulled it closer. "I don't know. It got busy, but I saw them together at a corner table. They were friendly at first, but then their expressions changed, and I could tell they were mad. That's not unusual though. They fought all the time."

"Did you hear any of the conversation?"

She swallowed and pulled another tissue from a box. "I couldn't hear the argument, but I heard what she said to him when she left."

"What was that?" Daniels almost crossed his fingers, hoping he'd get something to implicate Scott.

"She said 'I'll just go find Remalla and see what he thinks.' Then she smiled and walked out. Scott didn't look happy. That's when he called somebody."

Daniels' stomach twisted. "She said that, about Rem? You're sure?"

"That's what I heard." Her face fell, and she held her mouth. "And now she's dead." She stifled a sob. "She found your friend, and he killed her."

Daniels' heart sunk.

· · • • • · • • · · ·

Daniels pulled up to Herndon's Auto Body and parked. He got out of the car and before going inside, he debated how to handle Scott. Their last encounter had been the bar fight and now Sharon was dead, and Rem accused of her murder. Scott would likely be reluctant to answer his questions, and if he was the murderer, may not answer them at all. Daniels had to talk to him, though. Even if Scott lied, Daniels would hopefully be able to see through it. Guys like Scott killed out of impulse and when the law came calling, they typically crumbled under the pressure.

He squared his shoulders and entered the shop. A skinny man with oily hair and wearing a yellow shirt with the name Wilson sewn into the pocket greeted him. Daniels introduced himself and asked to see Scott Herndon. Wilson's face fell and he asked what it was about.

Daniels put his hand on the counter. "Sharon Belafonte was murdered last night, and Scott was one of the last people to see her alive. I need to ask him some questions."

He nodded. "We heard about Sharon. It's terrible and Scott's pretty upset about it. Didn't they arrest some guy already?"

"They did, but I still need to talk to Scott. Is he here?"

"He's in the back." He shot a thumb toward a door behind him. "But I don't think he's up for answering questions."

"It's never a good time when someone close to you is dead, but this can't wait. You mind if I go back?" He stepped around the edge of the counter.

Wilson stammered. "I don't...uh...think...maybe...I..."

"Thank you." Daniels walked to the door and opened it. He saw a cluttered desk in the corner, a TV on the wall and a couch across from it. One dirty window provided the only light and Scott stepped out of a small bathroom, his eyes red and his hair ruffled. He held a wet hand towel and wore the same yellow shirt with his name sewn into the pocket. He stopped when he saw Daniels. "What the hell are you doing here?"

Daniels closed the door. "We need to talk, Scott."

"The hell we do. Get out of here." He waved the towel at Daniels. "Your buddy killed Sharon, and for all I know, you helped him."

Daniels put his hands on his hips. "Rem and I did not kill Sharon."

"Deputy Shaw says Remalla did it."

"I know what Shaw says, but he's wrong." He pointed. "You were one of the last people to talk to her. Word is you two argued, and I want to know about what."

Scott's face tightened. "You're trying to blame me, aren't you? To save your buddy. You think I killed her?"

"I think it's possible. You and Sharon have a history. She hung all over Rem to make you jealous, and then you two argued again right before she left. That sounds suspicious, Scott. You could have followed her, killed her, and planted the weapon."

Scott gripped the towel. "You son-of-a-bitch. I loved Sharon."

"You got a funny way of showing it."

Scott's face turned red, and he took a step toward Daniels. "You better get the hell out of here."

"What are you going to do? Kill me, too?"

Scott straightened and his eyes narrowed. "Don't think I—"

The door opened, and Daniels turned to see two big guys, both wearing the same yellow shirts, enter the room. Based on their pockets, one was Bart and the other was Ricky. They glared at Daniels. "What are you doing here?" asked Bart.

Before Daniels could answer, Scott sneered. "This guy was at the bar last night. He started the fight with me and then his friend murdered Sharon, and now he's trying to pin it on me to save his friend's ass."

"Is that so?" asked Ricky. He faced Daniels, his burly shoulders stretching the seams of the shirt.

Daniels looked between the three of them and realized Gin was right. This town would definitely protect one of their own. "I may have started the fight, but he's wrong about my friend. Somebody else murdered Sharon."

"Me, right?" asked Scott.

Daniels prepared himself. "If the shoe fits." He paused. "If you killed her, Scott, it will come out and it's better to come clean now, because if you make me work any harder, it's not going to be good for anybody, especially you." He aimed a steely stare at Scott but kept his peripheral vision on Bart and Ricky.

Scott's brow furrowed and he chuckled. "Your friend's going to prison. Get used to it."

"And you're leaving, asshole," said Ricky to Daniels. "Right now."

Daniels braced as Ricky and Bart advanced.

Chapter Thirteen

REM SAT ON THE small cot and stared at the cell. This time around, he was in the larger one with a sink and toilet. Laying his head back against the cement wall, he wondered how in the hell he'd added a murder charge to his already substantial collection of shit-ton problems in such a short period of time. He tried to recall his last interaction with Sharon the previous night, but a lot of it was a blur. He did recall the fight, but not much after it. A good prosecutor would love that. He also recalled Daniels waking him in the woods outside his shack that morning. How he'd ended up there was a mystery.

Sighing, he wondered what Daniels was doing. Once Shaw had brought Rem to the jail, he'd taken Rem's phone and watch, put him in the cell and then he'd disappeared. He hadn't asked Rem a single question. Bored, Rem had been staring at the walls ever since.

Rubbing his eyes, he heard footsteps and sat up. The door to the cells opened with a clang and Shaw stepped in with Aunt Genevieve beside him. "You've got five minutes," said Shaw.

Aunt Gin scowled at him. "Five minutes? That's all?"

"Be glad I let you in at all." He shot an ugly look at Rem and walked out, closing the door behind him.

Rem stood and approached the bars. "You shouldn't have come."

Gin walked up. "Don't tell me what to do, young man. I'm still your aunt." Her face softened. "Are you okay?"

Rem grabbed a bar. "It's been an invigorating morning. I've counted three dust bunnies and heard four cars drive by."

"Has he treated you well?"

Rem shrugged. "He hasn't done much at all, other than call me a murderer."

Gin adjusted the strap on her purse that hung on her shoulder. "If I was brave, I'd slip you a file."

Rem had to chuckle. "Maybe on your next visit."

"I brought you something else, though." She eyed the door and slid her purse off her shoulder. She opened it and pulled out a plastic bag with two brownies in it. "Here. You need to keep up your strength."

Rem smiled. "Aunt Gin, you may have just saved the day." He took the brownies.

"Don't tell Deputy Doom. He won't be happy."

"Don't I know it." He slid out a brownie and took a bite. He sighed and closed his eyes. "That's delicious."

"Eat fast."

He took another bite. "Don't worry." He chewed and swallowed. "Where's Daniels?"

"He's out trying to prove your innocence."

Rem broke off more brownie. "Is he having any luck?" He ate another bite.

"I don't know. I haven't heard. I know his first stop was Amy, Sharon's roommate, but after that, I don't know."

Rem nodded and chewed. "He'll find Herndon. That's what I'd do. Odds are, he's the killer."

Aunt Gin sighed. "I wish he'd wait till Joe gets here. I spoke to Joe by the way. He's looking into the whole thing. Said he'd call Shaw and find out about the investigation, but he can't be back any sooner than tomorrow."

"Thanks, Gin. I appreciate that and Sheriff Joe's help. But I want you to lay low and stay out of this. Daniels and I can handle ourselves, but I don't want Deputy Doom making you a target of whatever grudge he has against me."

Gin patted his hand. "Don't you worry about me, dear. I've handled worse than Shaw. He can try whatever he likes, but he won't get far with me."

Rem swallowed another bite. "I know you and Sheriff Joe are close, but you can't rely solely on that. Guys like Shaw will find a way if they're determined. Especially if he doesn't like Joe, either."

"I can't imagine what Joe would do if Shaw threatened me."

"Just be careful, okay? And don't worry. We'll figure this out, and I'll be free in no time. Maybe I'll still be able to get some of your lasagna if Daniels solves the crime." He kept his tone casual to keep his aunt calm but in the back of his mind, he hoped his partner wasn't doing something stupid to prove Rem's innocence. "But once you leave, do me a favor and call Daniels. I want to be sure he doesn't end up in the cell next to mine."

"I will. It worries me that he's out there by himself. He's an unknown around here and you know how this town can be."

Rem recalled how Merrimac had turned on him in the past. "I do know, but I also don't think they want a murderer in their midst, even if he's local." He hoped that was true but couldn't help but think of Daniels out there without backup.

"I agree, but I'll check in on him. I suspect he'll be visiting soon so he can tell you what he's learned."

Rem ate another bite. "If we're lucky, maybe Herndon will confess."

"I hope so." She looked back toward the door. "Have you had any insight as to what might have happened to Sharon?"

"My guess?" Rem grabbed the remains of the second brownie and popped it in his mouth. He chewed and handed the bag to Gin who stuffed it in her purse. Wishing he had a soda, he swallowed. "Sharon pissed Herndon off one too many times. She left the bar, and he followed her. They ended up in the woods, and he killed her. I doubt it was premeditated. He likely just snapped. Then he panicked and figured he'd dump the weapon at my place."

"You think the weapon was there before you left the shack this morning?"

"I doubt it. I made the bed. I think I would have seen it."

She nodded. "What about Sharon? Did she mention anything to you about Scott being violent?"

"We never talked about Scott." He groaned, remembering his drunkenness. "At least not that I recall."

She nodded, her face somber. "What about me? Did she say anything about me?"

Rem frowned. "You? Why would she say anything about you?"

Gin started to answer when the door swung open, and Shaw entered. "Times up. Let's go, Genevieve." He waved at her.

"But I just got here," said Gin. "You know Joe would let me stay longer."

He hooked his thumbs in his belt. "Well, Joe's not here, is he? So get your scrawny ass out of my jail."

"Hey," said Rem, his anger rising. "Don't talk to her like that."

"It's okay, Aaron," said Gin, narrowing her eyes at Shaw. "I've heard worse."

"No, it's not okay," said Rem. He glared at Shaw. "Apologize to her."

Shaw snickered. "What are you going to do, Detective? Kill me?" He shot out a thumb and glowered at Aunt Gin. "Move it."

Gin patted Rem's hand again. "I'll come back tomorrow."

"We'll see," said Shaw. "He acts up, I may have to prevent any more visits. This man is dangerous, and I wouldn't want you to get hurt."

Gin's face tightened. "The only one I fear in this room is you." She walked toward the door, and he stepped aside as she walked through.

"You're a lot smarter than you look," said Shaw, and he grinned at Rem and shut the door behind him, leaving Rem in silence.

·•·•••·•••·

Daniels faced Ricky and Bart, prepared to stand his ground. He felt confident he could handle them, but if Scott joined the fray, then it would get dicey. Bart grabbed his arm and Ricky reached for the other when Daniels swiveled and brought his elbow back into Bart's ribs. Bart grunted and let go just as Ricky punched Daniels in the gut and Scott grabbed his other shoulder and shoved him back into the wall. Daniels hit it with a thud and prepared to slug Scott in the face when a booming voice echoed through the room.

"What the hell is going on in here?"

Daniels held his stomach, Scott froze, and Ricky and Bart straightened and widened their eyes.

An older man resembling Scott but with gray hair and a receding hairline stood at the open door with an anxious Wilson standing behind him.

"Dad," said Scott.

"Mr. Herndon," said Bart, holding his ribs.

Daniels realized this was Herndon, Sr., the owner of the auto body shop. He pushed off the wall. "Mr. Herndon?" he asked, breathless.

Scott's father stepped into the room. "You want to tell me why you idiots are ganging up on a detective in the back office?"

"Detective?" asked Ricky. He pointed at Daniels. "Him?"

"Shit," said Bart. "How come you didn't mention that, Wilson?"

"You're blaming Wilson?" yelled Scott's dad.

Ricky slumped his shoulders.

"And why in God's green earth would you three feel the need to beat up on one man?" asked Herndon.

"Dad, listen...," said Scott.

"Shut up, Scott," said Herndon. "What happened, Bart?"

Bart didn't hesitate. "This guy is accusing Scott of killing Sharon last night."

Scott jumped in. "His friend is the one who did it. Shaw arrested him this morning."

Ricky pointed at Daniels. "He's blaming Scott for framing his friend. We were just setting him straight. Guy needs to mind his own business."

Herndon glared. "All of that could be handled with words instead of fists."

Daniels smoothed his shirt and spoke up. "I just wanted to ask your son a few questions about what happened last night at the bar."

Herndon eyed all of them.

"Dad—" Scott took a step toward his father.

"Sit down, Scott," said Herndon. "Bart. Ricky. Get your asses back to work. We got two cars going out today that still need work. Move it."

Bart and Ricky nodded. "Yes, sir." They jogged around Herndon and left the room.

"Wilson, you go with them," said Herndon.

Wilson turned quickly and left, closing the door behind him.

Scott raised his hands. "Listen, I—"

"I told you to sit. So sit," said Herndon. "Now."

Scott sighed, frowned at Daniels and sat on the couch.

Daniels rubbed his stomach and walked up beside Scott, waiting to see what would happen next.

Herndon eyed Daniels. "Tell me who you are again?"

Daniels filled Scott's dad in about who he was and why he was there.

Herndon nodded and walked up to Scott, who sat back against the couch. He scowled at his son. "Did you kill her?"

Scott dropped his jaw, and Daniels waited to hear his answer.

"I didn't kill Sharon," said Scott.

"Do you know who did?" asked Herndon.

"Dad, this is ridiculous. Why are you asking me that?" yelled Scott.

Herndon squinted his eyes. "I knew that girl was nothing but trouble. I told you but you wouldn't listen."

"Sharon and I—"

"I don't give a shit about Sharon and you. There is no more Sharon and you."

Scott hung his head.

"And if you've got nothing to hide," said Herndon, "then why not answer the man's questions?"

Daniels waited, glad Scott's father seemed somewhat rational. If he'd backed up Bart and Ricky, Daniels may have ended up in the hospital.

Scott raised his head. "He's trying to make it look like I did it. He's protecting his friend, who's the real killer."

Daniels tensed. "My friend didn't kill Sharon, Scott. I talked to Amy. After Rem and I left the bar, she said Sharon stuck around. She hung out with you, then you two got in an argument and she left. Then you called someone on the phone, and it looked like you were still angry, and you left not long after Sharon. I want to know why you and Sharon argued, who you were speaking to on the phone and where you went after leaving the bar."

Scott gripped his thigh with his fingers and looked between his father and Daniels. "Dad, are you gonna—"

"Answer the man's questions, son, so we can all get back to work. We've wasted enough blasted time as it is. If you're innocent, then what the hell does it matter?"

Daniels wondered if the reason Scott was so belligerent was because he knew more than he was saying.

Scott sighed and jabbed out a hand. "It's none of his damn business."

Scott's father cursed. "Your ex is dead. Your business is now under scrutiny, so tell him so he can go find someone else to bother because this is eating into my profits."

"Fine." Scott huffed. "We argued about Sonya."

"Sonya?" asked Scott's dad. "Who the hell is Sonya?"

"Some girl I met last week when I dropped off those parts across town. She was staying at the Millers' B&B. I told Sharon because she'd been hanging all over his buddy. Sharon got pissed, I told her to get over it and that's when she left."

"And the phone call?" asked Daniels, not believing a word of what Scott said. He felt sure Scott had been stalling to come up with a good story.

"I called Sonya. Asked to see her and she blew me off. That's when I left. I went back to my place, went to sleep, woke up and came here, and that's when I heard about Sharon." He scowled at Daniels. "Sharon even said she was going to see Remalla when she left. That's how I know your friend's guilty." He sat back on the couch, his expression a mixture of cockiness and overconfidence.

"That should all be easy to verify," said Daniels. He pulled out a small notepad and pencil from his jacket pocket. "What's Sonya's number?"

Scott's expression fell.

"I think you've got all the information you need," said Scott's dad. "He said he didn't do it, he answered your questions, and you got what you came here for."

"With all due respect, sir," said Daniels, "I think there's an excellent chance that your son may be concealing the truth."

Herndon bristled. "You're calling my son a liar?"

Scott sat up again, and his smug smile returned.

Daniels faced Scott's dad. "Alibis have to be proven, sir. Anybody can say one thing and do another. And to be blunt, it would have been easy for your son to have followed Sharon, killed her, panicked and planted the weapon at my friend's place." He eyed Scott. "And if he wants me off his back, he better be prepared to prove everything he just said."

Herndon narrowed an eye at Daniels. "You're a detective?"

"I am. My partner and I work in San Diego."

"Then you are out of your jurisdiction."

Daniels held Herndon's look. "It may not be my jurisdiction, sir, but it's my partner's future on the line."

Scott smirked. "Then maybe you should go find another partner because this one's not lookin' too good."

"Shut your mouth, Scott," said Herndon.

Scott's smile faded, and Herndon sized up Daniels. "I want to see your badge."

Seeing where this was going, Daniels deflated. "I don't have it. I'm currently on administrative leave pending a shooting investigation."

Scott snickered. "You shot someone? Hell. It looks like you and your partner are cut from the same cloth, only this time he got caught."

Herndon shot a harsh look at Scott, and Scott closed his mouth. "Get back to work," said Herndon to Scott.

"Work?" asked Scott. "Dad, Sharon is dead. I was going to take the day."

Herndon snorted. "You can cry when you go home tonight." Scott hesitated. "Go," yelled Herndon. Setting his jaw, Scott stood and left the room.

"I'd like to get Sonya's number," said Daniels.

Herndon offered a mirthless laugh. "I bet you would, but I think it's time for you to leave."

Daniels bit back an ugly comment and told himself to stay cool. "Scott's not off the hook, Mr. Herndon."

"He is as far as you're concerned." He gestured toward the door. "I suggest you leave now before I call Deputy Shaw. I'm sure he'd be happy to put you in the cell right next to your partner if I insisted."

Daniels tensed, but realized he'd taken his questioning as far as he could for now. He stepped around Herndon. "Then I'll see myself out." He paused at the door. "But if your son is guilty, sir. I'm going to find out."

Herndon glared. "Get out."

Daniels held his stare for a second, then turned and left.

Chapter Fourteen

REM TOOK A SIP from his water bottle. An hour earlier, Shaw had brought him a sandwich and the water and then he'd left without saying a word. Hungry, Rem had eaten the sandwich. His headache had faded, but his fatigue had remained. He'd tried to take a nap on the cot, but his mind wouldn't settle. Images of Sharon dead in the woods plagued him, and he couldn't help but worry about Daniels. If whoever had done this believed Daniels was getting close to the truth, would they retaliate?

Giving up on sleep, he'd sat on the ground with his back against the wall and made himself sip his water. After his substantial alcohol intake the last few days, he suspected he needed fluids. Drinking from it, though, brought up images of sitting in that dark room with the rodents after being taken by Victor D'Mato. The longer he sat in the cell, the harder it became not to be reminded of his terror-induced state while he'd waited for Victor's goons to come for him. He still dealt with the nightmares and PTSD from his assault and this situation wasn't helping. Knowing he'd be spending the night in jail, he hoped there would be some light in the room. He didn't do too well in darkness.

Time passed, and breaking out in a sweat and bouncing his knees, he tried to think of something else when the door to the cells opened and Shaw appeared.

"You have a visitor," he said.

Rem stood as Daniels entered, glaring at Shaw. He walked up to Rem's cell. "Hey."

Rem sighed in relief. "Hey."

"I'll let you two enjoy your talk since it's probably one of your last," said Shaw. "But make it fast." He paused for a second and then walked out.

"I really hate that guy," said Daniels.

"He makes it easy."

Daniels looked back. "You doing okay? Hanging in there?"

Rem gripped the bars. "Just great. At least he brought me some food." He dabbed his sleeve across his brow.

Daniels studied him, the cell and the water bottle. "You sure you're okay?"

"Just havin' a moment," said Rem. "But I'm working through it." He shook out his hands and blew out a breath. "Enough about me, though. What did you find out?"

Daniels' face furrowed. "We're going to get you out of here. I talked to Lozano. Kate knows someone who can represent you, but they can't make it here until Monday morning. They'll be there for the arraignment."

"Shit. That feels like a lifetime from now."

"I know, but it's the weekend, so we'll have to wait. Has Shaw questioned you?"

Rem shook his head. "He hasn't done a damn thing. I've been sitting in this cell ever since he brought me in. All he did was read me my rights, take my picture and fingerprints and confiscate my watch and phone, and I've been studying the ceiling ever since."

"I talked to Gin. He went through your car, too."

"Great. He's got my dirty underwear and my gun. Badge, too."

"He's only got forty-eight hours before he has to formally charge you," said Daniels.

"And he's gonna use all forty-eight of them." Rem ran a hand through his hair and paced in his cell. "You having any luck?"

"Not as much as I'd hoped." Daniels filled him in on his encounters with Amy and Scott. "After leaving the auto body shop, I went to Jimmy's. I talked to him and anybody else I could find who might have seen what happened last night after we left. They all pretty much corroborated Amy's account though."

"Sharon said she was going to see me?" asked Rem.

"Apparently. Do you recall seeing her at all after I left your room?"

Rem groaned. "That's the problem. I don't recall much of anything after the fight. I have a vague recollection of puking outside the bar, but that's it."

"You think she could have snuck in while you were sleeping? Or maybe you woke up and followed her outside, and that's why I found you in the woods this morning?"

Rem sighed. "I don't know. The only reason I can think of as to why I might have been outside is I had to use the bathroom or throw up again."

"You realize you had indoor plumbing."

"Yeah, well," Rem hugged his elbows. "That shack was a little claustrophobic. To be honest, I felt a little enclosed in that space. If I got spooked...I might have gone outside."

Daniels nodded. "If you did, then you may have encountered Sharon."

"But then what? What happened after that? Her body wasn't near the shack. I didn't have any signs of a confrontation with her."

Daniels put a hand on one of the bars. "Well, that might not be true."

Rem heard the tone in his partner's voice. "What do you mean?"

Daniels eyed the door. "When I did your laundry this morning," he looked back and lowered his voice, "I saw blood on the sleeve of the shirt you'd been wearing. I didn't think much about it because I figured you'd cut yourself." He paused. "I washed the clothes, but the stain is still there."

Rem tried to think. Had he cut himself? "I don't remember any injury, but that doesn't mean it isn't my blood."

"Maybe, but I went back to the shack after I left Jimmy's, just to look around. It's taped off and I couldn't go inside, but I found the tree where you were this morning and checked the area. I saw a few drops of blood not far from there, leading off into the woods."

Rem's belly flipped. "Are you saying...do you think...?"

"I don't think you did anything." Daniels rested an elbow on the bar and leaned in. "What if Sharon did find you last night, either in your shack, or in the woods? What if Scott followed her and saw you with her, but you'd passed out again. He confronted her, they argued, and she ran into the trees, but she was injured and dripping blood at the same time. Scott caught up to her and finished it. Then got the bright idea to plant the weapon in your shack."

Rem cursed. "It's smart. Especially since I can't remember a damn thing."

"Better to keep that to yourself." He paused. "When you made up the sofa bed, are you sure there was nothing there?"

For the thousandth time, Rem reviewed his morning. "I didn't see anything, but you know the state I was in. It's possible I missed it."

Daniels nodded. "We're just going to have to keep pushing buttons. Somebody in this town knows something." He paused. "I'm going to find Scott after he gets off work. I want to know if he lied about this Sonya gal. If I can get him alone and make him sweat, I may be able to get him to talk."

"Check the Millers' B&B," said Rem. "Maybe you can confirm if there actually is a Sonya."

"That's a good idea."

"You should also talk to Rocky Whistler, the sheriff's brother."

Daniels scrunched his face. "Why him?"

"He owns the barbershop. He came in one night at Jimmy's. Guy cuts everybody's hair and knows everything about this town. You never know what he's overheard or what secrets he's keeping to himself."

"Okay. I'll talk to him, too."

The inevitable worry crept up Rem's spine. "Just be careful, though. Bart and Ricky may not take too kindly to you sticking around. And if whoever killed Sharon feels threatened, you could make yourself a target."

"Aunt Gin said the same thing," said Daniels. "She told me to stay out of the woods after dark. Can you believe that?"

Rem's worry turned to fear. "She's right."

Daniels rolled his eyes. "Not you, too. You were the one wandering around outside last night."

"I was still in town, and drunk. Believe me, if I'd been sober, I would have locked my doors. The woods have a vibe after dark. I've heard a few stories since I got here, and the locals take it seriously. You heard about the challenge?"

Daniels' face fell. "Marvin got me up to speed."

"Just do me a favor and don't get cocky, Aunt Gin's right. Somebody could dump your body and blame the witch and her hound, and this town wouldn't blink an eye. If somebody wants to get to you, that would be a way to do it."

"Nobody is going to get to me. And if they did, that just sheds more light on a killer that's obviously not you. Besides, Sheriff Joe will be back tomorrow, and he'll pick up where I left off. Gin trusts him, and says he'll check into the details. That's where I'm at a disadvantage. I didn't see the body or the crime scene. Hell, we don't even know how Sharon died or what kind of weapon was found."

"Yeah, I get it. Just humor me, okay? I'm not there to back you up, so you need to stay alert."

Daniels shook his head. "You're the one in jail, accused of murder, and you're worried about me?"

Rem leaned a shoulder against the bars. "I just want a partner to return to. I don't have the patience to break in a new one." He picked at the iron of the bar. "And don't even get me started on the parenting advice I might need soon."

"I thought we weren't going to mention kids until we got through the next six months."

"It's amazing how a little jail time compels you to consider the future."

Daniels eyed the room. "I guess you can't catch up on the latest TV series or read that book you've been putting to the side."

"Not really."

Daniels sighed and gestured toward the door. "How come you think Shaw hasn't questioned you?"

Rem shrugged. "You got me. Maybe because he knows I won't say anything? Or maybe he doesn't like my sparkling personality."

"I find that hard to believe."

Rem smirked. "You and me both."

Daniels straightened. "I booked my shack again, so I'll be nearby. I'll be here tomorrow to check on you and let you know what I found out. You going to be okay tonight?"

Rem swallowed, uncertain of the answer. "I don't think I have a choice."

Daniels gestured at the barred window at the top of Rem's cell. "It'll be a full moon, so you'll have some light."

Rem eyed the small opening, already feeling his chest constrict. "Don't tell Shaw. He'd probably cover it." He rubbed his face, wishing he could be anywhere else but in that cell.

"Hang in there. Remember what the shrink told you. Long, slow breaths. You'll get through it." He held the bar. "I'll keep digging, and Joe will be here tomorrow. I can get more information from him. Then, if nothing else, we'll get you out of here on Monday."

"You're assuming I'll make bail." Rem didn't want to think about what he would do if he didn't get out of his cell after Monday.

"You'll make bail. Try not to think the worst."

Rem chuckled sadly. "After what I've been through the last few years, and now this?" He raised a hand. "I'm beginning to think that dark cloud hanging over my head is permanently attached."

The door opened, and Shaw emerged. "Time's up, Detective." He stuck out a thumb. "Let's go."

"See what I mean?" said Rem.

Daniels glowered at Shaw but looked back at Rem. "I'll be back first thing tomorrow. Just stay cool and try not to worry. We're gonna figure this out."

Shaw grinned. "I bet you believe in unicorns and fairies, too." He stepped to the side. "After you."

"Remember what I said. Be careful," said Rem.

Daniels nodded. "I will." He walked out, Shaw followed, and still sneering at Rem, Shaw shut the door with a clang.

Chapter Fifteen

DANIELS PARKED ACROSS THE street from the auto body shop and sat in his car. After leaving Rem, his first stop was the Millers' B&B. He'd called Gin, and she'd told him where to find it. After arriving, he'd attempted to talk to the owners about their recent guests, but they were reluctant to speak with him. Once he'd explained why he was there, they were even more dubious and said they'd prefer to discuss any customer issues with Sheriff Joe. Realizing they weren't going to trust an outsider, he'd left and returned to the auto body shop. After watching for a few minutes, he'd called the shop, and learned that they closed at four o'clock on Saturdays. Nearing four o'clock, he waited, wanting to catch Scott Herndon leaving.

Sure enough, Scott walked out at closing, still wearing his embroidered yellow shirt. He got into an older model, brown Trans Am and drove off. Daniels followed. Within minutes, Scott pulled into an apartment complex. Eyeing the tall grass, peeling paint and rusty iron fences, Daniels guessed this was the cheaper place to live in Merrimac. Scott exited, ran up a flight of stairs, and disappeared into a second-floor apartment.

Daniels remained in his car and observed his surroundings. The complex was quiet for a Saturday. There were no joggers or dog-walkers, and nobody came and went from the parking lot. After fifteen minutes, Daniels eased his door open, figuring he'd given Scott enough time to relax, change his clothes, pop a beer and start to grieve for Sharon, when a car, loud music blaring, pulled into the lot.

Daniels closed his door, slid down into his seat, and saw Bart and Ricky emerge from the vehicle, each holding two six-packs of beer. Laughing, they headed toward Scott's staircase and climbed it.

Groaning, Daniels watched them knock. Scott answered, and Ricky and Bart entered the apartment. Glad he'd waited, Daniels figured Bart and Ricky were trying to cheer their friend up by getting him drunk, which meant they'd be together the rest of the night. Daniels would have to wait until tomorrow to get Scott alone. He hoped it would work to his advantage if Scott was hungover when Daniels questioned him.

Accessing his phone, he pulled up the location of the local barbershop. Now was as good a time as any to talk to Rocky Whistler.

He found his way back to Main Street and drove two streets over. After finding the shop, he parked in front of the barbershop pole and went inside. It was a small space, with big mirrors, two barber chairs and a small desk up front with a beat-up black leather couch across from it. A young guy who looked to be in his twenties sat on the couch, looking at his phone, and there was an elderly customer in one of the chairs. He had a cape around his neck, and a middle-aged man with a slim mustache, bushy eyebrows and dark-framed glasses was holding scissors and combing the man's gray hair.

"Can I help you?" asked the barber. "I can get you in for a trim if you can wait about twenty minutes. I'll be done with Whit here soon."

The guy with the phone didn't even look up. Daniels walked over to the chair. "Rocky Whistler?"

The barber lowered his comb. "Yes?"

Daniels glanced at the customer. Judging by his deep wrinkles, drooping skin, thin frame and shaky fingers, Daniels put him somewhere north of ninety. Despite that, he still had a decent head of hair. Daniels introduced himself to Rocky and told him why he was there.

Rocky shook his head with a sigh. "I heard about Sharon this morning. Such a terrible thing. It surprised me when I realized they'd arrested your friend. When I met him, he seemed like a nice guy."

The old man in the chair chuckled. "I got arrested once." He smiled but didn't elaborate.

Daniels raised a brow at him, but then spoke to Rocky. "My partner is a nice guy and he's innocent. He told me he met you and that you might have heard a few things. You might be able to shed some light on Sharon and Scott."

Rocky resumed combing. The elderly man hooted and raised a hand. "I love a good mystery."

Daniels frowned at him.

"Don't mind Whit," said Rocky. "He's a few years past his prime. He's ninety-two and the town's oldest resident so we all give him some leeway. His filter's gone and he'll say things that don't make sense, but I think he just disappears into his memories, which I guess would be a nice place to go." He gestured toward the couch. "That's his great grandson, Justin, up front. They come in every month like clockwork to get Whit's hair cut and then they get a coffee across the street before heading back to Whit's granddaughter's house. She takes care of him, which isn't easy because Whit likes to wander sometimes. I think he forgets where he is."

Daniels nodded, trying not to show any impatience. At any other time, he might have engaged with old man Whit, but he kept thinking of Rem locked up in that damn cell and hated wasting time. "Nice to meet you, Whit."

Whit played with edge of his cape and didn't respond.

Rocky started to cut Whit's hair. "You sure your friend didn't kill Sharon?" he asked. "I saw them together. They looked pretty close."

"I saw them, too. Did you also see Scott Herndon shooting laser eyes at the both of them?"

Rocky snipped some hair. "You don't need to tell me about Scott. He and Sharon were on a collision course from day one." He eyed Daniels. "You shouldn't worry so much. My brother will get to the bottom of it. He's good at sniffing out Shaw's bullshit."

"Yeah, well, your brother is currently out of town and my partner's pacing in a cell for something he didn't do. And Shaw seems perfectly content to sit on his ass."

Rocky chuckled. "That's Shaw for you. Once he decides he doesn't like you, he'll turn whatever screw he can find. He and his sister were a lot alike."

"You mean Sybil?' asked Daniels.

Rocky nodded. "Joe's former wife. She disappeared into the woods one day and hasn't been seen since."

"I like the woods. I walked through them once," said Whit. "There's a lot of trees."

"Very true, Whit," said Rocky. He combed Whit's hair again. "Once Sybil vanished, Shaw showed up, angry about his sister, but also looking for work. My brother's guilt complex took over and he hired him. He's been regretting it ever since."

"There's birds, too," said Whit. "I like it when they sing."

"There's nothing stopping your brother from firing Shaw," said Daniels.

"Try telling him that," said Rocky. He gathered some of Whit's hair and snipped some more.

Arguing about Shaw was pointless, so Daniels got to the point. "You talk to a lot of the locals in this town. You hear anything that might make you think twice about Shaw's alleged story about what happened to Sharon?"

Rocky patted Whit's shoulder when the old man tried to remove his cape. "Not just yet, Whit. I'll let you know when I'm done."

Whit settled and put his hands down. "I saw a chipmunk, too," he said.

"I'm sure you did," said Rocky. He pointed at Daniels with his scissors. "You're partner's right about my knowledge of random information. I hear the rumors about who's sleeping with who, who's shoplifting from the retail stores and who's behind in their credit card payments. Is any of it true? I don't know, but I listen and don't judge. I think that's why people confide in me."

Daniels crossed his arms. "What were the rumors about Scott and Sharon?"

Rocky shrugged. "They were hot one minute, cold the next. But they definitely had a lot in common."

"Like what?" asked Daniels.

Rocky moved to the other side of Whit and snipped more of his hair. "They both wanted out of Merrimac. Scott's been talking about it since his youth but hasn't gotten any further than the body shop with his dad. Then Sharon showed up and stirred up all that angst in Scott. Scott came in for a haircut about a month ago and talked about what they would do once they had some money. He wanted to open a bar on some Mexican resort and said Sharon would join him. She'd serve drinks, lie on the beach in her bikini, and basically live to make Scott happy." He paused in mid comb. "I think Sharon may have had different ideas about how to enjoy herself, though, and Scott wasn't necessarily part of the picture." He sighed. "Young love."

"I saw a pretty girl once," said Whit.

Rocky patted his arm. "You sure did. Your Nancy was beautiful. God rest her soul."

"She was in the woods," added Whit.

"Nancy did love the woods," said Rocky.

Listening to Rocky, Daniels perked up. "Are you saying that Sharon wasn't just spending time with Scott? That maybe she was planning on disappearing with someone else?"

Rocky moved to the back of Whit. "Maybe. She was hanging out with your friend."

"My friend showed up five days ago. That may be long enough to do some foolish things, but I can guarantee you that one of them wasn't running off with Sharon."

"She may have hoped otherwise."

Daniels snorted. "Rem is a cop and isn't exactly rolling in dough. Sharon struck me as a woman who didn't want an average lifestyle."

"For someone who just arrived in town," said Rocky, "you know a lot." He lowered his voice. "I like you, Detective, so I'll give you a little help." He paused. "I heard a rumor that Sharon was telling her friends that she planned to leave town soon, but whether Scott was part of her escape, I can't say."

"How soon?" asked Daniels.

Rocky wiped Whit's neck with a towel. "Depends on what you believe. I heard as early as next week. After the Dandelion Festival."

Daniels considered that. "If that's true, she'd need the cash to do it, but from what I know, she worked as a teller at the bank. Not exactly a cash cow for income."

Rocky grabbed some clippers and turned them on. He began to shave the hair from Whit's neck.

"I didn't see cows in the woods," said Whit.

"I'd be surprised if you did," said Rocky, continuing to shave Whit's hair. He glanced at Daniels. "Just between you and me, I think Sharon had another man in her life. One who told her one thing, but maybe did another." He waved the clippers. "But again. That's based on rumor and innuendo, which is a nasty byproduct of Merrimac."

Daniels stilled. "Any chance that byproduct could suggest who that man is?"

Rocky shaved the hair beneath Whit's ear. "You might check out Sharon's boss at the bank. Tyler Barnstone. Word is, he'd been planning on firing Sharon, but he never got around to doing it."

Daniels straightened. "You think Sharon was offering him more than her forty hours?"

"Again, this is all based on rumor," said Rocky, "but a bank manager must make decent money."

"I can't say much about that," said Daniels, "but he sure as hell works around a lot of money and probably a nice big vault."

Rocky's eyes widened. "I didn't even think about that." He turned off the clippers. "I like the way you think, Detective. Joe would be impressed."

"So is the woman in the woods," said Whit.

Daniels checked his watch. "What time does the bank close?"

"It's Saturday. They close early," said Rocky. "But I have it on good authority that Tyler stays late on Saturdays. You go now, you might catch him before he heads home."

Daniels nodded. "Where's the bank?"

"You can walk it from here." Rocky gave him directions.

"She saw what happened," said Whit.

Daniels turned to leave.

"She wants to talk to you," said Whit.

Daniels stopped and turned. A chill ran up his back and he eyed Whit. "Is he talking to me?"

Rocky leaned over. "You okay, Whit? Who saw what happen?"

"The woman in the woods." His gaze bore into Daniels and Daniels chills turned into shivers. "Take the trail."

"Just ignore him," said Rocky, combing Whit's hair. "He's back in the past."

Whit continued to stare, and Daniels debated asking Whit to explain what he meant, but then Whit's shoulders relaxed, and his gaze drifted. "Nancy always said to be careful in the woods," he said, his voice soft.

"She was right, Whit," said Rocky. "Especially around here."

Daniels hesitated, but then looked back at Rocky. "Thanks for your help, Rocky."

"Good luck, Detective." Rocky went back to cutting Whit's hair. "To you and your partner."

· · • • · • · · ·

Daniels followed Rocky's directions and headed across and down the street. At the next intersection, he walked a block over and saw the bank on the corner. He jogged over and up to the door. A sign on the glass read 'Closed,' but Daniels tried the door and it was unlocked. He swung it open and walked in.

The small lobby was empty and the lights behind the tellers' stations were off. He saw an office with an open door and a light on. He approached it. "Hello?"

A tall, thin man stepped out, wearing a crisp shirt and tie. His brown hair was combed back, and his goatee and polished shoes gave him a dignified look. "I'm sorry," he said, "but we're closed for the day."

"Tyler Barnstone?" asked Daniels.

He nodded. "Yes. That's me."

Daniels introduced himself. "I'm investigating the murder of one of your employees. Sharon Belafonte."

Tyler tensed and took hold of the counter. "You're investigating Sharon's death? What happened to Deputy Shaw?"

"Deputy Shaw feels it's better to let someone else do his job for him, so I volunteered."

Tyler's eyes widened. "You're the friend, aren't you?"

"Excuse me?" asked Daniels.

"It's all over town. That officer was arrested for Sharon's murder, and his partner is harassing everyone he can find to prove his innocence."

"Harassing? That's a bit of a stretch. I just want to learn the truth. Isn't that what anyone in this town would want?"

Tyler drew his shoulders up. "Sharon is dead. As shocked as I was to hear the news, I have to admit, it wasn't a surprise. I'd heard about her and your friend's antics at Jimmy's the last few nights and none of it sounded good.

Obviously, things got out of hand and your friend took matters into his own hands."

Daniels took a step toward Tyler. Tyler tightened his grip on the counter but stayed where he was. "I wasn't aware you had so much knowledge about Sharon's murder," said Daniels.

Tyler fidgeted.

Daniels encroached. "How did Sharon die?"

Tyler didn't answer.

"Where did she die?"

Tyler pursed his lips.

"Did you see her with my friend? Were you a witness to the crime?"

Tyler's cheek reddened.

"Do you know anyone that was a witness?" Daniels paused. "Do you know my friend, or his background, or why he's been in that bar drinking himself into a stupor the last few nights with a woman who was hanging all over him just to make her occasional boyfriend jealous?"

Tyler spoke softly. "I didn't say Sharon didn't have her vices. She took stupid risks."

"So, it's her fault she was murdered?"

"That's not what I meant, but everyone has to face the consequences for their actions. Your partner included."

Daniels set his jaw. He told himself to stay cool, but his impatience with some of the people in Merrimac was wearing on him. "My partner left the bar while Sharon was alive and well. He went to bed, and Sharon hung out with her BFF, Scott Herndon, and you want to blame my friend for her death because Shaw said so?"

"I heard they found the murder weapon on your friend. Sounds pretty damning to me."

Daniels snorted. The rumor mill was in full swing in Merrimac. "You heard wrong."

"I'm just telling you what I know."

Daniels' impatience grew. "Which is why you're a fool, Tyler, along with anyone else around here who is prepared to believe an idiot like Shaw and accuse an innocent man without getting the facts first."

Tyler set his jaw and scowled at him. "Why are you here?"

"You're Sharon's boss, right?"

"I was."

"What can you tell me about her? What kind of an employee was she?" Daniels figured he'd start with the easy questions first.

Tyler hesitated, but finally answered. "Lousy. She'd show up late if she even showed up at all. And when she was here, she was usually on her phone."

"Then why didn't you fire her?"

Tyler shifted and studied the floor. "I was going to, but recently, her work performance improved."

"Improved? How so?"

Tyler crossed his arms. "I don't have to answer any of your questions. I don't even know you. For all I know, maybe you helped kill Sharon."

"Nice pivot, Tyler, but I'm not here to defend myself. If Shaw wanted me in jail, I'd be there." Daniels gestured at Tyler. "If you've got nothing to hide, then what's the big deal? It's either talk to me now, or Sheriff Joe tomorrow. Take your pick."

Sighing, Tyler loosened his tie and undid the shirt button at his neck. He paused. "The last few weeks, Sharon had been arriving on time. She ate at her desk, didn't leave early, and even put her phone away when I asked. She even asked to work this weekend, which was unusual since she hated working on Saturdays."

"Something special about this weekend?" asked Daniels, wondering if Sharon's behavior had anything to do with her plans to leave town.

"Nothing, other than the festival. More tourists mean more business."

Which means more money, Daniels thought to himself. "Did Sharon have access to your safe?"

Tyler widened his eyes. "What? Of course not."

Daniels noted the sheen of sweat on Tyler's forehead. "You sure about that?"

Tyler's expression shifted from certainty to doubt. "I'm not that stupid."

"Where is the safe?"

"It's in my office."

"Has Sharon been in your office?"

Tyler's cheeks flared red. "On occasion, yes, but only because I asked her in...you know...for business reasons."

Daniels held Tyler's look with a hard stare. "Business reasons? Is that all?"

Tyler stammered. "I...I don't...what...what exactly are you implying?"

Daniels tipped his head. "Pardon my bluntness, but were you sleeping with her?"

Tyler's mouth fell open. "I...I...can't believe...how dare you say that."

"Spare me your indignity, Tyler. You said yourself that Sharon took risks. She sucked as an employee, but yet you kept her on the payroll. And don't tell me it was because she suddenly became a pristine worker in the last few weeks." He let Tyler stammer. "How long were you sleeping with her?"

Tyler jutted out his jaw. "I don't have to listen to any of this."

"Did you have sex in your office? Could she have gained access to information she shouldn't have had while you relaxed in post-coital bliss?"

"That is outrageous," yelled Tyler. He patted his pockets. "I'm calling Deputy Shaw. You have no business asking me that."

"Go ahead and call. Just be sure you're ready to answer some questions about Sharon when you do, because when Sheriff Joe gets back, he's going to get an earful about what I know." He leaned in. "This is a small town, Tyler," said Daniels. "Did you honestly think this would stay a secret?"

Tyler gritted his teeth. "Get out."

Daniels eyed the lobby of the bank. "Enjoy your remaining time here, Tyler, because I got a feeling when word gets out, your status as a respectable bank owner is going to take flying leap into the toilet."

His voice shaking with anger, Tyler pointed. "I said get out of here."

"On my way." Daniels headed toward the door. He put his hand on the knob and turned. "And you should know, Tyler. You're now a murder suspect. Better you stay in town until we get this sorted out."

Tyler's eyes flared and he insulted Daniels' mother as Daniels walked out of the bank.

Chapter Sixteen

DANIELS WALKED DOWN THE street, deep in thought. He now had reason to suspect not only Scott, but also Tyler, Sharon's boss. Did Tyler know more about Sharon than he was admitting? Or was Sharon using him the way she'd used Rem? Were Sharon and Scott involved in some crazy plot to steal money from the bank and then take off to Mexico? Or was Sharon planning to run off with Tyler, or even by herself, leaving Scott and Tyler to handle the fallout?

Rubbing his tight shoulders and neck, Daniels headed back toward his car, which was still parked outside Rocky's barbershop, and debated what to do next. He couldn't confront Scott until tomorrow, and he'd pushed Tyler as far as he could for now, but he had no doubt that one of them knew something. And even more likely, one of them, if not both, were responsible for Sharon's murder and planting the weapon at Rem's.

He returned to his car and leaned back against it. Frustrated, he blew out a breath. Rem was going to have to spend the night in that cell and his only connection to the outside world was the lunatic Deputy Shaw. Daniels wondered what else he could do. Should he talk to Rocky again? Maybe there were others that Sharon had manipulated.

Thinking back, Daniels recalled the elderly Whit sitting in the barber chair and remembered the old man's words. *She saw what happened. She wants to talk to you. Take the trail.* Whit had stared at him like he'd known Daniels all his life. Recalling it, more chills broke out on Daniels' skin. What had Whit meant? Did it mean something important?

Telling himself he was overthinking the random comments of a ninety-two-year-old man with obvious signs of dementia, Daniels pushed off the car, planning on returning to Rocky's, when he heard a bell tinkle. He looked over to see the door to a coffee shop across the street open. Whit and his great grandson, Justin, walked out, both holding disposable cups. Justin held Whit's elbow as they headed slowly down the sidewalk. Daniels remembered Rocky saying that Whit and Justin would stop and get a coffee before heading home.

Something tugged at Daniels and making up his mind, he jogged across the street and ran up next to Justin, who was guiding Whit toward a car parked in a handicapped space. "Hey, Justin. Hey, Whit. Remember me? Detective Daniels? From Rocky's?"

Justin paused. "Who?"

Daniels almost rolled his eyes. "I was talking to Rocky while he cut Whit's hair." He waved a hand. "Hi, Whit."

Approaching the car, Whit put his hand on the hood, his freshly cut hair blowing in the breeze. He paused and stared. "You're the woods guy."

"That's right," said Daniels. "I'm the woods guy."

"I like the woods," said Whit.

"We got to go," said Justin. "Mom is waiting for us."

"Uh, Whit," said Daniels, hoping he could get some clarity on Whit's comments. "You mind if I ask you about what you said in the barber shop? About the woman in the woods?"

Holding his coffee, Whit rested a hip against the car.

Spying a bench, Daniels raised a hand. "Why don't we sit for a second? You can enjoy your coffee and tell me about the woman."

Justin scoffed. "Dude, he doesn't know what he's talking about. He mutters about all sorts of stuff." He took Whit's elbow. "C'mon, Grandad."

Whit frowned. "I want to sit on the bench."

Daniels hid a satisfied smile. "It will only take a second. I promise." He began to wonder if his desperation was making him do crazy things. Talking to a ninety-two-year-old man, hoping to get a clue, seemed to confirm that.

Whit turned and Daniels took his elbow and helped him up to the bench. "There you go," said Daniels. "Have a seat."

Justin pulled out his phone. "I'm calling Mom."

"Tell her I said hello," said Whit.

Daniels sat beside him. "How's your coffee?"

Whit eyed his cup. "My Nancy made better, and she didn't charge five dollars for it. It's highway robbery."

Daniels decided Whit was smarter than most thought. "I agree."

Whit sipped his drink. "You find out what happened to that lady?"

Daniels shifted to face Whit. "You mean Sharon? No. Not yet."

Whit gestured at Justin, who spoke on the phone. "That's my great grandson."

"Yeah," said Daniels. "We've met."

"He likes the woods, too."

Daniels watched as Justin hung up with a groan. "Now Mom wants a coffee." He stepped up on the sidewalk. "Can you stay with him until I get back?"

After expecting to be told to get lost, Daniels breathed a sigh of relief. "Of course. Take your time."

Justin nodded and turned back toward the coffee shop. "Be right back."

Whit settled back on the bench. "It's pretty here," he said.

Daniels took a second to eye the big shade trees, small shops and colorful flowers lining the streets. "I guess it is." He hadn't had much time to appreciate Merrimac since arriving. "It's a nice town."

Whit shrugged. "Nice towns don't mean nice people."

Daniels raised a brow. "What do you mean?"

Whit smiled and sipped his coffee. "I saw her. Nancy, too."

"Saw who?" Daniels leaned in. "You saw Sharon?"

"Who's Sharon?"

Confused, Daniels shook his head. "Who did you and Nancy see?"

"She was in the woods with her dogs. And then Nancy died." Whit's shoulders slumped and he hung his head.

Daniels tried to understand. "Did Nancy die in the woods?"

"She died in the hospital." Whit looked up, his eyes wide. "I don't like hospitals."

Determined to be patient, Daniels leaned back on the bench. "Not many people do, Whit." He realized that Rocky was correct. Whit was lost in his memories, and he was only remembering bits and pieces of his past. He patted Whit on the wrist. "Justin will be back in a second. Then we'll get you in the car and you can go home."

"The woman knows." Whit sighed. "She knew about Nancy."

Daniels humored him. "What did she know?"

"That she was sick."

Daniels perked up. "The woman in the woods knew Nancy was sick?"

"She knows things. She knows about your friend."

Daniels' stomach tightened. "How does she know about my friend?"

"She can see." Whit looked over at him. "She told me."

Daniels squinted. "When did she tell you? Have you seen her today?"

"No," said Whit with a smirk. "I heard her." He scoffed. "Sheesh."

Daniels rubbed his temples, having no idea what Whit meant.

"You need to find her."

"Find her? How?"

"She likes the woods. Like you. Follow the trail."

The warnings Daniels had heard about the forest flared in his mind. "I thought the woods were dangerous. Everyone says to stay away from them, especially at night. I've been told about a witch and her hell hounds. Are you saying that I need to go out there?"

"Detective...." Whit held his gaze and stared with the same intensity as he had in the barbershop. "...if you don't, you won't live to see the sunrise."

Daniels held his breath and gripped the edge of the bench. "What do you know, Whit?"

Whit's expression softened and the dull look returned to his eyes. "Did Justin leave?" he asked. "He's supposed to take me home."

Disappointed, Daniels sighed. Whatever part of Whit's brain that had fluttered to life to warn him had flickered and gone out. Daniels put a hand on his wrist. "Justin will be right back, Whit. I'll stay with you."

"Thank you," said Whit. "You're a nice man." He sipped his coffee.

· · · ●·●·●·● · ·

After leaving Whit, Daniels returned to Genevieve's home. She'd insisted on feeding him while he gave her an update on his visit with Rem and what he'd learned from Scott, Rocky and Tyler. All the while though, Whit's words echoed in his mind. He told Genevieve about meeting Whit, but not what the elderly man had said. He figured if Gin knew he was considering taking Whit's advice, she'd argue with him and never let him leave.

Still considering his options, he told Gin he was returning to his shack to get some sleep and would visit Scott and Rem again in the morning. And once Joe returned, he would speak with him about the evidence against Rem. Satisfied that Gin was up to speed, and if something did happen to him that night, whether it was in the woods, or elsewhere, Daniels knew she could update the sheriff.

He'd left just before sunset, and stopping at the intersection, he chose to turn in the opposite direction from the town and head toward the trail. The least he could do was check it out.

A few minutes later, Daniels pulled into the small rocky clearing in front of the trail head. There were no other cars and he parked, turned off the ignition, and sat, wondering what the hell he was doing. Was he actually considering walking the trail, just as the sun was setting?

Uncertain, but telling himself he didn't have to do this, he got out of the car and listened. The wind rustled the tree branches and an occasional bird cawed, but beneath that there was only silence. The trail disappeared into dense woods, and he again recalled Whit's warning. *If you don't, you won't live to see the sunrise.* Had he upset the applecart enough that Sharon's killer planned to kill him, too? Or was Whit only pulling the string of some old memory where someone had died, and he'd connected it to Daniels?

He thought again of those who'd walked the trail after dark in the past. They'd either never returned or if they did, vowed never to go back. Amy and her friend had attempted it. Their fear had stopped them, and terrified, they'd rushed home, but they were alive. Daniels figured if they could do it, so could he. If he saw something, he'd just run like hell.

And Whit had kept mentioning a woman in the woods. Was she real, or just a figment of Whit's imagination? Could she help Rem or was Daniels' desperate need to clear his friend's name creating false hope?

A rumble of thunder made Daniels look up. Dark clouds had gathered in the distance, and he cursed, thinking of Rem in his cell, knowing those clouds would obliterate any moonlight. Rem would have to get through a dark night, fighting against potential flashbacks. Daniels hated knowing that and frustrated, he realized the only way to help Rem was to follow every lead, and if that meant taking this trail, then he would do it. It was better than waking up in that shack the next morning, wondering what to do, or worse, not waking up at all.

Thunder rumbled again, and he told himself not to worry about silly tales of witches and hell hounds. If Rem could get through a tough night, then so could he. Making up his mind, he shut his car door, took a deep breath, and walked into the woods.

Chapter Seventeen

REM BARELY REGISTERED THE metallic clang. Hearing it a second time, he cracked an eye open. He saw the sink and toilet in his cell, but nothing else. Trying to wake up, he blinked, and saw the tray outside his door. Shaw had left him breakfast.

He moaned and covered his eyes with his hand, recalling his awful night. It had started out well enough, considering where he was, but it hadn't been long before he'd heard thunder and eyeing his small window, he'd prayed the storm would head in another direction. After nightfall, the moon was still out, and he'd thought he'd dodged a bullet. He'd slept fitfully until a crack of thunder had roused him, and he'd opened his eyes to darkness, broken only by the occasional flash of lightning.

His chest had tightened, and forcing himself to breathe, his mind had flashed back. Seeing himself in the dark room again, he'd sat up, gripped his pillow, and had told himself to remain calm. He'd repeated the mantra he'd memorized. He was no longer there, and no one was coming for him.

It had worked for a while, but then the storm had gained strength. The driving rain and the inky darkness made the cell seem more confining. Fighting against panic, he'd ended up in the corner against the wall. Strangely, It was the only place he'd felt safe. He'd remained there, shaking, telling himself he was okay, until the storm had passed, the clouds cleared, and the moonlight returned. His cell had brightened, but it had taken Rem a good hour before he could get himself to return to the cot and lie down. His muddled brain had eventually succumbed to his fatigue just as the first signs of sunlight had emerged.

His cell now bright with light, he stretched and moaned, feeling the aches and pains of an uncomfortable night. Eyeing the tray, he could see a boxed orange juice and milk, a bowl with dry cereal, another bottle of water, and an apple. He sat up and sighed in dismay. He'd give his life savings for a huge cup of coffee and a hot shower. Swinging his legs off the cot, he stretched his neck, wondering what this new day would bring, and praying it would be better than the previous one. Sheriff Joe would return, and Rem hoped he would shed some light on this situation. If Daniels had uncovered other suspects and Joe was open to learning the truth, maybe Rem could get out of here, unless Shaw threw water on it in an attempt to convince Joe that Rem was the killer.

His stomach rumbling, he forced himself up. The clock against the far wall said it was almost nine o'clock. He ambled toward his cell door, pulled the tray through the narrow opening at the bottom, sat and ate his breakfast.

· · • •· • • • ·

Two hours later, Rem paced with nervous anxiety. He hadn't seen or spoken to anyone. Shaw had not appeared, nor had Daniels or Gin. He'd heard muffled voices through the door about thirty minutes earlier, but they'd faded, and no one had entered the cells.

Knowing that Gin and Daniels had planned to visit, Rem had to assume that Shaw was preventing them from seeing him. He didn't understand why, though, since Shaw had let them in the previous day. Was this some attempt to wear Rem down, or to assert his dominance before Joe arrived and took over? Weary and worried, he told himself to relax. Joe would arrive soon, and so would Daniels, and then they would figure out their next steps. His thoughts drifted and thinking about spending another night in the cell, he shivered. Massaging his knotted shoulders, he sat on the bed and continued to wait.

· · • •· • • • ·

Hours later, Rem eyed the time. It was two o'clock, and he debated banging his head against the bars. Nothing had changed since that morning. He'd seen no one and heard nothing. Shaw had not emerged, and no lunch had been delivered. His mind creating a barrage of scenarios, he began to wonder if the zombie apocalypse was upon them. Were Shaw and the people of Merrimac victims and now wandering the forest as the undead? He imagined Daniels and Gin as zombies roaming the woods in search of fresh meat. Forgotten, Rem would die in his cell of either hunger or whatever discovered, murdered, and ate him.

Anxious, he'd yelled a few times, trying to get someone's attention, but with no results. Where the hell was everyone? Remembering the same fear when he'd been captured by Victor's followers, he reminded himself that this situation was different. He hadn't been kidnapped and someone would eventually come for him. Shaw was probably making him sweat and enjoying every moment of it.

Determined not to give Shaw the satisfaction, Rem returned to his cot and sat cross-legged. Bouncing his knees, he tried to think about his next hamburger and beer and how much he would appreciate them, when he heard a familiar creak and the door to the cells opened.

Rem jumped up, praying he had a visitor, and saw Shaw step inside, his face flat and his eyes dull. He entered and then closed the door behind him with a clang.

Rem walked to the bars. "Nice of you to stop by."

Shaw raised the side of his lip. "Lonely?"

"You could say that. It's been a little quiet."

Shaw stepped closer. "I suspect it has." He stared at Rem.

Rem grabbed a bar. "What's going on out there? Where's Daniels? Where's Gin? Is Sheriff Joe back?"

Shaw's smile grew. "You really shouldn't put all your hopes on Joe."

A kernel of unease flickered in Rem's belly. Shaw had a strange look on his face that he couldn't interpret. "You're going to try and convince him I'm guilty, aren't you?"

Shaw raised his right brow. "It's not going to be as hard as you think." He stepped closer to the bars, and he rested his palm on the butt of his gun.

Rem's heart began to thump. "All I want is the facts to come out, and you'll realize I didn't do this. The killer is still walking around out there."

Shaw squinted. "Your partner ruffled a lot of feathers yesterday, but he didn't prove anything. The evidence still points to you."

"With all due respect, I think I'd rather talk to my partner first. Something tells me I won't hear the full story from you. Did you stop him from visiting? Because that's only a temporary solution. I'll see him eventually."

"I didn't stop him from anything. He didn't come by." He rubbed his palm on his gun belt. "Genevieve was here, but she annoys me, and I told her you were sleeping and to come back later. She didn't like it, but who cares?"

Rem wanted to gripe at Shaw for denying his aunt's visit, but his worry about Daniels overrode it. "Daniels didn't show?" he asked. "Is that the truth or are you lying just to make me squirm?"

"I haven't seen him, Detective. Nor has anyone else. I haven't received a single call or complaint, unlike yesterday." He smiled. "Maybe your friend gave up when he couldn't prove your innocence and went home." He shook his head. "Such a shame. Betrayal can be a bitter pill to swallow."

Chills broke out on Rem's skin. "You need to go look for him. There's no way he wouldn't have stopped by."

"Look for him? I'm certain your partner can handle himself. He seemed competent enough, although I use that term loosely."

Rem gripped the bars. "Listen to me. If Daniels got too close to the truth yesterday, the killer may have gone after him. At least go to the shack where he was staying and make sure he's okay."

Shaw tipped his head. "Maybe later, if I'm bored."

Rem brought his face up to bars. "He could be hurt. Somebody needs to check." Images of Daniels wounded or worse flared in Rem's mind and his heart raced. "Please." Hating that he had to rely on Shaw for help made Rem feel completely useless.

"Bet you'd like to go check on him yourself, wouldn't you?"

Rem pulled on the bars in frustration. "This is important..."

Shaw stepped up to the door. "Maybe I can accommodate you, since it's so crucial." He pulled out a key, inserted it into the lock and turned it. He opened the door.

Rem stepped back, itching to leave, but uncertain of Shaw's intentions. "What are you doing?"

Moving backwards, Shaw stepped away, giving Rem ample room to walk out of the cell and into the front room of the Sheriff's office. "You want to check on your friend?" He pointed. "Now you can." He held the butt of his gun.

Rem's flicker of unease turned to worry. As much as he was tempted to simply walk out and find Daniels, something told him to stay put. "And what happens when I do?"

Shaw's eyes narrowed. "Let's find out."

Rem swallowed, baffled by Shaw's motives. Did Shaw plan to kill him? He didn't know what to think. "Are you saying I'm free to go? Are you dropping the charges?"

Shaw glared. "Stop stalling, Detective. Time is short. You want to leave, so leave. Go check on your partner. Go check on Genevieve. Isn't that what you want?"

Rem tried to think. His gut told him if he took one step outside of his cell, he'd be a dead man. Was Shaw that crazy? Or did he just want to accuse Rem of trying to escape so he could add another nail to Rem's coffin? Was Shaw that desperate for a conviction? None of it made sense. Rem spoke softly. "Maybe I should wait for Joe."

Shaw stared, his face flat. "You think you're smarter than me, standing there, pretending you're innocent and worried about your partner?"

Rem swallowed, unsure of what to say.

"I've known cops like you. So damn smug. Talking to me like I'm stupid. Judging me like I'm some backwoods rent-a-cop." He set his jaw. "Not this time, though. This time, people are going to see you for what you are. I saw it the night Joe dragged you in here, so drunk you barely knew your own name. It's about time somebody else saw it, too."

Rem spoke carefully. "Shaw, listen. I—"

Shaw erupted. "I said get the hell out of here. Now."

Feeling the blood leave his face, Rem raised his hands. "I don't want any trouble, Shaw. I want to leave, but the right way."

Shaw's face relaxed, and he seemed to gain control of his anger. He took a deep breath. "You're a curious man, Detective. How do you manage to irritate me so easily?"

Rem made a nervous chuckle. "I'm sure Daniels could give you an explanation. It's a rare talent."

Shaw paused. "I'll give you thirty seconds, then your window of opportunity closes."

Rem debated what to do. Shaw obviously had some misplaced beef with him and had a bad history with law enforcement. Was he risking his life by staying or going? "What about my stuff? My wallet and gun and badge? Can I get it?"

Annoyed, Shaw set his jaw. "Now it's twenty seconds."

Rem took a step toward the open door but stopped when Shaw tensed. "Maybe I should stay," said Rem, his voice shaky. "I'm sure Daniels will be here soon."

"Ten seconds." Shaw's grip on his gun tightened.

Prepare to flee to save his life, Rem said a small prayer to get out of this situation when a distant loud voice boomed.

"Shaw? Where the hell are you?" The door to the office swung open, and Sheriff Joe appeared at the door. His height, broad shoulders and barrel chest almost spanned the whole frame. His gaze flicked between Rem and Shaw, who hastily dropped his hand away from his gun. "What the hell is going on in here?" he asked.

Chapter Eighteen

SHERIFF JOE WHISTLER'S WEEKEND had been a long one. After arriving at his mother's on Friday and getting settled, he'd woken early on Saturday to check her into the hospital for minor surgery. After the procedure, while Joe had waited for her return to her room, he'd called his brother Rocky to give him an update. During the call, Genevieve had left him a voicemail. Once his mom was settled back in her bed, he'd listened to Gin's frantic message, hearing how her nephew Aaron had been arrested by his deputy for the murder of Sharon Belafonte.

Not sure he'd heard correctly, he'd listened to the message again and then called Gin back. She'd been just as frantic and then reiterated what had happened. Perplexed, Joe couldn't answer her questions because he hadn't heard one word from Shaw. After assuring Gin he would get to the bottom of it, he hung up and contacted his deputy. Shaw had confirmed Sharon's death and Remalla's arrest and had said he was handling it while Joe took care of his mother.

Still in disbelief over the news, Joe asked Shaw several questions, wanting to get as much information as possible. Shaw had filled him in on the discovery of Sharon's body, the crime scene, calling in a forensic unit and coroner from the neighboring county for help, the search of Remalla's room and Remalla's subsequent arrest. Joe had found a pen and notepad in his mom's purse and took numerous notes. He'd told Shaw that once he got his mom home the next day, he would return to sort things out. Shaw had assured him that everything was sorted, and felt confident they'd caught the killer, despite Genevieve's insistence otherwise.

Joe had hung up, shocked and alarmed by all that happened since he'd
left, and immediately began to make phone calls. He'd contacted the
forensic team and the coroner and then called Jimmy at the bar. He'd
wanted to know what had happened that night with Sharon and Remalla.
Jimmy had filled him in, and then Joe had called Gin back, telling her he
was investigating and he would know more soon. Although she continued
to insist that Aaron should be freed, he'd managed to calm her and
ensured that once he learned more, than he would decide what to do next.

That morning, after the hospital released his mother and he'd got her
back home and settled, he'd hit the road, making more phone calls on the
way, and learning a lot more about the details of Sharon's death, the crime
scene and weapon. By the time he'd returned to Merrimac, he had a lot of
questions for Shaw to answer.

Now, standing at the door to the cells, he eyed his deputy, who stood at
one side of the room, and Remalla in his cell on the other. Remalla looked
pale and nervous, and Shaw slapped a smile on his face.

"You're back, Joe," said Shaw. "I wasn't expecting you until later."

Joe wondered why Remalla's cell door was open. "I got Mom home
early."

"How is she? Everything okay?" asked Shaw.

Joe crossed his arms. "Why is his cell open? He still under arrest?"

Remalla didn't answer but Shaw did. "We were just talking. I figured he
might like to have a discussion without bars in his way."

Joe regarded Remalla, remembering the last time he'd seen him. He'd
been sleeping off his drunken state on one of the cots. "You slow down on
the drinking, Detective?"

Remalla eyed Shaw warily. "I did, but in hindsight maybe I shouldn't
have."

"I hear you've got yourself in a pickle," said Joe.

Remalla nodded. "You could say that."

Joe remained in the doorway, uncertain about what was going on. It felt
as if he'd missed something. "What were you two talking about?"

Remalla looked at Shaw, who stared back. Remalla spoke first. "I was
telling Shaw that I was worried about my partner, Detective Gordon
Daniels. He didn't come by this morning when he said he would."

Shaw huffed. "His partner was a general nuisance yesterday, riling up the townspeople, accusing everyone of killing Sharon except his partner. It wouldn't surprise me if he got a little drunk himself and he's sleeping it off."

Remalla shook his head. "I may be stupid enough to handle my problems with booze, but not Daniels. If he says he's going to do something, he does it. Somebody needs to check on him."

Shaw snorted. "The only person you need to be concerned about is yourself." He walked forward and began to shut the door to Remalla's cell. "Our talk is over. I need to speak to Joe."

Joe took a step inside. "Hold up there, Shaw." He grabbed the cell door before Shaw could close it. "You wanted to talk to our inmate here? Then let's do it." He pulled the door back open.

Shaw hesitated. "But he's a killer."

Joe regarded Remalla. "Can you handle a discussion about your case without trying to escape?"

Remalla approached the door. "I'd welcome any information about my case. Just check on Daniels afterward, if that's okay."

Joe nodded. "You got it." He turned back toward the office and grabbed one of the office chairs and rolled it inside the room and toward Shaw. "Have a seat."

Shaw stopped the chair's progress. "Joe, I think it's better we talk alone."

Joe stepped back into the office and opened a closet door. He pulled out two folding chairs and returned to the cells. He handed one to Remalla. "I think it's best we get everything out in the open, don't you? I mean, it's his life we're talking about here. He should know what he's up against."

His face regaining some color, Remalla took the chair and opened it. "Joe, if you were a woman right now, I'd be tempted to kiss you."

Joe almost smiled, but judging by his deputy's face, he kept his amusement to himself. "Save your PDA, Detective, until you hear what I have to say." He unfolded his chair and sat.

Remalla sat along with Shaw, who looked uncomfortable. "I still think he should be in his cell," said Shaw.

"You started the open-door policy," said Joe. "Let the man relax."

Shaw sneered at Rem, who ignored him.

"Let's start with the body," said Joe. His chair squeaked with his weight. "Just so Remalla's up to speed, you said two tourists found Sharon early yesterday morning on their way to go fishing."

Shaw nodded. "Yes. They called it in. I went over, identified the body, and contacted the neighboring forensics unit and coroner."

Joe nodded. "What made you investigate his shack?" He nodded at Remalla.

Joe paused, looking annoyed that he had to explain himself in front of Remalla. "You and I both know Sharon had been hanging all over him." He aimed a thumb at Remalla. "I went and talked to Jimmy and learned that when Sharon left, she'd planned to see him." He eyed Remalla with another sneer. "I went to his shack. I didn't find him, but a quick search revealed the weapon under the couch."

"The weapon?" asked Remalla. "What was it?"

"Like you don't know," said Shaw.

"It was a knife," said Joe. "Sharon's blood was still on it."

"When I saw the knife," said Shaw, "it was obvious Sharon had met up with Remalla, they'd gone out into the woods and he'd stabbed her, hid the knife and then planned to leave town with his partner."

Remalla squinted. "That is the stupidest scenario. Why the hell would I have brought the knife back to the shack when I could have tossed it anywhere in the woods?"

"He's got a point, Shaw," said Joe. "It doesn't make sense."

"Murderers don't always make sense," said Joe. "Maybe he planned to return later to dispose of the knife once he distracted his partner. He probably didn't expect Sharon's body to be found so soon."

Joe nodded, and Remalla sighed. "I'd have to be one stupid detective," said Rem.

"If the shoe fits," said Shaw.

Joe eyed Remalla's sneakers. He pointed. "Those your only shoes?"

Remalla lifted a sneaker. "Yes. They're the ones I brought with me."

Joe leaned over and Rem lifted his foot higher. Joe straightened. "You find any other shoes, Shaw?"

Shaw shook his head. "No. I confiscated his phone and clothes, badge and gun, wallet and watch. That's it."

Joe crossed his arms and tapped his elbow. "You notice anything else when you went into the shack?"

Shaw paused. "What do you mean?"

"I got the preliminary report back from the forensic team," said Joe, "and I stopped by the shack on the way here and looked around."

Shaw shifted in his seat. "And?"

Joe eyed Remalla who waited to hear what Joe would say. "You happen to notice muddy footprints leading to the couch?"

Remalla looked over at Shaw, who shrugged. "It's possible."

Joe pointed. "His shoes aren't muddy." Remalla lifted a sneaker again as if to check. "They're also not the right tread," added Joe.

Shaw's shoulders dropped, and Remalla's rose.

"I suspect whoever put the knife under the couch walked through some mud on the way. There was mud near the body, but not near the shack, at least not that I can see from the crime scene photos."

Shaw sat still, and Rem's eyes widened. "I like the way you think, Joe," said Rem.

"So he had another pair of shoes and he tossed them," said Shaw. "Not that big of a leap."

Rem snorted. "So I toss the shoes but not the weapon? Are you serious?"

"Are we done?" asked Shaw.

"Not quite," said Joe, adjusting his position in the chair. "I called in a few favors and got the autopsy done this morning. I talked to the M.E. on the drive back. Based on his initial findings, Sharon died from blunt force trauma. Somebody hit her over the head, probably with a rock."

Remalla widened his eyes, and Shaw tensed.

"She wasn't stabbed?" asked Rem.

"But the knife...," said Shaw.

"The knife wound was postmortem," said Joe. "Somebody stabbed her after she was dead, then walked through the mud and put it in Remalla's shack. I suspect the actual murder weapon, a bloody rock, is somewhere in the stream."

Shaw didn't speak and Remalla straightened. "You believe me?" asked Remalla.

Joe held his elbows and leaned back. The chair creaked again. "I think the evidence is pretty clear. Somebody encountered Sharon in the woods, hit her on the head with a rock until she was dead, and then tossed the rock. Realizing what they'd done, the killer stabbed her to make it look like the knife was the murder weapon. Then put that weapon where it could be easily found in order to draw our interest toward another suspect."

Shaw leaned forward. "That is ridiculous." He pointed. "He's the one who met her in the woods, he beat her with the rock and stabbed her."

"And then he kept the knife but tossed the rock and shoes?" asked Joe. He raised his voice. "Are you willing to stake your reputation on that? Unless you've got a witness or can link his DNA to the crime scene, which right now we can't, any good defense attorney would rake our so-called evidence over the coals. And I haven't even gotten to the good part. There were no fingerprints on the knife. It had been wiped clean."

"Then he wore gloves," said Shaw.

"You find any?" asked Joe. He leaned in. "C'mon, Randal. I talked to Jimmy, too. Remalla was so drunk, he could barely stand. And Herndon was watching him and Sharon the whole night. You talk to Scott yet? Does he have an alibi?"

Shaw gripped the chair's armrests. "I didn't find the murder weapon on Herndon."

"You didn't find it on him, either," said Joe, tipping his head toward Rem. "You found a knife in his shack, after he'd already left."

"That doesn't make him innocent," yelled Shaw.

"It sure as hell doesn't make him guilty either," yelled Joe. "We don't have enough to hold him."

"But he's lying," said Shaw.

Remalla aimed a steely gaze at Shaw. "I'm not lying. I told you all along. When I left that bar, Sharon was alive, and I never saw her after that. I don't know what happened after she left Jimmy's, but I suspect someone heard her say she was coming to see me. They followed her, killed her and they framed me."

"He's right," said Joe. "I'm inclined to believe we've got a murderer on the loose in Merrimac, but it isn't Detective Remalla."

Shaw shot out of his seat. "I can't believe this." He glared. "Are you going to release him?"

Rem gripped his knees, and eyed Joe with eagerness.

"I don't have a choice," said Joe. "You're free to go, Remalla." He stood. "Come with me and I'll get your things."

Rem jumped out of his seat. "Get ready for some PDA, Joe."

Shaw's eyes glittered with anger. "You're making a mistake," said Shaw.

"I'm doing what's right," said Joe. "And after I go home, talk to my mom and Rocky and get a good meal and night's sleep, you and I are going to start looking for Sharon's murderer, and our first stop is Scott Herndon."

Remalla stood by the door. "Thanks, Joe."

Shaw stood in mute fury, but Joe figured he'd see the light eventually and calm down. He spoke to Remalla. "Your first assignment is to talk to Genevieve. She's been burning up the phone lines trying to prove your innocence. Put me out of my misery and call her, please."

Remalla nodded. "I will."

"Joe...listen...," said Shaw. "Think this through."

Joe paused at the door. "I've been thinking this through all day. I know you've got your issues with cops, Shaw, especially with him, but not all of them are bad. This is the right thing to do, and you know it. You can't force a round detective peg into a square murderer hole. It never works, no matter how much you dislike someone." He cocked his head. "If you need to take the rest of the day, then take it, but first thing tomorrow, we start looking for a killer."

Chapter Nineteen

AFTER JOE RETURNED HIS things, Rem called Daniels from the station. It went straight to voicemail. His worry growing, he called his Aunt Gin, telling her he was free and to pick him up outside Daniels' shack. Rem almost hoped Shaw was right, and his partner was sleeping off a hangover, but he knew that was unlikely. Daniels' shack was down the road from the station and if Rem ran, he could get there in about the time it would take Gin to drive there.

Rem stuck around long enough for Joe to tell him to stay close to Merrimac and avoid doing something stupid until they could solve the case. Without agreeing to anything, Rem thanked him again, and raced out and down the street. He made it to Daniels' shack in record time. After knocking, he opened the door but didn't see Daniels. The room was empty except for Daniels' small bag which remained packed. There were no personal items in the bathroom, the towels were dry, and the sofa bed didn't look like it had been touched. His stomach churning with worry, he heard the beep of a car horn, grabbed Daniels' bag and went outside. His aunt had pulled up, and Rem got in her car.

Teary eyed, she expressed her relief that he'd been released. While she drove, Rem gave her a quick update on what Joe had learned and Shaw's disgust. She told him how she'd tried to visit earlier, but Shaw had refused to let her in when he'd discovered she'd brought Rem coffee and donuts. She'd expressed her outrage by calling Shaw a few names Rem's grandmother would not have approved of.

After arriving back at the house, Rem called Daniels again with no luck and then asked Gin about Daniels. Gin told him she'd seen him the previous evening and she conveyed where he'd been, what he'd discovered and that he'd told her he was heading back to his shack to get some sleep.

Rem almost hopped in his car and sped away to start his search, but his aunt insisted he eat since Shaw had denied him lunch. Although anxious to find his partner, Rem realized Gin was right. He'd missed too many meals already that week and he would need the energy. He also needed to call Lozano, charge his phone and take a shower.

After cleaning up and changing into fresh clothes, Rem returned to the kitchen where Gin had a serving of hot lasagna waiting for him. He sat and ate fast.

Gin sat beside him. "Where are you going to start?"

Rem chewed and spoke. "Scott Herndon."

She nodded and wrung her hands. "Would you listen to me if I told you not to go alone?"

"Aunt Gin—"

"Aaron, Gordon has disappeared. What if you do, too?"

Seeing her concern, Rem tried to slow down long enough to put her at ease. "I have to go. I can't wait for Joe to look. He's busy trying to find Sharon's killer. If Daniels is hurt, I have to find him." He refused to believe Daniels could be dead.

She studied her hands. "I know."

Anxious to leave, Rem took another big bite of lasagna. "I'll be fine. Try not to worry," he said through a mouthful.

Her face pensive, she looked over. "Aaron. I have to tell you something. I...I may have done something stupid. I wanted to tell you earlier..."

Rem stopped chewing. "What is it? Do you know something about Daniels?"

She shook her head. "No. It's not about Daniels. It's about Sharon."

Rem stabbed more lasagna. "What about her?"

Gin put her face in her hands. "I was dumb. I let my anger get the best of me." She looked up. "I saw Sharon the day before Gordon arrived. I went to the bank. When she was the teller that helped me, I let my emotions get the best of me. I knew she'd been harassing you to get back at Scott. I told her what I thought and suggested she leave you alone." She paused. "I may have called her a few names, too."

Rem studied her and swallowed. "It's okay, Aunt Gin."

"It's not," she said, her face somber. "I've been beating myself up over it. What if it's my fault that she was bothering you that night, because I confronted her? What if, for some reason, she targeted you because of me, and maybe that pissed the killer off, and he murdered her and framed you." She held her temples. "I feel terrible. Like this is somehow my fault."

Eyeing the clock again, Rem put his fork down and put his hand on her back. "None of this is your fault. Your argument with Sharon had nothing to do with her getting killed or me being arrested. That would have happened regardless. You can be a handful, Gin, but I don't think you made the killer snap." He paused. "Although I'm learning more and more about your temper. I heard a rumor you pushed Joe's ex, Sybil, into the fountain."

She groaned into her palms. "Don't remind me. That was another one of my better moments that I regret." She sighed and eyed Rem. "And then she disappeared."

"Maybe you've got more mojo than you think."

She put her hand over his. "When I confronted Sharon, I was only trying to help. You know that, don't you?"

He squeezed her fingers. "I used to think I got my 'punch first and think later' gene from the Remalla side of the family, but now I know the truth."

She smiled softly. "It's a Reverton curse."

"Or maybe a blessing." Glad his aunt appeared more settled, Rem wolfed down another bite. "I've got to go."

"You haven't finished."

Rem stood and found his phone. "I've had plenty. Once I find Daniels, we'll both be back for more."

"You've got Scott's address?"

"I do. In my pocket."

She stood as he grabbed his jacket and slid it on. "Aaron," she said, "please be careful."

"I will." He kissed her on the cheek. "I'll keep you posted. Try not to worry."

She nodded and he picked up his keys and darted out the door.

• • • • • • • • • •

Rem pulled up to Scott Herndon's apartment complex, believing it was his best hope at finding Daniels. Although Gin had told him Daniels had come here but backed off after seeing Bart and Ricky, he also knew his partner had planned to return. But had he waited until that morning or taken a swing by after leaving Gin's? Whatever had happened, if he'd encountered Bart and Ricky, then Daniels could be lying in a ditch somewhere needing medical attention. He watched for a few minutes, but the lot was quiet and the only person he saw was an older woman walking her dog. Not seeing anything suspicious, he got out and eyed the unit number on the paper Gin had given him, then tossed the paper back into his car and shut the door. Praying he would find Daniels unharmed, he headed toward Scott's apartment.

After passing the dog walker and climbing the stairs, he found Scott's door and knocked. Unlatched, the door slid open. Alarmed and his cop instincts kicking in, Rem stepped to the side and pulled his weapon. He knocked again and called for Scott but didn't hear a response. Carefully, he pushed the door wider and peered inside. Beer bottles and fast-food bags littered the floor. Rem slid around the frame and entered but didn't see anyone. Couch cushions were laying on a worn rug and there was a rumpled sheet on the sofa as if someone had slept on it. Rem closed the door behind him and quietly walked through the apartment. More beer bottles and a half-filled bottle of vodka were on the kitchen counter and an empty pizza box was in the sink.

Hearing a moan, Rem turned, holding his gun, and headed toward the bedroom. He stuck his head in and saw Scott sleeping in his bed, his naked upper torso and neck tattoo exposed and a sheet covering him from the waist down. Beside him in the bed was a woman covered by a blanket, with only her curly blonde hair and mascara-smeared eyes visible.

Stepping into the room, Rem tucked his gun into the back of his jeans and studied the couple in the bed. Seeing another beer bottle on the end table beside Scott, Rem picked it up and shook it. Happy there was beer in it, he lifted it and poured the remains over Scott's head.

Scott came awake instantly, sputtering and cursing. His sheet slipped down to reveal a bare hip, and he sat up, wiping at his face. "What the hell?" he yelled.

The woman raised her head and pushed herself up, her eyes half-slits. Seeing Rem, she turned and sat, holding the blanket against her torso and bare shoulders.

"What are you doing?" shouted Scott. He pulled the sheet up and blotted his face and chest. He blinked, saw Rem and his eyes widened.

"Who is this guy?" asked the woman, her black-ringed eyes were as wide as Scott's.

Rem waved. "Morning, Scott. Or rather afternoon." He set the bottle back on the table. "I figured I'd finish what my partner started."

"Wha...what are you doing here?" asked Scott. "You're supposed to be in jail."

"Surprise," said Rem, wiggling his eyebrows.

"Who the hell are you?" yelled the woman.

"Housekeeping," said Rem. "Your boyfriend here is a slob, and probably a murderer, too." He shook his head at her. "You really should vet your boy toys before you sleep with them."

"Get out of here," said Scott. "I'm calling Shaw." He reached for a cell beside the bed.

"Murderer?" asked the woman. She squinted at Scott. "Him?"

"He's the murderer." Scott fumbled with the phone and dropped it. It hit the table and fell beneath the bed. "Shit." Scott reached for it, but the sheet pulled away. Scott tugged on it, but the woman was sitting on it. "Georgia, move." Scott tugged again.

The woman scowled. "My name is Gretchen."

"Don't be shy on my account, Scott," said Rem. "I'm sure there's not much to hide." He raised the side of his lip. "Right, Gretchen?"

Gretchen, shooting Scott a dirty look, pulled her blanket closer. "Honestly, I don't recall."

"Ouch," said Rem with a flinch. "She wasn't too impressed, Scott. Can't say I'm surprised."

Gretchen scooted to the edge of the bed. "I don't know what the hell's going on, but I'm outta here." She sat up, adjusted the blanket around herself, and stood.

Scott didn't argue but held his head and aimed a red-eyed stare at Rem. "You killed Sharon. You need to get out of here. Now." The sheet free, he stood, holding it at his waist. He stooped to get his cell while Gretchen disappeared into the bathroom and slammed the door.

"Make sure you contact Sheriff Joe," said Rem. "He can explain to you the details of my release and how he plans to visit you next."

Scott found his phone and straightened. "Sheriff Joe is back?"

"He sure is," said Rem. "He did his due diligence, unlike poor Gretchen, and decided I wasn't the killer. Shaw wasn't too thrilled, but he'll get over it." He took a step toward Scott, who moved back toward the bed, bumped into the end table and knocked the lamp over. It teetered and fell, and Scott, still holding his phone, tried to grab the lamp, but the sheet slipped, and he caught that instead. The lamp fell and hit the floor.

Scott pulled the sheet tighter and pointed. "I didn't kill Sharon and you know it," he said, his face pale. "Is that why you're here? To get me to confess?"

The bathroom door flew open, and Gretchen strode out, wearing a skimpy black dress and holding her heels. "Don't call me." She barely looked at Rem or Scott as she stomped out of the bedroom.

"I don't even have your number," yelled Scott as his apartment door slammed shut.

Rem smiled. "You really know how to pick 'em, Scott." He eyed the room. "I'm sorry you're so overcome with grief that you got wasted and had a one-night stand."

"Give me a break." Scott groaned and rubbed his head. "My buddies showed to cheer me up and we ended up in a bar and then a dance club. That's where I met Georgia."

"Gretchen," said Rem.

"Whatever," said Scott.

Rem took another step, and Scott scooted back toward the wall. "Your friends," said Rem. "They do anything else?"

Scott adjusted his hold on the sheet. "They got drunk. Ricky took off with Geor...Gretchen's friend, Marsha, and Bart passed out on the couch."

Rem nodded. "Is that it? No other stops?"

Scott aimed a weary gaze at Rem. "Look...I don't know why you're here but if it's about Sharon—"

Rem walked up to within inches of Scott. "I don't give a shit about Sharon at this point, Scott. I want to know where my partner is."

Scott opened his mouth, and for a second, nothing emerged. "How should I know?"

Rem fought back the urge to knock Scott into the wall. "I heard about what happened yesterday. You and your buddies got in my partner's face. You were going to beat him up until your dad interrupted."

Scott tensed. "Listen, we were just—"

Rem took another step. "He was going to come here. I want to know what happened."

Scott furrowed his brow. "He came here? When?"

Rem set his jaw. "My patience is wearing thin, Scott, and I'm not a patient man to begin with. Daniels planned to talk to you. Did you see him? Did your buddies show and decide to finish what they started? Or did you three go and find him first?" He glared. "Did you hurt him?"

Scott stammered. "I never saw him. He never came here. I got off work and Bart and Ricky got here not long after. We never went near him and if your friend planned to visit, then he changed his mind." He held up a hand. "I swear it."

Rem studied Scott, letting his gaze bore into him, and judging his truthfulness. "Do you know where Daniels is?" He narrowed his eyes and lowered his voice. "And think very carefully about your answer."

Scott stepped back again and bumped against the wall. "I'm not lying. I never saw him after what happened at the shop. I swear." He scoffed. "Maybe he got in somebody else's face and pissed them off, too. He's good at that."

His restraint at a breaking point, Rem walked up, grabbed Scott by the throat and pushed him hard against the wall. He brought his face up to Scott's. "You listen to me, Scotty boy. You better be telling the truth because if I find out you're lying to me and you had something to do with Daniels' disappearance, there isn't going to be a trash heap deep enough for you and your buddies, Bert and Ernie, to hide in. Do you understand? I don't care how disgusting the slime is, I'll dive in and pull you out by your tongue if I have to."

Scott clutched at Rem's wrist. "I don't know anything. I didn't see him. Let me go." He pulled to free himself, but Rem didn't budge.

"You hear anything about where he might be, you call Sheriff Joe or me immediately. You got that?" He squeezed, and Scott flinched. "I find out you knew something and did shit about it, I'm going to pay you a visit, and this little pleasure palace you live in will be your final stop before you're knockin' on the gates to hell. You got it?"

"I got it. I got it." Scott screeched. "I promise I'll tell you or the sheriff."

Rem nodded and let him go. Scott gasped and held his throat. Rem reached into his pocket, pulled out a card and put it on the side table. "Good." He studied Scott again, who straightened and eyed Rem warily.

Rem stared back, ensuring Scott had gotten the message. He walked to the bedroom door and paused. "And do your neighbors a favor and take out the trash," he said. "Your apartment stinks."

Scott dropped his head, and Rem turned and left.

Chapter Twenty

FRUSTRATED, REM RETURNED TO his car and sat, thinking about what Scott had told him. If everything he'd said was true, then he had to wonder where Daniels had gone. And if he hadn't confronted Scott, then where did he go?

Rem knew Daniels had stopped at the Miller's bed and breakfast to ask about Sonya who Scott supposedly called the night Sharon died. Gin had said, though, that the Millers would only talk to Sheriff Joe. Rem doubted the Millers would have any cause to hurt Daniels, so he didn't feel a need to visit them.

His next option was either Rocky Whistler or the bank manager, Tyler Barnstone. The bank was closed, though, and Gin didn't have an address for Tyler since he lived outside of Merrimac. She thought Rocky might know where he lived, but the barbershop was also closed on Sunday. Gin had provided Rocky's address, though, and Rem started the car to head in that direction when his phone rang. He sighed when he saw it was his aunt and not Daniels. He answered, and Gin told him she'd gotten hold of Rocky, and he'd said he'd be at the barbershop to do some paperwork and Rem was welcome to stop by. Rem thanked her, pulled out of the lot and headed toward town.

Ten minutes later, he parked outside the barber shop and got out. He jogged up to the door and entered, seeing Rocky at the front desk, writing on a piece of paper. He looked up. "Detective. How are you?" He set the paper aside.

"Hi, Rocky," said Rem. "I guess you remember me from Jimmy's."

"Remember you?" he asked. "You're a hard man to forget. You bought me three drinks, along with everyone else at the bar."

Rem sighed, feeling embarrassed. "Not one of my prouder moments."

Rocky smiled and sat back. "It was one of mine. I had fun that night." He chuckled. "You told some bawdy jokes."

Sheepish, Rem shook his head. "I bet."

"I'm glad to hear you've been cleared of any wrongdoing, though. I found it hard to believe you'd kill anyone, even Sharon."

"I may make some stupid choices, but I'm not that stupid," said Rem. He eyed the quiet shop. "I heard my partner, Detective Daniels, came in to see you yesterday."

Rocky nodded. "He did. He was asking questions about Sharon and doing his damnedest to clear your name. He's an intense man."

"Yeah, well, when he's on the trail of something, he won't let up until he finds what he's looking for."

"I could see why some might find him intimidating. I bet he's happy you've been released."

Rem put his hands on his hips. "That's just it. I can't find him. That's why I'm here. I know he talked to you yesterday. Any idea where he went after that?"

Rocky's face fell. "You can't find him?" He paused. "Did you talk to Scott Herndon?"

"He was my first stop, but Scott swears he didn't see him." Rem spotted the couch behind him and sat on the armrest. "Aunt Gin also said Daniels went to see Tyler Barnstone, the bank manager, but I don't have an address on him. She thought you might know where I can find him."

"I do," said Rocky. "I have his address." He pulled out a notepad from a drawer and flipped through it. "Here it is." He scribbled on a pad. "But before you see Tyler, I think you should talk to someone else first." He flipped through some more pages and scribbled again.

"Someone else?" asked Rem, standing. "Who?"

Rocky finished writing and ripped the page out of the notebook. "His name is Allen Whitlock, but everyone calls him Whit. He's ninety-two years old and has some dementia." He handed Rem the paper.

Rem studied the addresses, seeing Whit's. "Why would I want to visit Whit?"

"Because he and your partner had an interesting exchange yesterday. I was cutting Whit's hair when your partner arrived. Whit kept saying something about a woman in the woods. I just thought he was rambling but then he said the woman wanted to see your partner."

"What woman in the woods?" asked Rem. "Does someone live in the forest?"

Rocky shrugged. "Not that I know of. I didn't think it meant anything and your partner left. But then when I was closing up yesterday, I saw the two of them on the bench across the street."

"Daniels and Whit?" asked Rem. "Across the street?"

Rocky nodded. "Yes. They were talking. And your partner had that intense look on his face. I'm sure you're familiar."

"Very," said Rem. He eyed the paper. "Whit lives nearby?"

"Five minutes away, with his granddaughter Wendy who takes care of him. I'd say he's your best shot at finding your partner. Tyler may be a lousy manager who sleeps with his staff, but the odds of him incapacitating your partner and concealing his location are slim to none. I doubt Tyler could conceal himself in a game of hide and seek."

Feeling a little hopeful, Rem folded the paper. "Thanks, Rocky. Can you do me a favor? Can you call and let Wendy know I'm coming? I doubt she'll be too thrilled to open the door to the man who was a suspect in Sharon's death."

"You bet. I'll call her now." He reached for his phone. "And good luck, Detective. I hope you find your partner soon."

Rem hoped the same and headed out of the shop.

· · · ● ● · ● ● · ·

Rem pulled up to the curb in front of Whit's granddaughter's house. It was a two-story brick home with big windows and a porch with a swing out front. Getting out of the car, Rem saw an elderly man with uncombed gray hair on the swing, pushing it back and forth.

Rem headed up the walkway and made it to the front steps when the door opened, and a middle-aged woman stepped out. Her hair was up in a bun, and she had an apron on. "You're the detective?" she asked.

"You're Wendy?" Rem introduced himself and showed his credentials. "Rocky told me your grandfather spoke to my partner yesterday. I was hoping Whit could tell me about what they talked about."

She studied him, and he wondered what was going through her mind. "My granddad isn't always easy to talk to and his short-term memory is shot," she said.

"I understand," said Rem. "But I'd still like to try."

She put her hand on the door frame. "This have anything to do with what happened to Sharon Belafonte?"

Rem opened his mouth, uncertain how to answer. "It might. But to be honest, I'm not sure."

Her eyes narrowed, and she looked back at Whit, who continued to push himself back and forth on the swing. "Don't pressure him or he gets confused. And if you stress him out, the talk's over. He doesn't handle stress well."

"I understand," said Rem. "Thank you."

She hesitated. "I'll be watching from the window."

"That's fine. This shouldn't take long."

She paused, then stepped outside and walked to the swing. "Granddad?"

Whit stopped swinging and looked up at her.

Rem walked over, and she pointed toward him. "This man would like to talk to you. He's a friend of the man you spoke to yesterday. A Detective..." she eyed Rem.

"Daniels," said Rem. He leaned around her. "He's my partner, Whit."

Whit resumed pushing the swing with his leg. "I'd figured you'd come."

His granddaughter raised a brow at Rem, who widened his eyes and shrugged.

"I'll be in the kitchen if you need anything," she said, patting Whit on the shoulder. She turned and went inside the house.

Rem sat next to Whit on the swing and helped him push. "Hi, Whit. My name's Aaron Remalla."

Whit stared off. "You Miss Reverton's nephew?"

"I am."

Whit scratched his knee. "I heard you killed someone."

The statement took Rem by surprise. "That's the rumor. I spent a night in jail."

"A night? For murder?" He scowled. "Things have changed since I was a kid."

Rem almost smiled. "I didn't do it, so they let me go."

Whit stared off. "You plan on killing anyone else?"

Rem thought of Scott Herndon. "Not unless I have to."

Whit scratched his other knee. "Some people in this town might need killing." He paused. "It'll give you something to do."

Interested, Rem sat up. "Is that what you talked about with my partner?"

Whit frowned. "Who?"

Rem bit back a sigh. "Big guy, with broad shoulders and gelled-back blonde hair? Kinda looks like he could bench press King Kong?"

"Oh, that guy," said Whit.

Rem waited, but Whit kept swinging. "What did you two talk about?" asked Rem.

"He likes the woods."

Rem told himself to be patient. "He does. A lot more than me."

"Nancy liked the woods, too, until she died."

"Who's Nancy?"

"Nancy was pretty. We were married fifty-five years."

Pensive, Rem stilled and relaxed back against the swing, thinking this might take longer than he thought. "That's a long time."

"It is." Whit put his hand on the armrest. "You married?"

Recalling his past, Rem shook his head. "No."

"Kids?"

Rem swallowed. "No. Not yet, at least."

"One day."

Rem pursed his lips. "Yeah, maybe."

"No. Not kids. One day you'll be happy."

Rem raised a brow at the elderly man beside him and questioned the depths of his dementia. "You sure about that, because I'm not."

"Happiness is in the eye of the beholder. Nancy always told me that."

Rem interlaced his fingers but didn't answer.

"And I always told her she was full of shit." Whit chuckled, and Rem chuckled with him. Whit continued to push the swing. "But then she'd tell me I was walking on two good legs, seeing with two good eyes, and smiling with a handsome face. I had good people in my life, a roof over my head, food in my belly and money in the bank. There's a lot of people in this world who can't say that, she'd say." He paused. "Then she'd tell me to stop bitchin' 'cause it was getting on her nerves."

Rem eyed a leafy potted plant on the porch and thought of Jennie. "Nancy sounds pretty amazing."

"I miss her every day."

"I can see why."

They moved back and forth for a few seconds in silence. "Did you lose someone, too?" asked Whit.

Surprised, Rem cleared his throat. "You're a perceptive guy, Whit. How'd you know?"

"Grief has a feeling, Detective. I may not always find the words, but I can still sense things." He paused. "Your partner can, too."

Rem shook off his memories and leaned forward. "Tell me about Daniels. What did you two discuss?"

Whit blinked against the sun. "He wanted answers and the woman has them."

"What woman?"

"She sees things. She sees me. I can hear her."

Uncertain, Rem wondered what to think. "Tell me about her."

"She's in the woods."

"Where in the woods?"

"Take the trail."

A cold slice of dread ran up Rem's back and he shivered. "What trail?"

Whit made eye contact with him. "You know what trail."

"Is that what Daniels did?" asked Rem, suddenly anxious. "Take the trail?" He clenched his fingers. Had his partner been that stupid?

"He wanted answers and she has them." Whit leaned close and smiled. "Just be careful of her dogs."

Rem broke out into a cold sweat. "You told Daniels to go out into the woods to talk to some woman who could supposedly help me?"

Whit's eyes softened. "He was worried."

Rem put his elbows on his knees and dropped his head into his palms. "Hell, Whit. Why couldn't you have told him to go to the ice cream parlor instead?"

Whit scoffed. "They make lousy hot fudge sundaes."

Fatigued, Rem raised his head. "How are their banana splits?"

"Delicious." Whit stared off again. "Did I tell you about my Nancy?" He took hold of the chain that connected the swing to the porch roof. "She loved the woods."

Rem's head began to throb.

· · · ● ● · ● ● · · ·

Pulling into the trailhead, Rem cursed when he spotted Daniels' car. He parked next to it and got out, eyeing the woods around him and the path that led deeper into them. It was getting late, and Rem was intensely aware of the setting sun. "Daniels," he yelled, and listened. He yelled again but got no response.

He closed the car door and debated his next move. Should he call Sheriff Joe and report his partner missing? Should he call Aunt Gin and organize a search party? Neither option seemed promising. Both parties would tell Rem to wait until morning before heading into the forest, but Rem didn't want to wait. If Daniels was injured or worse, he needed to be found.

He walked to the trailhead and looked around but saw nothing that revealed Daniels' presence. Taking another chance that Daniels might answer his phone, Rem called him again, but with the same result. It went to voicemail.

Muttering to himself about how he'd gotten himself into this mess and questioning whether or not a partner was really necessary, he stared at the thick woods. Some part of him wished he was back in jail, but then he changed his mind. He'd follow ten of these trails if it meant staying out of that cell and finding Daniels. So long as they both came back alive.

He pulled out his gun and checked it, and then returned it to its holster. He considered calling Aunt Gin to tell her his plan, but knew she'd panic if he told her where he was headed, and she'd likely want to help Rem with the search. He didn't want to have to worry about her, too, so he told himself to stop over-thinking it. He'd probably get a mile in, find Daniels with a busted ankle, and help him out. Then they'd have dinner at Gin's after getting Daniels medical attention and they'd leave Merrimac the next morning, despite the sheriff's urging that Rem stay in town. Rem couldn't wait to get home and sleep in his own bed. With everything he'd dealt with the last few days and now facing a stroll through a haunted forest, Allison Albright and her antics didn't seem all that bad. Maybe Nancy was right. Happiness was in the eye of the beholder. He'd have to remember that if he survived this little excursion.

Standing at the trailhead, Rem squared his shoulders, stretched his neck, and shook off his nerves. He eyed the rocky path leading further into the trees and told himself he would find Daniels, get him back here, and they'd go home. Nervous, but faking confidence in his plan, he started walking.

Chapter Twenty-One

A LITTLE OVER A mile in, Rem stopped and sat on a log. He'd remained on the trail and had so far seen several squirrels, a chipmunk and possibly a snake, but he didn't stick around to be sure. He periodically called Daniels' name but never got a response. The last tendrils of light slowly dissipated, and he said a brief thank you to himself for thinking of the flashlight. He'd turned back and taken it from his trunk before resuming his walk.

Sitting there, he wondered what he would do if he got to the end of the trail and never found Daniels. Would it be worth the risk to go off trail to find him? And if he did, where would he start? The only tracks he could capably follow were his own when he stepped out of the shower. Pulling his jacket tighter around him as a cooler breeze blew, he stood and told himself to keep going. He'd figure it out once he got to the end.

Trying to hold off as long as possible before turning on the flashlight in order to conserve the battery, Rem heard a shuffling behind him. He swiveled but the shadows made it hard to see, so he flipped on the light and saw two raccoons digging in the dirt. Their eyes reflected the light, and Rem yelped and stumbled backward, putting plenty of distance between him and them. Anxious, he turned and resumed his walk but left the flashlight on.

As darkness descended, he became hyperaware and aimed his light at every noise. The wind rustled the trees, but the birds had gone quiet, and the crickets had begun to chirp. Taking long, slow breaths to calm himself, he swung the light back and forth, on and off the trail and stopped when he caught sight of something shiny beneath a tree. Taking cautious steps, he moved toward it and squatted. His heart thumping, he picked it up and realized it was Daniels' cell phone.

"Shit," he whispered. He tried to use the phone, but it was dead. He slid it into a jacket pocket and stood, shining the light. "Daniels?" he yelled again, but there was no response.

Continuing along the path, he looked for any indication of Daniels' whereabouts or why he'd lost his phone, but Rem didn't see anything. Had Daniels made it to the end? Had he dropped his phone by accident or had something spooked him?

Darting his gaze around the area, Rem kept going. The last thing he wanted was to leave the trail because he feared not finding it again. He'd heard the stories of people vanishing, and he figured it's because they'd gotten lost, couldn't find their way back, succumbed to the elements and had become bear food.

Thinking of bears, Rem cursed. That was the last thing he needed to worry about. On edge and his senses on high alert, he kept walking.

After a while, the regular sounds of the forest became more bearable, and he didn't startle every time he heard a rustle or a creaking branch. A bit more relaxed, he reminded himself that he could do this. He'd dealt with a lot of scary things in his life and had survived, and this would be no exception.

His throat dry and wishing he'd brought some water, he stopped and called Daniels' name again but only the frogs and crickets croaked and chirped in response. Rem began to fear that his partner could be unconscious and may not be able to hear him. If that were true, Rem would have to contact Joe and organize a search party because Rem couldn't cover this amount of space by himself.

A louder creak made him pick up his pace. Telling himself it was just a swaying branch, he kept his eyes forward, wondering how much farther the trail went. Was it four miles or five? He couldn't remember.

The creaking stopped, and Rem's heart rate slowed. He was getting there. Just one step at a time. His stomach rumbled, and he again thought about that burger and beer. Once he and Daniels got out of this mess, that was Rem's first stop and Daniels was buying. He spotted another dead log and taking a second to collect himself, he waved the flashlight around to ensure there were no animal neighbors and sat. Spotting a leafy bush beside the log, he aimed the light and studied it, and saw what looked like raspberries among the leaves, only they were smaller and redder. Hungry, he plucked one off and ate it. It was sweet and juicy. Rem plucked a few more and ate those too. Then he put some in his pocket for later.

About to pop another berry in his mouth, he stilled when he heard a low rustle and then a soft snap behind him. That sound was not familiar, and he dropped the berry, stood and swung the light behind him. All he could see were roots, vines, rocks and various other thick foliage. His heart raced.

"Hello?" he yelled. "Daniels?"

Everything went quiet. The wind still blew but the crickets and frogs no longer chirped or croaked.

Rem gripped the flashlight with a shaky hand. "Hello?"

Another rustle from the other side of the trail made him whirl. The hair on his body raised, and he had the sense he was being watched.

Another soft snap made him whirl around again and this time he thought he saw something in the trees, but it had darted off the second the light had hit it. Rem swore he'd seen fur.

Rooted to his spot in fear, he trembled. "Hey," he said, his voice not projecting the amount of confidence he'd hoped. "Listen. If this is some kind of joke or prank, it's not funny, okay? I'm looking for someone who might be injured."

Soft footfalls encroached, and Rem swiveled again, his whole body on edge. "Who's out there?" he yelled. Desperate and terrified, he forced himself to start moving again. Maybe whatever it was would get bored and leave him alone.

It took a monumental effort to get his feet to cooperate, but when they did, he took off in a fast walk. Hearing the footfalls keep pace, he broke out into a run, sure that he was being followed. Gasping, he prayed to make it back alive, and stopped abruptly when his light flashed into the trees, and he spotted two red glowing eyes staring back.

Frozen in place, he fought back panic. It had to be an owl or another raccoon and he was overreacting. Then he remembered the witch and her hellhound. Were the rumors true? Is that what he was seeing? Was the witch's hound stalking him?

The eyes didn't move and in some small part of Rem's remaining logical brain, he told himself to pull it together. It was just a curious forest animal.

But then he heard the growl. A low snarl, deep and menacing. And the eyes moved closer.

Abandoning any sense of courage or will, Rem shrieked, turned, abandoned the trail, and raced into the trees. Dashing through the brush and not paying attention to where he was going, Rem tried to direct the light, but his furious pace made it difficult. He managed to dodge roots and low hanging branches but hearing something running behind him, Rem sprinted faster. He swore he heard panting, too, and his mind raced with images of some enormous monster tracking him, waiting for him to tire, and when he did, it'd pounce, and Rem would become hound food.

His terror motivated him, and he raced deeper and deeper into the woods, but the thing kept up. He almost fell when his foot snagged a vine, but he righted himself and kept going. Branches and leaves swiped at his face, but Rem barely noticed. All he cared about was putting some distance between him and whatever the hell was chasing him.

Gasping for air, he pushed himself faster, when the unthinkable happened. His arm caught a branch, and the flashlight was ripped from his grasp. Plunged into darkness, Rem used his arms to guide him, but his foot caught on a rock, and he stumbled onto the ground, grunting when his ribs hit something hard.

The footfalls encroached, he heard more panting and a low snarl, and feeling a sudden weariness overtake him, he curled up into a fetal position, covered his head with his hands, and whimpering, waited for the monster to kill him.

Chapter Twenty-Two

A BIRD TWEETED, AND another responded to its call with a melodic song. Distant water gurgled and something tickled Rem's nose. Becoming aware, Rem clenched his eyes against a bright light and then opened them, seeing the sun.

Squinting, he felt the hard, rocky ground beneath him, and leaves pricking his skin. Disoriented, he tried to remember where he was. Was he dreaming? Had he fallen asleep at Aunt Gin's? Or was he back in his shack? He couldn't be though because he'd been looking for Daniels.

Remembering his partner, he jolted awake and groaned when he moved. His whole body ached, and a lancing pain shot through his ribs. Moaning, he blinked and looked around. He was lying in the dirt and leaves with large trees around him. A shaft of sunlight cut through the foliage and illuminated him as if were in a spotlight. Sucking in a breath, he held his side and tested his other body parts, ensuring they still worked. He tried to think and recalled his dash into the woods, his terror and the thing chasing him. He held his head and gripped his throbbing temples. Where the hell was he? And more importantly, where was the monster? Would it return? And where the hell was Daniels?

His stomach growled and remembering the berries, he patted his pocket. Tired and hungry, he sat up carefully, reached into his pocket and pulled one out.

"I wouldn't eat that."

The voice scared the shit out of him, and he swiveled and darted away on his butt all in one swift movement. He bumped up against a tree and froze when he saw a woman sitting cross-legged on the ground near where he'd been sleeping. "Who...who the hell are you?" he asked, breathless.

She smiled at him and stood. A long dark braid that reached to her waist swung over her shoulder and she pushed it back. She wore a long plain cotton brown dress that Rem thought looked handmade, and he put her age at around forty, although he couldn't be certain. She wore no makeup or jewelry and tendrils of hair that had escaped her braid framed her narrow face, round dark eyes, and strong chin. "Do...do I know you?" His mind whirled. Had he seen this woman the previous night? Had she chased him through the woods? Judging by her small stature and lean frame, he doubted she'd been the one to snarl at him.

"No," she said, studying him. "But I know you. Or at least know of you."

Rem fought to get his bearings. "Where am I?"

She picked up the berry that he'd dropped. "I believe you're in the woods."

Rem wanted to curse. Of course he was in the woods. "Where in the woods?"

She held the berry. "You shouldn't eat these. They're poisonous." She tossed it into the dirt.

"Poisonous?" Rem held his stomach. "Are you serious? But I ate some last night." He groaned. "Oh, God. I'm going to die out here, aren't I? Either by some damn toxic berry or some crazy hellhound." He put a hand to his head. "My poor aunt is going to think I deserted her, and then one day years from now, they'll find my decomposed skeleton under these godforsaken trees."

"You're a bit melodramatic, aren't you?"

Rem looked up, wondering when the berries would kill him. Would it be painful?

"The berries are poisonous in high quantities," she said. "But just a few make for a nice sleep. You'll simply drift off. I put one in my tea at night. Have too many, though, and you won't wake up." She wiped her hands on her dress.

Rem eyed the berry in the dirt. "I thought they were raspberries."

"They look like them, but they're not. I'm not sure of their exact name, but I've always called them rain berries. They flourish around here, especially after a good rain."

Realizing he wasn't going to die, Rem relaxed. His side ached though, and he clutched it. "I guess that's why I slept so well, despite being chased through the woods by some hellish monster." He stilled. "You should be careful. I don't know what you're doing out here, but something lurks in these woods, and it ain't small."

Her gaze darted behind him. "It's true about the size, but I wouldn't call them hellish."

Rem heard a snort behind him, and his hair rose. The snort came again, and Rem felt a tickle of warm air against his ear. His heart thumping, Rem summoned his courage, and slowly turned. Sitting right behind him was an enormous animal. It looked like a dog, but judging by its immense size, Rem figured it had to be a wolf. It's thick black hair and large bushy tail rose when Rem looked at him, and Rem got the sense it was studying him, too. The dog sniffed his hair, and Rem didn't move. The beast's face was bigger than his, and Rem prayed he'd pass inspection. The dog stood and sniffed Rem's shoulder and then his chest, and Rem didn't even breathe. One bite from this animal would render him dead in seconds.

"She's safe," said the woman. "She won't hurt you."

Rem let go of a held breath when the dog stopped sniffing and walked to the woman's side. Its haunches came up to her waist. "What's her name?" asked Rem. "Godzilla?"

She scratched the animal's massive head. "No. This is Ripley."

Rem forced himself up with a muffled groan. "Hey, Ripley," he said softly. "Nice pooch." Ripley stared at him. "Are you the one who chased me last night because you're very good at it."

"No," said the woman. "That was Hicks."

Rem stared in shock. "There's two of them?"

"They come in handy when you need to keep the curious at bay, and the hikers on the trail."

"And when you want someone to shit their pants."

"That, too." She smoothed Ripley's fur. "They're very smart and loyal. They know these woods better than me."

Rem looked between her and the dog. "Who exactly are you? Other than a woman who owns two massive animals, helps strangers in the woods and is obviously an *Aliens* fan."

She smiled. "It's one of my favorite movies. Hicks and Ripley are good names for two badass dogs."

"I don't disagree."

"As for me, I haven't gone by my given name in a long time," she said. "But you can call me Ivy."

Rem tried to stretch but moaned when his side pulled. "Hi, Ivy. I'm—"

"Detective Aaron Remalla." She paused. "I know who you are."

Rem dropped his jaw. "How did you—"

"I've been expecting you." She ruffled Ripley's ears. "Sorry about having to scare you but at least you're not too damaged. How are your ribs?" She walked closer and put her hand on Rem's chest. He gasped when she touched him, and Ripley stood and trotted to Ivy's side, watching Rem.

"Easy, Pooch," he said, gritting his teeth. "Your mom's fine. I'm not too sure about me though."

She prodded him for a second. "Two fractured ribs. It'll hurt for a while, but you'll heal." She stepped back. "I suspect you're hungry. Follow me and we'll get you patched up and fed."

Surprised, Rem watched her start to walk away. "Hold up," he said with a wince. "I appreciate your diagnosis, but I should probably find a doctor. And I don't suppose you've seen a big irritating blonde guy wandering around out here? The whole reason I'm even in these damn woods is to find him. And when I do, I'm going to give him a few broken ribs of his own."

"Detective Daniels is at the house. He complains about as much as you do." She waved at Ripley. "C'mon, girl." Ivy headed into the woods, Ripley trotting beside her.

"He's what?" Rem stared in disbelief. "Wait a minute...," he said, and holding his throbbing ribs, he followed her.

• • • • • • • • • •

Daniels sat up on the edge of the cot and touched his bandaged forehead. His head still ached but he could at least move without wanting to throw up. The small house was quiet, and he stood. Wobbling slightly, he waited to see if his dizziness would return. When it didn't, he walked toward a wall with a dingy mirror and studied himself. The large bandage almost covered his left eye, and he could see bruising near his hair line. His scratched face gave him a zombie-like look, and along with his messy hair, he could only imagine what Rem would say if he saw him. Carefully, he peeled the bandage off and examined his injury. He had an ugly cut above his left eye, but the redness had faded, and it appeared less swollen. His eye was red and bruised and the cuts on his face had scabbed over.

Feeling stronger and less fatigued, he walked into the tiny kitchen. He didn't see Ivy and for a moment, he considered leaving. He needed to get back to Merrimac and let Rem know he was alive. If his timeline was correct, his partner would be arraigned that morning, and Daniels wouldn't be there. He could only imagine what his partner and Gin were thinking and how worried they must be. Daniels hadn't told anyone where he was going. He suspected Gin would eventually locate his car and start a search party. Daniels knew if his partner were free, he'd scour the woods himself to find Daniels.

After Ivy had brought him here, he'd tried to leave, but he'd been in no physical shape to do it. He could barely stand straight much less walk. And when he'd tried to sneak out the previous day, the damned wolf had growled at him. Knowing he'd lost the battle, he'd gone back to bed and had slept through to this morning.

Realizing he must be in the house alone, he opened the door and peered out. There was no sign of Ivy or her animals. Could he leave now? He had to get back and call Marjorie and let Rem know he was okay. He couldn't afford to wait. He returned to the small front room, found a shirt Ivy had left him and his shoes and hastily put them on. He went back to the door. Opening it, he listened for any sound and then stepped outside and down the porch steps. Prepared to run into the woods, he stopped short when he heard a low growl behind him. Sighing, he turned to see Hicks sitting to the side of the door. He would never understand how such a huge animal could be so quiet.

"C'mon, Hicks. I have to go."

The wolf stood and faced him. He growled again.

Daniels debated whether to challenge the animal or not. If he left, what would Hicks do? He took a step back. "I'm just going into the forest. I'll be right back. I promise."

The wolf growled some more.

Daniels took another step. "C'mon, big guy. Give me a break here. I've got to get back. It's important." He moved again, and Hicks barked, bared his teeth and ran in front of Daniels.

Daniels froze and held out his hands. "All right. Nice doggie. Point taken. I'll stay."

The dog growled until Daniels backed up to the door, went inside, and returned to the kitchen, just as a wave of dizziness hit him and he sat at the table. He took deep breaths until his head stopped spinning and wondered again what to do. How could he get word to Rem? Daniels had to get the hell out of there.

He heard barking, and a second animal joined in. Guessing Ivy and Ripley were returning, Daniels sat up and smoothed his unruly hair with his fingers, determined to convince Ivy that he was well enough to leave. He wished he'd washed his face because that would have helped.

The door opened, and Ivy entered. Ripley sat outside next to Hicks and they both panted and stared toward the trees.

"You're up," said Ivy. "How do you feel?"

"Better," said Daniels, leaning forward. "Listen. I appreciate all you've done, but I have to—"

"Are you kidding?" asked a male voice from outside. "You call this a house?"

Daniels knew that voice. He gripped the edge of the table. "Rem?"

His partner walked in, holding his ribs, his face and clothes dirty and his shirt ripped. He froze. "Daniels?"

Daniels carefully stood. "What the hell are you doing here?"

Rem's eyed widened. "What am I doing here? I've been looking for you. What are you doing here?"

"Trying to prove your innocence."

Rem looked him over. "I don't think it's going too well. You look terrible. What happened to your head?" He pointed toward the wolves. "Did they try and eat you?"

Daniels looked down at himself. His pants were blood stained and he wore an oversized *Hello Kitty* t-shirt. Ivy had taken his shirt to wash it and he didn't know where it was. "They didn't, but they scared the hell out of me." He touched his head. "I ran into a tree branch in a driving rain and fell into a thorny shrub. Ivy found me." The dizziness returned and he sat.

Rem stepped into the kitchen, his gaze darting around the small room. "You and I should write a book. Thankfully, I only fell on a rock and broke my ribs."

"Have a seat," said Ivy. "I'll get you both something to eat and find something to wrap your ribs." She began to move through the kitchen.

Rem sat across from him with a groan. "What happened after you hit the trail?"

The dizzy spell eased. Daniels' head hurt and he wished he could take a shower, but he told Rem how'd he made it about three miles when he'd encountered one of the wolves and knocked himself out in his panic to escape. Ivy had helped him to the house, told him he had a concussion and despite his objections, had insisted he rest and recuperate after she'd treated and bandaged his head. Nauseated and disoriented, he'd been unable to do much else but sleep until that morning.

"How'd you find me?" asked Daniels, fearing the worst. "Please don't tell me you broke out of jail and are a fugitive."

Ivy set cups of water in front of both of them. "Drink up. You both need it."

Daniels and Rem both drained their cups and Rem set his down. "What happened to Mr. Positivity?" he asked.

"He's out to lunch," said Daniels. "Maybe after I've had a shower, a meal and a good night's sleep, he'll make an appearance."

Rem grunted. "I'd give a million dollars for that plus a cup of hot coffee."

"I can get you some coffee," said Ivy. She opened a wood burning stove and tossed more wood onto a small flame.

Rem widened his eyes. "Add a shower and a burger and I'll marry you and take you away from all of this." He waved his hand and grimaced.

Ivy stoked the flames. "Why would I want to leave?"

Rem raised a brow at her. "Your choice, but I'll definitely take that coffee, please." He eyed Daniels.

"Me, too," said Daniels. "Thanks. So, you're not a fugitive?" he asked Rem.

"Sheriff Joe returned and did his own digging into Sharon's murder. Once he got the facts, he let me go." Rem went through the details of Sharon's death. "Shaw was furious."

"I bet he was."

"I immediately started looking for you. I found my way to Whit, and he told me about the woman in the woods." He looked at Ivy. "I'm guessing that's you."

Ivy smiled and put a kettle on the stove. "Whit's a gentle soul."

"He said you talk to him," said Rem.

"I do," said Ivy.

"But I thought you said you rarely leave the woods," said Daniels.

"That's true," she said, adding more water to their cups from a pitcher.

Rem frowned. "What am I missing here?"

"Whit told me you knew what happened," said Daniels to Ivy. "And that you could help me."

She nodded. "He's correct." She added water to the kettle. "But we don't talk physically."

Daniels swiveled to face her. "What other way is there?"

She reached for a canister on a shelf and pulled it down. "I hear him, and he hears me." She popped the lid open and scooped out some coffee grounds into an empty pitcher. "It's easy with the elderly and with children. Not so easy with others. They're too closed off and distracted by their thoughts."

"Are you saying this is some sort of telepathy?" asked Rem.

She closed the canister and put it back. "I suppose."

Daniels regarded Rem, whose eyes widened. "Wait a minute..." Rem pointed at her. "Are you..." He paused. "Are you the witch?" He stared out the open front door. "And those are the hellhounds?"

"You're just now figuring that out?" asked Daniels. "Some detective you are."

"Witch is a complicated term," said Ivy. She checked the fire and added more wood. "It has such derogatory connotations. I don't think of myself as anything other than a woman with unique gifts, but if I have to depict myself or my dogs as frightening mythical creatures in order to keep people away, then I will."

Daniels recalled what Amy had told him. "A woman at the bar said she'd seen your house and it glowed red."

"So do the dogs' eyes," said Rem.

Ivy opened a drawer and pulled out a red sheer fabric. "If the dogs alert me, I dampen the lights and drape these over the windows. It provides a nice eerie glow. Then Hicks and Rip do the rest. Their eyes glow red all on their own. It's a nice touch." She returned the fabric to the drawer.

Rem shivered and winced. "It sure the hell is." He sipped more of his water. "You got quite a story going. No one wants to be near these woods at night."

"You responsible for the disappearances, too?" asked Daniels.

Reaching for two mugs, she stilled. "No." She grabbed the mugs and set them on the table. One of them had a big sun with a smiley face on it and the other said *Don't even bother until I have my coffee*. "That has nothing to do with me."

Daniels eyed Rem who raised a brow again.

She smiled. "You two practice a little telepathy yourselves." She set a bowl of sugar down with a spoon. "Sorry. I don't have any cream."

"I'll survive with the sugar," said Rem.

"I can hear your minds whirling," she said. "Those disappearances have a cause but it's not me. I'm not the only one with gifts around Merrimac." She checked the kettle. "The water will be ready soon."

"What do you mean about you not being the only one with gifts?" asked Daniels. "Are you saying someone else is responsible for the people who vanished?"

"Like it was intentional?" asked Rem. "And they didn't just get lost?"

Ivy shrugged. "Maybe, but maybe not." Steam began to rise from the kettle. "But there's something about Merrimac that's dangerous. For most, it's just a quaint town to spend a long weekend, but for others, it's their last stop."

"How do you know this?" asked Rem.

"It's something I've sensed," said Ivy.

"Sensed?" asked Rem. "You mean like the way you sensed I have two fractured ribs and he's got a concussion?"

"Something like that," said Ivy. "I've always had the ability to intuitively make a diagnosis. The curing part is not my strength, though."

Rem clutched his side. "That's unfortunate."

"These disappearances," said Daniels. "You don't know who's doing it or why?"

She shook her head. "I'm very careful with where I direct my energy, Detective. If it doesn't feel right, I avoid it."

"Why's that?" asked Rem. "If someone is doing this intentionally, they should be stopped."

Ivy watched the kettle as steam began to emerge from the top. "I'm not sure I agree."

Daniels narrowed his eyes. "These people were murdered."

Ivy picked up the kettle with a towel. "Who said anything about murder?" She added the hot water to the pitcher with the coffee grounds.

Rem frowned. "If they're not dead, then where are they?"

Ivy returned the kettle to the stove. "I don't know."

Daniels touched his injured forehead, wondering if he'd been hit harder than he'd thought. "I'm confused."

"Join the club," said Rem.

Ivy opened a drawer and pulled out what looked like cheesecloth. "All I can tell you is that they disappeared and maybe for good reason. I don't look any further than that because I choose not to. It's not my business. I keep to myself for a reason. Coming forward to reveal that some people vanished by another's hand would bring unwanted attention." She paused. "I don't have any proof anyway."

Rem shifted in his seat with a groan. "Well, this is a surprise."

"You said they disappeared for a reason. So, they were targeted?" asked Daniels.

"Like I said. I only know so much. I can't say for sure why they didn't return, but I have my suspicions." Ivy set the cheesecloth down and peered out a back window. "I'll be right back." She opened a back door and stepped outside.

"What do you think about all this?" asked Rem.

"I don't know what to think," said Daniels. "She took care of me though, when I could still be roaming the woods, so that's something."

"You believe the whole telepathy thing?"

"Whit did tell me to find a woman in the woods and he was right, so unless he's got some secret cell phone to converse with her, which I doubt, then there's something to it."

Rem added some sugar to his mug. "I feel like we're in *The Twilight Zone*. Rod Serling is going to step out of a closet at any second."

"Yeah, well, tell Rod we need to go home. Can he blink his eyes and take care of that?"

"That's *I Dream of Jeannie.*"

"Figures. Where's Jeannie when you need her?"

"In her lamp," said Rem. "Which we don't have."

"Just our luck. We only have a witch and her hellhounds."

"You need to stop hanging out with me. Then your luck might change."

"I'll keep that in mind."

The door opened, and Ivy returned, carrying several ripe tomatoes. "I hope you like tomatoes."

"Love them," said Daniels.

"They're bearable," said Rem.

She set them down on the counter and picked up the cheesecloth. "Ready for your coffee?"

"I've been trying not to drool," said Rem.

Ivy put the cloth over the mugs, picked up the kettle, and began to pour the coffee.

Rem eyed the drink with eagerness. He spooned out more sugar and added it to his mug.

"I don't know what to think about any of what you said, Ivy," said Daniels.

"You and me, both," said Rem. "But maybe once I get some food in me, I'll start to care. Right now, though, I'm desperate for this cup of coffee."

Ivy finished pouring and slid his mug over. Rem smelled it and sighed. After taking a sip, he smiled. "That's delicious."

Daniels sipped his own coffee. It was hot and strong.

Rem took another sip and expelled another deep sigh. "If you're not up for marriage, then how about a year's supply of dog food," said Rem. "This is great coffee."

"Not bad for a witch in the woods," she said. "But Ripley and Hicks don't eat dog food."

"What do they eat?" asked Rem.

"Pretty much whatever they want," she said.

Rem blanched. "That makes sense." He held his stomach. "What does a witch in the woods serve for breakfast?"

Daniels scoffed. "She's not your mother."

"She mentioned breakfast." Rem grimaced and gripped his side. "I'd be happy to help but my ribs are killing me, and you look like you can barely stand."

"It's fine," said Ivy. "I'm your host and I'll happily make breakfast. How about some toast and jam? I think I even have some eggs. I can throw in a tomato, too."

Daniels nodded, knowing Rem was right and he wouldn't be much help. "That would be great. Thank you."

"Add a hot shower and, since marriage and dog food are a hard no, I'll buy you a..." He looked around the rickety house. "I don't know... everything."

Ivy grabbed a jar from a shelf. "I know it's not much. This house is probably a hundred years old. I don't have running water or electricity, but I make do. At first, it was rough, but I got used to it, and now it's home." She opened a small bag and pulled out some slices of bread. "I baked this the other day, and I canned the jam."

"I hope it's not made from rain berries," said Rem.

She raised the side of her lip. "No, it's not."

"How'd you end up in the woods?" asked Daniels. "I mean, you have some things that you've obviously bought in a store."

"And you've seen *Aliens*, so you're not totally exiled from the world," added Rem.

"Aliens?" asked Daniels. "What aliens? In the woods?" He smirked. "Don't tell me. They made those people disappear?"

Rem rolled his eyes. "No, you idiot. The dogs," said Rem, pointing toward the door. "Their names? You know. From the movie?"

Daniels stared in confusion, and Rem huffed with impatience. "Never mind. Remind me to introduce you to the *Alien* universe when we get back."

"Is this going to require me to sit in front of a TV for several hours in prolonged agony?" asked Daniels.

"I'll buy the alcohol."

"Damn right, you will. And I'll bring the ear plugs."

Rem smirked back at him.

Ivy slathered jam on the bread. "I wasn't always secluded like this. I lived a very normal life for a while. I had a job, a boyfriend, money in the bank, and I traveled. I did all the things everyone else does, only I was miserable." She picked up another piece of bread and added jam. "I couldn't figure out what was wrong with me. I was depressed, underweight, lethargic. I tried therapists and medication, but none of it worked. It got so bad, I quit my job and laid in bed for weeks. I finally decided to end it all but didn't know how to do it." She put the bread on two plates and set them on the table. "Until I found myself in Merrimac one day. I'd heard the stories of people walking into the woods and not returning. I'm sure a lot of it was rumors and over-exaggeration, but that's when I knew." She picked up the pitcher and cheesecloth and added more coffee to their mugs. "I went home and sold everything, came back here and walked into the woods. I didn't tell anyone. I simply left."

Rem sipped his coffee. "What happened?"

"I walked," said Ivy. "And when nothing bad emerged, I walked some more. I left the trail and kept going, waiting for whatever took people or killed them to come after me, but it never happened. Instead, I found this house. It was old and decrepit, but it was a shelter. There's a brook nearby with fresh water and I ate roots and berries. When I wasn't dead after a few days, I walked through the woods and realized something that changed everything."

Daniels leaned in. "What was that?"

"I wasn't depressed. In fact, I was happy. It was quiet and I could think for the first time since...ever. That's when I realized what had been wrong with me. I had been taking on the pain and suffering of others. Their thoughts, feeling, worries, doubts, all of it had ravaged me. I'd always had the ability to pick up on stuff. I could hear things or see images. I thought it was normal, but I had no idea the toll it was taking on me until it finally stopped. Then it became clear what I needed to do. I would stay. I could work on the house but live off the land. I knew how to garden, and I was handy. I found an overgrown trail and cleared it and then bought an old car that I still hide in the woods. At first, I used it to take occasional trips into the city outside Merrimac when I needed things, but as time passed, I did it less and less often. Now I leave maybe twice a year to pick up any essentials. It's better if I stay away from people though, or the depression returns."

"What about the dogs? How'd you find them?" asked Rem.

She picked up a basket and set it beside the sink. "I was walking through the woods one day, just enjoying the silence when I heard whimpering. I'd encountered wildlife out here and figured it was a possum or even a doe, but when I looked, I found two wolf cubs. They were hungry and appeared to have been abandoned. I took them in and raised them, and now they're my best friends. They know the woods and hunt for me, and they come in handy when nosy tourists or curious thrill seekers want to test their skills and wander the woods at night. Hicks and Rip scare them away." She removed some eggs from the basket and set them to the side.

"Thus, the tale of the haunted woods with the witch and her hounds was born," said Daniels. "I knew there was a simple explanation."

"You call this simple?" asked Rem. "It's a helluva story, and let's not forget the whole telepathy thing which landed you and me smack dab in this spooky tale. You realize everyone's going to think we've disappeared, too."

Daniels thought of Marjorie and knew he needed to contact her. Aunt Gin would be worrying about Rem, as well. "He's got a point, Ivy. We need to get back."

"They've cleared me," said Rem, "so I'm good to go. We can go home now. Thank God."

Ivy found a skillet and set it in on the stove. "It's not that simple, gentlemen." She started to crack the eggs into the skillet. "You're not out of the woods yet, so to speak."

Daniels stopped in mid-sip of his coffee. "What do you mean?"

Ivy finished cracking the eggs and wiped her hands on a towel. "Because someone out there still wants you both dead."

Chapter Twenty-Three

REM NARROWED HIS EYES, unsure he heard right. "Excuse me?"

"Who wants us dead?" asked Daniels.

Ivy stirred the eggs in the pan as they began to sizzle. "I don't know." She grabbed a shaker and dusted the eggs with a powder. "I sensed it not long after Remalla arrived in town." She picked up a tomato, found a knife, and began to slice it.

Rem tried to shift into a more comfortable position. "What exactly did you pick up on?"

"I felt it from Whit, but others, too. The festival was on this weekend, and I can sense the shift when others come and go. But this was something different. I homed in on it because it felt off, but then it merged in with the crowds and I lost it."

"And it had to do with me?" asked Rem.

"I wasn't aware of you at first, but then Sharon's murder happened. That's when I zeroed in on you."

"Through Whit?" asked Daniels.

She nodded and added the diced tomato to the eggs. "Whit hears and picks up on a lot more than most realize. Plus, I can see through others' eyes when they're quiet. Have you ever had a moment when you catch yourself daydreaming and then realize several moments have passed without realizing it?"

"Sounds like Rem at work," said Daniels.

Rem shot him a dirty look. "Watch it."

"It's those moments that allow me to see." She stirred the eggs, pulled down two more plates and set them beside the stove. "They're brief but helpful. I knew immediately you didn't kill her."

"How so?" asked Rem. "That spooky sense of yours?"

"You carry a lot of weight on your shoulders, Detective, but not enough to murder someone." She stirred the eggs again and took them off the heat.

Rem sipped more of his coffee. "You sure about that, because I've been close a few times."

"We've all been there," said Daniels. "But she's right. You would never purposely harm anyone out of anger."

Rem sighed. "I guess there's still hope." He picked up a piece of bread with jam. "You think whoever killed Sharon is after me and Daniels?"

"Do you know who killed Sharon?" asked Daniels.

She scooped the eggs onto the dishes. "I can't be sure about anything. All I can tell you is that Sharon's murderer is still free, but whether that's the person who wants to harm you, I can't discern."

"If you're able to discern I didn't do it, then how come you can't tell who did?" Rem bit into his bread.

She picked up the plates with the eggs and set them in front of Rem and Daniels. "It doesn't work like that. It's like the disappearances. Unless I choose to open myself and probe people's energy, then maybe I could find out more, but even then, if someone is closed off, I won't see a thing. And if I do open myself up, then it drains me terribly. I'll end up in bed for days."

Daniels pulled one of the plates toward him. "Whit said you saw what happened and that you could help me." He picked up a fork Ivy had placed on the table.

She tensed and held her elbows. "I sensed Sharon's pain. Sometimes I'll pick up on things when I sleep. I woke up that night aching, feeling like I'd been fighting a boxer in the ring. All I wanted to do was cry. I didn't understand it until I'd learned later what had happened." Her face paled. "It shocked me. Normally I can block that sort of interference, but not that night."

Rem picked up his own fork and slid his egg-filled plate over. "We ought to introduce you to the Redstones. You and Mikey would hit it off and Mason would be intrigued."

"The Redstones?" asked Ivy.

"Friends of ours, with amazing gifts of their own," said Daniels. "I bet Mikey's blowing up your phone by the way." Daniels took a bite of his eggs.

"Last I saw, she'd left a couple of voicemails," said Rem. "She's going to give me hell when I finally call her back." He took a bite of his own eggs, chewed and moaned. "These are delicious."

Daniels nodded. "Best eggs I've had, and Marjorie's a pro."

"I add my own combination of spices and herbs I grow in the garden," she said. She grabbed a mug and poured some coffee for herself.

"You're not eating?" asked Rem between bites.

"I'm an early riser. I already ate." She grabbed some cloth napkins, set them on the table and then pulled out a chair and sat.

Daniels grabbed a napkin. "Getting back to the somebody wants us dead," he said, wiping his mouth. "That's one of the reasons I came out here. Whit told me I wouldn't survive the night if I stayed. Was that based on this same threat?"

"It is," said Ivy. "I think someone planned to link you to Sharon's murder."

"But how?" said Daniels.

"My guess? By making it appear as if you'd committed suicide. They'd want people to think you'd killed yourself over guilt. Maybe the sheriff would have found a note implicating Detective Remalla in the murder."

"I wouldn't have written that," said Daniels, his face paling.

"It would have been typed," said Rem. "And your signature forged. You think once Sheriff Joe and Shaw had something like that, they'd dig any deeper? Hell. You'd be dead and I'd still be in that damn cell." His skin prickled at the thought.

Daniels touched his swollen forehead. "Guess I shouldn't complain about a throbbing head."

"Be glad it's still in one piece," said Rem.

Daniels nodded. "Don't misunderstand, Ivy. I'm grateful for your help and glad we're both well enough to be sitting here, but we can't stay. We need to let our loved ones know we're all right. Otherwise, you're going to have a big search party in these woods that you might not be able to hide from."

"And Aunt Gin will lead it," said Rem, taking another bite of his eggs.

Ivy set her chin in her hand. "I've considered that."

"Rem and I have been in difficult situations before," said Daniels. "If we're aware of the threat, we can keep an eye out for it. If it's Sharon's killer, then my money's on Scott Herndon. And we sure as hell can handle him."

"I'd welcome it," added Rem.

"It's more than that," said Ivy. "I think you're facing worse than just a killer."

Rem swallowed his bite of eggs and sipped his coffee. "This have something to do with the people who disappeared?"

Daniels added a piece of bread to his plate. "Maybe you need to tell us exactly what you know."

After a pause, she put her elbows on the table and interlaced her fingers. "As I said, Merrimac has a feel to it. When I first arrived, I sensed something, but I jumbled it into all of the other mixed emotions I was carrying around at the time. But as I adjusted to my new surroundings and the heaviness began to lift, that sense of foreboding remained. Whatever it was I picked up on is still here, and it's powerful." She studied her hands.

Rem grabbed his own napkin. "So, we're back to those lost people. Somebody eliminated them."

She nodded. "Which is why nothing happened to me when I entered the woods, and why others come and go freely along the trail. They aren't targets."

"Hold up," said Daniels, laying his napkin along his lap. "Despite what you may or may not sense, people disappear all the time in the wilderness. It's not that uncommon."

"But to have no bodies turn up?" asked Rem. "You have to admit that's odd."

"But it does happen. It is the woods. There are predators," said Daniels. "I talked to Marvin at Jimmy's. He said if the people who'd disappeared walked far enough, they could have made it to the next town and then just gone home or flew to some remote island because they wanted to escape from their lives."

"These people didn't go home," said Ivy.

Rem moved and winced when the pain flared. "I might buy it if one person or even two flew off to some magical destination, but the numbers are suspicious. It's too many. You can disappear from anywhere if you want. Just walk out your front door and go. Why Merrimac?"

"Then maybe they got lost. There's thousands of acres of forest around here," said Daniels. "And I'm not sure I agree about the numbers. Hell, maybe they did what you did, Ivy. They intentionally planned to vanish and never be found. Life will do that to you."

Rem recalled his week. "Tell me about it."

"I wasn't referring to you," said Daniels. "You may disappear and get drunk for a few days, but you eventually find your way back."

"That's because you came looking." Rem pushed a bite of eggs around his plate with his fork. "Maybe if I'd known more about the disappearances, I may have considered what Ivy did."

"Nice try, partner, but you wouldn't have come near these woods with a twelve-foot pole. I don't care how desperate you might have been."

Rem set his fork down. "I came after you, didn't I?"

"Because that's the guy you are," said Daniels. "You'll risk life and limb for the people you love, but without it, you'll stick to indoor plumbing every time."

Ivy picked up her mug. "And you wouldn't have vanished anyway. You weren't a target. At least, not at the time."

"Then let's get back to the person doing this," said Daniels, "If we're buying this theory, then who is it? Who would be capable of it?"

"I suspect these people made someone angry," said Ivy.

"But how do they vanish without a trace?" asked Rem. "Does this person hide the bodies?"

"I've wondered about that," said Ivy, "and I don't think anyone's been hidden. I've studied the phenomena over the years. There is such a thing as a person who can make objects, or what's called apports, appear or disappear. I've read about it. It's popular in Spiritualism and occurs when a medium causes things to materialize or dematerialize during a séance. In the past, though, those experiences have always been proven to be fraudulent, but it doesn't mean it isn't possible."

Rem waved his napkin. "Okay. Wait a minute. Are you saying someone just waved their hands, went 'poof,' and these people were gone?"

"Well, it may be a little more complicated than that," said Ivy, "but, yes. That's what I'm saying."

Daniels pushed his plate back. "I have to agree with my partner here, Ivy. Granted, he and I have seen a few things over the years—"

Rem pointed. "His granddad's house was haunted."

"Maybe," said Daniels.

"Maybe, my ass," said Rem. "And don't even get me started on Jill, Madison, Jace, and that other asshole." Rem thought of Rutger, and his stomach twisted. He didn't like to say his name. "And there's Mason and Mikey, and their psycho sister Margaret."

"Psycho sister?" asked Ivy. "Sounds like an interesting family."

"Mason and Mikey are fine," said Rem. "They have their gifts, but Margaret Redstone is a different breed. She's in a psychiatric facility." Thinking about her wild eyes, cackling laugh, and demented attraction to him, Rem shuddered despite the ache in his ribs.

"Like I said," said Daniels, "we've seen a few things, but this seems a little farfetched."

"A little?" asked Rem.

"Oh, it is," said Ivy. "This sort of skill would require an enormous amount of power and the ability to direct it with scary accuracy."

Trying to think, Rem scratched his head and sighed. "Let me see if I get this straight. You believe some powerful medium who makes things disappear like a magician is in Merrimac. Is this the same person targeting me and Daniels?"

"I don't know," said Ivy. "It's hard to tell. Whatever I sensed after you arrived has now merged with the people in the town. I can't delineate between the two. If it's someone separate, they're good at shielding themselves, but if it isn't, and you've angered the wrong person..."

Rem groaned. "Then why are we still here? Wouldn't we have vanished by now?"

"I doubt it's easy to do. Planning would have to be involved," said Ivy. "Maybe if they'd known you were heading into the woods...but I'm assuming neither of you told anyone where you were going."

"Or...," said Daniels. "...this whole thing is silly. There is no crazy magician. Someone is pissed because they wanted Rem to take the fall for Sharon's murder. It didn't work, though, but they're still hoping to make both of us look guilty." He picked up his coffee. "And the people who vanished got careless and died when they didn't take nature seriously."

"Or maybe it's both," said Rem. "The magician that made those people disappear murdered Sharon and is after us."

Daniels rolled his eyes. "And maybe Ripley and Hicks are werewolves."

Rem grunted at Daniels and spoke to Ivy. "Who are the people that vanished?" he asked. "Do we know anything about them?"

"Marvin told me," said Daniels. "There was a couple from nine years ago, then Sybil, the sheriff's wife, and two years ago, a guy named Doug."

"They have anything in common?" asked Rem.

"Not that Marvin mentioned," said Daniels.

"Not that I know of," said Ivy.

Rem took the last sip of his coffee. "Then here's the deal. If there is some creepy Magic Man roaming the streets of Merrimac, which I agree with Daniels, is doubtful, then unless we know who it is, there's nothing we can do about it. My guess is Scott Herndon's pissed I'm no longer a suspect and would love to make Sheriff Joe doubt his decision to release me. Deputy Shaw doesn't like it either. He'd rather be right than find the actual bad guy."

"We need to notify our families we're okay," said Daniels. "Once we're in Merrimac, we'll watch our backs for Herndon and Shaw." He set his napkin on the table. "But we plan on going home."

"Lozano is probably wondering where we are, too," said Rem.

"If we leave now and take our time, we can get back before this evening," said Daniels.

"And don't worry," said Rem to Ivy. "We'll keep your secret. No one will know you're here."

Ivy shook her head and closed her eyes. She went quiet and Rem made eye contact with Daniels, wondering if they should interrupt. "Ivy?" asked Rem. "You okay?"

She opened her eyes. "Something isn't right. This is about more than Sharon and Scott. You have to stay."

"Ivy...," said Daniels.

Ivy's face lost its color. "If you don't, you'll die. I don't know how or by who, but I can feel it. You're in danger." She set her coffee cup down. "You have to believe me."

Rem tapped at the table, feeling a little anxious. As much as he wanted to return, he also didn't want to end up dead. "What do you propose we do? Stay here forever?" He and Daniels waited for her response.

She pursed her lips. "Can you give it twenty-four hours?"

"Ivy, we have to contact our families," said Daniels.

"I can do that," said Ivy. "Do you have your phones?"

"Phones?" asked Rem.

"Mine's lost," said Daniels.

"No, it isn't." Rem reached into his pocket. "I found it on the trail." He handed it to Daniels and pulled out his own phone.

Daniels studied his cell. "It's no good if it's dead."

"Mine, too," said Rem. "But it wouldn't matter anyway because there's no service out here."

"Give them to me." Ivy held out her hand. "Write down who to contact and what you want to say. I'll take Hicks and go to your cars. I assume you have chargers in them?"

"We do," said Daniels. "What's your plan? Start our cars long enough to use the phones, shoot out a text telling people not to worry, then return?"

"Yes," she said. "It would be easy enough. Your people will know you're alive and you can take the twenty-four hours you need to rest and get better while I can hopefully dig a little deeper and possibly determine the threat."

Rem had to admit that hiking through the woods with his injured ribs didn't sound too appealing. "What do you think?" he asked Daniels, noting his partner's weary features, pale pallor and nasty cut on his forehead. "You could probably use another day to recover. You fall over out there, I'm in no shape to carry you."

Ivy clasped her hands together. "Please. Give me and yourselves some time. I'd rather have your families worry a little instead of planning your funerals."

Daniels blew out a breath. "When you put it that way..." He regarded Rem. "You're sure you're okay with spending the night?"

"I'm not sure about anything," said Rem. "But I'm willing to wait if you are."

"Okay," said Daniels. "You win, Ivy." He raised a finger. "But Magic Man or not, by this time tomorrow, we're out of here."

Chapter Twenty-Four

REM AND DANIELS WROTE out quick messages. Rem's would be sent to Gin and Daniels to Marjorie. They simply told them not to worry, they were in a remote location but safe, and would return the next day to give them more details.

Ivy grabbed a knapsack and added their phones and car keys to it, along with water and some snacks. She called Hicks to her side and told Rem and Daniels she would move fast and would be back before nightfall. Looking them over, she suggested they clean up at the stream, wash their clothes and hang them to dry on a line behind the house. A trunk in the front room stored various shirts and pants, some of which had belonged to her dad. They could go through it and find something to wear while their clothes dried. Then she'd found a bandage she'd used for Ripley after Ripley had encountered a bear and told Rem to use it for his ribs. She suggested they rest, and she would use her time in the woods to focus and try to learn more about the threat and would hopefully know more by the time she returned. Then she and Hicks disappeared into the trees.

Rem had taken her advice and went to the stream to clean up while Daniels rested. Ripley went with him, and Rem abandoned all hopes of taking a dip when he stuck his toe into the freezing cold water. Instead, he used the towel he'd brought to wipe himself down and then changed into a pair of baggy sweatpants and a ragged t-shirt with old stains on it. His ribs protesting, he rinsed out his clothes as much as he could and then laid them on a rock to dry and did his best to wrap his aching chest.

Spent, he laid beside Ripley in the sun next to the stream and dozed until Daniels jostled him awake and they switched. Rem went back to the house to eat a sandwich while Ripley remained with Daniels as he cleaned up and changed clothes.

The remainder of the day was spent not doing much of anything and as the day waned and the sun descended, Rem sat on the small porch in a creaking wooden chair and studied the woods while Ripley slept beside him. Not long after, Daniels joined him, sitting in the creaky chair next to him.

"Our clothes are almost dry," he said.

Rem reached down and patted Rip's head. "Good."

"I added more wood to the fire in the stove and lit the oil lamps. It should give us plenty of heat and light for tonight."

"Thanks," said Rem, grateful he wouldn't be sleeping in a dark room. "How's your head?"

"Better. Dizziness is gone and it's not throbbing. How're your ribs?"

Rem shifted in the chair. "Pretty uncomfortable."

"Your bandage tight enough?"

"Probably not."

"Stand up." Daniels rose out of his seat.

Rem frowned at him. "Don't torture me."

"You want it to feel better, don't you? Especially tonight when you're trying to sleep."

Rem sucked in a breath and stood. He raised his arm while Daniels adjusted the bandage, pulled it tight and secured it. Rem gasped while Daniels tugged.

"Better?" asked Daniels.

Rem had to admit, his ribs felt more secure. "Yeah. Thanks."

"You have to be able to walk out of here tomorrow," said Daniels, sitting down again.

Rem sat carefully. "I know." He thought about their situation. "You worried about what Ivy said?"

Daniels shrugged. "I've certainly thought about it. Do I believe there is some sinister force making people disappear in Merrimac? No, I don't. But God knows, we've been surprised before."

Rem recalled their previous cases. "If Rudy could shoot electricity out of his finger and Margaret could curse statues, who's to say someone couldn't make an enemy vanish into thin air? Never mind *The Twilight Zone*. I think we're in an episode of the *X-files*."

Daniels lightly touched his forehead. "The X what?"

Rem sighed. "Never mind."

"Magic Man or not," said Daniels, "if we are in danger, then it has to do with Sharon's murder. You didn't take the fall so now the killer's going to plan B."

"Murder us and make it look like we're Sharon's killers?" asked Rem. "It's a tall order. We're detectives. We won't make it easy."

"Exactly. Which is why I think Ivy is right to be concerned, but I think she's overreacting."

"I've been thinking about Sharon," said Rem. "I know Scott is our number one suspect, but I don't see him as some sort of mastermind killer. He's not the type to murder and frame us."

"I've wondered about that, too," said Daniels. "If it's not Scott, then maybe it's Tyler, the bank manager."

"You get murder vibes from him?" asked Rem.

"Not really, but some people are good at hiding it." Daniels rested an ankle on his knee. "What about Amy?"

"The roommate-friend?" Rem tipped his head. "It's possible."

"She cried a lot of tears when she saw me."

"Some people can cry on cue." Rem looked over. "What if she and Scott were a little closer than anybody thinks?"

"And Amy got jealous of Sharon and killed her?" Daniels shrugged. "Could be."

Rem recalled his encounter in the jail cell. "There's someone else to consider." He shivered at the memory. "Deputy Shaw."

Daniels turned his head. "Are you serious? I know the guy's got an attitude problem, but you think he's a killer?"

Rem bounced his knee. "He freaked me out the day Joe released me." He gave Daniels an account of Shaw opening the door to his cell and acting strange while keeping his hand on his gun.

"What do you think he would have done if you'd left?" asked Daniels.

"That's just it. I don't know." Rem thought back. "Maybe he had the same info Joe did and knew it wasn't enough, so he came up with some crazy scheme to make it look like I'd tried to escape to give Joe reason to hold me." Rem paused, recalling Shaw's intense stare. "Would he have actually shot me? I'm afraid to ask."

"Then he's definitely on the radar. That guy needs meds. What if he killed Sharon, framed you, and when he realized the evidence against you wasn't strong enough, he planned to kill you before Joe arrived. Then Shaw could have made up whatever story he liked."

Rem picked a leaf off his sweatpants. "Or maybe he just takes his job a little too seriously and thought he'd have a little fun scaring the shit out of some big city detective. He definitely harbors a grudge against cops."

"Either way, it's better we steer clear of that guy."

"You won't get any argument from me," said Rem.

"I wonder if Ivy knows anything about him, or any of the suspects?" asked Daniels. "We should ask."

"She does have some spooky gifts, doesn't she?" asked Rem. "She knows I have two broken ribs and you have a concussion?"

"Maybe she's just making it up. Our injuries aren't that difficult to figure out."

"She sure the hell knows a lot of things for someone who rarely leaves this house." Rem eyed the woods. "How do you suppose she's stayed hidden all this time? They had to have sent search parties when Sybil and the other guy...Doug, went missing. She was living out here by then."

"They probably did. The question is, how far did they search?"

"Judging by what I heard about Sybil, maybe not that far."

"And Doug was an outsider," said Daniels. "Plus, if the wolves did their thing, they may have kept searchers from getting too close."

"They probably did. I wouldn't want to bump into one of them in the middle of nowhere."

"Whatever she's doing, it's working."

Rem scratched his unshaved jaw. "I'd be lonely as hell out here, but I have to admit I can see why she stays. It's nice and peaceful."

"It doesn't hurt to have Rip and Hicks hanging around, either," said Daniels.

"No. It doesn't. I would love some hot water, though, and a toilet. That outhouse has spiders in it." Rem shuddered.

"It's not the Ritz, that's for sure." Daniels settled back in his chair. "But there's something to be said about unplugging for a while. No phone, no

TV."

"No power. No running water." Rem shook his head. "I'd rather be at your grandfather's house."

"You sure about that?" asked Daniels, looking over, his brow raised.

Rem shuddered again. "No. Not really."

"Just relax, partner." Daniels lifted a hand. "Enjoy the silence. After today. God knows when we'll get it again."

Ripley stirred and sat up.

"What is it, girl?" asked Rem. "You hear something?"

Her tail began to wag, and she bounded into the woods.

"Where's she going?" asked Rem.

"Probably found Big Foot," said Daniels.

Rem made a face. "You just had to bring that up, didn't you?"

"I'm surprised you hadn't already."

Barking sounded from the trees, and Rem saw Ivy emerge with Hicks and Ripley beside her. "She's back," said Rem.

Daniels stood, and Ivy approached the house. "How'd it go?" asked Daniels. "Any problems?"

She stepped up to the porch and removed her knapsack. She opened it and pulled out two dead squirrels. Despite his aches and pains, Rem stood and backed up. "What the hell is that?"

"Hicks brought us dinner." She walked into the house.

Rem pointed, his eyes wide. "We're gonna eat that?"

"You eat meat all the time, Rem," said Daniels. "How is this any different?" He patted Rem on the shoulder. "C'mon." He smiled. "If you're lucky, maybe you can help her clean them." He entered the house.

Rem stomach churned. "Just one more day," he muttered, and followed Daniels inside.

Ivy was in the kitchen and had set the squirrels on a table in the rear of the kitchen. Hicks and Ripley remained outside.

"Sit," said Ivy. "We need to talk." She poured water from a pitcher into a basin and washed her hands.

Daniels sat at the small table, and Rem joined him. "Everything okay?" asked Rem, eyeing the squirrels.

"Yes and no." Ivy dried her hands on a towel. "I made it to the cars. No one was around, so no search party yet."

"I don't know whether to be happy or disappointed," said Rem.

Ivy sat at the table with them. "I started up the cars and let the phones charge. Then I found Marjorie's number and texted her. She responded wanting to know more but I just told her that you were involved in a case and cell service was bad, but you loved her and would be in touch tomorrow."

Daniels sighed. "Great. Thank you."

"I texted your aunt next," she said to Rem.

"Did she respond?" asked Rem.

"She did." Ivy's face furrowed. "She had disturbing news."

Rem waited. "What is it? Is she okay?"

Ivy clenched her hands. "Scott Herndon is dead."

· • • ● • ● • • • ·

Daniels straightened. "You're kidding."

"No, I'm not," said Ivy. "Your aunt said he was found in his bed this morning, a gunshot wound to the head. Sheriff Joe and Deputy Shaw want to talk to you both."

Rem stared in disbelief. "I bet they do."

Shocked, Daniels tried to think. "They think we did it?"

"I don't know," said Ivy. "I'm just relaying what Genevieve said."

"I don't believe this." Rem groaned. "I threatened him, and you almost had a fight with him and his buddies." He looked at Daniels. "Gin knows we were both searching for Scott. If she tells that to Sheriff Joe, then we're obvious suspects."

"But we're out in the middle of nowhere," said Daniels, his voice raising. "That's a substantial alibi."

"Says who?" asked Rem. "Her?" He pointed at Ivy. "You going to make her reveal herself?"

"We don't need Ivy," said Daniels. "Joe and Shaw can say whatever they want, but we weren't there. They have no witnesses, and the gun obviously wasn't yours."

Rem rubbed his eyes. "I think in this town, mere suspicion can get you thrown in jail. If somebody's trying to frame us, there's no telling what else Joe and Shaw have." He dropped his head and cursed. "Shit. I left my card at Scott's, and a dog walker saw me." He raised his head, his eyes weary. "That's a point in their favor."

"Maybe we're overreacting," said Daniels. "It could have been suicide."

"I hate to say this, but let's hope so," said Rem.

Unnerved, Daniels rested his head in his hands. "This is crazy."

"Now you understand why I want you here," said Ivy. "Someone is conspiring against you."

"We can't stay forever, Ivy," said Rem. "We don't have a choice. We still have to go back."

"If it isn't suicide, we have to clear our names and find out what the hell is going on," said Daniels.

"How are you going to do that if they arrest you?" asked Ivy.

Daniels sat up. "We'll have to get a hold of Lozano. Tell him what's going on. That way someone will be on our side in case they bring us in."

"How do you plan to investigate a crime in a town where everybody is going to think we're guilty?" asked Rem. "No one will talk to us. As much as I hate to admit it, we're going to have to rely on Joe to do his job."

"While crazy Shaw tries to convince him otherwise?" asked Daniels.

"Nice, huh?" asked Rem. He groaned. "Looks like going home isn't happening anytime soon."

"Don't forget the other threat," said Ivy. "I tried to get more clarity on the Magic Man in Merrimac, but he, or she, hides well. I'm certain there's something there, though. Something that is watching for you."

"No offense, Ivy," said Daniels, "but our Magic Man is the least of our problems."

"I think you're picking up on Deputy Shaw," added Rem. "That's guy's an asshole who's had it out for me since day one." He regarded Daniels. "He'd love to see us both take the rap for murder."

"If they don't find us," said Daniels said to Rem, "they'll think we took off. They could issue a warrant for our arrest."

"They may already have," said Rem. He grimaced and massaged his ribs. "Remind me next time I need to escape to check out Death Valley. I think I would have fared better there."

Daniels could only shake his head.

Chapter Twenty-Five

ON THE VERGE OF a scream, Remalla opened his eyes. Gasping and unsure of where he was, he blinked, seeing a dark room softly lit by oil lamps. Recognizing Ivy's house, he pushed the blanket away with a shaky hand and wiped his sweaty brow. The dream still fresh in his mind, he sat up, and his breath caught when his ribs pulled. Seeing Daniels asleep on the cot across the room, Rem stayed quiet and took a second to get his bearings.

Taking slow breaths, he recalled the previous evening after Ivy had told them about Scott's death. Daniels had helped Ivy clean the squirrels and prepare the meal while Rem took Ripley in search of more wood to burn in the stove. After everything had been prepared, they'd had a quiet but decent dinner despite Rem's reluctance about the squirrel meat. While eating, they'd discussed their plan to return to town the next day. He and Daniels would leave in the morning, go to their cars, drive to Gin's house and call Lozano. Then they'd find out what was happening with Scott's case. They would contact Sheriff Joe and answer any of his questions and trust him to handle the investigation. When Joe asked about where they'd been, they would tell him about Whit's message to Daniels and how Daniels had gone to the woods, ended up injured and lost and how Rem, after talking to Whit, had followed. After breaking his ribs, Rem had found Daniels and never having discovered a woman in the woods, they'd spent a night in the forest before finding their way out.

Satisfied with their plan, they'd gone to bed. Ivy had made up a pallet on the floor for Rem to sleep with enough cushion to support his ribs, and Daniels had brought in two oil lamps to ensure the room wasn't too dark.

Once settled in for the night and after Ivy had gone upstairs, they'd talked for a while until fatigue had set in and Daniels had begun to snore.

Rem had eventually drifted off, but the nightmares had returned. Still trying to shake off the dream, he wished he were home. If he had been, he would have gotten up and flipped on the TV, but he didn't have that option at Ivy's.

Daniels stirred and mumbled. "You awake?"

Rem rubbed his face. "Yeah. I'm fine, though. Go back to sleep."

Daniels opened an eye. "Nightmare?"

Tired, Rem sighed. "They'd stopped with the binge drinking, but I guess they're back."

Daniels opened the other eye. "Bad?"

"Not great."

Daniels sat up and swung his legs over the cot. He looked around the room. "What time is it?"

"Hell if I know."

Daniels arched and stretched with a groan. "Be glad you're not on this cot. I feel like I'm sleeping on rocks. He stood. "You want some water?"

"No. I'm good. Go back to sleep."

"I will, but I'm thirsty." He grabbed an oil lamp.

"Well, if you're getting some, then get me a glass, too."

"Okay." He took some steps toward the kitchen and stopped short. "Shit." He grabbed his chest.

Alarmed, Rem sat up and winced with the movement. "What is it?" He leaned to look.

"I almost tripped on the enormous wolf in the room."

"Where?" Rem squinted to see and made out the dark fur which blended into the wood floor. "Is that Ripley or Hicks?"

"I can't tell," whispered Daniels. "But he scared the hell out of me."

Rem looked closer. "She. I think that's Ripley." Ripley barely registered Daniels' presence when Daniels stepped around her and went into the kitchen.

Rem heard him move around and a minute later, he brought Rem a glass of water. "Thanks," said Rem.

Daniels returned to the kitchen and came back with the lamp and his own glass. He sat on the edge of the cot, drank from it and set it on the floor. Ripley continued to sleep. "How can she sleep through me moving around and over her, but she hears a squirrel a mile away and her fur raises?"

Rem gulped some water, thirstier than he expected. "You're not a threat and you're not food."

"I suppose." Daniels stifled a yawn. "How are your ribs?"

"They hurt. How's your head?"

"Okay." Daniels touched his injured forehead. "You want to talk about your nightmare?"

Rem shrugged. "It was extra special." He recalled the dream and shivered. "I was being chased through the woods. Someone was after me, but I couldn't see who it was. I kept running but couldn't go fast enough. Then I ended up in some clearing." He squeezed his temples, remembering the rest. "I saw Allison. She was holding a baby." He paused. "I stopped when I saw her." He cleared his throat and took a breath. "Then I saw you and Mikey. You two were on the other side of this clearing."

"What happened?"

"D'Mato ran out of the woods. He had big snarling teeth and he was holding a torch. He...uh...he told me to choose." Recalling the fear, he took a deeper breath. "One of you would die and I had to decide which."

"Hell."

"I couldn't do it, and Victor turned into a wolf and attacked Allison and the baby. That's when I woke up." He paused. "I guess this is what I can expect for the next six months...or longer."

"Maybe not. It's still fresh and you're trying to process it. Give it time."

"Mr. Positivity returns." Rem fluffed his pillow. "Maybe I should go back to drinking."

"You could," said Daniels, "but then your days would suck instead of your nights. Which do you prefer?" He picked up his glass. "And keep in mind. Your day job doesn't mesh well with the booze."

"That's why I keep you around. Your logic comes in handy."

"Once you get back, talk to the shrink again. Get back into a routine. Work some cases. It'll get better."

"And then the trial will start."

"But you'll be ready."

"And then the baby will be born..."

"We're not worried about that right now, remember? When we know more, then we'll deal with it."

Rem drained the rest of his water and held his glass. "One step at a time."

"One step at a time." Daniels finished his own water. "Let's try and get some sleep. I have a feeling morning will be here soon, and we're going to have a long day ahead of us."

"Let's hope it doesn't end with us in jail."

Daniels laid down and pulled the sheet up. "Let's hope we're in our own beds this time tomorrow.

Rem imagined being home. "That would be great." He pulled on the blanket and began to carefully lean back when Ripley sat up.

Rem stopped with a groan. "What is it, girl?"

Daniels looked over.

Ripley stood, stared at the door and began to growl.

Rem tensed, and Daniels raised up. "Something's got her spooked," he whispered.

Rem straightened and debated reaching for his gun. "What do we do?"

Daniels stood and walked toward the dog. Ripley continued to stare and growl. "What's out there, Rip?"

Rem's heart thudded. "You think we should—"

Ripley quieted and sat. She stared a second more, then lay back down and lowered her head.

"What the hell...?" asked Daniels.

Relieved, Rem rested his head back against the pillow. "Probably just an animal."

Daniels studied the door. "Yeah. Probably."

Rem listened but didn't hear anything. "We should try and get some sleep."

Daniels nodded, and after a pause, returned to the cot. "Probably a bear."

Rem put a hand on his forehead. "Thanks. That helps."

Daniels settled himself and pulled the sheet back up. "Whatever it was, it's gone now. And nothing's getting past Ripley. We're safe. Get some rest."

Rem blew out a breath. "I'll try."

"And no nightmares."

"Right. No nightmares." Seeing Ripley relax, Rem adjusted the blanket. He tried not to think about a bear wandering around outside. "Night."

Daniels turned on his side. "Night."

· · • • · • • · · ·

Daniels opened his eyes as sunlight brightened the room. Wondering what the day would bring, he yawned and pushed back the sheet. He'd slept fitfully after dreaming of being chased down the wooded trail by Scott and his buddies, all of which had red glowing eyes.

Grateful the sun was up, Daniels got out of bed, eager to start the day and get back to civilization despite where it might lead. Missing Marjorie and J.P., he hoped he'd see them soon. Stretching, he rubbed his eyes and ruffled his hair. Hearing Rem snore, he quietly left the room and went into the kitchen. Looking out the window, he saw the sun-dappled trees and the trickling brook in the distance. He searched for a towel, wanting to head down to the water to wash his face and clean up before they had breakfast and returned to town.

He opened the door and saw one of the dogs sleeping on the porch. "Morning," he whispered. The dog sat up. "You Ripley?" The dog didn't react. "Or Hicks?" The dog stood, and Daniels smiled. "Hicks it is."

A basket of apples was sitting on the front steps, and Daniels figured Ivy had taken Ripley in search of food for breakfast. He grabbed the basket, brought it inside, grabbed an apple, then picked up his towel and went outside.

"Care for a walk, Hicks?" He stepped onto the dirt and strode toward the stream, taking bites of the apple along the way. Hicks whined, and Daniels bit off a few bites and fed them to the dog, who eagerly ate them.

Once at the stream, he wet the towel and washed his face, neck and chest, wiped his hair back and combed it with his fingers. Feeling more awake and refreshed, he put his shirt back on, tossed the apple core and returned to the house. Hicks reclaimed his spot on the porch, and Daniels went inside.

Rem stood at the stove, heating some water.

"Morning," said Daniels.

"Morning," said Rem with a yawn. "You're up early."

"It's the fresh air," said Daniels. "It's invigorating." A trickle of sweat ran down his neck and he wiped it away. "How do you feel? Any more nightmares?"

Rem hovered over the kettle as if willing it to boil. "Feel okay. No more nightmares, and I slept better than I thought. Ribs still hurt, but I'm not complaining. Sleeping in that jail cell was a lot worse." He found the canister with the coffee grounds and opened it. "I'm making coffee. You want some?"

"Sure," said Daniels, wiping off another trickle of sweat. "Is it hot in here to you?"

"No, actually. I'm a little cool. I'm glad Ivy gave me that extra blanket." He scooped grounds into the pitcher.

Daniels opened the front door to get some air. The room almost felt claustrophobic. "I think I just need a breeze."

"You seen Ivy?" asked Rem.

"No. I'm sure she's out with Rip looking for food."

"I wouldn't mind some more of those eggs," said Rem. "Those were good."

Recalling the eggs from the previous morning, Daniels' belly churned. He held it and wiped a trickle of sweat from his brow.

"You okay?" asked Rem.

Daniels straightened. "Yeah. I think I'm still dealing with some concussion aftereffects. I'm sure it will fade."

"I hope so. We've got a long walk ahead of us today." He took the kettle off the heat and added the steaming water to the pitcher. "And God knows what else after that." He closed his eyes. "I'm praying I don't end up back in that cell." He opened his eyes, set the kettle down, and found the coffee mugs.

"Let's not assume the worst," said Daniels, sitting in one of the chairs. He pulled at his shirt to get more air on his skin. "I've decided that Ivy's got us freaking out over this whole Magic Man theory or whatever it is that's out to get us. I bet Joe's already figured out what happened to Scott, and we'll be on our way home this afternoon." He dabbed his forehead with his shirt sleeve. "If you're lucky, you may even get another one of

Gin's brownies before we head out." At the mention of brownies, Daniels' stomach gurgled.

"Don't tease me," said Rem.

A dog woofed, and Daniels saw Ripley bound up to the porch and sit beside Hicks, who continued to lie on the porch. Ivy entered the house carrying a small bag. "Good morning."

"Morning," said Rem.

"Morning," said Daniels, blinking. Everything had gone blurry for a moment, but then his vision returned to normal. What was the matter with him?

She laid the bag down. "I found some fruit, plus plucked some vegetables from the garden. We can eat them with the eggs," she said. "You two still planning on leaving today?"

"That's the plan," said Rem. He picked up one of the apples from the basket on the table. "You can save the veggies for Daniels, but I'll have one of these." He raised it to his mouth but Ivy swatted it away before he could take a bite. The apple hit the floor with a thud, and it rolled into a corner. "What the hell?" asked Rem. "You got something against apples?"

"Where did you get those?" asked Ivy as she grabbed the basket. "These don't grow here. Where did they come from?"

Daniels held his stomach as it churned some more. "They were on the front steps."

"Front steps?" Ivy looked outside and stared, then turned, her face white. "Did you eat one?" She eyed Daniels and squatted next to him.

His mouth dry, Daniels tried to swallow. "On the way to the brook. I gave Hicks a few bites, too." Daniels exhaled slowly as more sweat popped out on his skin.

Her eyes widened.

"What is going on?" asked Rem. He came around the table and studied Daniels. "You're sweating worse than me after Lozano threatens to cut my hair." He pulled a chair over and sat. "You look terrible."

Ivy ran outside. She knelt next to Hicks, who didn't move, and put her hand on him. Her face fell and she returned to Daniels and put her palm on his forehead. "You're both feverish."

"I've felt better," Daniels whispered. "Stomach hurts." He wiped more sweat from his brow.

"Can you stand?" asked Ivy. She stood and went to the water basin where she wet a towel and brought it over. She wiped Daniels' face with it.

"I think so," said Daniels. His body began to shake with chills. "But not sure for how long."

"You want to tell me what's happening?" asked Rem, his face a mask of concern. "He was just fine a few minutes ago."

"Help me get him back to bed," said Ivy, grabbing Daniels' arm.

Daniels attempted to get up, but his legs wobbled. Rem held his other arm and supported him back to the cot. Daniels sat and laid down. Ivy covered him with blankets, and he shook some more although his body felt like it was on fire. "What's happening to me?" whispered Daniels.

Ivy sat on the edge of the bed, dabbed his face with the wet cloth and rested it on his forehead. "It's the apples."

Rem pulled a chair over and sat. "What's wrong with the apples?"

"They didn't come from me," said Ivy.

"Were they there when you left this morning?" asked Rem.

"I went out the back door to the garden, so I don't know."

"Well, if you didn't put them there, then who did?" asked Rem.

Instead of answering, Ivy held Daniels' hand and went still.

Daniels closed his eyes and tried to relax, but the shivers worsened, his throat hurt, and it was hard to swallow.

"Ivy?" asked Rem. "Are you saying someone left poisoned apples on your porch for us to eat?"

Daniels moaned when a cramp shot through his stomach. He couldn't remember feeling this bad since he'd eaten his sister's pasta with white clam sauce. "Who?" he managed to ask.

Ivy stared off, her face flat, then blinked and seemed to come back to the present. She hesitated before regarding Daniels. "Someone with enough capabilities to walk up to the house without alerting me or the dogs." She pursed her lips. "I underestimated our nemesis. They must have been waiting by the cars yesterday and followed me back. I never sensed them."

Rem eyed Daniels. "Ripley. Last night. She heard something."

Daniels nodded, not able to do much else.

Ivy widened her eyes. "What happened?"

Rem told her about Ripley growling at the door earlier that morning.

Ivy shook her head. "They were out there."

"You're scaring me, Ivy," said Rem. "What exactly are we dealing with here? Daniels is going to be okay, isn't he?"

When she didn't answer, Daniels gripped her hand. He wanted to push the blankets down to cool off but didn't have the strength. Another chill rippled through him, and some innate sense told Daniels he was in trouble. "Tell him," he whispered.

Ivy bit her lip and looked at Rem. "I don't think so, Detective."

• • • • • • • • • •

Rem heard her and almost laughed. "You don't think so? What do you mean you don't think so? It's a damn apple." He stood, ignoring the flare of pain in his side.

"It's not just an apple," said Ivy.

Rem began to pace. "Then tell me what it is, so we can fix it."

"It's not that simple," she said.

"What is this? Some sort of Sleeping Beauty nightmare?" He jutted out a hand and stood over Ivy. "What are you telling me? He's going to die?"

"Rem," whispered Daniels. His cheeks were flushed and a drop of sweat slid down his neck. "This isn't her fault."

"I don't give a shit about fault," said Rem. "I just need to know what to do." He paced again, his muscles tense and his fear rising. He sat again. "Just tell me what he needs. Whatever it is, I'll do it."

Ivy's eyes watered. "I want to fix this, too. Hicks isn't any better off. I can't lose him."

Frustrated, Rem clenched his fingers together. "Then let's make sure we don't." He told himself to stay calm. "He ate a stupid apple. You can't tell me he won't get better. That's crazy." He ran his hands through his hair. "Think, Ivy. Whoever did this isn't all-powerful and all-knowing. They must have a weakness. What is it?"

Ivy studied Daniels who winced and blew out a breath. "I can only tell you what I sense," she said. "And it isn't good. If it were just poison, I might be able to help, but it's more than that. By eating the apple, your partner opened a link between him and the one who brought the basket. That link is what's making him and Hicks sick. Whether it's the Magic

Man or something else, they're strong enough to use that link to…" She rubbed her forehead.

"To what?" asked Rem.

"…to break them down physically," she said. "This is just the start. The longer the link is open and the person doing this has access, it will only get worse. Their bodies will begin to weaken and then their organs will shut down and…and…" She dropped her head.

"I get the point," said Rem, trying not to think about it. "So all we need to do is break the link. How do we that? There has to be a way."

Ivy straightened, closed her eyes, opened them and stared off for a second. "I can't do it from here. I'm not strong enough to challenge whoever this is."

"Then I'll do it. Just tell me how," said Rem sitting on the edge of his seat.

Ivy hesitated. "From what I'm feeling, only those on either side of the link can break it, so that's Daniels, or the one who created it, who's unknown."

"Great. So how do we do that?" asked Rem.

She aimed a sharp gaze at Rem. "You want the hard truth?"

Rem glared back. "What else would I want?"

She spoke flatly. "The only way to sever it is death. You're going to have to kill whoever is on the other side to save your partner, unless he dies first."

Chapter Twenty-Six

REM DIDN'T MOVE BUT his mind raced. He looked at Daniels who blinked at him with bleary eyes, and Rem made his decision. "Okay," he said with resoluteness. "Who do I kill?"

"No," whispered Daniels. "You can't..."

"Mind your business. You let me handle this," said Rem. He narrowed his eyes at Ivy. "Who?"

"Rem, please—" said Daniels.

"Shhh," said Rem. "I'm talking to Ivy."

Ivy's shoulders dropped. "That's just it. I don't know who."

Daniels appeared to relax.

"Then how do we find out?" asked Rem. "If what you're saying is accurate, then whoever this is has to be emitting some serious energy to maintain the link and transmit whatever crap they're directing at Daniels. That has to be a big signal. How do we locate it?"

Ivy shook her head. "I haven't been able to determine the source." She paused. "There may be another way, though."

"What is it?" asked Rem. He clutched his hands together, eager to do something.

Ivy picked up the cloth and wiped Daniels' face again. "The link goes both ways. By keeping it open, the creator makes themselves vulnerable as well."

"Can we poison them, too?" asked Rem, hopeful.

"No. Daniels doesn't have that ability, but what he can do is focus enough to pick up on who is on the other side. If he concentrates, he may be able to see who it is, but it may weaken him. He'll have to move quickly."

Rem made eye contact with Daniels. "What does he have to do?"

Daniels shivered, and Ivy pulled up the covers. "Can you close your eyes and be still?" she asked Daniels. "Let your mind relax until you're almost in a sleep state. I can help to guide you. I'll hold your hand and try to ease the discomfort as much as I can until you can engage with the other side."

Daniels swallowed with a grimace, and Rem stood and went into the kitchen. He filled a glass with water and brought it back to his partner. "You thirsty?"

Daniels nodded, and Rem helped him sit up and handed him the glass. Daniels drank almost all of it, and Rem lowered him back down. "Better?"

"A little," said Daniels, his voice shaky.

"Can you try to connect?" asked Rem. "I need to know who's doing this."

"I'm not sure I want to," said Daniels. His gaze focused on Rem, and Rem understood his concern.

"You let me worry about the bad guy, okay?" said Rem. "I just need you to tell me who he is."

"You're going to kill him." Daniels set his jaw and moaned. "I can't let you throw away your life to save mine."

"That's not up to you," said Rem. "This is my decision. I know what I'm doing, and I accept responsibility. Don't lie there and tell me you wouldn't do the same for me."

"And you'd try and stop me," said Daniels, his voice weakening.

Desperate, Rem tried to think of what to say. "But I'd fail, just like you will. Stop thinking the worst and help me out, partner. I'm not going to sit here and watch you die. I'd rather go to prison."

"And I couldn't live with my myself knowing you'd be in that prison because of me." Daniels shivered again. "Don't make me do that."

"If I'm in prison, then at least we'll both be alive. You can visit me on the weekends."

"That's not funny," said Daniels.

"I know," said Rem, "but keep in mind, I doubt whoever's doing this will stop with you. I'll be next on the list. This is saving both of us."

Ivy dabbed Daniels' forehead and cheeks with the wet towel. "If we're going to try, it has to be now. He's getting weaker."

Rem squatted next to Daniels. "Listen to me, you idiot. You have to help me. I swear I'll do my best not to kill anyone. I promise I'll try and break the link without violence. Do you trust me enough to try and save your life without losing my own?"

His eyes watery, Daniels blinked at Rem. "You swear on Jennie's soul? If you can't do this without breaking the law, then don't do it."

Rem bit back a curse. "You're so damn obstinate." He shut his eyes. "Fine." He opened his eyes. "I promise. I'll find a way without breaking the law. Now relax and focus."

Daniels hesitated. "If you're lying to me, I'll haunt you forever."

"I'll take the risk. Now close your eyes."

After a pause, Daniels settled into the pillow, and Ivy wiped the sweat from his skin. "Relax," she said. "Empty your mind and let yourself go."

With a last glance at Rem, Daniels closed his eyes. Anxious, Rem bit his lip.

"Take it easy," Ivy's soothing voice helped Rem relax, too, and he returned to his seat to wait. Ivy continued. "I want you to take a long deep breath and allow the pain to fade." She paused. "It's in the background, and you can barely feel it."

Daniels breathed in and out.

"Put yourself somewhere beautiful," said Ivy, squeezing his hand. "You're with your wife and child. You're happy and peaceful."

Rem bounced his foot.

Ivy continued to talk, easing Daniels into a cocoon of his own making, surrounded by happy memories and better times.

"Now," said Ivy. "When you're ready, look around and find the tunnel. It's emitting beautiful light, and it attracts you. Walk toward it."

Daniels' eyelids clenched.

"Don't worry. It's safe. Do you see it?" she asked.

"Yes," Daniels whispered.

"Step into the tunnel," said Ivy, "and let it carry you. You're light as a feather, and you float. Follow the tunnel until you reach the other side."

Daniels' breathing slowed, and his grip on Ivy's hand appeared to ease. Rem wished he could do something but told himself to stay put.

"Are you at the end of the tunnel?" asked Ivy. "Squeeze my hand if you are."

Daniels squeezed.

"Good," said Ivy. "I want you to look around. Study what you see. Are you looking?"

Daniels squeezed her hand again.

"Memorize it to bring back with you." Ivy paused. "Do you see a person?"

Daniels jerked and moaned.

Rem slid to the edge of his seat. "What is it? What's wrong?"

Daniels jerked again.

"Remember, you're safe," said Ivy, although her face reflected worry. "They can't hurt you."

Daniels tensed. "Get me out," he whispered.

Rem came off his seat. "Get him out."

Ivy leaned in. "Follow the sound of my voice. Go back to the tunnel. Stay relaxed. Find the tunnel."

Daniels whimpered. "Where is it? I can't see it."

"It's full of light," said Ivy. "Only you can access it. Jump on and it will take you. It's right in front of you. Stop searching and let it find you."

Daniels clenched her hand. "I see it."

"Get on, Detective," said Ivy. "Right now."

The room suddenly felt oppressive as if energy had begun to build. Rem started to sweat. "Get on, Daniels," he said. "Move it."

Daniels began to breathe heavily as if he were running. "She sees me."

"Go to the tunnel," said Rem. "Forget her. You're faster. Run and jump on. Hurry."

Daniels panted and more sweat poured down his face. "I'm there. I'm on."

"Ride it back," said Ivy. "It's okay now. You're coming back to us. No one can hurt you. You're light and free and relaxed."

The strange vibe in the room began to dissipate, Daniels' rigid body softened, and Rem exhaled. "Are you back?" he asked. "Daniels?" He jostled his partner's shoulders.

Daniels grunted and opened his eyes. He blinked as if confused. "Rem?"

"I'm right here." Rem leaned over him. "You okay?"

Daniels eyed him with worry. "Am I back?"

"You are," said Ivy. "Do you remember anything?"

Agitated, Daniels tried to sit up. "I saw her. I know who it is."

"Take it easy," said Rem, trying to ease Daniels back down. "Who?" he asked. "Who did you see?"

"Ru...Rudy's girlfriend." Daniels trembled. "My God, Rem. It...It's Ginger."

Chapter Twenty-Seven

"WHO'S GINGER?" ASKED IVY.

Rem stared in dismay and horror. Why hadn't they considered that? "Are you sure?"

"I'm sure." Daniels fell back against the pillow.

"Who is she?" asked Ivy again.

Rem pushed back in his seat, remembering the woman who'd spiked his coffee at the police station. "On our last case, Daniels and I recently encountered a kidnapper and murderer named Rudy who had some crazy abilities of his own. He could manipulate electricity. He'd targeted us, but we'd figured out how to stop him, and Daniels shot him." He aimed a glance at Daniels. "You saved me, remember?"

"That was different," said Daniels, his skin beaded with sweat.

"Rudy was Ginger's mentor," said Rem to Ivy. "She had similar abilities and was just as dangerous, but he'd abused her. We never caught her and we'd assumed after Rudy's death she'd move on and maybe enjoy her newfound freedom, but apparently we were wrong." He dropped his head and gripped his temples. "Ginger's pissed. She must have followed me to Merrimac." He sighed. "But how in the hell is she capable of doing this?"

"Many with abilities have more than just one," said Ivy. "Rudy either taught her more than you realize, or she had another mentor." She wiped Daniels' face again.

"You can't fight her," said Daniels, gripping the blanket, his face blazing with heat.

"We thought the same about Rudy." Rem looked up. "But we stopped him."

Daniels cleared his throat but he still whispered. "We were working together and had a plan. You're doing this on your own. Rudy wasn't easy to kill, and Ginger won't be any different. It could be worse." Another trickle of sweat ran down his neck. "She's probably waiting for you, knowing you'll come."

"Then let's not disappoint her." Rem took hold of the armrests and paused. "How do I find her?" he asked Ivy.

"Rem...don't...," said Daniels.

"Be quiet and rest," said Rem. He waited for Ivy to answer.

Ivy looked between them. "I don't know, but Daniels might." She adjusted the blankets and spoke to Daniels. "What did you see after you left the tunnel other than Ginger? Any indication of where she could be?"

Daniels looked away.

Rem almost cursed and set his jaw, knowing what Daniels was doing. "Ivy, can I have a few minutes with him?"

Ivy nodded and reached for the glass and the cloth. "I'll check on Hicks, get you some more water and re-wet this."

"Thanks," said Rem.

Ivy stood, and Rem took her place beside the bed. Daniels continued to stare at the wall as more sweat beaded on his skin. "You need to tell me where she is," said Rem.

Daniels looked back. "It's a death sentence. You know that."

"And you're not already dying?"

"Better it's just one and not both of us."

"Ginger is not going to stop with you. I'll be next."

Daniels tried to push the blanket down. "Maybe, but at least you'll have some time to plan how to stop her. This...this is just running into a wildfire with no water."

"You really expect me to make a plan against Ginger if you're dead?" Rem pulled Daniels' blanket back up. "I've made it through a lot, but that will be the last straw. I'll welcome her arrival."

"No, you won't," Daniels whispered. "It'll be hard, but I need you to watch over Marjorie and J.P. That will keep you going."

Rem swallowed back a lump in his throat. "That's exactly why I have to do this. You have a wife and kid. I can't look Marjorie in the eye if I didn't do everything in my power to protect her husband and J.P.'s dad." He softened his voice. "You have to understand that."

"And if we both die?" asked Daniels.

"Don't count me out yet. I'm doing this to prevent both our deaths. If I can stop Ginger, we can both go home, but it can't wait. You're declining fast. I need to know what you saw."

Daniels sucked in a breath with a shiver and clenched his eyes shut. Rem found his hand and gripped it. "You realize you're doing exactly what you don't want me to do," said Rem. "Dying to protect me."

The shiver passed, and Daniels' tension eased. He opened his eyes and spoke with a shaky voice. "I like being the hero."

"You've been the hero enough," said Rem. "You've gotten me through some rough spots. Give me the chance to get you through this." His throat tightened and he cleared it. "Please trust me. We've always found a way before. I'll find a way again."

Daniels hesitated. "God, you drive me nuts."

"And I intend to continue that, but not if you don't tell me what you know."

Daniels held Rem's gaze. "If this doesn't work, and I don't make it, but you do, I want you to keep on living, okay? Take the time to grieve but don't give up on life. Find Mikey and tell her how you feel. Be happy." He squeezed Rem's hand. "Promise me."

Rem fought to hold it together. "Shit."

"Rem..."

Rem groaned. "Fine. I promise."

A few seconds passed, and Daniels sighed. "There was a hummingbird."

Relief coursed through Rem. "What else?" Daniels' grip tightened on Rem's hand, and he shuddered. "Take it easy," said Rem.

Daniels exhaled. "A trellis with roses...and...a blue rock. It sparkled in the sun." He paused. "I don't remember anything else.

Rem nodded, knowing it wasn't much. "Okay. That's something to go on." He put his free hand over Daniels' fingers. "You stay here and watch over Ivy and the dogs, okay?"

Daniels almost smiled. "I will." He blinked watery eyes. "You be careful."

Thinking of his situation, Rem released his own shaky breath. "Listen... before I go...I have a crazy request..."

"What?" Daniels looked like he could barely stay awake.

"If...if...something happens and I don't make it, but you do..."

"Rem..."

"Just listen." Rem bit his lip, wondering if he was doing the right thing. "I know you're unsure about another kid, but if Allison's baby is mine..." His voice caught.

Daniels' eyes briefly widened, and he nodded. "I hear you." His grip weakened. "I'll fight like hell to take care of your child."

Grateful and realizing this could be their last talk, Rem sniffed. "Thank you."

"Try not to die, though. Okay?" asked Daniels, his voice barely audible.

"You, too," said Rem.

Daniels closed his eyes and released his grip. Letting his partner rest, Rem extricated his hand and wiped at his eyes.

Ivy returned with a glass of water and a fresh cloth. "I'll watch out for him," she said. "But you need to hurry." She set the glass down and composing himself, Rem stood.

"I don't suppose a hummingbird, a trellis of roses and a sparkly blue stone remind you of anything?" he asked, looking for the clothes he'd cleaned in the stream the previous day.

"No, they don't." Ivy sat beside Daniels and dabbed at his face with the cloth. "But my advice is to follow your gut. It will tell you where to go."

"I don't think I have much choice." Rem began to gather his things.

"There's something I want to give you, Detective." Ivy laid the wet cloth on Daniels' forehead.

Rem changed into his own shirt. "Please tell me it's something good." He sat to put on his shoes.

She stood, walked over, and reached into her skirt pocket. She pulled out a small glass tube with a stopper.

"What's that?" Rem got his shoes on, grabbed his jacket and slid it on.

"Rain berry juice." She shook it and Rem could see clear liquid inside. "One drop will help you sleep...but the whole thing..." Holding his gaze, she held it out to him. "Use it as you wish. The juice won't be detected in the bloodstream."

Rem hesitated. He stared at the tube, a myriad of conflicting emotions running through him. Was he really about to find and kill Ginger? And would this juice even work against her?"

Ivy didn't wait for a response. She opened his jacket and slid the tube into his inside pocket. "It's just between you and me."

Rem didn't argue. "Thanks."

She nodded. "And one more thing..."

He held his aching ribs. "I'm afraid to ask."

"I meditated this morning, to try and learn more about what was happening in town," she said, her voice somber. "I spoke with Whit."

Rem found his gun and tucked it into his waistband. "How's Whit doing? Hopefully he's better than us."

She paused. "He had bad news."

"Why am I surprised?" asked Rem. "What is it?"

"A warrant has been issued for your and Daniels' arrest for Scott's murder. You're now a fugitive, Detective."

• • • • • • • • • •

Rem raced through the woods, but in the opposite direction of his car. After Ivy had told him about the warrant, he'd had to rethink his options. He couldn't drive his own vehicle because he'd be picked up by Shaw or Joe in no time. If he got arrested, Daniels would die. He had to find Ginger first and then he could worry about jail.

Ivy offered him her car that she'd hidden in the woods not far from the house. She'd given him directions, made him a quick peanut butter and jelly sandwich and tossed that and a thermos of water in a bag. Giving him the bag and her car keys, she'd wished him luck and he took off, running as fast as he could despite his damaged ribs.

Finding the landmarks she'd mentioned, he turned and almost ran right by the car. Because it was covered by branches and shrubs, he'd almost missed it. He quickly uncovered it, seeing it was an old four-door sedan and hopped in. Giving thanks when the engine turned over easily, he backed out. After seeing the narrow-rutted path that led out of the woods, he took it. It wasn't long before he spotted the two-lane road that led back to Merrimac. Before he turned onto it, though, he stopped and wondered where to go. How was he supposed to find a hummingbird, rose trellis and a blue rock?

His gut provided the only sensible start. He'd have to go to Aunt Gin's. She'd know better than anyone if those three things made sense. He'd have to be careful though, because Joe or Shaw would likely be watching for him.

Making up his mind, he made the turn and headed toward Merrimac.

Chapter Twenty-Eight

REM APPROACHED AUNT GIN'S street and keeping an eye out, he slowed at the intersection and stopped. Looking down the quiet road, he saw exactly what he feared. A police cruiser was parked not far from Gin's house underneath a large tree. He couldn't tell who was behind the wheel, but whoever it was, they were obviously waiting for him and Daniels. Did they actually expect them to just pull up to the house if they'd been trying to hide?

Debating his next steps, Rem turned in the opposite direction and found another side street that led to the road behind his aunt's. Staying alert, he found the alley where the trashmen accessed the trash bins and stopped at the curb beside it. Not wanting to get stuck in case he was spotted, he left the car and walked down the alley, doing his best to stay out of sight. The last thing he needed was to be caught by a nosy neighbor.

A dog barked, and he crouched beside a bin. When no one emerged, he resumed his walk until he made it to his aunt's back gate. Approaching it, he listened for any voices or sounds but hearing nothing, he popped the gate open, slid inside, and closed it. He carefully walked through the backyard and eyed the small guest home behind the main house, hoping whoever had stayed for the weekend had checked out. He saw no one though and stepped up to the porch. Peering through the glass of the rear door, he eyed the kitchen. It was empty and he tried the door, but it was locked.

Saying a desperate prayer that he wouldn't be caught by a guest, he softly knocked. There was no movement and he wondered if Gin was home, and if she wasn't, what would he do?

He knocked again and this time, a woman poked her head around the corner, and he recognized his aunt. Her eyes widened and her mouth opened, and she hurried toward the door and opened it.

"Aaron," she said. "What are you doing?"

Rem slid inside. "Hey, Aunt Gin."

She closed the door. "They're looking for you. Do you know that?"

"I heard." He looked around the house ensuring no one was there.

"Are you okay?" she asked. "Why the cryptic text yesterday? I was worried sick about you and Gordon." She looked toward the back. "Where's Gordon?"

Rem tried not to think of his sick partner back at Ivy's. "He's not doing too well."

Gin's face fell. "What is going on? Where have you been? You know they believe you and Gordon killed Scott? They think you both took off after murdering him and now Shaw's trying to convince Joe that you were both involved in Sharon's death. I tried to talk to Joe about how that was ridiculous, but he won't listen to me. He said his hands are tied, but he's willing to listen if you turn yourself in." She paused and watched Rem pace. "Why are you holding your chest? Are you hurt?"

"I'm okay. It's not serious."

She waited. "Are you going to turn yourself in?"

Rem stopped pacing. "Listen, Aunt Gin. I need your help."

Her eyes widened more. "Oh, my God. You didn't actually kill him, did you?"

Rem almost moaned and flinched when his ribs flared. He'd barely felt them on his trip over. "No. We didn't kill Scott."

Her gaze narrowed. "You're in pain."

"It's just a couple of broken ribs. No big deal."

"Aaron, you should sit." She pulled out a chair. "You're scaring me."

Rem shook his head. "I can't sit. I need to ask you something." He paused. "It's important."

Gin wrung her hands. "What is it?"

He hesitated, wondering what to say. "I need to find someone. Daniels' life, and maybe my own, depends on it."

Her jaw dropped. "What on earth?" She shook her head. "Where is Gordon? What's wrong? Is he in the hospital?"

Rem bit back his impatience. "I can't explain it right now. Time is running short. But I will tell you that there is a woman named Ginger who is targeting us. It has to do with a previous case Daniels and I were on. She's angry, holding a grudge and capable of doing a lot of damage. She made Daniels sick and if I don't find her and stop her, he's going to die." He put a hand on the counter and gripped it, painfully aware of the passing time.

She stammered. "How...how am I supposed to help?"

"I have some clues but have no idea where to start." He paused. "I know it sounds strange, but I'm looking for a hummingbird, a rose-covered trellis and a blue rock. Do you have any idea where I might find those things together in Merrimac?"

She furrowed her brow and put her hand on the back of the chair. "Aaron...I..."

"Aunt Gin, please," he said, his worry growing. "Just try. You're the only one I can think of who might know. If you don't..." He held his breath, feeling his fear rise. "I don't...don't..." Terrified he'd reached a dead end, he dropped his head, finding it hard to speak.

"The Miller's bed and breakfast."

Rem shot his head up. "What?" A small kernel of hope bloomed.

She nodded. "The Miller's open their house to their guests, but they live in a small cottage in the back of the property. I've been there before. They have a trellis with roses, a hummingbird feeder, and a blue rock on their back patio." She stepped forward. "But why does it matter? I don't even think they're home now. I remember them saying they were going on vacation after the festival ended."

"Could they still have guests in their house?" Rem's heart thudded. Was Ginger staying at the Miller's B and B?

"I...I don't know," she said, breathless. "I suppose they could if they hired someone to help."

Rem searched for a paper and pen. "What's their address?"

"Aaron, are you sure you should go alone? Let me call Joe—"

"No," yelled Rem. She jumped, and he softened his voice. "I can't take the risk of getting arrested. And this could endanger Joe. I have to go alone." He found a notebook and pencil near the phone.

"I don't like this. How will I know you're safe?"

"You won't. Not until I take care of her."

Her face paled. "Who is this Ginger? Why is she so dangerous?"

Rem sighed. "I wish I had the time to tell you, but I don't. You'll have to trust that I know what I'm doing." He held out the notebook and pencil. "Just tell me where I'm going."

Aunt Gin stared, her gaze darting between Rem's eyes and his hands. After a pause, and with trembling fingers, she reached for the notebook.

· · · · ● · ● · ● · ·

Rem pulled up to the Miller's bed and breakfast and parked. He took a few minutes to study the house, trying to get a feel for its layout. He looked up and down the street but didn't see any police cars or unmarked vehicles. Feeling more comfortable, he opened the car door and got out. Trying to act casual, he walked up the front steps and knocked. The Millers had met Daniels before when he'd questioned them about Sonya and Scott's supposed phone call, but they hadn't met Rem, so he hoped they would talk to him. He knocked again, but no one answered.

Anxious, he eyed the neighborhood. He didn't see anyone around or any prying eyes at the neighbors' windows. Hopeful he wasn't being watched, he stepped around the side of the house. Spotting a wooden gate, he walked up to it and tried the latch. It opened, and with a last look to ensure no one saw him, he slipped into the backyard and closed the gate behind him.

Standing still, he listened for any indication that someone was around. Hearing only silence, he took quiet steps toward the yard. Peering around the side of the house, he saw a large porch and a small cottage behind it. Blue curtains covered the cottage windows and there was a small outdoor sitting area to the side of it.

Rem tried to go slow, but he wanted to run into the house to find Ginger. He stopped himself though, realizing he'd have to be careful. Remembering Ginger's abilities, he would only have a brief window of opportunity in which she would be vulnerable. He patted his jacket pocket, feeling the glass tube Ivy had given him, wondering if he could use the juice against Ginger. He thought of Rudy. If Rem could manipulate

Ginger the way he and Daniels had Rudy, then he and Daniels might just make it out of this alive. He patted his waistband, feeling his gun.

Saying a small prayer for guidance, he stepped out into the yard. Big windows at the back of the house made him hesitate, and he slid up to the side of one of them. He peeked in, but the house was dark and quiet. He didn't see anybody.

Taking a breath, he moved forward, passed the windows, and stepped up to the back door. His heart pounding, he turned the knob, but it was locked. Looking inside, he could see an alarm panel on the wall. A red light glowed from it and Rem cursed. The Millers had an alarm, and it was set. He couldn't go inside without alerting the neighborhood and the police.

Frustrated, he realized just as quickly that if someone were inside, the alarm probably wouldn't be on. Gin had said the Millers had left town. Was the B and B closed? Did that mean Ginger wasn't here? Uncertain and anxious, Rem paced along the back porch. She had to be there. His aunt had said she'd recognized the hummingbird, trellis and rock. Spying the cottage, Rem stopped. He stepped down the porch steps and approached the small side yard beside the cottage.

Looking around, he frowned. He didn't see a hummingbird feeder, the trellis along the gate was bare of flowers, and the only rocks were the pebbles that lined the steppingstones leading to a small garden.

Confused, Rem looked some more but couldn't find anything that matched Daniels' description. Had Gin given him the wrong bed and breakfast? Had she been thinking of someone else?

Dismayed and scared that time was running out, he ran out of the yard and back to his car. Determined to figure out what the hell was going on, he headed back to his aunt's.

• • • • • • • • • •

Daniels shivered and moaned. His body felt like thousands of needles pricked at him, and all he wanted to do was curl into a ball against the pain and cry.

Something cold and wet touched his forehead, and he forced his eyes open. He saw a blurry image of a woman and wondered where Rem was.

Was Marjorie here? Was she trying to help him? He whimpered when another searing cramp tore through his gut.

"Shhh," said a female voice. "Breathe and try to relax." She wiped the cool cloth over his skin.

"Marjorie?" He blinked, and she came into focus, but it wasn't his wife. "Wh...where's Marjorie? Where's Rem?" Sticky with sweat, he tried to remember where he was.

"I'm Ivy," she said. Her soft voice soothed him. "Your wife's at home, and Rem's looking for Ginger. Remember?"

Hearing the names, the memories returned, and he moaned again. "Is he back?"

"No," she said. "You want some water?" She held his head, and he tried to take a drink, but he choked and coughed. "Go slow," she said. He managed a few sips, and she lowered his head back to the pillow. "Hicks won't drink much either." Her eyes weary, she set the glass down.

Having a brief moment of clarity, Daniels turned his head to see Hicks lying on the floor while Ripley sat beside and sniffed him, as if waiting for him to get up and play. His chest hurting, Daniels took a labored breath. "I'm sorry about the dog," he managed to say. "I didn't know."

She stepped away to check on Hicks and pet his head, then returned to sit beside Daniels. "It's not your fault." Her eyes watered, and she swiped at one of them.

Seeing her somber face, Daniels knew his time was short. His mind fought to stay conscious. "It's getting close, isn't it?"

She sniffed and nodded. "You're getting worse."

Fear bubbled up. He wasn't ready to die, and he didn't want to be alone. "Stay with me."

"I will. I won't leave you." She blotted the sweat from his face.

He swallowed and needed a distraction. "Can you talk to me?"

She stilled and put the cloth back on his head. "About what?"

He blinked again when she went out of focus. "Tell me about your family."

Adjusting his covers, she smiled softly. "There's not much to tell."

"You have one, don't you?"

"I do."

Sensing her hesitancy, he raised his trembling hand, and she took it. "I just need to hear your voice. It makes me feel better," he said.

She looked away. "It's complicated, and there are things I'm not proud of."

He sucked in a breath when his stomach knotted. "I think your secrets are safe with me," he whispered once the pain faded.

She studied him and squeezed his hand. "You may think less of me. My secrets might shock you. I've never been an easy person to live with, not even as a child."

"I'm not one to judge, especially now."

Sighing, she paused, but then started to talk. Daniels focused in on her voice, trying to stay connected to the here and now. He listened as she spoke of her past and her mother and father. Struggling to stay conscious, he drifted in and out, hearing some things but not all, and not sure he believed others. His muddled mind tried to grasp everything, but he found it more and more difficult.

She quieted and then offered him more water, but he declined. He had so many questions but didn't have the ability to ask them. "Thank you," he said.

She nodded. "You're welcome."

Thinking of Ivy's revelations, he couldn't help but think of Rem, and Daniels wished he'd said more to his partner. He did his best to summon enough energy to speak. "I know you're trying to hide from the world, but I need to ask you a favor." He paused and clenched her hand when the needles became knives. He gritted his teeth and fought through it until the pain eased and he could continue. "If Rem doesn't make it either, I need you to tell my wife and son that I love them." He shook with sadness, finding it hard to believe he was having this conversation. His emotions surfaced and he fought back tears. "They need to know I was thinking of them at the end. They're the best thing that ever happened to me."

She sniffed and wiped away a tear that ran down her cheek. "I'll find a way to get the message to them. I promise."

"Thank you," he said, barely able to finish. Fighting to breathe, he whispered. "And if he does make it, tell Rem I love him, too."

Her tears falling faster, she took the cloth and dabbed at his face again. "He already knows, Detective, but I'll tell him."

He wished he could say more. His chest tightening, he shuddered and moaned. Sensing he was close to the end, he thought of his family, sad that they would have to grieve for him, and prayed his partner would know that he'd held on as long as he could.

More needles jabbed at him, and he gripped the sheet, his joints throbbing with tension. Everything hurt, his bones ached, his head pounded, and his heart raced. He fought to get more air in his lungs, and scared he was about to die, he pushed back against the darkness, determined to stave off his demise. *Not yet, Daniels. Give Rem time.* He wheezed, and Ivy still held his hand, although he barely felt it. Her eyes bleary with tears, she leaned over him. "It's okay. You can go if you want. He'll understand."

Daniels tried to swallow but his throat stuck. "Not yet," he tried to whisper, but nothing emerged. She slowly faded from view, and a bright white light replaced her image. A warmth flooded through him, and he waited for the next sharp stab of pain, but it never came. His body began to relax, and his muscles eased as the tension released. Feeling better, he took a solid breath, and studied the intense bright light. For a brief moment, he though he saw his sister Melinda, but didn't understand why because she'd died when he was a teenager.

Taking another long needed, full breath, he finally spoke without discomfort. "Melinda," he asked. "Is that you?"

Something touched his arm, and not wanting to leave his sister, he ignored it. "Melinda?" he asked again. The tugging became more insistent, and Daniels swiped at whatever was pulling at him.

Feeling stronger and the pain gone, he sat up, prepared to join his sister, when a loud voice shouted in his ear. "Detective Daniels."

He startled, feeling a pull on his stomach, a sudden lurch, and an almost thump as his butt hit something soft. He opened his eyes and saw Ivy beside him. He was sitting up, his body was slick with sweat, and the bedsheets were rumpled at his waist. Breathing hard, he darted his eyes around the room.

Ivy sat back in surprise. Disoriented, Daniels gulped in air. "Ivy?"

She held her chest and Hicks popped his head up. Ripley stood and bounced up and down. Ivy looked over. "Hicks?"

The dog stood slowly. He sniffed Ripley and then walked over to Ivy, who petted his head with a smile.

Daniels tried to get his bearings. "What happened?"

Hicks trotted off with Ripley and Ivy stared at Daniels. "You lost consciousness for a second, and I thought...I thought..." she paused, her eyes wide, "...and then you stirred, asked if I was Melinda, and just sat up."

Daniels recalled seeing his sister and the light. He did a quick check-in on himself and noted that he felt better. His muscles didn't ache, his head didn't throb, he'd stopped sweating and he could breathe with ease. He pushed back the covers and Ivy stood to let him get out of bed.

"You sure you're strong enough?" she asked.

He made it up and wobbled for a moment but then straightened. "It's fine. I can stand."

Ivy handed him his water, and he drank the whole glass.

She took the glass back. "Hicks is better, too."

Daniels thought of Rem. "He did it." His elation was quickly replaced with worry. Was Rem okay? What had happened with Ginger? His legs shook, and feeling dizzy, he sat back on the bed.

"You need to take it easy," said Ivy. "I'll get you more water and something to eat."

Daniels nodded. The dizziness subsiding, he prayed Rem was alive as Ivy headed into the kitchen.

Chapter Twenty-Nine

REM PARKED IN THE same spot as before and ran down the alley to Aunt Gin's. He accessed the gate and entered her backyard. Darting up the porch steps, he stopped when he heard and felt glass crunch beneath his feet and spotted her shattered sliding door. He froze, thinking of his aunt. What had happened? He ran inside. "Aunt Gin?" he called, running through the house. "Aunt Gin?"

A bathroom door opened, and she stepped out into the hall.

Relieved, Rem ran over, and gasped when he saw her. Her flowery dress was streaked with blood, and she held a bloody towel against her temple. "My God," he asked. "What happened?" He immediately thought of Ginger. Had she attacked his aunt?

Gin waved at him. "Don't worry, dear. It's worse than it looks." She pulled the cloth away and he saw the ugly gash. "Head wounds always bleed a lot."

Rem struggled to make sense of it. "Who did this? Did someone break in?" He guided her toward a kitchen chair. "You should sit."

"I'm fine. Really. No need to worry." Gin didn't sit but went into the kitchen.

Rem followed. "What the hell happened here?" he asked. "Who broke your glass?"

Gin rinsed the bloody rag. "It's nothing for you to concern yourself about. Did you find who you were looking for?"

Rem stared, feeling like he was missing something. "No. I didn't."

She squeezed out the rag. "I'm sorry to hear that." She put the rag back against her temple.

"I didn't see a trellis, hummingbird or a rock." He gripped the edge of the counter and thought of Daniels. "The Millers didn't have any of that."

Gin frowned. "I'm so sorry, dear. I guess I must have been thinking of someone else." She looked away. "Give me a second and I'll see if I can remember the correct bed and breakfast."

Rem's stomach clenched when he realized his aunt was lying. "Aunt Gin. This is important. What is—" He stopped when a hummingbird darted past the kitchen window behind Gin.

Cold shivers ran down his arms and he eyed the shattered door.

"Aaron?" asked Gin.

He didn't respond and stepped away. Looking for the hummingbird, he headed out the broken door.

"Aaron...wait..." Gin followed.

He stepped down the porch steps and strode toward the guest house. The bird was gone, but the water fountain gurgled, and he stopped beside the gazebo, where a large rose-covered trellis covered the back side of it. Hanging next to it was a hummingbird feeder. The hummingbird returned, took a quick sip, and flew away. His whole body tingled, and he swiveled toward the guest house.

"Aaron," said Gin. "Come back inside."

He ignored her and walked up to the guesthouse entry. Beside it was a large blue rock which sparkled in the sun. The chills on his skin raised into daggers, and he threw open the door. He barely stepped inside when he saw the damage. The front room was in ruins. The furniture was overturned, dishes and glasses were in pieces on the floor, there were holes in the far wall and anything unattached was broken and splintered. Barely able to breathe, he stumbled over a shattered vase and held the wall to keep from falling.

"Aaron," said Gin. "I can explain."

He turned toward his aunt, feeling a little shaky. "She was here, wasn't she? Ginger was here."

His aunt tried to take his elbow, but he pulled away. "Please," she said, her face stricken. "Come back to the house."

His fear for Daniels bloomed, and he pushed off the wall and checked all the rooms. "Where is she? Where did she go? Did she get away?" He held his head, terrified he'd failed. Ginger had disappeared, and Daniels was dead. "Oh, God. What have I done?"

"Aaron, get a hold of yourself. It's fine. Everything's fine."

His frustration boiled over. "It's not fine," he yelled. "She killed him. I could have stopped her. And now she's gone. Why didn't you tell me she was here?" He stomped through the front room, tossing whatever he could find. "Why didn't you tell me?" he screamed.

"Because she would have killed you, too," Gin screamed back. "You would have been dead, and I couldn't allow that."

Overwhelmed, Rem clenched his hands into fists. "So Daniels' sacrifice was worth it because I'm alive? Is that what you're saying?" He smacked his chest. "I'm the one that should be dead. Not him."

"He's not dead, you idiot," yelled Gin.

Feeling sick, Rem tried to register what Gin was telling him. "How do you know that? How could you possibly know that?" He kicked at an overturned potted plant. "The only way he's okay is if Ginger is—" He stopped, eyeing his aunt with her bloody face and dress. He studied her and unflinching, she met his gaze.

"Dead?" she asked.

Rem fought to think. What had Aunt Gin done? "She's not...but you... how could you...?" His mind spinning, he attempted to understand.

She stepped closer and took his arm again. He didn't pull away and she tugged on him. "Come inside. I'll make you some coffee and we'll talk."

Rem attempted to speak but didn't know what to say.

Gin waited and patted him on the shoulder. "I'll go start the coffee, then. You come when you're ready." She turned and left.

Rem took in the wrecked room, trying to come to grips with his aunt's disclosures. Was Ginger really dead? Was Daniels okay? Taking several long, slow, deep breaths, he realized he needed answers. Determined to get them, he left the small house, walked through the yard and entered his aunt's home.

She was standing in the kitchen, making the coffee. Rem stood there, still confused.

"Sit," she said. "I'll bring you a brownie."

"I don't want a damn brownie," said Rem.

"Then just sit. You look like you're about to pass out."

Believing that was true, Rem pulled out a chair and sat. Dropping his head, he squeezed his temples.

"Relax," said Gin. "I promise Gordon is okay."

Trusting her, Rem fought to think. "Where's Ginger? What happened to her?"

Gin fiddled in the kitchen, and Rem heard drawers open and close. "She's gone," said Gin. "She won't bother you again."

Exhausted, Rem raised his head. He asked the question he dreaded. "Did you kill her?"

He heard a soft laugh. "Heavens, no. I just sent her away."

Rem's hair hung in his face. He pushed it back and put his elbows on the table. "I don't understand."

She came around the counter and set a plate with a brownie in front of him. "Just in case you change your mind."

Weary, Rem just needed the truth. "Please tell me what is going on."

Gin sat beside him and took his hand. "You need to rest."

Rem pulled his hand back. "I won't rest ever again until you tell me what you did."

Her face serious, she paused and sighed. "She arrived Saturday afternoon after your arrest. I didn't know who she was, but I immediately didn't like her. She'd rented the back room, though, and was quiet and kept to herself. I didn't see much of her. I just dropped off her breakfast basket in the morning and that was it. She was supposed to leave Sunday but then asked to extend her stay. The room wasn't booked, so I agreed. There was something about her, though. The way she looked at me – it was like she knew me, or something about me. It was unnerving."

Rem held his aching ribs. His whole body hurt. "Ginger has been staying here this whole time?"

Gin nodded. "Maybe if you hadn't been arrested and then disappeared, I would have paid more attention and realized she was bad news, but I'm getting older, and I don't sense these things as well as I used to."

Rem sunk in his seat. "Just tell me what you did, Gin. I promise I'll do everything I can to protect you, but I have to know the truth."

She remained quiet but faced him. "You'd protect me?" she asked. "You'd keep my secret?"

Rem debated what to say. Would he turn his aunt in if she'd killed Ginger? Could he do that? Dejected, he sat back. "I won't say a thing."

She patted his wrist. "Revertons stick together. We protect our loved ones at all costs, don't we?"

Rem's worry for Daniels was replaced by worry for his aunt. "Where's the body? Did you hide it?" He thought of Shaw. If the deputy learned what his aunt had done, there would be nothing Rem could do for her. Considering the warrant out for his own arrest, he'd likely be in the cell next to her.

"Don't worry about that. There is no body." She stood. "I'll get our coffee."

Rem closed his eyes, terrified his aunt had crossed over into complete madness. "Aunt Gin...You have to tell me. Let me help you." He stood and went into the kitchen. "You can't hide a body."

"I'm not hiding anything, dear." She pulled two mugs from a cabinet.

Confused, Rem shook his head. "Then where is Ginger?"

"I don't know." Gin opened the sugar container. "You take three scoops?"

"Forget the damn coffee," yelled Rem. "And tell me what happened."

She stopped in mid-scoop. "Don't yell at your aunt." She resumed her scooping.

Rem ran his hands into his hair and grabbed his neck. "Gin—"

"When you came here, all upset and scared," she said, "I realized that the woman in my guest house was the woman you were looking for, so I sent you away." She opened the refrigerator and took out some cream. "I knew she was the one hurting Gordon, and I knew she'd hurt you, too, so I needed you away from here."

Rem tried to understand. "Aunt Gin, Ginger is—"

"Was," Gin corrected. "Dangerous. I'm aware. Why do you think my door is shattered and the guest house a mess?" She added cream to the mugs. "I confronted her and told her she'd messed with the wrong family. I took her by surprise because she looked rather shocked."

Rem stammered. "You...you confronted her? She could have killed you."

"It did turn ugly quickly, but I was ready for her. She fought to escape, which is why the guest room is a wreck and my door's broken. A piece of glass cut me, but I hung on and kept her in there until I finished what needed to be done." She paused. "I may be older, but I have still have a few tricks up my sleeve. Especially with someone so naive. Younger sensitives tend to be a little pretentious." She scoffed. "They think they're untouchable. She should have known better."

"Younger sensitives?" asked Rem in shock. "Are you telling me...have you done this before?"

"Not quite like this. But yes, the Revertons aren't slouches, dear. The women of our family have some mojo. I won't go into details because it isn't my place."

"Isn't your place?" Rem couldn't seem to do anything but just sputter and stare.

"Your mom has it too, but it scared her, and she chose not to pursue it. I, on the other hand, couldn't resist." She put the cream back and narrowed her eyes at Rem. "What's the point of having gifts if you're not going to use them? Don't you agree?" She sighed. "I wish your mom had made a different choice, though. I would have made your father disappear faster than a frightened rabbit." She picked up the pot of coffee. "I'm sorry. I shouldn't have said that, but my filter is thinning rapidly."

Rem gripped the counter, his heart thumping faster. "Did you say disappear?"

Pouring coffee, she nodded. "Yes."

Rem held his breath. "Like, *gone*—disappear?"

"What other disappear is there?" She put the pot back, stirred the contents of the mugs with a spoon and handed one to Rem. "Here you go. Drink this. You'll feel better." She lowered her voice. "I added a touch of Irish Whiskey to take the edge off."

Rem took the mug, not sure he could stand much less drink. He thought of what Ivy had told him, and about the people who'd vanished in the woods. "Are you...did...did you...?" He told himself it wasn't possible. The Magic Man couldn't be his aunt. Feeling dizzy, he swayed. "I need to sit."

"You do, dear. Take my hand."

Rem blindly took it and let Gin guide him back to the table where he returned to his chair.

Gin took Rem's coffee and set it down, sat beside him, and sipped on her own. "You okay?"

Rem's tried to keep up. "You made Ginger disappear?"

"It took some doing because I didn't have a lot of time to prepare, but my anger made up for it."

"Where did she go?"

Gin shrugged. "I don't know. I don't know where any of them go. Maybe another dimension. Maybe the past or the future. Or maybe they're just transported to another planet. Who cares? All I know is they're not coming back here. And that's all that matters."

Rem dropped his jaw. "The couple who vanished, and Sybil, Joe's wife, and the other guy...did you...?"

Staring off, she made a face. "That couple was atrocious. They stayed at my previous B&B briefly and tried to convince me I should sell. When I didn't budge, they turned mean. I threw them out, but not before snooping through their things. You should have seen their computers. Smut and porn. That was bad enough, but then I discovered they were scamming the elderly. Taking their life savings and if I'd been the slightest bit gullible, I would have been next. They went to a different bed and breakfast, but I'd mentioned to them the trail and the dangers it posed and implied they didn't have the guts to take it. They took the bait and all I had to do was wait. They eventually went out there, walked for a while, and before they knew it, they were walking somewhere else. Wherever they landed, I hope it was hot." She sipped more coffee while Rem gawked at her. "Sybil was sent away for obvious reasons. God what an awful woman. Joe was lucky to be rid of her."

"What did you do with Sybil?" asked Rem.

"I'd put up with her as long as I could. As you know, we'd had a fight and I'd tossed her into the Main Street fountain. She was livid, but so was I. The next day, she called me. Told me she knew I liked her husband, but I would never have him because Joe was too honorable to leave her. Then she said she'd dedicate her life to making him miserable. That's when I dared her to meet me in the woods. I told her if she wanted me gone, she'd have to fight me. If she won, I'd leave Merrimac. She laughed and accepted." Gin eyed her coffee mug. "I'm pretty sure she may have planned to kill me, but she never got the chance. I vanished her the minute she walked into the trees." Gin exhaled. "It was quite satisfying. Joe searched and grieved, but once he recovered, we started dating and have been ever since."

"You vanished her?" asked Rem.

"Yes. It's an appropriate term, I think." She grimaced. "And that man, Doug. The minute I met him, I sensed his evil tendencies. He'd done things. To women and children. And animals. I couldn't prove any of it, but I didn't have to. I just made sure he never returned home to hurt anyone else."

Rem stared, openmouthed, not believing what he was hearing.

"I figured I'd vanished my last person after him. It saps me of energy and it's a lot of wear and tear on the body, but never say never." She stretched her neck. "I'm going to be sore for weeks." She touched the gash on her head. "I left the towel in the kitchen, but I think it stopped bleeding." She turned her face. "How does it look?"

Rem sat in shock. His fatigue made it hard to focus, but he tried to form some words. "Gin...what you've done..."

"What have I done, Aaron?" She set her coffee down. "The world no longer has to deal with a couple of scammers who ruin people's lives, a bitchy and cruel woman who wouldn't know kindness if it licked her ass, a monster who harmed innocent victims, and a crazed sensitive who'd hurt others and wanted to kill you and Gordon." She shook her head. "Good riddance if you ask me." She studied him. "I have no regrets about any of it. Are you telling me you wouldn't have done the same? You're a cop, Aaron. God knows the things you've seen. Don't sit there and tell me there haven't been people in your life you would have happily made disappear if you'd had the chance."

Rem considered what had happened to Jennie, the pain Victor and Allison had caused him and others, and Margaret Redstone and her madness and cursed statues and the damage they'd done to him and Daniels. Would he have done what Gin had if he'd had the opportunity? Uncertain, he shook his head. "I don't know what I—"

A loud crack boomed, and the front door banged open. Rem and Gin jumped. Gin stood abruptly, bumping the table and spilling her coffee. Rem turned and his stomach dropped when he saw Deputy Shaw standing at the entrance, his gun drawn and aimed at Rem.

Chapter Thirty

DANIELS FINISHED THE FOOD Ivy had made him and drank more water. Feeling stronger and more alert, he stood. "I have to go." He tested his legs and was glad when he didn't feel woozy.

"Are you sure?" asked Ivy.

"I am." He headed into the other room to change into his own clothes. "I've got to go back. I have to call my wife, contact my captain, and locate Rem." He found his shirt and looked for his shoes. "You still sense he's alive?"

Ivy found his shoes and handed them to him. "I do. But I'm not picking up on anything more than that."

Relieved that Ivy could at least sense that much, Daniels nodded. "I'll take whatever I can get."

"What if Remalla returns here?" asked Ivy.

"Then tell him to meet me at his aunt's. That's where I'll go."

"But the arrest warrant..."

Daniels sat to put his shoes and shirt on. "All the more reason to get back." He thought about what Rem had told him about Shaw when Rem had been in jail. "If Shaw is somehow involved in this, he could be dangerous. And if Rem's been arrested, he'll need help."

"You can't be much help if you get arrested, too."

"And I can't be much help from here, either. I'll figure it out when I get there." He stood and grabbed his phone and car keys. "Any chance you can tap into Shaw and learn what he's up to?"

She shook her head. "I tried once. He's a closed book, and he leaves a bad taste in my bones. He's not a nice man."

"At least you tried."

"I'll try again, though. Maybe Whit can give me some information, or maybe I can connect with someone else."

Daniels walked to the door and opened it. "I can't wait. Something tells me Rem's in trouble." The nagging feeling hadn't left him since he'd sat at the table to eat, and he wished he'd left sooner.

"If I pick up on something, I'll find a way to get word to you."

Daniels wondered how she'd do that but didn't have the time to worry about it. "How do I get back to the trail?"

"Rip," she called. The big dog walked up to the entry. "Take him to his car." Ripley woofed and bounced on her front legs.

"Thanks," said Daniels, pausing. "Rem and I owe you, Ivy," He wondered if this would be the last time he'd see her. "I feel pretty certain if you hadn't taken us in when you did, we would be dead."

"You two found your way here, so I can't take all the credit."

Daniels recalled what she'd told him before he'd recovered. "I remember what you said...about your family."

Her face fell. "I thought you were out of it."

"Not all the way." He paused at the door. "It's not my business but maybe it's time to reconnect." He studied her, sensing her indecision. "If you don't, you'll wake up one day wishing you had, and it will be too late."

Nodding, she pursed her lips. "I'll consider it." She sighed. "You take care, Detective."

"You, too." He headed out the door. "After you, Rip." The dog ran into the trees, and Daniels followed.

• • • • • • • • • •

Rem stood and Gin cursed. "What the hell are you doing?" she yelled. "You broke my door."

Shaw held the weapon on Rem. "You're harboring a fugitive." He smirked. "Next time, close your curtains." He sneered at Rem. "Looks like you've been caught again, Detective, but this time, you won't be so lucky." His eyes narrowed. "Let's go." He pulled out his handcuffs.

Rem's heart pounded. The thought of returning to that damn jail made him feel sick but being in Shaw's custody scared him worse. "Shaw...

listen...," said Rem. "I was just checking in on my aunt." He waved at the shattered door. "She had a break-in."

"Shut up, Detective. I'm tired of all the games." He jabbed the gun toward Rem. "Assume the position."

"Shaw," said Aunt Gin. "This is ridiculous. There's no need to treat him like a common criminal."

"He's a murder suspect," said Shaw. "Scott Herndon is dead, and your nephew and his partner likely killed him, and probably Sharon, too." He eyed Rem. "Are you armed?"

Moving slowly, Rem removed his gun and let it swing from his finger.

"Aaron..." said Aunt Gin.

Rem kept his hands visible. The last thing he wanted was for his aunt to get hurt. "It's okay," he said. "Contact Joe. Tell him I've been arrested. Then contact my captain at my precinct. His name's Lozano. He'll know what to do." Rem thought of Daniels but had no idea how to get in touch with him or what shape his partner would be in.

"Move," said Shaw. "Up against the wall."

"I'll call Joe now." Gin found her phone.

Rem walked over with his hands up. Shaw took Rem's gun and tucked it under his belt while Rem put his hands on the wall. Shaw patted him down, removed Rem's phone and put it in his back pocket. Shaw found the glass tube, took it out and shook it. "What's this, Detective? A magic potion from your aunt?"

Rem eyed the tube. "It helps me sleep."

Shaw sneered and put it back in Rem's jacket pocket. "You can keep it for now. I think you're going to need it."

Relieved Joe had returned it, he eyed Gin as she held her phone to her ear.

Shaw raised the handcuffs. "Call all you want, Genevieve, but Joe won't be any help. He's at the Herndons', helping a grieving family make funeral arrangements. I doubt he'll even answer." He took Rem's wrist and pulled it down.

"Do you have to use handcuffs?" asked Gin, lowering her phone. "He's not resisting. Don't you have any decency?"

Shaw regarded her and studied Rem. "You're right, Genevieve. He is a fellow officer." He leaned close to Rem and Rem tensed. He didn't like

Shaw near him. "I'll make you a deal, Detective. You come peacefully and I won't arrest your aunt for protecting you."

Gin's jaw dropped. "Arrest me?"

"I'll come peacefully," said Rem. "Just leave her alone. She didn't do anything."

Shaw's mouth twisted. "Good." He stepped back. "You win, Genevieve. No handcuffs." He grinned at her. "See? I can be a reasonable man."

Rem slowly turned toward him. "It'll be okay, Aunt Gin."

Her eyes wide, she hit a button on her phone. "I'll get a hold of Joe and be there soon."

"Take your time," said Shaw. "Your nephew and I have a lot to discuss." His eyes gleamed. "Like where is your partner? You hiding him?" He chuckled. "Or did you kill him, too?"

Rem grit his teeth. "If we're going, then let's go. You're wasting time." He tried to stay calm. Joe was in town and would keep his eye on Shaw. He wondered about Daniels and what he would do once he learned Rem had been arrested again.

"I couldn't agree more." Shaw lowered his voice. "Say goodbye to your aunt, Detective." He eyed Gin, who was trying again to call Joe. "You never know when it might be the last time."

Rem glared. "You touch her, and no jail cell will stop me from killing you." He thought of his aunt's revelations. "And if you hurt me, be prepared to vanish."

Shaw raised a brow. "Threats, Detective?"

"No," said Rem. "Promises."

"Good to know," said Shaw, scowling. "Let's go."

· · · ● ● ● ● ● · · ·

Sitting in the back of the patrol car again as Shaw drove away, Rem reminded himself not to think the worst. Ginger was no longer a threat, his aunt would contact Sheriff Joe and Lozano, and Daniels was safe in the woods with Ivy. Somehow, this mess would get sorted and he'd go home. His conversation with his aunt still shocked him, but now it seemed less important. Her justifications that she'd removed some ugly people from this world made more sense. How she'd done it still baffled him, but right now he had bigger issues to handle.

Shaw pulled up to the end of the street and stopped at a stop sign. After getting Rem in the backseat, he'd remained silent, his eyes narrowed at the road. Rem had not engaged because it only seemed to irritate Shaw more, so he'd stayed quiet, although his mind raced.

Shaw idled at the intersection, and Rem looked both ways but didn't see a car. He wondered about the holdup but didn't ask. If Shaw wanted to take his time before returning to the jail, Rem wouldn't argue.

More seconds passed and flicking a gaze at Rem in the rearview mirror, Shaw pulled out and turned left.

Rem tipped his head. "The jail's the other way."

Shaw didn't respond but kept driving.

"Where are we going?" asked Rem. He shifted uncomfortably. Something about Shaw's demeanor worried him. "Shaw?"

Shaw gripped the steering wheel. "I think it's time you and I had a heart to heart." He eyed Rem again through the mirror. "And tell each other the truth."

Rem watched the road. The trees became thicker as the distance from Merrimac increased. He realized the road they were on led back to the trail. "I did tell you the truth. I didn't kill anyone."

"Where's your partner?"

Rem set his jaw. "He's recuperating. He was injured."

"That's not what I asked."

"He didn't kill anyone either."

Shaw scoffed. "I spoke with Scott before his death. He said you threatened him."

Rem gripped the back of Shaw's seat. "I was looking for Daniels. I thought Scott had hurt him." The trees whooshed by outside the windows. Anxious, Rem realized he was stuck with no way to get out.

"That's motive."

"I was wrong, though. Scott hadn't done anything. Daniels had been hurt and needed time to recover."

"So you know where he is."

The car bounced over a pothole, and Rem held his aching ribs, glad he wasn't handcuffed. "Where are we headed?"

"To find your partner."

"Listen. You take me to jail, and he'll show up. You just have to wait. He'll come looking for me."

Shaw slowed the car and turned on to the rocky dirt road that led to the trailhead. The vehicle bounced as they approached the small parking area. Rem's and Daniel's cars came into view.

"Well, well, well," said Shaw. "Lookie here. Your and your partner's car." He slowed, pulled up next to Rem's vehicle and parked.

"What are we doing here?"

Shaw shifted to look back. His dark eyes reminded Rem of their encounter in the jail. "You're going to tell me where you hid your partner's body." He unbuckled his seat belt, tossed Rem's gun and phone into the passenger seat, and got out.

Rem began to sweat. "I didn't kill Daniels. He's fine. I didn't kill Sharon or Scott, either."

Shaw shut his door, pulled his gun and opened Rem's door. He aimed the weapon on Rem. "If you didn't kill your partner, then you're going to show me where you're hiding him." He glared when Rem didn't move. "Get out."

Rem's anxiety bloomed into full grown fear. He hesitated. "What are you doing?"

Shaw yelled. "I said get out."

Rem jumped and made some uncomfortable deductions. Shaw could shoot him and tell Joe whatever story he wanted. Wondering how to get out of this, Rem held out his hands. "Take it easy." He slowly slid out of the car. Would Shaw actually kill him or was he just trying to scare him? Something told Rem that Shaw was not new to killing anyone.

He stood while Shaw stepped back, still aiming the gun. "Move," said Shaw. "Toward the woods."

Rem had to slow this down. "You're the one who murdered them, aren't you? Sharon and Scott."

There was the smallest flicker in his eyes, and he stilled. "I said move."

His heart rate zooming, Rem stepped away from the vehicle and toward the trail but kept his eyes open for an escape route. Ivy's home was too far away, but he wouldn't want to endanger her anyway. If he could get to the woods, he might have a shot of running and hiding until someone came looking. But for now, he'd have to keep Shaw talking. "You and Sharon have a thing going?" he asked, walking. "She chose Scott, though, and you killed her?"

He heard Shaw chuckle from behind. "You think I'd kill anyone over Sharon? She was a means to an end, Detective, and my meal ticket out of here, until you showed up."

Rem stepped into the woods. Shaw continued to follow. "Meal ticket?" asked Rem. He thought about what Daniels had told him. "Because she was sleeping with Tyler at the bank?"

He heard a snort behind him. "She slept with Tyler at the bank to learn how to get to the money. She slept with me because I actually made it worth her while. She slept with Scott because she was bored, and thought he'd eventually marry her, and they'd leave this stupid town."

Rem made some more deductions. "Was it her idea to rob the bank?" Shaw didn't respond.

Rem walked slowly down the trail. "I thought we were out here to tell the truth." He paused. "Or was robbing the bank your idea?"

After a long pause, Shaw answered. "Sharon knew that with the festival there would be a lot more money in the vault. She told me and Scott and we came up with a plan to take it. She knew how to get to the safe, Scott knew how to rig the cameras and I would handle Tyler's call when he reported the theft. We'd lay low for a while until the shock abated and then we'd go our separate ways."

Listening, Rem eyed the woods in case he got the chance to run. "You three planned on taking off into the sunset together?"

"I didn't care what they did. They could go one way and I'd go another. They just had to keep their mouths shut. They kept up their arguing and breaking up and as the festival neared, I thought we might actually have a shot at pulling this off, and then you arrived."

Rem heard the derision in his voice. "Daniels has always said I have perfect timing." He continued to follow the rocky path. "Let me guess. Sharon got a little too close to me and a little too drunk. Scott got jealous. That last night, after the bar fight, she and Scott argued for real." He paused, thinking. "Did Sharon threaten to tell me everything? Is that why she told him she was going to find me?"

Shaw's voice hardened. "Scott called me after Sharon left, panicked that she would reveal our plan. That bitch was going to ruin everything, and worse, tell a detective."

"You decided to stop her?" asked Rem. He still couldn't remember anything after getting sick in the bushes. Had Sharon found him?

"I figured she just wanted to piss Scott off, but I also knew she did stupid things when she drank. To be safe, I headed to the shacks. Sure enough. I found her outside yours. You were passed out against a tree, but I thought she was talking to you." His tone deepened. "I grabbed a rock, thinking she'd told you everything. She stopped and saw me, and her demeanor changed. She acted like nothing was wrong and thought her smile and seduction would sway me." He paused. "She tried to tell me she'd seen you on her way home and was just out to have some fun. I confronted her about what Scott had said, and she denied it. I called her a liar and asked her if she'd told you anything. She got angry and started threatening me. Telling me that Scott and I couldn't do anything without her. She was the hinge of the whole operation, but she was having second thoughts. She suspected that if it went south, we would turn on her, so she was going to tell you everything."

Rem couldn't recall hearing any arguments that night. "I didn't hear a thing."

"That didn't stop her from trying to wake you. I knew she was just drunk, but I was pissed and told her to back off. She ignored me and shoved me back. I hit her with the rock, but not enough to stop her. She ran off and I followed. When I caught up to her, I finished the job."

Rem knew then that he was a dead man. Shaw had just confessed murder and he wasn't going to allow Rem to leave the woods alive. Wondering when to make his move, Rem kept walking and let Shaw talk. "How did Scott play into all of this?"

"He'd been nearby and saw me chase her. He showed up after she was dead and panicked. I had to calm him down. It took some time to get him to think ahead. He didn't have the sense to determine what to do next, so I told him."

"Make me the patsy," said Rem.

"I'd tossed the rock in the water, but I needed a weapon, so I told Scott to return to the shacks, and find the one used for cleaning fish, grab a knife and bring it back. He needed something to do so he did it. After he returned, I stabbed Sharon and handed him the knife. Told him to go to your shack and hide it. I couldn't do it because Joe was out of town, and I had to get back. He hesitated until I mentioned that he would be the obvious suspect once Sharon's body was discovered. That got him moving. Damn idiot didn't pay any attention to his muddy shoes though. I'd told him to wipe down the knife but didn't think about the mud." He paused. "My mistake."

Rem took a nervous breath, trying to think straight. "You honestly thought that would work?"

"Yes. I think it would have. You were drunk and had been all week. Sharon had been hanging on you like a wet rag. She'd said she was going to see you that night and, post-mortem or not, a weapon with her blood on it was found in your shack. You were passed out in the woods with no alibi. Pretty open and shut."

His shoes crunching on the rocks, Rem thought of Scott. "You warned Scott about the muddy shoes, didn't you?"

"I had to. After Joe released you, I visited Scott. He was shaken after his encounter with you. I told him to get rid of the shoes and stay calm. But I knew he would never survive Joe's questioning. He was too weak. Sharon's death terrified him, and his guilt was tearing him up. I had to go back and take care of him. I'd seen your card at Scott's and knew about your partner's altercation at the auto shop. With you and Daniels missing, it was another nail to add to your coffins."

Rem's stomach churned, and he paid attention to his surroundings. When he ran, he'd have to pick the right spot or Shaw could easily shoot him. "Then why are we here? Why not take me to jail and let the courts take it from there?"

"I'm not stupid, Detective. I know that people will doubt your guilt. Your aunt will make a scene about it, and Joe listens to her. I didn't know where you'd gone or if you had an alibi. Since finding you, though, the more I've thought about it, the more I realize it would be easier to get rid of you." He paused. "The way I see it, you offered to take me to your partner. I agreed. But then you tried to escape. I chased you through the woods and you attacked me. I shot you in self-defense. No one can argue any of it. Maybe your partner shows. Maybe he doesn't. But it doesn't matter. Sharon and Scott's murderer will be dead, and neither Daniels nor Joe will be able to prove different. Even if Daniels is your alibi, it would be easy to make it look like he's guilty himself and only protecting you. Your partner will go home, Genevieve will grieve, and the town will move on."

Desperate, Rem took slow steps, trying to slow his progress down the trail. "This is crazy, Shaw."

"Crazy works, Detective. More often than you think." His footsteps stopped. "Right here. Turn around."

Rem stood still, his hands raised. His fingers shook. "You're going to shoot me right here? That doesn't support your escape theory."

"I said turn around."

Rem bit his lip and slowly turned. His heart pounded when he recognized the blank look in Shaw's eyes. "C'mon. Think about this."

"It's all I've done. Now's the time for action." He straightened his aim. "Run."

Rem froze instead. "Run?"

Shaw scowled. "You have thirty seconds. After that, I follow."

"You're going to chase me?"

"It's your only hope, Detective. You get lucky enough, you might make it. But I grew up in the woods and I'm a good tracker. If I catch you, you're dead."

"What if I don't run?"

"Then I'll shoot you where you stand. At least this way, you have a tiny shot at survival." He aimed an ugly grin at Rem. "It makes it interesting." He paused. "You should know though, that I have no intention of letting you leave these woods alive."

Rem debated what to do. Should he face down Shaw or take his chances in the forest? Shaw would be in his element, but Rem might get lucky if he rushed Shaw. Rem figured his chances were slim either way.

"Your choice." Shaw studied him and his eyes narrowed. He spoke softly. "Thirty...twenty-nine...twenty-eight—"

Rem ran.

Chapter Thirty-One

IVY SAT CROSS-LEGGED ON the ground outside the house while
Hicks lay beside her, breathing softly. Relaxed and comfortable, she
allowed her mind to still. As the external world drifted away and her mind
quieted, she relaxed and took deep breaths. From here, she could go where
she wished, connecting to those who were open enough to receive. Finding
Whit, she communicated long enough to know that he had little
information other than what she already knew, so she left him to see if she
could find others. The deputy was only a blank space which didn't
surprise her. Very few people had minds silent or open enough for her to
reach. She moved on but had little luck. Telling herself to be patient, she
remained quiet and calm, and floated in the silence, but stayed aware for
any potential openings.

Sitting and listening, she shivered when her skin tingled, and a chill ran
through her. It was if someone had nudged her to get her attention. The
nudge felt familiar, and she questioned the source, doubting whether this
person was actually reaching out to her. While it was possible for someone
to communicate with her in the same way she'd communicate with others,
it was extremely rare, and it hadn't happened in years. Ignoring it failed,
though, when the nudge became a shove. Concerned, but curious, Ivy
allowed a cautious opening and listened. A message came through
instantly and was so forceful, Ivy opened her eyes and gasped. Taking a
second to absorb what she'd heard, she didn't move, but after sensing it
was true, she realized what she needed to do. She jumped up and ran for
the house. Hicks ran with her and waited as Ivy grabbed her knapsack,
threw several items in it, tossed it over her shoulder and ran back out.

Hicks stood and watched, his head cocked to one side, but then the dog turned toward the woods, as if understanding.

"C'mon," said Ivy. "We need to hurry."

Hicks darted into the trees, and Ivy raced to keep up with him.

•••••••••••

Rem sprinted off the trail and into the forest, aiming for the thickest cover he could find that he could also successfully navigate. Branches snagged at his clothes and leaves whipped at his face, but he kept running. He had no sense of direction and didn't know if he was heading toward the cars or away from them. Not that it mattered. He doubted he could safely get to his vehicle and drive off without getting shot. He'd be too far out in the open, and he sensed Shaw would be waiting for that. So he ran deeper and deeper into the woods, trying to put as much distance between him and Shaw as possible. He felt certain he was nowhere near Ivy's house since he recalled being farther down the path the night he'd ran after seeing the glowing eyes. He didn't want to endanger Ivy or Daniels anyway, so it was better to lead Shaw away from them. In his frenzied state, though, he wished he had a destination in mind where he could get some help. Merrimac was too far away even if he knew where he was going. Unfortunately, he was on his own.

Breathing hard and clenching his side, he kept going. Despite his injured ribs, he couldn't afford to slow down, but he couldn't run forever. He had to consider where to stop and rest. It would have to be heavily wooded where he could conceal himself long enough to catch his breath. Not feeling safe yet, he kept pushing, dodging twisty roots, thick vines, thorny shrubs and trees heavy with low hung branches. He finally had to stop behind a cluster of overgrown and leafy shrubs. Doubling over, he gasped for air, trying to collect himself. Hot and sweaty, he slid off his jacket, wrapped it around his waist and debated where to go next when he heard the soft crunch of leaves.

Alarmed, he bolted just as a shot rang out. Darting out of the shrubs, he felt a pinch in his shoulder and raced deeper into the trees.

•••••••••••

Daniels ran behind Ripley, doing his best to keep up. They'd been running since leaving Ivy's house and although he was tired, his energy levels remained high despite any lingering effects of Ginger's illness. Grateful they were getting closer and would be back to the trailhead soon, he almost ran into Ripley when the dog suddenly stopped.

Catching his breath, he stood beside her. Rip stared off, as if listening. "What is it, girl?" asked Daniels. "You hear something?"

He listened, too, but all he heard was a woodpecker and the tweeting of a nearby bird. He waited, expecting Ripley to move on, but when she didn't, he patted her head. "It's okay. What is it? A squired or rabbit? You can hunt on your way back." He paused. "We've got to go."

The dog didn't react, and Daniels was about to nudge her for encouragement when Ripley's fur raised, and she began to bare her teeth and growl. Daniels tensed. "Who's out there?"

Ripley's body went rigid, and her growling deepened. Daniels wondered what to do. Was there a bear or another wolf nearby?

"Easy, girl," he said, anxious.

He'd barely finished speaking when a shot rang out, and Daniels jumped. The sound reverberated through the trees and, alarmed, Daniels froze. The woodpecker stopped pecking and several birds screeched and flew from their branches. His own hair raising, Daniels watched as Ripley shot off into the woods, leaving Daniels behind.

· · · ● · ● · · · ·

Gasping for air, Rem kept running. He knew now that if he stopped, he'd be dead, so he pushed himself faster. Sweat poured down his face, his clothes were ripped, his shoulder ached, and his ribs screamed at him in pain. He felt warmth running down his arm and figured he'd been hit, but it wasn't serious enough to impede his progress. Not yet at least. His ribs hurt far worse.

Clenching his side, he darted to the right, hoping that changing directions frequently would make him harder to track. He looked for areas on the ground that might make it difficult to leave footprints, so he aimed for rocky terrain. He knew he was snapping branches and he tried to avoid them as best he could, but his speed made it difficult. His energy waning, he forced himself to keep going. The warmth traveled down his arm and hand and a quick glance confirmed he was bleeding. Realizing the drops of blood would lead Shaw directly to him, he pulled his hand in and wrapped it in his shirt, hoping that would prevent more drips of blood from falling for at least long enough to get farther away.

Finally getting to a point where he had to stop, he spotted a dense thicket of trees and foliage where a fallen log laid amongst a large pile of leaves. Desperate to rest, he slowed and stopped at the log, and collapsed beside it. He hunkered into the shrubs, trying to hide himself. His ribs flared again, and he bit back a moan and grit his teeth. Touching his shoulder, he felt his wet, warm sleeve. He could still move his arm though, which told him it wasn't serious.

Listening intently, he prayed he'd put some distance between him and Shaw, but knew Shaw wouldn't be far behind. Exhausted, Rem prayed this stop wouldn't cost him his life. Alert and prepared to flee if needed, Rem gazed out at the woods. Hearing nothing, he said a silent prayer of thanks and closed his eyes. A few seconds passed and for those brief moments, Rem wondered if he'd succeeded. Had he outrun Shaw and managed to escape? And if he had, could he get back to the cars and get help? How would he ever find his way out of these woods?

Hope slowly blossomed and he started to consider where to go next when he heard the distinct sound of footsteps.

• • • • • • • • • •

Daniels raced after Ripley, but the dog had vanished into the trees. He wanted to call out but feared that whatever danger the dog had sensed would be alerted to Daniels' presence and something told him that wouldn't be good. He tried to follow the dog's trail, but it was pointless. Ripley was gone, and Daniels was officially lost. He had no idea where to go. Eyeing the position of the sun in the sky, he made a projected course of what direction to follow and headed toward it, careful to make as little noise as possible. He kept an eye out for Ripley but didn't see anything. Continuing to walk and listen, he stopped when he spotted a drop of blood on a leaf. He touched it and felt the warmth. It was fresh. Was it

Ripley's blood or another animal's, or was it human? Spying another drop, he followed it. Was this what Rip had sensed? Was someone injured in the woods?

Daniels studied the ground. The blood drops stopped but he spotted a broken stem from a nearby branch. Someone had been through here. His senses alert, he kept walking, and seeing another broken stem, he followed it and approached a heavy thicket of trees and a fallen log. Hearing a soft shuffle, he stepped closer and saw disturbed leaves. Keeping his eyes on the surrounding area and moving carefully, he turned to step over the log, and almost tripped over a sneakered foot.

· · · ● · ● · ● · · ·

Rem plastered himself into the log and didn't move as the steps encroached. If he ran now, Shaw would have a clear shot. He had no choice but to remain still and try not to breathe.

The footsteps grew closer, and Rem prepared for the inevitable. A shadow crossed the log, and Rem held his breath, knowing this was it. Despite the odds against him, he attempted to dart out from the log when he heard his name. It barely registered though, and he kept trying to scoot away when he heard it again.

"Rem. Stop. It's me."

The voice penetrated. Rem crawled up to and propped himself against the closest tree trunk. Breathing hard and trembling, he saw Daniels walking toward him. Relief coursed through him, and he gripped his throbbing ribs. "Daniels?" He blinked to be sure it was him and looked him over. "You're okay?" He put his head back against the tree. "You scared the hell out of me."

"I'm great. Feel fine." Daniels squatted beside him, his face furrowed. "What are you doing out here? You're a mess." He wiped leaves from Rem's shirt. "Did you fight Big Foot?"

Rem did a quick scan of himself. He looked like he'd just escaped a gauntlet of zombies after running through a muddy obstacle course. "I've had better days."

"Did Ginger do this?"

Rem kept his eyes and ears open for any indication of Shaw's presence. "No."

Daniels' gaze settled on his arm. "Your arm's bleeding."

Rem grimaced when Daniels touched his shoulder. "I'm aware. That happens when you get shot." Fearful that Shaw was near, he tried to stand. "We need to get out of here."

Daniels wouldn't let him up. "Take it easy." He probed at Rem's injury. "Who shot you?"

The sound of footsteps returned, and Shaw stepped out of the woods. He raised his gun and aimed. "I did, Detective."

•••••••••••

Seeing Shaw, Daniels' blood turned cold. He slowly stood and faced him. Shaw's pale face illuminated his dark eyes, and Daniels sensed the danger they were in. Seeing Rem's torn clothes, sweaty and scratched face, bloody arm and white-knuckled grip on his chest, he began to put two and two together. "What are you doing, Shaw?"

Shaw stared at Rem. "I arrested your partner for Scott Herndon's murder, and he told me he could lead me to you. I believed him, but as I should have suspected, he lied and tried to run. I tracked him here, and now I find you. Looks like Lady Luck is turning my way." He grinned.

Rem gasped when he attempted to sit up. "He's lying. He killed Sharon and Scott, and now he wants to kill you and me, and blame us for the murders."

Daniels kept his eyes on the gun. "Listen. This game you're playing is stupid. Joe and the rest of the town will see right through it. Nobody's going to believe that we killed anybody."

Shaw's aim never wavered. "I'm willing to take the risk." His grin fell and he sneered. "You and your idiot partner have wasted too much of my time. I had my fun chasing him, but playtime is over. Let's get this over with." He held the gun on Daniels and Daniels didn't move.

"Don't," said Rem. "He has a wife and kid."

Shaw's face tightened. "We all have families. You have your aunt, and I had my sister. Life is tenuous at best. No one gets out alive. Some of us just leave sooner than others." He glared at Rem. "But don't worry. You won't grieve long because you'll be next."

"Your sister may not be dead," said Rem. "She just disappeared."

"If she isn't dead, then she deserves to be," said Shaw. "Her cruelty almost exceeded our parents'." He paused and straightened his aim on Daniels. "I admired her for that."

Seeing Shaw's finger tense on the trigger, Daniels realized there was nothing he could do. He thought of Marjorie and J.P., knowing he would never see them again. Hoping to reach Shaw, he held out a hand. "Don't."

"Shaw. Stop," said Rem, breathless.

"Sorry, Detectives." Shaw focused his gaze on Daniels.

Daniels waited for the boom when he heard a thunderous raucous through the foliage, and a deep snarl. Ripley emerged from the woods and launched herself at Shaw just as the gun discharged.

Chapter Thirty-Two

DANIELS JUMPED AWAY JUST as Shaw fired and a ripple of air created from the path of the bullet caressed his cheek. He landed beside Rem who scooted back into the tree and grimaced as Shaw began to scream.

Daniels turned to see Ripley straddling Shaw. Shaw had dropped the gun; his legs were kicking at the dirt, and his hands were at the dog's neck in a desperate attempt to push her away. Shaw's high-pitched screams echoed through the woods and his body bucked as Ripley latched onto his throat.

"Rip," said Daniels, but the dog did not let up.

Shaw continued to scream, and Rem looked away. Daniels sat up just as Shaw made one last gurgling scream that abruptly stopped and then he fell silent. His body went limp, and Ripley stopped snarling although she still had Shaw by the throat.

"Ripley, come here," said Daniels. His heart was beating so fast, he worried he might pass out.

Ripley didn't move for a moment as if ensuring Shaw was no longer a threat, but then let go. Shaw's head fell back and rolled. Rip stood for a second, then trotted up next to Daniels, her snout and teeth bloody.

Rem stared at Ripley, his face white. "Is it over?"

Daniels eyed Shaw on the ground. "I'd say so." Ripley sat and panted.

"Is he dead?" asked Rem.

"It's hard to be alive when your throat's been ripped out." He reached over and rubbed Ripley's neck. "You saved our lives, girl."

Ripley licked his wrist.

"Good dog," said Rem. He made a face. "But gross." He shifted to move but sucked in a breath. "Let's get the hell out of here."

Satisfied Shaw was dead, Daniels got to his knees. "You're not going anywhere."

Rem's face fell. "I'm not staying here. I've had enough trees and nature this week to gag a grizzly. Help me up." He groaned as he tried to stand.

"You can barely move." Daniels put a hand on Rem's arm and guided him back down. "I'd have to carry you back." He eyed the dog who watched them. "Rip will guide me to the trailhead, and I'll get help. You just sit tight."

Rem's eyes widened. "How will you find me after you get help? The hell I'm staying." He tried again to stand but gasped. "Just get me on my feet. I can make it."

"Rem, listen to me," said Daniels. "We're not that far from the cars. I can get there a lot faster if you let me go on my own."

"You're going to take the dog and leave me here with Shaw? I'd rather eat your vegetable pie with tomato juice."

"If I thought that were true, I'd be tempted to take you." Daniels got to his feet and squatted next to Rem. "You're bleeding, exhausted, and your ribs are killing you. If you've reinjured them, you could puncture a lung. It's better you just sit and rest. I'll find my way out and get back here before dark." He petted Ripley. "Once I get to the cars, I'll send Rip back. She'll stay with you until I can return with help."

Rem's shoulders sunk. "You're really going to leave me here?"

"You know I'm right. It's better you wait."

Rem's gaze darted toward Shaw and the surrounding woods. "You know if you don't make it back before dark, I'm going to lose it."

Daniels nodded. "Which is why I need to go now." He patted Rem's knee. "Don't worry. I'll be back before you know it." He looked at Ripley. "You ready, girl?"

Ripley woofed, and then turned toward the woods and barked.

"See?" said Daniels. "She's excited."

"I think it's the fresh kill," said Rem, eyeing Shaw. "It's got her all worked up."

"She's like you and your Taco del Fuegos," said Daniels.

"I think it's a little different. She's a wolf."

"And you're not? I think Jennie thought otherwise." Daniels straightened, hoping Rem had relaxed enough to let him leave without freaking out. "I promise. I'll be back soon."

"You better." Rem scowled. "If I recall, the last time you said that, Lozano had asked us to finish a boatload of paperwork. I didn't see you for hours."

Daniels shrugged. He wiped the leaves from his pants. "Something must have come up."

"I found you sitting in the cafeteria, talking to Sergeant Wilford."

"He wanted to talk to me about the Billings' deposition."

"You two were playing cards," yelled Rem. The burst of energy made him wince.

Ripley yapped again. Her gaze on the trees, she paced and bounced on her front legs.

Rem tensed against the tree. "Oh, God. Now what?"

Daniels swiveled, looking in the same direction as Ripley. "I don't know. What is it, Rip?"

The dog woofed again, and then Daniels heard the crunching of leaves. He almost dove behind a tree when Hicks appeared out of nowhere, jumped and barked back at Ripley.

"What the hell?" asked Rem just as Ivy ran out of the woods.

• • • • • • • • • •

Rem stared in shock. "Ivy?"

Breathless, Ivy took in the surroundings.

"What are you doing here?" asked Daniels.

Seeing Shaw's body, Ivy stilled. "Are you two all right?" She stepped over to Shaw and leaned over him. She grimaced. "Did Ripley to do that?"

"Well, it wasn't Daniels," said Rem. "But I think he was tempted."

"Ripley got to him first," said Daniels. "How'd you find us?" He glanced at Hicks who sat next to Ripley. "Stupid question. Never mind."

Ivy stepped away from Shaw and came over to Rem. "I got a message that Remalla was in trouble." She slid her knapsack off and squatted beside Rem. "I came as fast as I could."

"Message from who?" asked Daniels.

Ivy hesitated. "It's not important. I grabbed what I thought I might need and ran." She took hold of Rem's bloody arm. "What happened?"

Rem set his jaw. "It's nothing. Shaw nicked me with a bullet. It looks worse than it is. My ribs are the problem. I can barely breathe without wanting to cry."

She pulled on the jacket tied around his waist. "Let's get this and your shirt off and let me look."

Daniels leaned over Rem. "I'm going. Ivy and Hicks are here, so you won't be alone. I'll take Ripley, get help and come back as soon as I can. Okay?"

Rem's face relaxed. "I'm good now. Just be careful."

Daniels regarded Ivy. "You'll need to disappear before I get back."

"I know," said Ivy. "Hicks will alert me when anyone's close and Ripley will return after ensuring you're safe. We'll be long gone by the time help arrives." She dug into the knapsack. "I'll patch him up while you're away and keep him comfortable."

Daniels nodded and recalled what she'd told him when he'd been sick. "And while he's waiting, now might be a good time to spill a few family secrets."

Ivy stilled as she dug through her bag.

"What secrets?" asked Rem.

Ivy didn't answer.

"He should know," said Daniels. "And you should tell him. Not me."

Ivy finally looked up at him.

"Tell me what?" asked Rem, clenching his side.

Ivy nodded. "Okay."

Daniels smiled back. "Good." He faced the woods. "You ready, Rip?"

The big dog woofed again. Hicks had licked her bloody snout clean, and Daniels eyed Shaw's body again and shuddered. "Let's go."

Ripley took off, and Daniels followed.

• • • • • • • • • •

Rem tried not to complain as Ivy dabbed at his injured shoulder with a cloth. She'd removed his shirt and was cleaning the wound.

"You're right," she said, pulling more cloth from her bag. "It's not that bad. It's deep though. You'll need stitches, but the bleeding is already slowing." She took a container from the bag. "I'll bandage it then rewrap your ribs."

Rem tried to focus, but his mind was hazy with fatigue. "When are you going to tell me this big secret?"

She flicked a gaze at him and opened the container. "Here. Eat this." She held a berry and a wide green leaf.

Rem stared at what she held with doubt. "Is that a rain berry?"

"It is. It's just one. It will help you relax. The leaf will assist with the pain. You need to chew it though and it tastes awful, but the berry will help."

Rem sighed but figured he could suffer through a bad-tasting leaf if it would help his throbbing chest. "Okay." He grabbed both and popped them in his mouth.

"Chew the leaf or it won't help."

Rem chewed and almost gagged. "God. That tastes awful. Did it grow in manure?" He debated spitting it out but forced himself to swallow.

Ivy smiled. "I suppose it could have grown up beside a dog turd. I can't be sure."

Rem blanched. "Good to know."

Ivy finished cleaning his arm and began to wrap it with the cloth. "I remember you once stepping in a dog turd. I thought you were going to throw up then, too."

Rem frowned. "You remember what? I stepped in a dog turd?"

"I had a dog named Foster. Tiny yippy thing. My dad hated him."

"A dog named Foster?" A brief memory flickered in Rem's mind. He was a young boy playing in a backyard. A small white wiry dog had been barking. "How do you know about Foster?" He watched while she wrapped his arm. "Have we met before?"

She tightened the cloth and tied it. "We have. I used to take your toys and you'd run screaming to my mother."

Confused, Rem shook his head. "Your mother? Who's your mother?" The memories began to surface. He recalled Foster and stepping in his dog poop. Disgusted, he'd yelled for his mom, but...he dropped his jaw when he remembered his Aunt Gin emerging from the house instead. He narrowed his eyes at Ivy. "Simone?" he asked. "Are you Simone?"

Ivy patted his elbow. "We used to play together."

Rem blinked. "Aunt Gin is your Mom? You're my cousin?" He tried to sit up but instantly regretted the movement. "What...? How...?" He breathed through a flare of pain. "I have so many questions."

"I know." She looked for the edge of the bandage on his chest. "Let's check those ribs."

Rem put up a hand. "Hold up. I need to understand." He paused. "Does Aunt Gin know you're out here? That you've been out here this whole time?"

She wiped her hands on a towel she'd taken from the bag. Hicks slept quietly beside her. Shaw's body remained where he'd fallen although Ivy had covered his face with some fabric from her bag. "I didn't think so, but apparently I was wrong. She's the one who sent me the message telling me you were in trouble." She sighed. "I guess I should have known. She's always been a step ahead of me." Her tone changed and her voice softened. "Some things never change."

Rem opened his mouth but didn't know what to say. His aunt could vanish people and his cousin was a witch with hellhounds hiding in an old house in the woods. It was a lot to absorb. "Why don't you start from the beginning."

Ivy stared off and then sat cross-legged in the leaves. "I remember those days when we were kids with fondness, but they didn't last long."

"All I can remember is that we used to hang out and then one day you were gone. Mom said you'd moved away."

Ivy sighed. "We did. My parents weren't getting along, and I think my mother was trying to make it work. But it only got worse. I can't even remember where we'd moved. I just recall the arguments and yelling. My dad became more and more disconnected but also more controlling. I didn't realize it at the time, but he'd separated my mom from everything she knew. Her family and friends. Her work. She'd become a shell of herself. We grew up like that, moving from place to place, until one of my dad's mistresses came to the door and confronted Mom. That was the tipping point."

Rem stared in disbelief. "I didn't know any of this."

"No one did. That was Dad's plan. Only back then, I didn't see it that way. He said things to me and my brother about Mom that made me think she was the cause of all the discord. I blamed her for a lot of it."

Rem recalled meeting Gin's last two husbands. "Gin left him eventually, though."

She picked up a brown leaf and fiddled with it. "Actually, he abandoned us."

Rem swallowed. "What do you mean?"

"After the mistress encounter, Mom and Dad had one last blow up. Sawyer and I had been sent to our rooms, but I recall the shouting, swearing and hearing things breaking. And then I heard Mom say she would never be treated like shit again and Dad needed to leave and not come back. He yelled that if he left, she'd never be safe. He'd take me and Sawyer and she would never see us again and if she tried to find us, he'd kill her." She broke the leaf and crumbled it in her hand. "Mom screamed at him to get out. And that's what he did. He left and I never saw him again. No letters. No phone calls. Nothing. It's like he fell off the earth."

Recalling his aunt's secrets, Rem wondered what to say. "It happens, you know? Some people aren't cut out to be parents. And considering how he treated Aunt Gin, maybe it was for the best."

Studying the ground, she shook her head. "I never thought he'd do that. I always thought he loved us."

"I'm sure he did. Just because he left doesn't mean he didn't care."

She picked up a twig. "I blamed Mom for everything. I was so angry. And then we moved again, and I hit puberty, and suddenly everything became dark and depressing. I didn't realize that I was dealing with my increased sensitivities and all that came with it. Mom tried to explain, but I wouldn't listen. I'd become surly and ugly, and made life miserable for myself and for her. And on top of that, she'd remarried. Then she moved back home to reconnect. I'd turned eighteen and I left. I didn't want anything to do with her or anyone around her. By then, I'd been getting battered by the emotions around me and I ended up in India where I could meditate all day and try to quiet the voices in my head." She traced the twig through the dirt. "I ended up with a lousy husband of my own, made dumb mistakes and sank deeper and deeper into depression. My husband left and I tried to regroup. I traveled, trying to find myself, but wherever I went, I couldn't silence the voices." She tossed the twig. "In some part of my mind, I thought if I came here and confronted Mom, and then ended it, I would find peace. But when I got here, I couldn't summon the courage to face her. That's when I'd heard about the couple who'd disappeared. I read up on people vanishing in forests and I wanted to disappear, too." She paused and ran her hand down Hicks' fur. "And...well, you know the rest."

Rem's thoughts whirled with all that he'd learned about his family. "Aunt Gin never reached out to you?"

"No," said Ivy. "At some point I guess she realized I was here. I don't know when, though. She's got a few gifts of her own, I suppose."

Rem almost chuckled. "Uh...yeah...I suppose she does." He suspected Aunt Gin had vanished her first husband. "She's got a way about her."

"That's very true. I don't know why I never considered that she may have similar abilities, and just found a way to cope."

"She found a way to cope, all right." Rem didn't want to think about what Simone...or rather Ivy, would do if she discovered what her mother had done to her father and the others. "But I know that her heart is always in the right place. She probably wanted to let you sort things out on your own and was waiting and hoping you would come to her."

Ivy reached for the bandage around his chest again. "Maybe one day. Right now, though, I prefer to remain lost. She and I will never be the mother and daughter we once were."

Rem didn't move as she adjusted his bandage. "It's not about what you once were. It's about where you are now. You're both grown women with your own unique strengths. Maybe it's time to put the past behind you and start reimagining a new future with someone in it. Someone who loves you." He thought of himself and Mikey and wondered if he should follow his own advice. "Life is short, Ivy. And regrets suck." He winced when his ribs pulled.

"You and Daniels know I'm here. You're welcome to visit any time."

He smiled. "That's nice, but after this week, I'm done with Merrimac and these damn trees for a while. Besides, it's not exactly an easy hike and I like my running water and electricity."

"It's no different from camping in the woods."

"Camping, like regrets, sucks. Ask Daniels. He'll tell you I need my dumb movies, greasy spoons, and an indoor toilet, or I get cranky."

"Well, the offer stands if you change your mind." She tugged and tightened the bandage.

"I appreciate that," he said through gritted teeth. "Did you know Aunt Gin likes to camp?"

Ivy sat back. "Mom? Likes to camp? Since when?"

"Yeah. With Sheriff Joe. They're dating by the way, but I guess you know that. She told me they go upriver and do the whole tent and campfire thing. Shocked the hell out of me." Rem blinked as a wave of fatigue hit him and tingles coursed through his limbs. "Said it was a Reverton thing. I told her that gene obviously bypassed me when it swam by."

"I'll keep that in mind." She studied him. "That leaf starting to hit you?"

Rem blinked again. "Everything's a little fuzzy."

"Is the pain better?"

He moved and didn't feel the urge to scream. "Bearable."

"Good." She handed him his shirt. "You can put this back on."

Groaning, he let her help him get his shirt and jacket back on. He was still a mess but felt more human. "Thanks, Ivy." He fell back against the tree with a weary sigh.

"You're welcome."

Rem's eyelids felt heavy. "And thanks for telling me everything. It's nice to know you're alive and well." He paused. "And I have yet another cousin." He stifled a yawn. "It's getting harder and harder to keep track of them all."

"That's another reason I stay in the woods."

He smiled. "You may be smarter than all of us."

"Rest," she said. "You need it. You'll still have to walk out of here after they find you."

He moaned. "Maybe Daniels will bring a stretcher."

She went quiet and after a second, she took his hand. "It's been good to see you again, and if we don't reconnect..."

He squeezed her fingers. "We will. Something tells me Aunt Gin won't wait forever. Especially now that she's reached out, and you know she's aware of you." He settled back against the tree. "Your car is still in town, by the way. We'll have to find a way to get it back to you. The keys are in my right pocket, though."

She reached in and pulled them out. "Thanks, Just tell me where you parked it and I'll manage."

Relaxing, Rem told her where he'd left the car. "Who knows? Maybe one day I'll visit, and we'll all go have dinner somewhere. Talk about wolves, family and Foster."

"Maybe," she said. "But in case we don't, you take care of yourself. And don't worry so much. You're in good hands." She tipped her head. "People love you, too, you know?"

He heard her words and wanted to ask her what she meant, but his eyes wouldn't stay open. "I guess," was all he could muster.

"Sleep," she whispered. "I'll stay until I know they're coming. You won't be alone."

Rem managed a nod, turned his head, and drifted off.

Chapter Thirty-Three

REM SAT AT AUNT Gin's table and sipped some coffee. He rubbed his sore shoulder, and his ribs were tender, but he was doing much better after getting out of the woods.

After Daniels had returned with the sheriff and a couple of other men from town, they'd helped Rem out of the forest. They had brought a stretcher but had used it to remove Shaw's body. By the time they'd wakened Rem, Ivy and her dogs were gone. Noting Rem's injuries and seeing he'd been bandaged, Sheriff Joe had given him an odd look, but Rem feigned sleepiness so he didn't have to answer any questions.

Daniels had taken him to a nearby hospital where they'd x-rayed Rem's ribs, stitched his arm and told him to go home and get some rest. Aunt Gin had offered both her upstairs rooms and he and Daniels had finally managed a hot shower and decent night's sleep.

The next day, they'd provided statements to Sheriff Joe, telling him about Deputy Shaw's involvement in the deaths of Sharon and Scott and explained how Shaw would have killed Rem and Daniels if it hadn't been for a wolf appearing out of nowhere and attacking Shaw. Afterward, the animal had disappeared back into the trees, and hadn't returned.

Daniels told Joe the story they'd concocted about each of them taking Whit's advice and going into the woods. Daniels had injured his head and gotten lost, and Rem had fallen and broken his ribs. Once they'd located each other, they'd spent a couple of days trying to recuperate and find their way back. Rem had managed to get to town after Daniels fell sick and was asking for Aunt Gin's help when Shaw had found him. Daniels told

Joe that he'd heard the gunshot and had found Rem injured after being shot by Shaw. Then Shaw had found them, and the wolf had appeared.

Joe had asked Rem about who'd treated him, and Rem told him he couldn't explain it. He'd passed out and when he'd woken, his arm and chest had been bandaged. Then he'd chuckled and said something about there really being a witch in the woods. He knew Joe hadn't believed a word of it, but it didn't take long for the town to hear about it. The rumors were already swirling about the benevolent witch who'd directed her killer wolf to protect them. The town was buzzing with excitement.

Amazed at how things had turned out, Rem grinned when Gin set a cinnamon roll in front of him. "It's not lasagna," she said, "but something tells me you won't mind."

Daniels, sitting next to Rem, sipped his coffee. "I may have trouble getting him out of here."

Rem pulled the plate closer. "No, you won't, but she's trying her best to woo me."

Gin sat across from him. "Everything's cleared up with Joe? Did he have any questions about Shaw?"

"He had plenty," said Daniels. "But luckily, Shaw left behind incriminating evidence. Joe found blueprints of the bank and a burner phone at Shaw's. It had plenty of racy photos from Sharon and texts from Scott on it."

"Plus, he found Scott's muddy shoes in the trash bin behind Scott's apartment complex," added Rem. "Between that and the stuff at Shaw's, it sealed the deal. We're in the clear."

"Thank God," said Gin with a sigh. "After all you've been through, are you sure you two don't want to stay another night? You're more than welcome. I won't have guests until this weekend."

Rem stabbed his fork into the roll. "Your hospitality is wonderful, but we've got to go home." He ate the bite and moaned as he chewed.

"Our captain is ready for us to get back," said Daniels. "I've finally been cleared to return to duty and Rem is already overdue."

"But you're still recovering," said Gin.

Rem swallowed and sighed. "I'll be okay. I'm already better. I'm sure Lozano will keep us at our desks for a while." He stabbed another bite. "Besides, I've got some things I need to handle. I thought running from it would work, but I learned the hard way that I should have stayed and faced the music."

"We all have our moments, dear," said Gin. "Lord knows I've made a few mistakes myself." She offered Rem a knowing stare.

Rem nodded and thought of Ivy. "You going to go talk to her?"

Quiet, Gin straightened in her seat. "I don't think so."

"Why not?" asked Rem.

Gin stared out her repaired patio door. "I'm not sure she welcomes my company."

"You might be surprised," said Daniels. "She's all grown up now, and quite capable of taking care of herself. She's found her place and she's happy. You two might get along just fine."

Rem chuckled. "She's the witch in the haunted woods of Merrimac who commands her hellhounds. That's a person you might like to get to know."

Gin smiled. "She is unique."

"She takes after her mother," said Rem. He paused. "You two have some rare skills."

Gin interlaced her fingers. "I'll think about it."

"Good," said Rem between bites. "I think she's doing the same thing." He considered something else. "You didn't mention what made you contact Ivy in the first place. How did you know I was in trouble?"

"I'd contacted Joe," she said. "He was just leaving the Herndons'. I told him what had happened, and he headed to the jail, but you and Shaw never showed. I knew then you needed help. I didn't know where he'd taken you, but something urged me to connect with Sim...I mean Ivy. I've learned to listen to those urges."

"I'm glad," said Rem. "That first step may be what you two needed." He sipped more coffee. "Even if I had to be chased through the woods by a madman to make it happen."

"You do have a flair for the dramatic," said Daniels. He leaned in. "There is something else. Neither one of you has explained what happened to Ginger. I keep asking and you keep dodging the question."

Rem eyed his aunt. "Care to take that one, Aunt Gin?" He took another bite of the cinnamon bun.

Gin reached over and patted Daniels on the hand. "Don't you worry your good-looking face about that nasty Ginger. She won't be bothering you anymore." She leaned back. "Now, can I get you two any food for the road? Maybe a sandwich and some chips?"

Daniels' mouth fell open. "She won't be bothering us anymore? What does that mean?" He eyed Rem. "You know what Ginger's capable of."

"I do," said Rem. "Aunt Gin took care of it, though. Ginger went on a trip, and she won't be back any time soon."

"Not ever," said Gin, standing. "I have turkey or ham."

Daniels narrowed his eyes, and Aunt Gin walked into the kitchen. Rem whispered to Daniels. "I'll explain later, but I doubt you'll believe it."

Daniels raised a brow. "After being saved by a witch and her hellhounds, plus everything else we've experienced, you might be surprised what I believe."

"We'll see," said Rem. He poked at the cinnamon roll, searching for the gooey pieces. "Hey, Aunt Gin."

"Yes, dear?" She poked her head around a kitchen cabinet.

"If I need someone else to take a long trip, you think you could help?" He winked at her.

She smirked. "I'm not a carnival act, dear. You can't rent me out for parties or whenever someone pisses you off."

"Too bad," said Rem. "I could think of a few people who could use a good trip."

"We all have a few of those," said Gin. "But you'll just have to put up with them."

"Figures," said Rem.

Gin returned to the kitchen, and Daniels stared. "What the hell are you two talking about?"

"Nothing, dear," said Gin from the kitchen. "Just a little Reverton secret." She opened a cabinet. "I have white or wheat bread."

"Nothing for us, Aunt Gin," said Rem. "Daniels is treating me to a burger on the way home. I've been craving one since sitting in that jail cell."

"Treating you, huh?" asked Daniels.

Rem made a face. "My ribs hurt, I was accused of murder and shot in the woods. I think that deserves a sympathy burger."

"Your ribs are healing, you were released from jail and you got eight stitches in your arm. I think you're doing okay," said Daniels. "And what about me? I almost died."

"I'll buy you some fries," said Rem.

Daniels rolled his eyes. "Gee. Thanks."

Gin came around the corner. "I can make you a burger."

Daniels raised a hand. "No need. I'll buy him one, because if I don't, he'll bitch all the way home."

"We're in two separate cars," said Rem.

"Then you'll call me and bitch by phone." Daniels eyed the cinnamon roll. "Eat up, Sport. If you want to get that burger on the way home, we need to go."

Rem took another bite and slid the plate away. "That was delicious Gin, but I need to save my appetite." He took a gulp of his coffee and set the cup down.

"You sure you two can't stay?" she asked, returning to the table.

"We're sure." Rem stood. "Merrimac and I need a little distance." He pushed his chair in and kissed his aunt on the cheek. "But I'll visit again, and if you need anything from me, you know how to reach me."

She gave him a warm hug. "You take care of yourself."

"I will," he said, hugging her back.

Rem pulled away, and Daniels walked over. "Thank you for everything," said Daniels. "You saved our butts, Genevieve."

Gin blushed. "Come here and give me a hug, you handsome fella." Daniels put his arms around her, and she squeezed him, too. "And call me Aunt Gin. We're family now."

Daniels raised the side of his lip. "Aunt Gin," he said. "I like the sound of that. I'm not close with my aunts."

"Well, now you've got a new one to love, right Aaron?" asked Gin, letting go of Daniels. "A Reverton takes care of their own, and you're now an official adoptee."

Daniels took her hand. "Thank you. I appreciate that."

"Guess what?" said Rem. "You now have over forty new family members. I hope you have some spending money at Christmas."

Daniels chuckled. "I hope they return the favor."

"Don't get your hopes up, unless you like socks." Rem raised a sneakered foot. He wore a blue sock covered with green and white polka-dotted frogs.

"Is that why you have all those crazy socks?" asked Daniels.

"Now you know my secret," said Rem. He gestured toward the door. "You ready, Tonto?"

"I'm ready, Kemosabe," replied Daniels. "Let's hit the road."

........·..

Two hours later, they stopped at a roadside diner outside of San Diego. Rem had found it and insisted they stop there. It was a small hole-in-the-wall, but the locals had rated it well. After studying the menu, the waitress took their orders and Rem sat quietly across from Daniels in the booth.

"You're not saying much," said Daniels. "How was the drive? Your ribs bugging you?"

Rem shook his head. "They're okay." He shifted in his seat and fiddled with the straw in his water glass. "You call Marjorie?"

"I did," said Daniels. "We talked for a while, and I caught her up with everything. She's anxious for me to get home."

"She still mad?"

"We definitely have some talking to do, but we'll work it out, no matter what we decide."

Rem nodded and stared at his glass.

Daniels rested his arm on the back of the booth. "You thinking about Allison again?"

Rem shrugged. "I've come to terms with it as best I can. There's not much I can do until I know more. Right now, I just need to prepare for trial."

"It will work out," said Daniels. "One step at a time."

"I suppose." Rem sat back. "I finally called Mikey back."

Daniels raised a brow. "Really? Is that why you're in a funk?"

"Am I in a funk?"

"You were excited to be heading home when we left Merrimac. Now you look like you lost a puppy." He paused. "How's Mikey?"

"My time away has been as eventful for her as it was for me. We weren't the only ones having a hard time." The waitress dropped off his soda. "Her brother Max was accused of murder, Mason was attacked by an evil spirit and Trick's in the hospital."

Daniels frowned. "Jeez. She did have a lousy week. Is everyone okay?"

"It seems so. She said she'd fill me in on the details later, but she had to go."

"Go? Go where?" Daniels understood Mikey well enough to know she would have given Rem hell for not returning her calls sooner and would have taken most of the drive time catching up. "Is she all right?"

Rem removed the paper from another straw. "She was on a date."

Daniels paused in mid-sip of his water. He set his glass down. "A date, huh?"

"It was just coffee with some guy named Kyle. She didn't want to tell me, but she's not good at hiding things, and I pried it out of her." He added the straw to his soda.

Daniels nodded. "Does that bother you?"

"I don't know." Rem paused. "I've been driving and thinking since we hung up." He crumpled the straw's wrapper. "I mean, we're just friends. She's allowed to go on a date."

"She is, but you're not acting like someone who's thrilled about it."

"I guess it just took me by surprise." He tossed the wrapper aside. "It's none of my business, though. If she likes this guy Kyle, then good for her."

Daniels almost moaned. "Would you listen to yourself? When are you going to admit that you like her? You've always liked her. You needed some time after everything that's happened. I get that. But maybe it's time to move forward."

Rem tensed. "Move forward? How am I supposed to move forward when Allison may be having my child? I can't ask Mikey to deal with that. That's not fair to her."

Daniels sat forward in the booth, determined to get through to his partner. "None of this is fair, Rem. Least of all to you. But if you keep waiting around for fair, you're going to end up alone in some rocker on a porch wishing you'd made a different choice. Besides, Mikey's a big girl. At least give her the option to decide for herself about Allison and what might come next. You can't assume anything."

Rem stared off. "Maybe...or maybe it's better if she finds someone else."

Daniels bit back a curse. "Martyrdom doesn't suit you, Rem." Frustrated, he decided his friend needed the hard truth. "If you want her, then go get her. Screw everything else and stop thinking so damn much. If you want to be happy, then choose to be happy. Stop letting everyone else dictate what should or should not happen to you. You can't change the past, Rem, but you sure as hell can change the future."

Quiet, Rem leaned back. "You know your eyes flare when you get mad. It's a little unsettling."

"Why do you think I'm so successful with interrogations?"

Rem chuckled and seemed to relax. "You think I'm thinking too much?"

"You could rival Einstein."

Rem slid his soda closer. "Okay. I see your point." He took a sip. "Maybe Mikey and I should talk when I get back."

"Maybe? You need to convince her to give coffee guy the boot. Show her the Remalla we all know and love. She'll swoon and then you'll be the guy to satisfy all her coffee needs."

"Swoon, huh?" Rem raised his brows. "I do like my coffee strong."

Glad Rem was coming around, Daniels pointed. "And she'll like it too, especially when you're supplying plenty of caffeine."

"She'll supply plenty of her own," added Rem.

"I don't doubt it, which is why you two are perfect for each other. I've just got to get you to pull the damn trigger."

Rem raised a hand. "All right. I hear you. I'll stop moping and take some action."

"The fun kind, not the wary kind. You want her, then make her want you back."

Rem blew out a breath. "I can do that."

"I know you can."

Rem eyed Daniels, his face serious. "Thanks for the pep talk."

"I've been wanting to say it for a while now. You just weren't ready to hear it." Daniels laid his napkin in his lap. "I'm kind of grateful for coffee guy. He's the catalyst you needed."

"Yeah, well. Let's hope he's not as charming as me."

Daniels scoffed. "That's simply not possible."

Rem smiled.

Daniels picked up an extra paper napkin that was on the table. "I'm halfway tempted to make you write it down on this and sign it so I can wave it in your face if you don't follow through."

Rem patted his pockets. "If I had a pen…" He frowned, stuck his hand inside his jacket and pulled out a small glass tube with a stopper.

"What's that?"

Rem studied it for a second and then shook it. Clear liquid jostled inside the tube. "It's…uh…rain berry juice." He paused. "I almost forgot. Ivy gave it to me."

"What's rain berry juice?"

He hesitated. "It's from a berry Ivy found. It…uh…helps you sleep." He continued to stare at it.

"That should be helpful. You use the whole thing?"

"Uhm…no. Just a drop. It's pretty potent."

"Then that should last you a while."

"Yeah," he said softly. "It should." Another second passed and Rem returned it to his pocket.

Daniels' phone buzzed. He pulled it out and eyed the display. "It's Lozano." He answered. "Hey, Cap."

"Daniels." Lozano spoke tersely. "Is Rem with you?"

"Yeah. He is."

"Put me on speaker."

The only other customers were at the opposite end of the restaurant. "Hold on." Daniels set the phone down and hit the speaker button. "Okay, Cap. Rem and I are on speaker."

"Hey, Cap," said Rem.

"You two on your way?" asked Lozano.

"We're about an hour from home. We stopped for a burger," said Daniels.

Lozano didn't mince words. "I need you to get back as soon as possible."

"Something wrong?" asked Daniels.

There was a brief pause before Lozano continued. "Yesterday morning, Margaret Redstone had a seizure at the psychiatric facility."

Rem's eyes widened and Daniels held his breath.

"They took her to the clinic," said Lozano, "but she declined rapidly, and they made the decision to transfer her to the nearby hospital for treatment. We kept round the clock surveillance on her, but as of last night, she was in a coma in ICU. Doctors didn't expect her to make it."

Rem dropped his jaw, and Daniels closed his eyes, hoping that the captain's next words would be what they needed to hear. "Did she make it through the night?" He opened his eyes and almost crossed his fingers. He didn't savor wishing anyone dead, but Margaret Redstone was the one exception.

"Worse," said Lozano. "She's gone."

Rem clenched the table's edge. "Gone? What do you mean gone?"

"Nurse went to check on her this morning. The bed was empty. The officer outside her door never saw a thing. They've searched the hospital, but they haven't found her."

Daniels' heart dropped. "Are you serious?"

Rem's face went white, and he clutched his stomach.

"Dead serious," said Lozano. "I've issued an A.P.B., but as of right now, Margaret Redstone is officially in the wind."

· · · · · ● · ● · · ·

Want more from J. T. Bishop? Sign up for her newsletter at jtbishopauthor.com. Get her first book, *Red-Line: The Shift* and the Daniels and Remalla prequel novella, *The Girl and the Gunshot* for free, in addition to extra content, plus opportunities for more free books.

I hope you enjoyed *Of Mind and Madness*, but there's more to come when Rem and Daniels are challenged by Margaret's escape and their hunt for a brutal killer who marks his victims with a mysterious symbol. Can they catch them both and stay alive at the same time? Get ready to find out in *Of Power and Pain*, now available for pre-order. Enjoy an excerpt below.

If you liked *Of Mind and Madness* and this is your first foray into the world of J.T. Bishop and her paranormal thrillers, then you're in luck. Check out the *Family or Foe* saga, which introduces Detectives Daniels and Remalla. A killer with powerful abilities is out for revenge against those he believes wronged him. Can he be caught before he kills again?

This series includes *First Cut*, *Second Slice*, *Third Blow* and *Fourth Strike*. Or grab all four in *The Family or Foe Saga Boxed Set*.

Or if you haven't already, jump straight into Daniels' and Remalla's own series, starting with *Haunted River*. The ghost of a woman whose murder remains unsolved haunts a small town with secrets. When another woman turns up dead years later, are Daniels and Remalla next? This book is followed by *Of Breath and Blood* where our detectives investigate a cult leader and will have to rely on each other to survive, and *Of Body and Bone*, where they'll hunt for a kidnapper whose unique abilities make him impossible to catch, but his connections to a dangerous foe creates a greater threat.

And if you like Mason and Mikey Redstone and their paranormal exploits, introduced in *Of Breath and Blood*, then grab *Lost Souls*, the first book in *The Redstone Chronicles*, a cross-over series with Daniels and Remalla. Chronologically, it follows *Of Breath and Blood*, but can be read on its own. In this book, Mason's estranged partner returns and asks for Mason's help to solve a murder, but can he be trusted? This is followed by *Lost Dreams* where Mason battles his inner demons while he and Mikey attempt to exonerate their brother after he's framed for murder. And in *Lost Chances*, book three in the series, Mason gets the help he needs but finds himself caught up in a dangerous web of deceit and death, and makes a dangerous enemy. Grab it now on pre-order. (For a list of all of my books in chronological order, see below.)

Or, do you enjoy an urban fantasy with light sci-fi and some paranormal romance thrown in? Then check out my first series, *The Red-Line Trilogy*, or the sister series to the Red-Line trilogy, *The Fletcher Family Saga*. Either can be read first. Take your pick. Boxsets are available, too!

A Note From J. T.

I love to hear from my readers about their experiences with my books, and I'd love to know what you thought about *Of Mind and Madness*. Continuing the Victor D'Mato and Allison Albright storyline is a thrill. I'm as excited to see where it leads as I hope you are. (Do I know for sure where it's going? Not yet, but I have some ideas.) In this installment, I thought it would be fun to get to know one of Rem's quirky relatives, so Aunt Genevieve was born. I figured she should have some abilities all her own, which makes sense for a Reverton, don't you think? I debated for a while what her talent would be since I like to come up with new things. At first, the people who disappeared in the woods were unexplained, but then the lightbulb went off and Aunt Gin became the culprit. It made for some interesting conflict. Does Rem support her because she's family or condemn her because he's a cop? If you've read the book, you know the answer.

I also like exploring the emotional side of Rem's journey as Allison's trial nears. The decision he has to make looms large and how he handles it allows the reader to get a deeper glimpse into his psyche. Of course, he relies on Daniels for some sage advice, a calming influence, and strong guidance, which we all need when going through a crisis. It's the most satisfying part of telling these stories – delving into their friendship.

What happens next with Margaret on the loose? You'll just to have to hang around for the next book to find out. I'm writing as fast as I can though! But in the meantime, stay tuned for *Lost Chances*, part three in *The Redstone Chronicles*. Since this is a crossover series with Daniels and Remalla, all the characters show up in both series and I write them in order. So, a Redstone Chronicle book follows a Daniels and Remalla book, and so on. For maximum reading pleasure, you can read one right after the other if you want to stay in chronological order. (See below for this list.)

Reviews are a huge plus and big help for an author and potential readers. I would love it if you could please take a couple of minutes to leave a quick review for *Of Mind and Madness*. And if you'd like, please leave a few comments, too.

As always, thank you for your time and readership. It is deeply valued and appreciated.

Now, on to the next book!

Acknowledgements

ANOTHER BOOK IS COMPLETE, and again, I have many to thank. This doesn't happen alone, and I am indebted to family and friends for their help, support and encouragement. It is truly appreciated.

I also want to thank my Beta and ARC teams. You guys keep me on my toes, ensure I write a great story, and help with early reviews. Thank you for being honest and offering your guidance.

I love writing about the bonds between loving family, deep friendships and the ties that hold them together. Plus, my fascination with the unknown thrown into the mix makes for a satisfying story and hopefully, adds a little more thrill for my readers.

I especially want to thank my fans. Hearing from you and knowing that you're enjoying my books makes all the hard work worthwhile. None of this would matter without your tremendous support. If I can help you escape from this crazy world for a short period each day, then I've done my job.

Here's to more stories, more fun, and more time for yourself. If you can have a little of that each day, you're on the right track.

Also by J. T. Bishop

The Redstone Chronicles
Lost Souls
Lost Dreams
Lost Chances...coming soon and available for pre-order

Books in Chronological Order

Although not required, in case you prefer to read in order...

Red-Line: Prelude to The Shift, a short story (free at jtbishopauthor.com)

Red-Line: The Shift (free at jtbishopauthor.com)

Red-Line: Mirrors

Red-Line: Trust Destiny

Curse Breaker

High Child

Spark

Forged Lines

The Girl and the Gunshot, a novella (free at jtbishopauthor.com)

First Cut

Second Slice

Third Blow

Fourth Strike

Haunted River

Of Breath and Blood

Lost Souls

Of Body and Bone

Lost Dreams

Of Mind and Madness

Lost Chances

Of Power and Pain

Enjoy an excerpt from Book Five of Detectives Daniels and Remalla, Of Power and Pain

ENSURING HE'D WAITED LONG enough, Oswald Fry slowly lowered the woman's limp body to the floor. Moving carefully, he supported her head and gently laid it against the tile of the kitchen, then smoothed her hair and clothes, and straightened her limbs. When he was done, he thought she looked like a sleeping doll, much like the one he'd given his niece a few days earlier at her fourth birthday party.

Smiling at his efforts, he looked around, pleased that nothing seemed out of place. Although she'd fought him, he'd prevented her from damaging anything and he had no scratches or bruises on his skin. Everything had gone just as he'd expected. Recalling his lack of academic and social skills from his youth, he was happy to note that he could do something well. It gave him a small sense of pride. In his mind's eye, he gave a middle finger to his old school teachers. He doubted any of them could have done what he'd just accomplished.

He took a moment to walk through the house, noting the family photos, the minimal furniture, the strange art on the walls, and the small room where the woman saw her clients. Pleased, he returned to the kitchen and sat on the floor beside his victim and closed his eyes. He sensed the energy of her and felt it mingle with his own. The moment she'd left, he'd felt her spirit join his, and it had been so gratifying. Breathing deeply, he enjoyed the essence of her, and when he felt fulfillment, he opened his eyes, and knew it was time to leave. Although he wanted to stay, he had to go before her lack of life force began to deplete his own, and he couldn't risk that.

He stood, took a last look around, then reached into his pocket and with his gloved hands, pulled out a black magic marker. After uncapping it, he squatted beside the woman and drew the symbol on her upper arm. Satisfied with the result, he stood, capped the marker and set it down on the counter. Then he took a plastic bag from another pocket, opened it, and removed a blank piece of white paper. He set it on the kitchen counter, took out the black bowtie and rested it beside the paper.

After uncapping the marker again, he wrote on the paper, recapped the marker and returned it to his pocket. Adjusting the paper and tie to sit beside each other, he smiled and sighed. Today was a good day.

Eying his handwriting, he was happy. The letters were big and clear and easy to read. Mrs. Montgomery, who'd taught him handwriting years earlier, would have appreciated his improvement.

Taking one last look at the body, he spied a silver bracelet on the woman's wrist. Seeing it sparkle, he walked over, removed it and slipped it into his pocket. Then, pleased with his handiwork and ready to go home and eat, he walked out the back door.

• • • • • • • • • •

Detective Aaron Remalla sat under the large shade tree on a bench in the cemetery. A row of tombstones stretched out in front of him, and Jennie's lay at the end. The marble stone had an angel and the name Jennifer Chapman etched into it, along with the years of her birth and death and the words *Gone too soon, but forever loved*. A single yellow rose lay in front of it.

Rem eyed the flowers in his hand. He'd brought her some lilies, which she'd always liked, but had yet to place them on her grave. He wondered about the rose and who had brought it. Her family would have contacted him if they'd been visiting, but they hadn't been in touch, and his partner, Daniels, would have told him if he'd swung by and left it. It could have been a friend, but in the various times he'd visited, he'd never seen flowers on her stone before, unless it was from family.

Shaking his head, he stopped staring at the yellow rose and sat his flowers beside him on the bench. Trying not to think, but failing, he reflected on the last several months.

He reluctantly recalled his encounters with Victor D'Mato and Allison Albright and his near death at their hands. His struggles with the PTSD, preparing for Allison's upcoming trial and her revelation that the child she carried was his. Then, when he'd thought he'd survived the worst of it, Margaret Redstone, a psychopathic follower of Victor, who had crazy blue eyes, a wild cackle and a demented attraction to Rem, had escaped the psychiatric facility where she was being held. Three months later, there was still no sign of her. He'd been doing his best to cope but there were times when he needed to escape, too, and he often found himself here, with Jennie. Although he knew Margaret could get to him no matter where he went, it was one of the few places he felt safe. Maybe because he figured if he died next to Jennie, he would be okay with that.

Sighing, he realized there was one bright spot in the hell of the last few months—Mikey Redstone, Margaret's sister. She was the only person who could relate to his trauma, and she was a good friend. She'd survived her own horrific experiences with Victor, and she'd helped him get through his recovery with an acceptance that he appreciated. He knew Daniels would stand behind him no matter what, but he never expected to find that same loyalty with anyone else.

Eyeing Jennie's tombstone, he wondered if Mikey could become someone he loved. Did he love her? He didn't know. So much had happened recently that it was hard to keep his thoughts straight. Mikey had begun seeing Kyle, but Mikey had informed Rem that it was strictly business between her and Kyle while her brother Mason was in rehab and Kyle had stepped in to help with Mason's business. But Mason had returned home a few days ago, and Rem wondered if Kyle hoped to resume his relationship with Mikey, and if Mikey did, too.

Rem wouldn't blame her if she did. From what he knew of Kyle and after their brief meeting, he could see why Mikey would like him. And with Margaret still at large, any potential relationship between Rem and Mikey was out of the question. If it meant attracting Margaret's interest or anger, then Rem wouldn't risk it. Mikey's safety was more important than whatever feelings he had for her. And he still hadn't found the courage to tell her about Allison's pregnancy. That alone would likely have Mikey running for the hills. Daniels disagreed with Rem about keeping his distance, but Rem couldn't help how he felt. He'd already lost one great woman in his life, and he couldn't imagine losing another. And Mikey sure as hell hadn't signed up to help Rem co-parent, nor would Rem expect it of her.

Rubbing his temples, he sighed again, wondering what to expect next. His mantra was to take it one day at a time, but there were moments when he desperately needed a reprieve. That's when he would come here and talk to Jennie. Sometimes it helped, but others, he'd descend further down the rabbit hole, and he'd go home and get drunk. Luckily, those moments were few, but when it happened, it would take him a day or two to resurface. Thankfully, he had a partner and a captain who understood, but he couldn't expect them to take care of him every time, so he did his best to stay positive or hide when the going got rough. In the past, Mikey had been a strong source of support, but with the two of them seeing less of each other, he'd kept his struggles to himself.

The trial loomed, though, and without any delays, would occur in three months. The prosecutor, Kate Schultz, had suggested offering a plea deal, which would mean no trial, but also a shorter sentence for Allison. Rem had considered it but had finally asked Kate not to offer it. Despite the fear and risk that Allison could be acquitted, Rem wanted the chance to face her in court and tell his truth. Mikey had reminded him that he'd done nothing wrong and between her and Daniels, he'd bolstered the strength to move forward and trust that a jury would believe him and not Allison.

Trying to relax, Rem closed his eyes, and listened to a bird sing in the tree above him. Several minutes passed, and feeling a little more centered, he opened his eyes and, blowing out a breath, he stood and picked up his lilies. He walked over to the tombstone and squatted in front of it. He slid the rose back and set the lilies beside it and again wondered who'd placed the rose.

"Hey, Jen," he said. "I brought you some flowers." He swiped some leaves away. "But it looks like someone beat me to it." He smoothed a petal on a lily. "I guess I'm glad someone else is thinking of you, though."

Rem sat cross-legged on the ground. "I'm feeling a little sorry for myself again, so I stopped by. You always help me feel better." The wind blew his long hair and he tucked a strand back behind his ear. "Not much has changed since I last visited. Maybe one of these days, I'll have some good news for you."

A cool breeze prickled his skin, and he rubbed his arms. "You here with me?" He smiled softly. "Sorry. Dumb question."

He sat for a minute, absorbing her presence, letting his mind quiet, and wondered what he'd do with the rest of his day off. In the past, he'd call Mikey and they'd go to a movie, but he couldn't do that now.

Feeling more at ease, he was about to say his goodbyes, when his phone rang. He pulled it out of his pocket, and saw it was Daniels. Shaking his head, he wondered how his partner always knew when he was at the cemetery. He answered. "Hey."

"Hey," said Daniels. "How's Jennie?"

Rem smirked. "Quiet, as usual. But still present."

"Good. How are you?"

"Taking a moment but hanging in there. You?"

"I'm hanging with J.P. while Marjorie runs some errands. She's on her way back, though, because I've got to go. And so do you."

"I do? Where are we going?"

"Lozano called. I hate to interrupt your moment but there's been a murder. He wants us on it."

"Us? Why us? It's our day off."

"He didn't elaborate, but said we'd understand when we got there. I'll text you the address and meet you there."

Rem rubbed his eyes, not anxious to go to a crime scene, but figured the distraction might be a good thing. "Okay. I'll head out."

"I'll be right behind you. See you soon."

"See you."

Rem hung up. He eyed Jennie's grave a second longer and stood. "Duty calls, Babe, but I'll be back soon. Enjoy your flowers."

A strange tingle ran up his spine and he had the odd feeling that he wasn't alone. His skin breaking out in chills, he scanned the area, but didn't see anyone. Only tombstones stared back. He stepped down a few rows and eyed the surrounding trees, but it was quiet. Figuring he was paranoid, he shrugged it off, but stayed aware just in case Margaret popped up from a gravestone and rushed at him, her blue eyes blazing.

With a last glance, he returned to Jennie's grave, and his heart thumping, he whispered a goodbye and left the cemetery.

CPSIA information can be obtained
at www.ICGtesting.com
Printed in the USA
LVHW081544170422
716434LV00013B/624